Dear Reader,

They say that people are the same all over. Whether it's a small village on the sea, a mining town nestled in the mountains, or a whistle-stop along the Western plains, we all share the same hopes and dreams. We work, we play, we laugh, we cry—and, of course, we fall in love . . .

It is this universal experience that we at Jove Books have tried to capture in a heartwarming series of novels. We've asked our most gifted authors to write their own story of American romance, set in a town as distinct and vivid as the people who live there. Each writer chose a special time and place close to their hearts. They filled the towns with charming, unforgettable characters—then added that spark of romance. We think you'll find the combination absolutely delightful.

You might even recognize *your* town. Because true love lives in *every* town . . .

Welcome to *Our Town*.

Sincerely,

Leslie Gelb

Leslie Gelbman
Editor-in-Chief

Titles in the Our Town series

TAKE HEART
HARBOR LIGHTS
HUMBLE PIE
CANDY KISS
CEDAR CREEK
SUGAR AND SPICE
CROSS ROADS
BLUE RIBBON
THE LIGHTHOUSE
THE HAT BOX

Titles by Deborah Lawrence
(who also writes as Deborah Wood)

GENTLE HEARTS
SUMMER'S GIFT
HEART'S SONG
MAGGIE'S PRIDE
HUMBLE PIE
THE HAT BOX

OUR · TOWN

THE HAT BOX

DEBORAH LAWRENCE

JOVE BOOKS, NEW YORK

THE HAT BOX

A Jove Book / published by arrangement with
the author

PRINTING HISTORY
Jove edition / March 1997

The Putnam Berkley World Wide Web site address is
http://www.berkley.com/berkley

ISBN: 0-515-12033-2

A JOVE BOOK®
Jove Books are published by The Berkley Publishing Group,
200 Madison Avenue, New York, New York 10016.
JOVE and the "J" design are trademarks
belonging to Jove Publications, Inc.

PRINTED IN THE UNITED STATES OF AMERICA

10 9 8 7 6 5 4 3 2 1

In loving memory,
Bess Hyatt Ellis,
a woman ahead of her time.

❖ 1 ❖

November 1851

MAKING HER WAY along the ocean-swept deck of the schooner *Julianna,* Emma Townsend kept a firm hold on the rail. Heavy fog cloaked the ship but did not calm the rough sea. Nonetheless, she relished the feeling of solitude. The captain's terse orders came through the haze like a beacon, and she wondered if his shouts sounded as disembodied to anyone else.

Staying well back from the ropes, the din of male voices, and the crew's rushing footsteps, Emma leaned on the port rail. She squinted in the direction of the northern California coastline, hoping for a break in the thick mist. She had so looked forward to seeing the familiar rugged bluffs and her home as they approached Pelican Cove.

The schooner pitched and shuddered violently. She gripped the rail with both hands, cocked her head, and listened for the captain's reassuring bellow. Instead, cries of alarm rent the air.

The ship rode up a large swell and plunged down into the trough. The deck tilted, then suddenly was awash, and she slipped to her knees. Saltwater plastered her wool cloak against her back and weighed her down.

One of the masts splintered and the heavy canvas sail

ripped. She crouched down and wrapped her arms around a rigging anchor. A wave broke overhead. She had always loved the tangy smell of the ocean, but now it filled her nostrils and stung her eyes.

The image of her brother, Bently, floated in her mind. More frightened of being confined to her cabin, as he believed her to be, than remaining on deck, she stayed huddled below the rail and prayed. Men ran past her. The ship seemed to be riding lower in the water. A clamor of hysterical voices reached her ear, and she looked back toward the ladder leading down to the lower deck. Shadowy figures poured out of the passageway like puffs of smoke rising from a boiler.

"B-e-n-t-l-y!" *Dear Lord, don't let him be trapped below, searching for me.* "B-e-n-t-l-y!"

Using the rail to guide and steady her, she made her way back to the ladder, calling her brother's name as she went. A thunderous crash jarred the ship, and the deck shifted at an odd angle. Until that moment, she had hoped they would clear the violent storm. Then she heard a horrible ripping screech, the way she believed it would sound if the *Julianna* were being torn apart.

"Emma! Thank God!" Bently grasped the rail on either side of his sister.

"Hit the deck and hold on!" A man yelled. "We're goin' aground!"

As if Neptune had waited for a signal, the ship reeled landward. Timbers groaned and began separating. The fog thinned, and dead ahead was a solid wall of dirt and rocks. Her brother shoved her down to the deck and held her there. The hull scraped bottom just before a wave carried the *Julianna* ashore. One moment there was deafening silence— the next, pandemonium broke out.

Bently leaned over to his sister's right side and stared down into her eyes. "Emma, what're you doing up here? Are you all right?"

She blinked. Before she could form an answer or warn him, a timber slid onto his back and knocked him out. Her scream joined others.

*   *   *

Kent Hogarth rode south to Pelican Cove. With a plug of luck and a bit of work, he'd have the information Mr. Wendell hired him to get and be on his way in a couple of weeks. The damned fog had soaked his clothes, and the giant redwoods would've blocked out the sun on a clear day. He knew he'd be more than ready to move on before the winter weather hit.

He'd never had a job like this before. But he hadn't had training to deliver letters and newspapers, either, until he'd hired on as expressman to several small gold mines. A wet-nosed kid, he'd mastered trapping the same way. There was no teacher like experience.

He needed to get hired on somewhere in the cove. Fit in. In a small town, he'd stick out like a blister on a man's nose if he didn't. And that would make his job even more difficult. The trail veered nearer the ocean. He stopped his horse and wiped a soggy handkerchief over his wet face.

The surf crashed somewhere below him. He shivered. One place he'd never be found was on a ship. Give him land, even wet, sodden ground, and he could make out okay. The thought of food, a dry room, and warm bed urged him on.

He hadn't ridden more than a couple of miles before the hair-raising wails reached him. Spurring his horse, Bounder, Kent followed the sounds until they seemed to come from below the bank. He tossed his hat aside and scrambled down through brush, over rocks, and into the surf. The fog thinned. He spotted a ship washed up against the bank.

He found the bodies of two dead sailors before he reached the ship. Good God! Where to begin? He thought he saw a man entangled in the rigging, but he wasn't sure. Another lay over the rail like a rag. He sloshed out of the water and climbed onto a boulder lodged in the sharp bow of the ship.

As he made his way onto the deck, agonizing moans and groans assaulted him. He knelt down and felt for signs of life in the three men in a heap at the bow. He moved the man on top off the others—they'd be meeting their maker anytime—and slapped the other's face.

The man grunted, winced, and his eyelids twitched.

"Come on, wake up!" Kent shook the man, none too gently. "I can't do this alone, dammit. You're goin' to help!" He shook the man like a dog would a fresh bone and left him to see about the others.

The next man he came to was alive but in no condition to help. Kent was making his way to a stairwell leading below when he slipped. He came down on his hands and knees—face-to-face with an unconscious woman.

She was breathing, but her face was stark white in contrast to the dark wet bonnet shielding one side. He pushed the hat back and blew on her cheek, his breath the only warmth he had at hand. She moaned softly and pressed her icy cheek to his face.

"Ma'am, can you hear me?" He freed one hand and brushed her dripping hair back from her eyes. "Ma'am?" She had a pretty face, but she looked younger than he expected, smaller, too. A man's body covered her and a timber across his back pinned them both down. The man was alive but unconscious. Kent sent the spar over the side. He then moved the man off the woman.

"Ma'am? Come on now, breathe deep."

He raised his hand but couldn't bring himself to slap her face. Instead, he took her frigid hands in his and rubbed them together. Damnation! Pulling men from a caved-in mine shaft was a far sight easier than dealing with a dazed woman.

Emma obediently inhaled. "Bently?" What had happened came back to her at once—his shielding her, pushing her down to the deck, and the beam . . . Her eyes snapped open, and she stared up, expecting to see him. Instead her gaze met that of a bearded man with brown eyes and huge shoulders—definitely not Bently.

"Please—" She struggled to sit up, but the man didn't move, and she was too weak to push him away.

Her voice was so soft Kent leaned forward to hear her. "Do you hurt?" She stared at him, clearly startled. The color of her eyes surprised him—light green, almost like new shoots of grass. "I didn't want to . . . well, you tell me where you're hurt."

"No. I'll be all right in a minute." She managed to pull one hand free of his grasp and brace herself on one elbow.

"I want . . . up." His hair was a lovely russet shade and so was his facial hair. He was actually gentle, but she had to find her brother, and the man was blocking her view.

From the wispiness of her voice, he doubted she had the strength, but he moved aside and helped her to her feet. "You sure you shouldn't rest? I need to see how the others are."

Emma felt steadied by his soothing warmth, but she stepped away from him and nearly tripped over her brother. "Bently!"

Kent braced her and glanced down at the man. "He's alive, ma'am."

She cocked her head, "What?" and watched his mouth. She was attacked when she was seventeen and had lost much more than the hearing in one ear, but that was easier to accept than the loss of her virginity. There was nothing she could do about that but she had learned to adjust to the loss of hearing. Under normal circumstances, she paid close attention to those around her and compensated for her loss by often turning her head or watching people's lips move when they spoke.

"He'll be okay."

She nodded. "Thank God." She worked the ties on her bonnet and cloak loose and let the sopping-wet garment drop to the deck. "I'll help after I see to Bently," she said and watched his lips. She shivered and clamped her teeth together.

Kent unbuttoned his heavy jacket. Her soaked garb exposed her thin body, and he wrapped his coat around her. "Sure you're okay?" It hung down to her knees and the sleeves covered her hands.

Holding the lapels of the sheepskin coat together over her breasts, Emma began to feel warmer and somehow safer. She nodded in response to the man's question. She and her brother had gone up the coast to Astoria to buy supplies. The trip had been uneventful—until now. She glanced around at the jumble of debris and people on the deck for the first time. Abject horror held her in its grip for a long moment. She knew there had been ten passengers but had never thought about the number of men that crewed the ship.

Bently stirred. "Emma?"

"I'm here." She watched him relax a bit, blink, and look up at her. She dried his face as best she could.

"Are we still afloat?"

"It doesn't feel like it." In the dim light it was difficult to see if his eyes were clear, but he seemed alert. She reached around, ran her fingers through his wet, light brown hair and felt the back of his head.

Bently sat up and repeated her action.

"I was sure that piece of wood hit your head but there's no lump. How's your back?"

He cautiously flexed and moved his limbs before sitting up. "Just stiff." He glanced beyond Emma's shoulder and stared. "Why didn't you tell me! My God! We've got to help them."

"I had to make sure you were all right first."

He struggled to his feet and helped her up. "Where did you get that coat, Emma?"

"Oh!" She held on to the lapels of the coat. "A man moved you so I could get up. It's his." She looked around and saw the man talking to a crewman.

"That is unlike you, Emma. He's a stranger." He eyed her. "Find your cloak and give the jacket back to him. I'll see if I can locate Captain Leonard."

She watched him walk away with one hand bracing his lower back before she went in the opposite direction. She stepped to her right, following the sound of a woman sobbing, and found the bearded man, whose coat she wore, bent over a middle-aged woman, Mrs. Lewis.

Kent tried again. "Please, ma'am, tell me what's wrong." He'd discovered two more sailors who hadn't survived, and he hadn't even had a chance to get down to the lower deck.

Emma stood by the prostrate woman. "Maybe she'll talk to me." She fingered the soft leather of his coat. She smelled a whiff of tobacco, pine from the woods, and the man's own scent. "Thank you for letting me wear this, but you need it." Bently was right. She didn't know this man, but she was very grateful he had come to their rescue.

"No. You keep it." With the jacket covering her from chin to knees, she looked like a child playing in her pa's clothes. But she was no child.

Resisting an urge to hug it around her first, she slipped the coat off and handed it to him. "My trunks are below," she said, kneeling at Mrs. Lewis's side.

Kent left the women and made his way down to the lower deck. It was dark, and sloshing through water didn't make his search any easier. He shoved at the first door he came to and it finally gave way. After stumbling around, he located a lamp and lighted it. "God A'mighty, how could a body stay in a space no bigger than a wolf's den?" he wondered aloud. There was no one there to answer, but that didn't matter. He was used to talking to himself. And that was fine—as long as he didn't answer.

The lamp swayed, the floor shifted, and he leaned against the wall. That wasn't too comforting. He lifted the lamp from the hook and searched two other empty cabins before reaching a door that was wedged shut. Applying his weight to it, he managed to force the door open enough for him to inch his way inside.

"Shit!" A woman dressed in her nightclothes lay on the floor between the door and a heavy trunk. He placed his fingers at the base of her neck. She hadn't had a chance. He picked her up and placed her on the narrow bed before leaving.

Emma wrung out the hem of her skirt and wiped Mrs. Lewis's face. "Better?"

"Thank you, dear. You don't have to fuss over me. It's just my arm, and it feels better now that you've bound it."

The woman's grimace when she tried to change position didn't confirm her words, Emma thought, but there were others still in need of attention. "I won't be far. Call if you need me."

The bearded man and her brother had seen to the others on deck, so Emma went below in search of a dry blanket. She waded through calf-deep water toward a wavering light at the far end of the corridor, coming from her cabin. By the time she reached the door, her bodice felt damp. She turned and stepped into *him*.

"Oh!" Staring straight ahead at his broad chest, she felt the heat of his body and swayed.

"Sorry, ma'am. I was just checking all these little rooms."

His resonant voice was easy to hear in the small cabin. "This one's mine." She tried to glance around, but he seemed to fill the small space. The *Julianna* groaned and in the next instant she felt his warm, reassuring hands on her shoulders.

"Come on, ma'am. We'd better get back up top." He held her as carefully as a china teacup, sure it wouldn't take much to snap her fine bones.

"Excuse me. I need to get a few things."

She was doing it again, he thought—whispering. Something must have caught her in the throat during the wreck, the poor little wren. There was no space to step aside, so he spanned her waist with his hands and picked her up. She quivered like a frightened animal. He turned around, trading places with her. "There you are. Don't stay down here too long."

In the blink of an eye, she stood inside her cabin, and he was gone. She was shaking as she reached for the blankets on her bunk. His hands were so large and strong, and his voice seemed to vibrate right through her. Just thinking about them made her quake anew. No man had touched more than her hand, except her brother, in the last six years. However, the man had moved so quickly, taken her by surprise, that she had not reacted in time to dodge him.

She was glad Bently had not seen what happened. Sometimes he could be so unreasonable. Still, she didn't know if she was more afraid of the man himself or her reaction to him. Just keep busy and you'll forget him. The cabin was a mess. She rummaged through both her trunks until she found a cloak, then she gathered several blankets and took them up to the top deck.

"Emma, there you are." Bently automatically moved to her right side. "Have you seen that bearded fellow?"

"Isn't he up here with you?" She continued walking toward Mrs. Lewis.

Bently gritted his teeth and matched her stride. "I need one of those for the first officer."

Emma handed him a blanket and set the other three down. "Sorry I took so long, Mrs. Lewis." She shook out one of the covers. "There must be a foot of water in the corridor and everything's a jumble."

Mrs. Lewis patted Emma's hand. "I'm fine now, dear, but I'm not sure about your brother."

Emma cast a glance in his direction. "A beam rolled onto his back. At the least, he'll be stiff and sore tomorrow. I'll see if I can't get him to rest."

"Oh, dear me! Look up there, Miss Townsend." Mrs. Lewis covered her mouth.

Following the woman's wide-eyed stare, Emma glanced up expecting to see a large gull. It wasn't. It was the bearded man swinging from a rope two thirds of the way up the remaining mast! She felt an icy wave of fear. She wanted to look anywhere but at him, but she couldn't tear her gaze away. "What is he doing?" she asked in a strained voice.

Mrs. Lewis pointed up with a shaky hand. "Up . . . there tangled in the ropes." She watched as if spellbound. "For such a large man, he's certainly agile."

"Yes, yes he is." And gentle, Emma recalled. Just then he dropped down several feet. She stifled a shriek.

Bently came up behind his sister and touched her shoulder. "What's going on?"

"That bearded man's up there. See?" She pointed to the rigging.

"And he said he didn't like ships."

"But there's a man caught up in the lines." Emma clasped her hands together. The bearded man was huge, but he now appeared much smaller and quite nimble.

Bently patted his sister's shoulder. "I'd like you to take a look at one of the seamen."

After another moment of staring aloft, Emma accompanied her brother over to the crewman, really just a gangly boy.

He was still unconscious. "Get one of the blankets." While Bently was gone, she carefully checked for broken bones but found none. He needed a doctor. They all needed a doctor, she corrected herself. As soon as the bearded man brought the injured sailor down, she would speak with him.

Bently spread the cover over the young man. "Is there anything you can do for him?"

She shook her head. "How many others are injured?"

"Five that I know of." He absently massaged his lower back. "Would you mind going down to the galley? Maybe there's some coffee left in the pot. There must be something to drink."

"Why don't you wrap a blanket around your shoulders and rest? I'll see if there's anything to drink."

Kent dropped another five feet and was almost even with the dead man. If he didn't look down at the water, he'd be fine. He'd rather be seated on his horse and riding for help, but this had to be done. He couldn't stand the sight of a body hanging overhead, and he was the only one who could do it. Just a little farther now. He could see how the man was entangled.

He inched down and looped the loose end of the rope around him to free his hands. Suspended like a fish on a line, he swung out and grabbed the man's arm, about the only part of his body that wasn't caught with a line. The rear of the ship was struck by a large wave and shifted.

"O-h-h n-o-o-o!"

He and the man swayed out over one side of the ship, then the other. It probably didn't take more than a minute; it only seemed like hours. When he was able, he pulled his knife from its sheath and cut the dead sailor free. The man had been hanging in a bent position. The sailor was slim and fit easily over Kent's shoulder for the descent.

Going down hand over hand, looping each in the rope as he went, kept Kent's mind off the water below. He stared into the distance, seeing nothing but fog, but that was better than knowing just how high up he was or how far he had yet to go to reach the deck. Another wave rocked the ship.

The sailor started to slip down Kent's arm. He let go of
the rope with the other hand and held on to the man's legs.
"I still got ya, friend. It shouldn't be much farther."

He rubbed his forehead against the back of his hand and
sighed. In that moment he got a glimpse of the deck. The
ship lurched again.

As if the rope had been greased, he slid straight down to
the deck. He landed with a thud. And, a definite crack.

❖ 2 ❖

EMMA WAS CROSSING the deck when she heard a shout and stared up in horror as the men fell toward the deck. She covered her eyes. It wasn't fair! The bearded man was their only hope. All of the survivors were injured, except for her. She stepped to the rail. Just before they'd crashed, someone had shouted, "We're goin' aground!" then she'd been pushed down to the deck. All she could see were large rocks and a bank. They should be just north of town, but it was impossible to tell in the gloom.

"You'll have to help me, Emma." Bently took her hand.

"What's wrong?"

"I can't lift the sailor by myself. Here." He took the dead man by the shoulders. "You take his feet. We've got to get him off the other one."

Gritting her teeth, Emma put a hand around each of the man's ankles. Her brother was only able to slide the man's shoulders off the other, but she managed to drag him several feet away. She caught her breath and motioned to their rescuer. "How is he?"

Bently straightened his stiff back and looked at the bearded man staring up at him. "This's a hell of a mess. You've been helping out and I don't even know your name."

He nodded to his sister at his left. "This is Miz Townsend," he said, slurring her title. "And I'm Bently Townsend."

"Kent Hogarth." He pulled himself into a sitting position against the mast and extended his hand. "Sorry I can't get up. Think my leg's broken."

He nodded to Miz Townsend. Her hair had dried some, but he still wasn't sure of the color. And she appeared to be better off than anyone else he'd seen. She was also a damned sight prettier than most women. Strange couple, though. The man's voice was almost as soft as his wife's.

Emma watched carefully while Bently talked with Kent Hogarth. She repeated "Kent" to herself and liked the sound of it. "Mr. Hogarth, would you like me to look at your leg?"

"'Scuse me?"

"Your leg. I've set broken bones. It should be done while the break is fresh." She glanced at Bently, resting on a nearby barrel.

"She's right."

Kent eyed her—small boned, hair that was beginning to remind him of dried corn, and she looked as if she'd missed more than her share of meals. Why not let her try? "I'd be obliged, Miz Townsend."

Emma put her cloak over the rail and knelt at Mr. Hogarth's feet. She might need Bently's help, she thought, then became even more determined to set Mr. Hogarth's leg herself. It was small repayment for his kindness.

"That's it, the right one."

She lightly ran her hand from his knee to his ankle and sighed. It wasn't as bad as she feared. "I will have to tear your trouser leg." She spoke without looking up. She didn't think he would object. He was strong—all over—his leg muscles almost rock hard.

"Use my knife." One good pair of pants shot to hell. He offered the handle to her.

She glanced at his face. "I'm sorry. I didn't hear you."

He extended his hand and leaned forward.

"Thank you." She set down the wide-bladed knife. Very carefully she slit the seams of his trousers up to his knee and handed the knife back to him, her attention focused only on his injury. The skin wasn't broken, thank God. She traced her fingers down the smooth flesh of his leg covered with downy soft reddish-brown hair. When her fingertips grazed the flesh a few inches above his ankle, he flinched. Ignoring propriety, she sat down on the deck with his leg between hers, resting on her skirt, and braced her outside foot on the weighted barrel at his side.

Her fingers were cool and felt like satin on the heat of his leg. They were distracting. She was the best medicine he could've hoped for. He inhaled, waiting for her to jerk the bone back in place and his rambling thoughts back to reality.

Emma knew he was watching her but refused to glance up. She didn't think the bone had moved, but she had to make sure. She wrapped both hands around his smooth, narrow ankle and pulled steadily until she felt certain the bone was in place. She lightly pressed her fingertips on the area of the fracture. She sighed and met his gaze. "You can relax now, Mr. Hogarth. I'll find some material and bandage your leg."

He realized she was stronger than she looked. "You finished, ma'am?"

She nodded and stood up. His voice was deep, and he had nice lips, easy for her to read, though she hadn't needed to.

"You sure have a gentle touch." He smiled. "Feels better already." At least it had while her cool hands had rested on his skin.

Bently waited until his sister had walked away before speaking. "Where are we? With this mist, I can't tell."

"South of the California line. I figured I wasn't too far from Pelican Cove, if that means anything to you." Kent rubbed his thigh. What a mess! From the way Townsend kept bracing his back, the fellow wasn't in much better shape than he.

"We're not far from town, then. Good. You have a wagon?"

Kent shook his head. "My horse's up there. So's my hat."

"I'll go for help. Shouldn't take too long." Bently leaned forward and stood but when he went to straighten up, he couldn't.

Kent watched Townsend and muttered. How did the man think he was going to leave the ship, let alone mount a horse? Kent decided he'd go over the side on a rope after he'd had his leg wrapped. At least his back didn't hurt, and he had two good arms, and a leg.

"Sit down, Townsend. You can't ride anywhere. Not tonight, anyway."

Emma returned and heard the last of Mr. Hogarth's comment. "Bently, what are you trying to do?"

He dropped back down on the barrel and reached around with both hands to massage his back. "I've got to go for help. Mr. Hogarth doesn't think we're far from town." He attempted to stretch his torso and gritted his teeth.

Working quickly so the tremor in her hands didn't show, Emma bandaged Mr. Hogarth's leg using strips of a bedsheet. She tied a piece of wood to his leg for support. "You'll need crutches." She spread a blanket over him and wrapped another around her brother.

"You have a horse nearby, Mr. Hogarth?"

"Up that bank. I'll lower myself to the ground with a rope. I can make a crutch from one of those broken poles."

"Good. That will keep you busy." She retrieved her cloak and put it on.

Bently stared at her. "Did you forget the coffee?"

Kent glanced from husband to wife and wondered why Bently suddenly called to his wife as if she were ten yards away. Strange couple.

Emma shook her head. "Everything's floating around or broken. You'll have to wait." She secured the cloak's ties at her neck and smiled.

"Look here, Emma, you are not setting foot off this ship until help arrives." He shook his head. "Why don't you see if there is anything to eat. Hogarth, are you hungry?"

Kent shrugged. He wasn't about to get between those two.

"I am going for help." She pulled a pair of gloves from a pocket and put them on. "I'd better leave."

Kent gazed at the embankment. "It's gettin' dark now. Why don't you wait till mornin'?"

"Some of the men might not be able to wait, Mr. Hogarth.'' She watched to see if he accepted her reasoning, then glanced at Bently.

''Don't be foolish, Emma. The Tolowas have been peaceful enough, but at night, who's to say?''

''They haven't bothered us.''

He locked his jaw and stood, his upper body still bent forward. ''I won't permit you to go!''

She stepped back out of his reach. ''One of us must. Mr. Hogarth has a broken leg, and you cannot straighten up. I'll take every caution.''

Bently braced his bad back and glared at her. ''Don't argue!'' He took two staggering steps and halted. ''It's too dangerous.''

Emma faced Mr. Hogarth. ''Do you have a rifle?'' She met his gaze and held her breath.

He nodded. ''On the saddle. Ever fire one?''

''Yes.''

''You never!'' Bently groaned. ''Don't fabricate, Emma.''

She squared her shoulders and glanced from Mr. Hogarth to her brother. ''I know how to load and fire a handgun and rifle. Ginny Talbert taught me.'' She smoothed her gloves and turned on her heel.

''Miz Townsend,'' Kent called out. ''I came over the rocks. They're slippery but it's the only way up, unless you want to use a rope.'' He watched her matter-of-fact nod and the easy sway of her skirt as she walked off. He hollered, ''Bounder's his name, and he'll take a strong arm!'' She was a little thing, but she had spunk.

Emma stood on an old piece of timber jutting out from the bank and grasped onto a fist-sized root to pull herself up. When she was young and watched the boys climbing trees and boulders, it had looked adventuresome. The reality was sore hands, scraped knees, and aching muscles. Furthermore, she learned long ago that she was not the mischievous type.

However, here she was about to embark on a ride, at night, on a strange horse through an area the Indians still claimed as their own. She inhaled deeply, brushed most of the sand from her clothes, and waved to her brother. Mr. Hogarth's horse was tethered a few feet away.

She spoke to Bounder and held her hand out while she unlooped the reins with her free hand. Mr. Hogarth must be over six feet tall, his black horse twenty hands high. They were both huge. A good match. After climbing atop a large rock, she successfully gained her seat.

The path was narrow but clear if you knew what to look for, and she did. Bently had insisted she become familiar with the territory around Pelican Cove. Now, she was grateful for his precaution.

When she nudged the horse, he took off like the devil was seated on his back. She gained little control over the stallion—just enough to dodge the low-hanging branches. He seemed to blend in with the night and run as if hurried on by a strong wind. The ride that she believed would take an hour took less than half that time.

She raced past her home at the edge of town with her hair and skirts flying. She pulled back on the reins with all her strength. Two long blocks later, she managed to slow the powerful horse as she passed her shop, guided him around the corner, and brought him to a halt in front of the general store. The new bat-and-board building with two split-log benches by the door never looked better. She dismounted and ran to the alarm bell at the corner of the porch.

She unwound the rope from the hooks and yanked hard. The bell tolled over and over, momentarily deafening her completely. With her head still ringing, she dashed to the store and banged on the door with her fists until it opened.

Emma pushed the door all the way back. ''Mr. Jenks, we have to form a rescue party!''

''Calm down, Miss Emma. Come on in and tell me what's happened.'' He took her arm.

She jerked free. ''Please . . . our ship wrecked . . . up the coast! People are hurt. We've got to help them! Don't you understand?'' Oh Lord, why didn't the man move faster?

''Why don't ya rest by the fire? I'll organize everyone. It takes time to harness up the horses, ya know.''

Emma nodded and allowed him to lead her through the small store into his living quarters in the back. Mr. Jenks was a kind man, past his prime, but his solid girth and ready smile made everyone welcome. She accepted a hot mug of coffee and gathered her thoughts while Mr. Jenks went out front to spread the news. Mr. Hogarth was a puzzlement. The man who had attacked her years ago was large, overpowering. So was Mr. Hogarth, and he was the kind of man she normally avoided, but he was tender and thoughtful. Had she been wary of the wrong things all these years?

Soon, the sound of people gathering and wagons arriving drew her outside. Men and women were chattering about the excitement. Two men started arguing about how many wagons were needed. Emma skirted the group and gave one good pull on the bell rope. There was immediate silence, and before their babble started up again, she went over by Mr. Jenks on the steps. Most of the faces were familiar, but a few new ones were mingled with the small number of townspeople.

Mr. Jenks raised his hands. "Listen up, folks, there's been a shipwreck north of here a ways. Miss Emma and her brother were coming home on it. We've got to get up there and get those people back to town. We'll need every man here and all your wagons."

"Miss Emma," one woman called out. "What d'ya want us t'do?"

Bently's house had been closed up for over a month, but it had more room than most. "Gather at my brother's house. We'll need supplies and a few more kettles to boil water. I know at least two people with broken bones. I'm not sure about the other wounds."

"Don't forget blankets and yor tools, gents. Let's git goin'!" Mr. Jenks eyed Emma. "Sure ya'll be okay? I can stop at yor house if ya like."

She smiled and touched his arm. "I'll be fine. Thank you."

"Well, git anythin' ya need from the store." He trotted back inside.

She went over to Bounder and rubbed his soft nose. "No need to run this time, boy. We're only walking two blocks."

She led the horse to the step, and mounted him. With a firm hand on the reins, she guided him around the corner and up the street to the single-story house she shared with her brother. He had promised her a mansion, in time, but theirs might be called that by Pelican Cove standards. She had a large bedroom, as did her brother, and there was also his office and a spare room. And the kitchen faced the ocean.

The town had only been in existence for seventeen months and had not grown in the last nine. Maybe the three new faces in the crowd were a good sign. And didn't Mr. Hogarth say he had been on his way here? He would definitely stand out among the other men, she mused and realized she was smiling.

Kent balanced on his good leg ready to try out the rough crutch he'd shaped. It made standing easier but when he tried to take a step, he went one way, it another. So much for resourcefulness.

Still resting on the keg, Bently watched Hogarth. "I doubt two would help on this deck."

"You're probably right. Can you use it?"

"Not unless you can strap it to my back. I never should have leaned forward." Bently gazed up at the top of the embankment. "I shouldn't have let her go, either."

Kent hobbled over near Townsend. "She seemed pretty determined. How could you've stopped her?" He leaned back against the mast and sighed. Of all the damned places to break a leg, he'd done it on a ship, but it wouldn't change his plans.

"Obviously, she didn't listen."

"Well, you must be used to that."

Bently shook his head. "Guess I never will be."

There was a stubborn streak in that woman that'd do a mule proud, Kent thought. But it wasn't his business if the man's wife was clever at outmaneuvering her husband. "She's probably setting off the alarm by now. Anyway, I hope so. We're a fine pair to play nursemaid."

"Hmph." Bently rubbed his chin and glanced around. "I'd better check on Mrs. Lewis. She hasn't made a sound."

He limped over to the woman and felt her brow. She was warm, warmer than that thin blanket warranted. "Mrs. Lewis, it's Bently Townsend. Wake up. Come on now, I just want to make sure you're all right." She moaned but did not wake. He pulled the cover up over her shoulder and went to check on the captain.

After checking the other injured men on deck, Bently made his way back to the keg and collapsed. "Help had better get here soon. One of the men died, and the others aren't doing too well. Damnation! You would think some of the Indians would have heard the wreck. Someone else must—"

"Shut up!" Kent hopped over to the rail. "Listen. Damned if that don't sound like wagons."

Joining Hogarth, Bently leaned over the rail, and craned his neck to see the roadway. "By God, you're right!"

"Hellooo . . . Bently, you down there?"

"Yes!"

Kent had never been one to join groups or spend much time in crowds, but the sound of those men coming down the bank was the next best thing to a bracer and a willing woman in a warm bed. He cupped his hands around his mouth and yelled, "Watch your footing! We've enough broken limbs."

Bently slapped Hogarth on the back. "Emma made it! But, by God, if she ever tries anything like that again, I'll tan her hide so she won't sit a horse for a month."

Kent would've bet Mrs. Townsend set Bently straight rather than the other way around. "First chance I get, I'm drinking a toast to her. Never did like boats. Now I know why."

"I'll pour that drink. I have a fine brandy at the house." Bently limped off to meet their rescuers.

Kent held on to the rail for support and hopped down to join the men who were climbing aboard. Four had made it onto the deck and five more were still on the ground. He glanced around at the injured, grateful the rescue party had arrived.

"You Hogarth?"

Kent held out his hand. "Welcome aboard."

"Charlie Jenks." He shook the outstretched hand.

"Miz Townsend made good time."

Mr. Jenks rubbed his jaw. "Never saw Miss Emma so riled up." He looked around and shook his head. "Guess she had good reason."

"Her husband's back's gettin' worse. This damned fog and cold aren't helpin' him much."

"Whose husband?"

"Miz Townsend's. Bently, over there."

Mr. Jenks chuckled. "Who told ya that? They're brother'n sister."

Kent stared at Townsend. "I must've misunderstood." In a snake's eye I did!

"I'd better check below." Mr. Jenks started for the stairs.

"Take a light. Don't know if the water's still rising down there or not." Kent continued his one-legged hopping gait until he reached a group of men. "How's the captain doing?"

One man pulled the blanket up and covered the captain's face. "How many on board?"

"Not sure. Miz Townsend thought at least twenty, but I haven't seen that many. Downstairs there're a couple more that didn't make it." Kent watched the men move off searching for survivors. A boy slid to a stop in front of him.

"'Scuse me, mister, but would ya mind kind of keepin' an eye on some of these people when we get them up to the wagons?"

Kent smiled. The boy didn't look to be more than nine, if that old. Tufts of fiery orange hair stuck out from the front of the lad's knit cap. "Don't mind at all. Do you think you can get me a good length of strong rope?"

"Sure thing." The boy ran off. He returned a short while later and held out his find. "Will this do?"

"Let's see." Kent took the cord and hung it over the side. "Just enough." He coiled it back over his arm. "Want to help me get off this dad-blamed ship?"

"Yes, sir!"

Kent hopped over to the mast and secured one end of the

rope around the base. He also picked up a strip of cloth that Miz Townsend had left on the deck and wrapped it around one hand. He used his kerchief to protect his other hand.

The boy watched in fascination. When Kent started hopping back to the rail, the boy stepped to his side. "Lean on me. Wouldn't like to see ya fall down. I don't know if I could get ya up."

Kent chuckled and put his hand on the lad's narrow shoulder. He continued on with the boy's help, though Kent didn't really put much weight on the youth. He secured the rope to the rail and dropped the length to the ground.

"What d'ya want me t'do, mister?"

"After I'm down, pull this back up and put it over by the mast. I don't want anybody tripping over the rope." He managed to keep a straight face when the boy nodded, as sober as an old-maid librarian.

Kent swung his broken leg over the rail first, then the other and grabbed hold of the rope. He was more careful this time and landed gently on his good foot.

"Okay, lad. Take it up."

He held the end of the rope so it wouldn't whip his face. It wasn't five feet above his head when he lost his balance and landed on his butt in the surf. *My own damned fault*, he thought. *Said I didn't care how soggy the ground was, as long as it was land.* His sore rump would attest to the hardness of this particular spot.

Thank God Miz Townsend wasn't here to try and bind this injury.

❖ 3 ❖

THE FIRE BLAZED in the new iron stove and the top was lined with large kettles of steaming water. Emma filled a cup with boiling water, sprinkled in a few spices, and carried it into the parlor to rid the room of the closed-up odor that still lingered. Logs were ablaze and warming the room. She had set the women to making bandages and sorting supplies. Pallets had been made up and placed a few feet apart.

She went to the front door for the ninth time in that many minutes to listen for the wagons. Was Bently able to make it up that embankment? Mr. Hogarth was strong but what if he fell climbing over the rocks? He didn't strike her as the type of man who would be held down for long. Alicia Simms joined her, opening the door even wider. She frowned, staring out into the foggy night. Emma fought the urge to smooth the lines marring her friend's pinched face.

"I hope we have enough bandages, Emma." Alicia rubbed her palms on her calico skirt. "What is taking them so long?"

Emma closed the door and started toward the fireplace. "The men will have trouble getting the injured off the ship and up that bank." She added more logs to the fire.

Alicia shivered. "I cannot imagine what you went through.

And the ride here!'' Another tremor shook her. "Weren't you frightened?"

"Mr. Hogarth's mount was so fast, it was all I could do to keep from falling off." Emma smoothed back a few strands of Alicia's black hair caught in her equally dark brows, then glanced around and smiled at Lettie, her dearest friend and partner in a women's accessory shop. They had named it the Hat Box, though they had only a few plain hats. Lettie's light brown hair was disheveled in an attractive way, and she too had worry lines.

"Emma, are you sure your brother wasn't hurt badly?"

"Reasonably. The spar didn't fall on him. It rolled onto him, knocking him out. The weight must have put his back out, though." Emma took a deep breath, praying she was right. "If it had fallen on him, his back would have been broken. He should be fine in a few days." She smiled at Lettie. Why she wouldn't admit she more than liked Bently, Emma hadn't been able to figure out. She went over to talk to Hannah Dunn, who was sorting the home remedies. "How are you at setting bones?"

"I've set a few," Hannah answered without looking up. "But didn't you say you'd set that one man's leg? Now what was his name?"

Kent Hogarth was as clear in Emma's mind as if he were standing next to Hannah. Her heart beat a little faster. "Mr. Hogarth. I did. And I think Mrs. Lewis's arm will be all right, but I wish you would look at her to make sure. I'm just not sure about the others." Hannah was plain of face with a heart of gold and a more than ordinary measure of common sense.

"Emma?" A hand touched her shoulder.

Emma whirled around.

"Why don't you lie down and rest a bit before the men get back."

"Oh, Pauline. You startled me." Pauline Young was a treasure. Her voice had a mellow tone to it and temperament to match. Emma sincerely hoped Nate, Pauline's husband, appreciated her.

"Go on. You had quite a day, and the night promises to

be long. I'm going to put on a large pot of coffee."

"That sounds good." Emma gave in to a nervous chuckle. "Thank goodness you're here."

"I brought a kettle of stew, some biscuits and bread."

"Thank you." Emma clasped Pauline's hand. "I didn't even think about feeding everyone. I'm glad you did. Bently was complaining about his stomach when I left."

"He seems to do a lot of that. Well, never mind. You take care of their hurts, and I'll fill their stomachs."

Kent sat in the back of a wagon along with five others. The driver, a tall, wiry fellow by the name of Nate Young, said he was going to take it easy so as not to jostle them too much. Kent's leg hurt like the devil.

It didn't take much imagination to know how the others felt. Even poor Townsend. He'd wanted to stay on board until his back was better. Of course he hadn't. And he probably wouldn't look kindly on Kent's quick right to the jaw for the peaceful ride back to town.

Nate glanced back at the passengers in the back of his wagon. "Everyone okay, Hogarth?"

"Most of them're out cold, includin' the kid. How much farther?" Kent smiled at Eddie. He was plum tuckered out.

"Not more'n five minutes."

"Mr. Young?" The redheaded boy ground his knuckles into his eyes.

"Yeah, Eddie?"

The boy was squirming. "I gotta piss . . . real bad."

"Hold on, boy. Won't be long."

Kent wiped the sleeve of his jacket over his damp whiskers. Eddie had found Kent's hat and had given it to him. That Eddie was a good kid. Kent shifted his rump and peered through the fog. The giant old redwoods did smell good, but he thought he also got a whiff of wood smoke.

"The Townsend house's just ahead. I can see the lights," Nate announced.

They turned off the road and continued for another couple hundred feet before coming to a stop. Eddie jumped over the side of the wagon and ran to the far side of some bushes.

The front door opened. A beacon of light from the doorway lit the yard, and four women rushed out. Kent found himself looking for one certain face. Before he saw her, he heard her voice.

"Bring everybody inside. Hannah, would you help Mrs. Lewis? Mr. Dunn, have you seen Bently?"

"Right here, Miss Emma." Mr. Dunn nodded toward Bently. "He's just coming around. There're some here that can't make it on their own."

Kent hefted himself over the side and dropped to the ground. Red-hot pain shot up his leg. He locked his jaw and waited for it to let up. Soon Eddie returned, and Kent was ready for him. "Son, would you mind helping me? I need to visit Joe, too." He nodded in the direction of the outhouse.

By the time Eddie helped Kent into the Townsend house, Kent's leg throbbed worse than ever, and he doubted Bently would keep good on that offer of brandy. But seeing Emma helped take his mind off his leg. She'd changed clothes and knotted her hair at the back of her head. A pity, but it did give him a clear view of her expressive eyes.

Emma stood by the door directing the placement of the injured and wondering what had become of Mr. Hogarth. Her neck was growing weary having to constantly turn her head to catch what was being said. Then, suddenly, *he* stood in front of her, and she smiled. "Mr. Hogarth, I wondered what had happened to you. How is your leg?" She hadn't realized how much she had been looking forward to seeing him again.

"It's been better." Kent stood on one foot with his hand on Eddie's shoulder. "Are there any empty chairs in here?"

Emma grinned. "We can do better than that. Eddie, help Mr. Hogarth over to that pallet by the settee." She had moved the table and chairs to the walls, making room for the makeshift beds.

She noticed him grimace and stepped to his left side. "Here, put your weight on my arm." His hand felt cold and rough on her sleeve. And like an iron clamp.

The first time he tried that, her arm dropped under his pressure.

"My shoulder's stronger." His large hand covered her

shoulder and spread an odd sensation down her spine. She
ignored the impulse to look up at him and braced herself.
The three of them hobbled across the room to the pallet that
was larger than the others.

Kent dropped down onto the makeshift bed and stretched
out. God, it felt good. He removed his hat and flicked it
under the sofa. Then he felt Miss Emma's light touch on his
bandaged leg. He hadn't spoken with Townsend since talking
with Jenks. Kent knew why the guy wanted him to think
"Miz Townsend" was his wife instead of his sister. Under
other circumstances, he would have thought it uproariously
funny. Hell, if he'd had a sister as pretty as her, he might've
done the same. As he watched her, he wondered what it
would take to make her laugh and how it would sound.

"It's no worse. Stay here. Mrs. Young will bring you
something to eat."

Emma edged by another pallet and stooped to feel a crewman's forehead. The man was more shaken up than injured.
She wouldn't give special treatment to Mr. Hogarth, even
though he had been a great help. Something about his gaze
and voice unsettled her in a way no man's ever had. She
motioned to Pauline.

"Ready for something to drink, Emma?" Pauline held a
tray of coffee cups and napkins.

"Later, but I think Mr. Hogarth"—she motioned behind
her—"would appreciate some."

Pauline stepped over to him and went down on one knee.
"Coffee?"

Kent nodded. "Smells good." Pelican Cove sure had its
share of pleasant-looking women. It might take him a few
days more than he'd planned to finish up here.

Pauline placed the cup and saucer within his reach. "I'll
get you a plate. Mrs. Simms is dishing out the food now. Be
right back."

Emma saw her brother propped up near the fireplace. Lettie was tucking a blanket around him. Emma went over to
check on another of the crewmen. Might as well give Lettie
a chance. Maybe Bently will lose his blinders.

Alicia tapped Emma on the shoulder. "Hannah went home

to get the smoked venison. These men eat like they haven't seen food in the last week.'' She was rubbing her hands together. ''Maybe I should send Franklin for more bread. At least it's filling.''

With all the noise, it was difficult to hear every word Alicia Simms said, but Emma understood the problem. ''Do what you think best. Before their stomachs quit rumbling, most of them should fall asleep.'' At least she hoped so.

Lettie came over next. ''Emma, your brother says his back is so stiff he can't lie down. What will we do?'' Her attention slid from Emma to Bently.

Emma stood up and moved her skirt away from the man at her feet. ''We'll bed him down on the floor. He can sleep on his side.'' She glanced around the room and didn't allow her gaze to linger on Kent Hogarth. The men were beginning to quiet down. She hoped they would sleep soundly with warm, full bellies. She knew she would, given the chance.

Emma squinted at the light coming through the window and pulled the quilt over her head. Still half asleep, she raised one knee and groaned. That opened her eyes. She experimented with her other limbs. She was sore and stiff from her neck down to her ankles and even on the inside of her thighs. It took her another moment to recall the shipwreck—the aftermath and Kent Hogarth.

Oh, what she would give to step into a deep, hot bath, scented and waiting for her. A frivolous wish, she realized, considering the injured men bedded down in the parlor. She forced herself from the warmth of her bed and hurried over to the washstand. Cold water completed the waking-up process.

She thought about Kent Hogarth and the slow smile that curved his lips when he had bid her good night. She splashed more cold water on her face, as if that would wash his image from her mind, and completed her toilet. Dressed, with her hair loosely pulled back, she went to the kitchen.

She wasn't accustomed to cooking for a large number of people. She stirred the fire in the kitchen and added kindling. Water needed to be heated, coffee made, and eventually grid-

dle cakes prepared. Soon she heard a wagon pull up in front
of the house and went out to investigate.

"Mr. Jenks, what is all this?"

"Those folks'll be hungry. Some of us wanted to help
out." He carried a barrel of flour into the house.

Emma went over and peered into the wagon bed. There
were onions, potatoes, turnips, salt, sugar, and two large
pieces of cured beef. She doubted there had been that much
food aboard the *Julianna*.

Mr. Jenks returned and saw her reach for one of the bushel
baskets. "I'll get that, Miss Emma. Ya'll have enough to
tote around in the kitchen cooking up all this." He laughed
and picked up the beef. "Roy Avery and Seth Dunn went
after the trunks and such."

She smiled and walked back to the house with him. "I
had better get started." She only glanced toward the parlor
on her way to the kitchen, not about to wake anyone. From
the variety of noises, she was safe for a while.

Kent looked around. The other men were gurgling, mumbling, or snoring. The noise really was terrible. Besides that,
he needed to make a trip outside. Another glance around told
him it wouldn't be easy to get to the door on one leg without
disturbing anyone. It was a humbling experience, not his
first, but he ended up scooting along between the pallets on
one knee and both hands.

He reached the door and pulled himself up to stand on his
good leg. He peered outside to see how far he had to go.
Forget the Joe. He'd settle for a bush. He shouldn't have
waited until Jenks left.

"What the hell?" Some things just can't wait. He braced
his hands on the doorjamb and hopped over the threshold.
The door banged against the wall, the iron handle out of
reach. He usually liked mornings, he thought grimly.

Emma had just left the kitchen to check on Bently when
the sound of the door startled her. She found Kent Hogarth
holding on to a post and jumping from the porch down to
the ground. Surely he had not grown even taller overnight?
Two steps above him, she was not more than a few inches

taller than he. But it was his winter-brown eyes that seemed
to almost touch her that bothered her most.

"Are you all right?" His gaze bored into her. She wanted
to turn away, go see if her brother was awake, and forget
she had gone outside. Instead, she stood watching the hem
of her calico skirt.

It was a hell of a mess when a man couldn't get himself
to the john. "I need to get over there," he growled, motioning to the small wooden building several yards away.

She steeled her dread—she really did not understand what
had caused it—and stepped down to his side. "Put your hand
on my shoulder."

Kent rested his hand on her narrow shoulder. She looked
scrubbed and pretty, good medicine for any man. He felt
better already.

He was *so* tall. She did not look up but stood perfectly
still, waiting to feel the pressure of his large hand. He
smelled of salt water, which was not offensive. His touch
was warm, and she was sure he wasn't putting his weight on
her.

Kent moved forward using Emma to steady himself. She'd
combed her hair back again, but more loosely so it softly
framed her face. The yard didn't look much different in the
daylight, except he now saw two outbuildings he hadn't seen
the night before. He frowned and concentrated on his footing.
He'd have to give her credit—she got him back to the parlor
and put a hot cup of coffee in his hands without any fuss or
prissy blushes.

Emma had just started a second pot of coffee and was
preparing the griddle cake batter when her brother hobbled
into the kitchen. "You shouldn't be up." She poured him a
cup of coffee. "I'll take this to the parlor for you."

"I'll drink it here." Bently sat down across the table and
clasped the hot cup with both hands. "How would I drink
flat on my back with my knees up? Or eat?"

"You'd manage." Emma carried the large bowl over to
the stove and dropped a little batter on the griddle. "I'll have
to serve everyone as the cakes are ready." She rubbed the

back of her hand over her brow. "I'm not used to cooking for so many."

"You'll do fine, Emma. Maybe you can spend the day at the shop. Lettie said she would bring her grandmother over to help out here."

That brought a smile to Emma's face. "Lydia Nance?" She flipped the testing batter into the bucket and poured four cakes on the hot griddle.

"She'll do fine."

"If she's distracted, she forgets how to make a pot of tea. She is sweet, and I adore her, but she cannot possibly handle everyone. Two of those men have something wrong with their innards and there isn't even a doctor within a hard two days' ride."

"Emma, you've done all a body can do. Besides, you know you're happier at the shop than around people you don't know." As he took a drink, he watched her over the rim of his cup.

She hadn't said a thing about being ill at ease, but he knew. He always knew. That's why he had encouraged her to open the shop, a shop selling only women's goods.

"I'll think about it."

She flipped the bubbling cakes over. The Hat Box was her solace. She felt sure her brother thought of the shop as a safe place for her, and it was. It was also a place where women could gather, have a cup of cocoa or tea, and receive support if they had problems, which most everybody did.

Kent dropped down on the sofa. Those who were able sat or wandered around the parlor. Townsend kept adding wood to the fire, and the room was warm, too warm for Kent. He preferred the outdoors, especially during the day. The fog had finally lifted. He had to admit that Townsend had chosen a perfect site for his house. It sat on top of a low bluff overlooking the Pacific Ocean and the bay. Quite a sight, when you could see more than ten feet.

Since Kent had nothing else to do, aside from handing someone a glass of water or a chamber pot that had been made available, he seated himself in a good place to watch the town. It was smaller than he'd been led to believe. The livery was on the far side of the Redwood Saloon. A barbershop and bathhouse stood on this side. There were also storefronts that looked vacant. What he didn't see were people.

Bently hobbled over and sat at the other end of the settee. "This must be pretty wearing on you."

"I can get around now." What was Bently up to? He struck Kent as a rather narrow-minded, suspicious sort of man.

Bently quickly added, "Sitting around. You look like a man who rarely dallies in a parlor."

Kent glanced down at his dirty boots and coarse pants. "You're right there." He turned his attention back to the town. "Where is everybody?"

"Digging graves. We've only had two burials here."

"Where's the cemetery?" Kent swept his gaze from one end of the town to the other. It was set in a lush valley with giant redwood trees to the north, grassland to the high mountains bordering on the east, and a good river to the south that fed into the bay.

"East of town." Bently stretched his arms out and tried to straighten his back. He stifled a groan. "Didn't you say you were headed this direction?"

Kent chuckled. "Yeah. By the way, do you know what Miz Townsend did with my horse?"

"She must've put him in the barn. I'll ask her." Bently propped his chin on his palm with his elbow on his knee.

Kent glanced at Townsend out of the corner of his eye. "This sure is a nice spot for a town. Surprised it isn't crowded with settlers."

Bently's hand curled into a fist. "When we came here, I thought Meyer's River would allow boats to carry supplies up into the mountains. I was wrong." He shook his head and sighed. "I sure was wrong. The packets even have trouble getting around that island out there." He pointed to the ocean.

Looking out to sea, Kent noticed the island for the first

time. "Lucky your ship didn't wreck out there."

"It's happened. There's only one skiff in town. It can't make it out that far in rough weather." The unmistakable sound of breaking glass echoed from the kitchen, and Bently cringed. "Mrs. Nance, are you all right?"

"Fine. Just fine."

Bently brushed at a speck on his pant leg. "She's Miss Morrissey's grandmother. Mrs. Nance tries, but her joints are stiff. She means well."

Kent heard Mrs. Nance's halting footsteps before she actually entered the parlor carrying a small tray. When he saw her he started to rise, then remembered he'd be of no help. Her face was lined and her hair white, but the light in her blue eyes made him smile. She must have been a beauty forty or so years ago.

Mrs. Nance handed a cup on a saucer to Kent. "You must be that young man Bently here wishes would leave town." She peered into his eyes and grinned. "I hope you don't, young man."

❖ 4 ❖

THE YELLOW BUILDING trimmed in white with the front bay window gave Emma a warm, welcome feeling. The small brass bell above the door jingled when she entered the Hat Box. It was really a house with the shop on one side and two bedrooms and a parlor on the other side, where Lettie and her grandmother lived. Emma surveyed the shop like a mother viewing the treasured faces of her children after a long separation. It had not changed in her absence, except for the display in the bay window. Lettie had been busy in her absence. There was a pretty hat box she must have re-decorated and a straw bonnet with silk violets.

The five slat-back chairs were still placed around the calico-cloth-covered pedestal table. Near the door stood a hall stand displaying two more bonnets, and an oak wardrobe displaying plain and lacy apparel. Across the room was a small cheval glass mirror.

She put her cloak and reticule away before straightening a small display of lace-edged handkerchiefs. They rarely sold one, but the women did enjoy looking at them. She heard Lettie enter and smiled. "It's good to be home, though I wish you had come with us." She checked their supply of collars and silk ribbons.

"Gram can't manage on her own and we both couldn't leave the shop for that long, or at least I'd like to think so." Lettie held up a chambray bonnet with blue and white plaid ribbons.

"Would you mind terribly if I didn't stay? Lydia shouldn't be tending those people." Emma tossed a silk shirtwaist in emerald-green into an open drawer and left one sleeve hanging over the side. Another frivolous item, one she would love to wear.

"You know Gram likes to visit. It will keep their minds off their grief and broken bones." Lettie picked up an intricately carved ivory fan and waved it in front of her face. "Think we'll ever sell this?"

Emma laughed. "I think we've purchased more than a few items we liked, rather than the more practical accessories." The brass bell rang out again, and Mrs. Talbert entered.

"Hello, Ginny."

"Emma! I was hoping you'd returned. How was your trip?" Ginny embraced Emma and stepped back before eyeing her.

Emma raised her hand to the neckline and began fingering the buttons on her shirtwaist. "What's wrong? Have I lost a button?"

Ginny shook her head. "You haven't changed. I was hoping to see a gleam in your eye—the kind you'd have after meeting a handsome man."

Emma shook her head. "Sit down, Ginny. You're too far along to be dashing about. Or trying to play matchmaker. Tea or cocoa?" Emma envied Ginny. She was eighteen years old, married to a nice man, carrying their first child and wanted everyone to be as happy as she was. Emma yearned to experience her friend's joy, but that could never be. She had accepted that long ago. She started for the kitchen and paused.

"Tea, thank you."

The shop was actually one side of Lettie's house in front of the kitchen. Emma returned with cups and a teapot. The sugar bowl was on the table along with linen napkins and spoons.

She poured three cups, passed them out and sat down near Ginny. "How's Will?"

"A wreck! He'll wear himself out before the babe is born." Ginny wrinkled her nose. "Before I forget, I came in for the lavender petticoat you had in your window. You haven't sold it, have you?"

Lettie laughed. "No. We put it away last summer."

"Oh, good. You did say that it was larger around than the others, didn't you?"

"I did," Emma said, stepping over to the wardrobe. "I'll get it for you." She grinned. Ginny always cheered her up.

Lettie set her cup down. "Ginny, did you hear about the shipwreck?"

"When?" Ginny frowned.

"Last night—"

"I thought I heard the alarm last night, but Will didn't wake up, so I figured I must've dreamed it. I've been sleeping like the dead lately. Was anybody hurt?"

Lettie glanced at Emma. "It was the ship Emma was returning on. It ran aground just up the coast."

Ginny was just setting her cup down. It clattered on the saucer, sloshing the tea. "Emma! Why didn't you say something? Gracious, no wonder you look peaked. Are you all right?"

"Yes." Emma handed the petticoat to Ginny and sat down. "Bently injured his back, and Mr. Hogarth, the man who tried to help everyone, broke his leg. Several of the crewmen and passengers are at the house. Lydia's there now."

Ginny scooted to the edge of her chair. "How can I help?"

"We could take turns." Lettie looked from Ginny to Emma. "That way you wouldn't have to do all the cooking and laundry."

Ginny absently massaged the small of her back. "Everybody survived?"

"No. I'm not sure how many died." Emma's lips quivered. How long would it take for the memory of those men to fade? She couldn't imagine what they would've done without Mr. Hogarth. "Mr. Jenks said he would organize the men to dig the graves. I hope Bently hasn't forgotten the pine boxes."

After taking two steps, Kent grinned at Jenks. "These'll do just fine. What do I owe you?" He turned, forgetting the newly acquired crutches. He teetered and swung the sticks to regain his balance

Mr. Jenks steadied Hogarth. "Easy. They'll take some getting used to, I imagine. They're yors while ya need 'em."

"Come with me. Townsend said my horse should be in the barn. I might have something to trade."

Kent moved across the dirt yard slowly at first. Walking on crutches was like trying to manage two extra legs. They reached the barn, and he found his saddle on the floor near one of two stalls.

"I won't take your saddle." Mr. Jenks stood in the doorway watching Hogarth.

"I'm not offering it."

Kent propped the crutches against the side of the stall and untied a bundle. "Three pure white rabbit pelts. Maybe you can sell them to the ladies for collars, cuffs, or such. Fair trade for use of these." He replaced the crutches under each arm. "God, it's good to move about on my own again."

Mr. Jenks slid his fingers through the rabbit fur. "Tell ya what. Ya're not goin' to be ridin' out for a while. There's an abandoned cabin 'cross the way. Ain't much, but ya might as well use it. The hotel's boarded up, but don't 'magine anyone'd mind ya stayin' there, either."

"Whose cabin is it?" After what Mrs. Nance said, this was probably the best offer he'd receive. Besides, it suited his needs perfectly.

"No one now. The fellow wasn't too sociable. Anyway, he took off last winter. Said there were too many folks around for him." Mr. Jenks shrugged. "Might as well use it."

"Think I will. Thanks for the offer." They walked back to the house. Kent hesitated at the steps. This might be tricky. "Could I trouble you for a ride over there? Don't think I'm up to mounting my horse just yet.'' He stepped up and brought up the crutches.

"Day after tomorrow okay? That place'll need airin' out, though.''

"Fine.'' By then, Kent thought, the pain in his leg should be down to a dull throb.

"Oh, we'll be buryin' those people from the wreck that day, too. Thought ya'd want to know.'' Mr. Jenks tipped his cap and started for his wagon.

Kent maneuvered around and faced the yard. "Wait up. Can you come by for me? I'd like to help.''

"Sure thing.''

Kent watched Jenks's wagon head for the road. Good sort. Friendly and not soft in the head. Kent wheeled around and went into the house. Having spent the day in the parlor, he wanted a change of scene, and enticing aromas were drifting from the doorway on his right.

He entered the kitchen and found Miss Emma standing in front of the stove stirring something in a large pot. He hadn't seen her since morning. Though she wore a dress that showed off her shape well enough, he didn't think much of the dun color. Her hair was still pulled back and fastened tight, as if it might fall out if it weren't.

Emma tasted the stew. Satisfied she had seasoned it sufficiently, she turned around to the worktable and started at the sight of Kent Hogarth in her kitchen. He was staring at her with an odd expression in his eyes—not quite a smile. Avoiding his piercing gaze, she grabbed a knife and the loaf of bread.

"Supper will be ready soon. If you're thirsty, the bucket is there.'' She pointed the knife at the end of the table.

He hadn't shaved off his beard. It had not filled out, and she suspected he didn't usually wear one. She glanced at him out of the corner of her eye, wondering what he would look like without it.

"Thank you, *Miss* Emma.'' He wanted her to know he didn't still believe she was married. Sure enough, her cheeks turned a nice shade of red and her eyes an angry green. He gulped down two dippers of water and left her gaping after him.

She had *never* heard "miss" sound so insulting in all her days! She raised the knife and chopped off the end of the bread. The remainder of the loaf followed in short order, but she was still angry. If only he had come in earlier, she would have had the vegetables cut in half the time.

While she dished the stew onto the plates, she remembered Bently had said Kent Hogarth would not stay with them until his leg mended. Maybe he would get a ride south to San Francisco, or east to the gold fields, or even up to Jacksonville. Ever since he'd come into her life, she found herself saying and doing things so unlike herself.

Emma served the recovering crewmen and passengers in the parlor, five besides Mr. Hogarth and Bently, then took a tray to Mrs. Lewis in the spare room.

"Mrs. Lewis? It's Emma Townsend . . ." Emma balanced the tray with one hand and eased the door open. The only other woman passenger was sitting up in bed dozing. Emma set the tray down on the small table by the bed and tiptoed out. The older woman's color was a little better, but she was listless, and Emma was at a loss as to what else she could do for her.

Emma glanced around the green, unfenced cemetery. The men who had perished in the shipwreck were being buried. Thankfully, the survivors were on the mend, although they weren't able to come with her and her brother. It was cool and foggy but everyone in town attended, including Kent Hogarth. He had changed into clean brown trousers and a blue shirt—and had trimmed his beard. Gracious, he was handsome, she thought, then suddenly remembered where they were. She stood at her brother's side, clutching her best handkerchief in her gloved hand.

Bently cleared his throat. "The Lord giveth, and the Lord taketh away; Blessed be the name of the Lord." He opened his Bible. " 'The Lord is my shepherd; I shall not want. He maketh me to lie down . . .' "

Emma had kept herself busy the last few days, but she could no longer avoid mourning the men. The tears finally came in a rush. A few moments later, Bently closed the Bible and lowered his head.

"Earth to earth, ashes to ashes, dust to dust . . ."

As the memory of another burial, that of their parents on the trail west, penetrated her thoughts, Emma grasped her brother's arm with one hand and tried to dry her eyes with the other. At least she and Bently still had one another. And for that she was most thankful.

Charlie Jenks, Franklin Simms, Nate Young, Will Talbert, John Pool, Seth Dunn, Roy Avery, and Virgil Chase went over to the coffins. The men paired off and began lowering the pine boxes into the freshly dug graves. To Emma's surprise, Kent Hogarth hobbled over to the markers, spoke with Mr. Jenks, and placed the first one in the soft earth. By the time the last coffin had been put to rest, the fog had lifted. The men were in shirtsleeves and wiping their sweaty brows.

She noticed her brother shifting his weight from one leg to the other. "Bently, please sit. There's a log just behind us."

"No. We don't even have a preacher. The least I can do is wait until those men are in the ground, properly buried, before I think of my own comfort." He eased his shoulders back.

"Then do it for me. My feet are numb, but I can't leave you standing here alone."

She had dried the last of her tears and silently said prayers for the deceased's souls and her parents. There was nothing more to be done for them now, until spring when she would place flowers on their graves.

"Bently . . ." She rested her hand on his sleeve. "You did all you were able to do." Their parents died when their wagon fell down into a deep ravine two months before they had reached Oregon, and since then he'd taken everything seriously, sometimes too seriously, and she had to reassure him that he had done his best.

"I tried, Emma."

*   *   *

Kent straightened the last marker and grabbed his crutches. It was rankling to pound markers into the ground and not be able to do more. He brushed off his trouser legs and started for Jenks's wagon. The old man had not only brought Kent out to the cemetery but was also taking him to the cabin.

The town was small, not more than a few blocks in any direction. He should be able to hobble anyplace he had to go. Once he got settled in, he would see about finding work. Everyone headed for their wagons. Jenks approached with the Townsends.

Kent tipped his hat to Emma before addressing brother and sister. "Nice service." He laid his crutches in the back of the wagon.

"A preacher couldn't have done better, Bently," Mr. Jenks added, and tossed his coat over the side of the wagon.

Kent held out his hand to Townsend. "Thank you for your hospitality. I won't be troublin' you any more." He dusted off his hat and met Emma's gaze. "Miss Townsend, you've been a real good doctor. My leg's feelin' better every day." He plopped his battered hat on his head and hefted himself up to the wagon seat.

Emma glanced from her brother to Kent Hogarth. "You have found a ride, then?"

"Ride, Miss Townsend?"

"Out of town." She slipped her finger under her collar and ran it around the neckline of her black dress. "I understood you were passing through."

"Not right away." He patted his bum leg. "Mr. Jenks told me about a cabin I could use. I can get around now, so there's no use my imposin' on you folks any longer." He arched one brow. Was she eager to get shed of him? If so, why? "But I'm looking forward to seeing you 'round town."

Jenks joined Kent on the wagon seat and started the horses moving. Kent tipped his hat to Miss Emma, then sat back with his bandaged leg resting on the footboard and made note of the surroundings.

Looking back beyond the cemetery, he saw a farmhouse quite a ways north. "Nice spread."

"Talbert farm. Will Talbert's the skinny young man with

big shoulders. Ginny, that's his missus, is a nice young thing. Always has a big smile for everybody. They'll be havin' their first young'un before long.''

Kent remembered the woman. She was cute, and her eyes held a spark even though her expression had been somber. Lucky man, her husband. The area was nice—big trees near the small cabin, plenty of water, and everything was green—just like above the state line in Oregon. He had his eye on a nice parcel of land north of Jacksonville. Now if he ever settled down, it'd be up there.

He didn't like that train of thought. He focused on the surroundings. The saloon was just ahead. Thank God they were back in town. After Jenks dropped him off at the cabin, Kent decided he would wander around. Get a feel for the town. Visit the saloon.

Mr. Jenks rounded the corner. ''Cabin's right up ahead, in those pines.''

The log cabin had character. The east and north walls were near two young redwoods—which were only about twenty feet tall. Kent climbed down to the ground as soon as the wagon stopped. He grabbed the crutches and went off to explore. The logs were of every size and gave him the feeling that the cabin listed westward as if it were windblown like the coastal pines.

Mr. Jenks followed at a slower pace with Kent's bedroll and saddlebags. ''It'll need to be cleaned out—more than I remembered. Like I told ya, no one's been in there since last winter.'' Mr. Jenks glanced sideways at Kent. ''Don't feel obligated to stay here if ya don't want to.''

''This will do.'' For the short time I'll be here, Kent thought.

''I'll leave yor things out here.''

Kent nodded. The stick-and-daub chimney looked good enough. He jabbed one crutch up at the overhang. As long as they didn't get a heavy snow he figured he wouldn't wake up with the roof on his blanket. The logs were weathered, and there were some spaces in the clay chinking. The door was solid and swollen. It took both men to get it open. Kent stood on the threshold and stared inside.

Opposite the door was a framed opening, less the glass, with a shutter and a bottle-glass window. But from what he saw, animals weren't responsible for all of the filth. The last occupant left a split-rail bedstead, a small wooden table, and what looked like a section of a tree trunk that made a good stool. Well, as long as the clay fireplace, roof, and walls held up, he'd take care of the rest. He turned and gasped for breath. Damnation, he hoped there wasn't a dead skunk or some other critter in there.

Mr. Jenks rubbed his stubbled chin. "It's worse off than I thought. If ya'd rather hole up in the hotel, I don't figure anybody'd mind."

Kent shook his head. "It'll clean up fine." He hobbled inside and opened the shuttered window. "Think Eddie'd want to earn some pocket money?"

"He's Seth and Hannah Dunn's boy. They live down First Street. Seth Dunn owns the livery. It's behind the house on Front Street." Mr. Jenks nodded, saying, "That Eddie's a good young'un. I'll ask next time I see him."

"I appreciate your help, Jenks. If you need any work done around your store, I'm handy with tools—long as it isn't the roof."

"Good enough." Mr. Jenks got back up on the wagon seat and went off down the path.

Kent rested against the trunk of an old tree. If the tract had been marked off, the cabin would be about three blocks due north of the Townsend house. Not a bad view, if there'd been a porch to sit on.

Emma settled back on the bench seat of their buckboard. "Bently, please collect yourself. I know less about Mr. Hogarth's activities than you." She recalled the twinkle in Kent Hogarth's eyes when he mentioned the cabin as she loosened the ties of her old black bonnet. Her heart began pounding. She would see him again.

"Hogarth's a troublemaker." Bently's gaze moved down from her bonnet to the tips of her black shoes. "I've managed to protect you from the likes of him since we came here."

''Yes, Bently.'' Sometimes, like now, she worried about her brother. Out of habit, or so she assumed, he walked her to and from the shop each day. Now that she thought about it, he was usually with her whenever she went anywhere.

He persisted. ''You didn't know he was staying in town?''

''No, Bently.'' She didn't dare let him know she was glad Kent wouldn't be leaving soon, and she'd better remember to use his last name or she'd never hear the last of it.

''I *do not* want you looking at that man *or* speaking to him. Is that understood?''

''Yes, Bently.'' She closed her eyes and breathed in the salty air, forcing her thoughts to what she would wear to the shop that afternoon.

Bently turned down the drive and stopped the buckboard in front of their house. ''Let me know when you're ready to go to the shop. I'll drive you.'' He glanced at his hand. He'd wound the reins so tight around his palm that it had started to ache.

Emma stepped down. When she started around the buckboard, she glanced at the old shack and wondered if that was the one Mr. Jenks had suggested. The building stood in shadow, but she could have sworn there was something different about it. It must be her imagination. Old Mr. Hayes had been gone since last winter and she was surprised the shack hadn't fallen down. She shaded her eyes and squinted. Kent? Her heart started pounding in her breast, then she shook her head.

Impossible.

Someone stepped outside.

She turned away. No one else in town looks like *him.*

She spun around. *It can't be! Not so close.*

Bently frowned at her. ''What are you smiling about?''

❖ 5 ❖

AFTER MISS EMMA entered the house, Kent grinned. He did like the view. But he couldn't spend all his time watching her house. He picked up the crutches and hobbled down the path to the road. If he was going to spend the night there, he'd need supplies. He should've thought of that earlier but the walk would do him good.

After he passed the pine trees between the cabin and the road, he cut through the bushes and came out on the road not far from a yellow house near the center of town. He had overheard Townsend talking to Miss Emma about her shop and decided it must be hers. Surely the town couldn't support two such stores. The Hat Box. When he passed it, he noticed women's gloves, a shawl, and gewgaws in the front window but no hats.

The general store was around the corner, centered at the end of the block with a vacant lot on either side. He kept the pace he'd set until he entered Jenk's store. It smelled good—oiled leather, tobacco, and vinegar. However, the aroma of hot coffee along with the sight of baskets of carrots and potatoes and smoked hams hanging from a low beam brought a rumble from his stomach. Tonight, after the cabin's been cleared out, he promised himself, I'll be having a real meal.

Mr. Jenks came out of the back room. "Hello, Hogarth." He set four lanterns on the floor near the shovels. "Come by for a cup of hot coffee?"

"That'll do for a start. I need a few supplies. A bucket, one of those lanterns, and plenty of oil for it, a shovel—"

Mr. Jenks laughed. "We should've stopped by here on the way over to the cabin." He set the cup of coffee on the counter. "Call out what ya want, and I'll get it for ya."

Kent sipped the hot coffee and kept his list to the basics, but the pile of supplies was more than he could carry back with him. "Might as well add a small ham. And a short length of twine to tie the shovel to one of the crutches. I'll put what I can in the bucket and come back for the rest later."

"The team's still hitched to the wagon, an' I don't have any deliveries today if ya want to take it."

"Thanks. That'd make it easier." Kent drained the cup and paid for the supplies. After he helped load the wagon, he climbed up to the seat. "See you in a little while."

Mr. Jenks stepped up on the board walk in front of his store. "I'm not worried. Take yor time, son."

Kent waved and guided the team around the corner and past the Hat Box. Townsend and Miss Emma were heading his way. When they were abreast, Kent tipped his hat. Townsend gave him a curt nod, but he thought Miss Emma started to smile. When Kent turned on the path to the cabin, he glanced back at the Townsends. Their buckboard was stopped in front of the yellow shop. It was close to the general store. The town was small. He'd definitely be seeing more of her.

After Kent ate a couple of slices of smoked ham, he returned the wagon before he began scraping layers of dirt and whatever from the bedstead, and the top of the table. When he cleaned out the fireplace, he discovered a chimney crane on the blackened sidewall that would make cooking easier. He had just replaced the ropes on the bed when Eddie called to him from the doorway. Kent smiled at him. "Hello. Come on in."

Eddie peered around the corner before he stepped inside. "Mr. Jenks said you might need some help."

"That I do." Kent secured the end of the rope and watched the boy. "Did you know the man who lived here?"

"Ol' Mr. Hayes." Eddie ventured farther into the cabin. "I seen him 'round. Never been in here b'fore, though."

Kent picked up the crutches and moved toward the open window. "Think you can scrape the floor clean with that shovel?"

Eddie nodded. "I clean out the stalls for Pa. Want me to start now?"

"Your parents know where you are?"

"Yes, sir. Pa'd tan my britches if I took off."

"My ma was partial to a switch." Kent grinned. "Think the job's worth five cents?"

"Oh, yes!" Eddie grabbed the shovel and started in one corner.

Kent picked up the bucket and went in search of the well or a creek. After circling the area, he had the sinking feeling he'd have to make a trip down to the river. While the boy worked, he plugged the holes he'd found in the chinking. He was surprised he hadn't found any dead critters. He wasn't particularly fussy about his surroundings, but if he was going to share the cabin, he'd rather have a two-legged roommate—one with nice curves and a whispery voice would be nicer than the four-legged variety.

It took the boy an hour to finish. The cabin now had a fresh floor and the place smelled a whole lot better. "You did a real good job, Eddie. I'll give you another five cents if you get some water for me. There doesn't seem to be a well around here."

Eddie grinned. "That's easy. It won't take me any time a'tall." He leaned the shovel against the wall and took off running with the bucket swinging from his hand.

Kent chuckled. If the boy brought back enough water to wash his face and hands, and make a pot of coffee, it would be enough for the night. It was close to sundown. He brought his gear and supplies into the cabin, lighted the fire and laid out his bedroll on the newly strung bed.

When he'd finished, he glanced around. It looked lived in. Hell, all it needed were gingham curtains and a dog. Well, by the time he could sit his horse, he'd know enough about the town to decide if it could support a shipping office. Then he'd be on his way.

Kent heard a wagon approaching and went outside. Eddie was in the back of the wagon.

"I got your water, Mr. Hogarth." Eddie jumped down to the ground and carried the bucket of water over to Kent. "See? It's almost full."

Kent smiled. "It sure is. Thanks, Eddie." He looked at Mr. Dunn. "I hope you didn't mind my asking your boy to get the water for me."

Mr. Dunn jumped down from the wagon. "Not at all. But that pail won't last long. I have an extra water barrel." He lifted the barrel from the back of the wagon and walked toward the cabin. "Thought you might need it. Brought a few more buckets of water, too. Eddie can get you more tomorrow."

"That's mighty kind of you, Mr. Dunn. You've got a good boy there." Kent moved aside.

"I kinda like him, too," Seth said with a smile. "You want this inside or out?"

"In. By the door is fine." Kent wasn't used to feeling about as useful as a third thumb.

Mr. Dunn set the barrel in the cabin and motioned for Eddie to pour the bucket of water in. "Jenks said you have a horse. I own the livery. If you want to board him with me, we can work something out. I also have a small forge, if you happen to need any ironwork done."

Eddie carried another bucket into the cabin, poured the water into the barrel, and went to the wagon for another one.

"I'd like to move Bounder from Townsend's barn." Kent offered his hand to Mr. Dunn. "I'll bring him over tomorrow. If there's anything I can do to help you, just let me

know. My leg's not much good now, but my back and arms
are fit.''

"Call me Seth,'' Dunn said, shaking Kent's hand.

"Kent.''

"If I think of something, I'll let you know.'' Seth motioned for his son to get in the wagon. "Want Eddie to get
your horse and bring him over? He's good with animals.''

Kent smiled but shook his head. "Bounder can be a handful.'' He was still amazed that Miss Emma had ridden him
to town without mishap. "I'll walk him over.''

Eddie leaned over the side of the wagon. "Mr. Hogarth,
do you wanna come see my dog? She had puppies in the
summer. Only two black ones but they're real cute.''

"I bet they are.''

Seth looked back at his son. "He'll see 'em later, son.
'Night, Kent.''

After they left, Kent looked out to sea. The horizon was
a golden blaze that faded to the lightest blue. With the last
burst of sunlight, he gazed at the Townsend house. A light
was on in the kitchen. As he stared, he remembered the afternoon he walked in on Miss Emma when she was slicing
bread. Her eyes flashed and her skirts swished about her trim
ankles.

He smiled and said, "See you tomorrow, Miss Emma,''
and went inside.

Emma finished washing the breakfast dishes, dried and put
them away. Since her brother's back still bothered him, she
wrapped her shawl around her shoulders and went to feed
the horses. The coast was blanketed with fog and on days
like this it was easy to believe they lived far from any other
living soul. She couldn't see past the bushes between the
house and the road. The surf sounded distant and even the
gulls were quiet.

The horses greeted her with soft nickers. After she had fed
them, she watched the stallion a moment and wondered about
Kent Hogarth. He had moved out of their house, but he
hadn't left her thoughts. She stroked the stallion's sleek neck

and whispered, "I fear your master's going to upset our quiet lives," then hurried back to the house.

She and Lettie were going to cut fabric needed for a couple of quilts. The nights were growing cold. She put on her yellow calico, coiled her hair on the back of her head, and buttoned her shoes before she stepped across the hall to check on Mrs. Lewis.

Mrs. Lewis scooted up on the pillow. "My, you look pretty on such a gloomy day."

Emma smiled. "Are you warm enough?" She straightened the bedcovers. "Can I get you something before I leave?"

"Don't worry about me, dear. I really must start doing for myself."

"My brother will be here for awhile. You might like sitting in the parlor. There's more light in there, and it's warmer." There was a renewed strength in Mrs. Lewis's voice, and Emma felt better about having to leave. She knocked on Bently's office door and peeked inside. "You won't forget to come by the shop for Lydia, will you?" Sometimes he became so caught up in his ideas and plans for the town he forgot about everyone else. As the town founder, he felt responsible for its success and was very disappointed when his hope to boat supplies upriver failed.

Bently glanced up from the ledger. "No, of course not."

"Then I'll see you later."

He checked his pocket watch. "Why are you leaving so early? I'll be finished here within the hour and drive you to the shop."

"Lettie and I want to get an early start. Don't—"

"I won't forget Mrs. Nance."

"I hope not," she said, closing his door. She came close to adding, "Lettie wouldn't mind if you called on her later," but Emma knew if she pushed him too hard, he'd run the other way.

She put on her favorite hunter green, octagon-button bonnet, wool cape, and left the house. The fog still hung in the air and dampened the ground. It also hid the old cabin from view. She held to her brisk pace and told herself that she was grateful *he* had rescued them. That was all. He was a stranger and surely wouldn't have any reason to stay in town after his leg healed. She recited that litany until she tapped on the front door of the shop, to signal Lettie it was her, before she entered.

The bell also rang out when Emma opened the door. The fire in the woodstove had taken the chill from the shop. She took off her bonnet and cape as she walked back to the kitchen and hung them on the peg. Lettie and Lydia were seated at the worktable. "Good morning. Something smells wonderful."

"I woke up early and started a kettle of soup." Lydia poured a cup of tea and set it out for Emma.

"Thank you." Emma sat down at the table. "Bently should come by for you within the hour, that is, if you still want to stay with the men today."

"Oh, yes, dear." Lydia smiled. "The young men are so nice but poor Mrs. Lewis." Lydia shook her head. "Her spirits have been so low."

Emma nodded. "She was badly shaken by the shipwreck, but she seemed better this morning. It might help if you could encourage her to keep you company in the parlor or kitchen."

Lettie met Emma's gaze. "Do you think Mrs. Lewis could have other injuries?"

"When I ask how she feels, she says she's fine. I can't force her to tell me what's wrong." Emma took a sip of tea. "At least the men appear to be recovering."

Lettie stood up, stepped over near her reading chair in the corner, and looked out through the back window. "You shouldn't have to put them up indefinitely. Bently should open the hotel."

"That's a good idea," Emma said. "Why don't you talk to him when he comes by for Lydia?" She started clearing the round pedestal table in the shop where they visited, shared a cup of tea, and, occasionally, hot chocolate.

Lettie's glance darted to Emma and back outside. "Oh, I couldn't. He might think I was prying into his affairs."

"Heaven forbid," Emma said, not caring if she sounded snippy, "you should speak of anything more personal than the weather."

"I'll ask him," Lydia said, grinning. "It will be something to talk about with him."

Emma laughed. "He has been out of sorts recently." She winked at Lydia. "I'll start cutting the pieces for the quilts."

Lydia glanced at her granddaughter. "Mrs. Lewis and I could crochet doilies or trim the hotel pillowcases."

"Mrs. Lewis may not feel up to it, Gram, but you could make a doily or two."

"Yes, dear," Lydia said absently, as if she were deep in thought.

Emma got the scissors and thread and set the pile of neatly folded scraps of fabric on the table. "Lettie, did you choose a design for your quilt?"

"I'm partial to the stepping stones." Lettie showed Emma two pieces of paper on the table. "Which do you like?"

"That's what I had in mind, too." Emma smiled. "If we made a dozen of the same pattern, no two would match."

Lydia went out into the shop and fingered a plain piece of cotton twill. "Lettie, would you mind if I cut a few squares from this? I would like to start a friendship quilt."

"Of course, Gram. That's a wonderful idea." Lettie laid out the fabric and cut several squares. "That should keep you busy for a while."

"Thank you, dear." Lydia went to her bedroom and returned with thread and two needles. She worked the needles into the fabric and folded it over the thread. "Oh, was Mrs. Lewis's trunk removed from the ship? I know she would be more comfortable with her own things around her."

"It's in her room—under the window," Emma said. "Did she ask about it?"

"Not really. She just mentioned missing her things."

Emma thought a moment. "I believe her shawl's on top, but it's the only trunk in the room."

Lydia picked up the rolled fabric and as she walked away said, "I'll speak with her. She may have just forgotten it was there."

Lettie waited until her grandmother had walked down the hall, then looked at Emma and laughed. "Gram enjoys helping out at your house, and visiting with Mrs. Lewis and the men. I wish she would be as nice with your brother."

"Sometimes I wonder if he's forgotten how to have a conversation with anyone." Emma laid out a piece of fabric and began cutting it into rectangles and squares.

"He's a serious man. He takes his responsibilities to heart." Lettie started trimming a small scrap. "You know how worried he's been about the town since the hotel closed."

Emma glanced at her. Everyone, at least the women, knew Lettie had a case on Bently. If Bently knew, he certainly didn't act like it. Emma thought they would make a good match and had hinted to him about Lettie's interest. Maybe he would notice her if they were locked together in the pantry.

A little while later, Bently came by for Lydia, and Emma met him at the door. "Mrs. Nance made a kettle of soup. Would you carry it out for us?" As Bently passed her, she touched his coat sleeve. "Lettie asked about you."

Bently leveled his gaze at her and said softly, "As, I am sure, she did about the other injured people at our house. She is most considerate. Matchmaking is unbecoming, Emma." And he walked back to the kitchen. "Good morning, Miss Morrissey."

Emma followed him, glaring at his back. Sometimes he could be a real toad.

Lettie smiled at Bently. "It's nice to see you, Mr. Townsend."

A moment later Lydia came into the kitchen. She looked from her granddaughter to Bently. "If you two chatterboxes are done, we can leave, Bently."

Moving quickly to Lydia's side, Emma linked arms with her. "I'll walk out with you."

Bently went over to the stove and reached for the pot.

"Wait—the kettle's hot. You'll ruin your gloves." Lettie handed him a towel and reached for a second one. "Gram can bring them back tonight."

"Thank you." He picked up the kettle. "This smells very good. I hope you saved some for your dinner."

"Yes, I did set some aside for Emma and me," she said, following him outside.

He set the pot on the floor of the buckboard and handed Mrs. Nance up to the seat, then he turned to Lettie and Emma. "I'll see you ladies later."

Lettie smiled at him. "Have a good day, Mr. Townsend."

Emma stepped behind Lettie. "You've known him more than long enough to call him by his given name. We aren't in Boston."

"I couldn't . . . not with him." Lettie turned and walked back into the shop. "He might think I'm overly bold."

Emma chuckled. "How could he? You've seen him nearly every day for a year and a half. I bet Ginny let her Will know she was interested in him."

"Ginny is so cute she can get away with saying the most outlandish things and everyone laughs." Lettie opened the curtain around the bay window.

Emma tied back the curtain on the side window. "Women have been allowing men to catch them for centuries. At least let him know he's in the race."

As Lettie removed the glass chimney from one oil lamp, she glanced sideways at Emma. "What about Mr. Hogarth? Does he know he's in 'the race'?"

Emma stared at her in amazement. "Why, Miss Morrissey, I believe you're trying to get a rise out of me." She opened the folding screen at the back of the shop to block the view of the kitchen. "You know I'm not interested in marriage." That wasn't true but it might as well be. She kept her hands busy so they wouldn't shake. As close as she was to Lettie, Emma couldn't tell her why she could never marry.

"If he catches you casting him one of your 'I'm not interested' looks, you'd better watch your step. I have the feeling he wins most of his races."

After breakfast, Kent made his way over to the Townsend house on his crutches. He knocked on the front door and waited to see if Miss Emma would answer. A woman's voice drifted out as the door opened.

Lydia smiled at him. "What a pleasant surprise. Please come inside, Mr. Hogarth." She opened the door wide. "Go on into the parlor. Everyone's in there."

"It's nice seeing you again, Mrs. Nance. Is Miss Emma home?"

"She's at the shop, just like every day."

He went in and joined the crewmen and passengers from the ship. Mrs. Lewis was seated near the fireplace, and he smiled at her. "It's good to see you up and around, Mrs. Lewis."

"Thank you, young man." Mrs. Lewis narrowed her gaze. "Aren't you the one who climbed up to rescue that poor crewman caught in the ropes?"

Kent nodded. "Someone had to do it."

"Sit down and rest your leg." She motioned to a nearby stool. "And tell me your name. I can't seem to remember it."

"Kent Hogarth, Mrs. Lewis. I don't think we were introduced the other night."

Lydia brought Kent a cup of coffee. "Will you join us for dinner, Mr. Hogarth?"

"Thanks for the invite, but I can't today." He took a drink of coffee and grinned at Mrs. Nance. "I want to see about finding work."

"You should speak to Bently." Lydia looked out the window toward town. "The hotel may need some repairs."

"I thought it was closed up."

"Oh, it is now." Mrs. Lewis shared a glance with Lydia. "She's trying to get him to open it for us so we wouldn't have to impose on his hospitality any longer."

"Of course, you would be welcome to stay there, too," Lydia said. "Bently said you moved to that old shack across the way. It must be drafty."

He chuckled. "Eddie Dunn helped me out. The cabin cleaned up pretty good. I'll be fine there." He finished the coffee and set the cup on a small table. "I came by to tell the Townsends I'm moving my horse to the livery.''

"I'll be happy to give Bently your message.''

"I'd appreciate it, Mrs. Nance.'' He got to his feet and set a crutch under each arm. "I'd better get going. Ladies, it was nice seeing you.''

Lydia stood up. "Why not let Bently take your horse to the livery tomorrow? It would be easier for him, and he goes to town every day.''

"There's no reason to bother him.'' Kent stepped over to where the passenger, Mr. Brice, was seated with two of the crewmen, Timothy Ross and Dave Kirby. "You're lookin' much better.''

"And you,'' Mr. Ross said. "How's the cabin?''

Kent chuckled. "Warmer 'n drier than camp. The fireplace even has a good draw.'' He shifted the crutches. "If you want to stretch your legs, come on by. It's across the road. You can see the place from the front door.''

"Just might, when I can get around a little better,'' Mr. Kirby said.

"You're welcome anytime.'' The crewmen, Kirby and Ross, probably weren't used to sitting around a house any more than Kent. "How're Green and Nash doing?''

Mr. Ross shook his head. "Determined to get down to San Francisco. Think they've headed back toward the ship-wreck today.''

Mr. Kirby glanced at Ross. "Mr. Green's been talking about gettin' the captain's log.''

"The wreck's a ways up the coast. Hope they're up to that trek.'' Kent turned and started for the door.

"Mr. Hogarth—'' Mr. Brice stood up slowly. "Would you mind if I walk into town with you?''

"Not at all.''

Lydia opened the door for them. "Do be careful, Mr. Ho-garth.''

"I always am, ma'am,'' Kent said, then took a step and added, "Well, most of the time.''

He made his way to the barn and saddled his horse. He wound the reins around his hand and started toward the road.

Bounder was well trained and patiently followed Kent's halting pace.

Mr. Brice fell into step with Kent. "Have you met many of the townspeople, Mr. Hogarth?"

"A few. Charlie Jenks owns the general store, and Seth Dunn the livery. They helped rescue us." Kent glanced at Mr. Brice. "Where were you headin'?"

"Not sure. Mrs. Brice passed on a year ago. One day I looked around and realized I could make shoes anywhere. I bought passage on the *Julianna* and decided to keep traveling until I found a good place that needed a shoemaker."

"You wouldn't have much competition here."

When they passed the Hat Box, Kent glanced through the window. He thought he saw Miss Emma, but he couldn't be sure it was her. At any rate, he didn't want to draw Brice's attention, and so he continued on around the corner.

❖ 6 ❖

EMMA ADDED THE long, narrow pieces of brown calico to the pile, stood up and arched her back. Lettie was at the table counting flour sacks they had been saving, and Hannah was crocheting new trim for her shawl. Emma added more wood to the woodstove and made a fresh pot of tea.

Hannah finished one side of the shawl and started on the next. "Emma, have you seen Mr. Hogarth since the burial?"

"I've seen him in passing." Emma refilled Hannah's cup. "Why do you ask?"

"I was surprised when I learned he was staying in Mr. Hayes's old shack. Eddie helped him move in the day before yesterday. Seth took him a water barrel and said Mr. Hogarth was going to board his horse at the livery."

"Mr. Jenks suggested he stay there. I wonder why he moved Bounder? He wasn't any trouble, and Bently didn't mention it to me." Emma sipped her tea wondering if her brother had asked Kent Hogarth to move his horse. Bently had made it clear he didn't want her seeing him, but had he been that rude? She hoped not.

"Mr. Hogarth walked by with his horse before noontime," Lettie said, watching Emma. "He was with that quiet man from the ship, the one with graying sideburns."

"Mr. Brice. It's good to hear he's getting around. At first I feared he had broken a rib, but he said he had been thrown against a barrel and was only bruised." Emma glanced at the side window. She hadn't seen Kent Hogarth. She caught Lettie watching her and shook her head. What difference did it make anyway? she thought.

"I'm glad the men are doing better." Hannah reached for her cup. "When they're feeling up to it, some of us could have one or two over for supper each night."

"They might like getting out." Emma finished cutting the scraps. "Have you seen the Olsens?"

Lettie shrugged. "I haven't. Hannah?"

"The river's been runnin' high. They probably can't cross."

The brass bell over the front door rang out, and Emma turned to see who had entered. It was Kent Hogarth. He stood to one side and closed the door. He looked fit. Handsome, actually, in a rugged sort of way. His russet beard looked a bit fuller and the hair around the edge was curly. She brushed her skirt and straightened her back. "Hello, Mr. Hogarth."

"Ladies. So this's where you disappear to every day, Miss Emma." The shop was more like a lady's bedroom than a store, warm and inviting, although Kent felt out of place with the lace, ribbons, and underclothes men usually saw in a different setting. He passed by a display of ladies' unmentionables and with care made his way over to the table. Miss Emma's cheeks were turning a nice shade of pink but her expression made it clear she didn't appreciate his comment.

"We work here, Mr. Hogarth." His comment sounded as if he'd accused her of hiding there, and Emma wanted to set him straight.

With a glance at Emma, Lettie pulled a chair out from the table. "Please be seated, Mr. Hogarth."

He nodded and sat down, moving his crutches out of the way. "You have me at a disadvantage. You know who I am, and I've seen you, but I don't remember your name." She was a pleasant-looking woman; strands of her hair had worked loose from the coil but not Miss Emma's. Her hair was bound securely.

"Miss Morrissey," she said, holding out her hand to him. "There were so many of us helping out at Emma's that first night it's not surprising."

"And her grandmother helps during the day," Emma added.

He smiled. "Mrs. Nance. She's quite a lady." He nodded to the third lady present. "I saw you the first night too at the Townsend house, didn't I?"

Hannah nodded. "I'm Mrs. Dunn."

"It's a pleasure, ma'am. Eddie and Mr. Dunn have been a big help." The boy didn't get his red hair from his parents, Kent thought, but the sprout had his ma's big brown eyes. She was a sturdy, sensible-looking woman, the kind his ma called the salt of the earth.

While he charmed Lettie and Hannah, Emma collected the pieces of fabric, turning her head so she could follow the conversation. When she talked with one or two people, she positioned herself so they were on her right or across from her so she could hear what was being said. However, when she was with more than a couple of people, she had to watch carefully.

Kent's gaze slid to Miss Townsend—Emma. She had cleared off the table and started dusting it without saying a word. "Miss Emma, I stopped by to let you know I moved Bounder to the livery. And thank you for taking such good care of both of us." She started to smile, at least her lips quivered, and she finally looked him in the eye. It was worth the wait.

He appeared quite comfortable visiting with women, but he must be used to being around them, she realized. "You're welcome, Mr. Hogarth. Bounder was no trouble," she said, then immediately wondered if she had sounded as if *he* had been trouble. It wasn't what she meant and hoped he wouldn't take offense. "Would you like some tea? I'm afraid we haven't anything stronger."

"No, thank you. I can't stay. I have another stop to make." He stood up and set a crutch under each arm. "Oh, if you need any work done around the shop, or the house,

Miss Emma, I wish you'd keep me in mind. I can't climb a ladder right now, but I'm good with a hammer and saw.''

Lettie waited for Emma to speak and when she didn't, Lettie said, "Indeed we will, Mr. Hogarth. And if we can be of any help to you, please don't hesitate to ask.''

"That goes for us too Mr. Hogarth," Hannah added. "We're a small town and watch out for one another." She stilled the crochet hook and smiled. "Welcome to Pelican Cove. I hope you stay with us a while.''

Emma noticed the wagon out front, then saw Ginny Talbert and her husband, Will. Emma quickly returned her attention to Kent Hogarth and found him watching her. He didn't miss much. She would have to be more careful around him. She glanced at his leg and the way he gripped the crutches. "You really shouldn't be on that leg too much for a while.''

"I'll try to remember, Miss Emma." He'd made his way to the door when it opened and a bright-eyed young woman, very much in the family way, burst into the shop. He teetered slightly and managed to step backward without falling on his rump.

Ginny immediately put her hand on Kent's arm to steady him. "I'm so sorry. All you all right?''

Kent chuckled. "Yes, ma'am. Just a little slow these days.''

"Gin," Will said, putting his arm around her shoulders, "I keep tellin' you to slow down." He urged her forward and held his hand out to Kent. "Will Talbert.''

"Kent Hogarth. Glad to meet you." The rangy young man shaking his hand had wavy brown hair, a strong arm, and a steadfast gaze. The young man and his wife appeared to be well suited.

"That's my wife," Will said, motioning to Ginny as she took the chair Kent had vacated. "You're from that ship that wrecked, aren't you?''

Kent shook his head. "I'm the one who found it.''

Will glanced at his wife and back to Kent. "Can I take you somewhere? She'll be here a while, and I feel about as comfortable in here as she'd be in the saloon.''

Kent laughed. ''I was just going to stop in the barbershop. Thanks, anyway.''

''How about stopping at the saloon for a lager first?''

Kent grinned. ''Sounds good to me.''

Will went over to Ginny. ''How're you feelin'?''

She grinned up at him. ''I'm fine.''

''Good. I'll have a drink with Mr. Hogarth, then.'' Will looked at Emma. ''If anything—''

''We'll get you.'' Emma put her hand on Will's arm. ''Staring at her will only upset her, and I'm sure you don't want to do that.'' The poor boy was a wreck waiting for the birth and had been driving Ginny to distraction. She was already as worried as any expectant woman would be.

He patted his wife's shoulder. ''I won't be long.''

''Take your time, Will.'' She pressed her cheek to his hand. ''Enjoy your beer while we solve everyone's problems.''

Kent waited for the young man and followed him outside. ''This must be your first.'' Fortunately, he thought, the wagon's close to the board walk. He hadn't realized how tired he was of the crutches.

Will gave a harsh laugh. ''I used to want a big family, now I'll feel blessed with one. I don't know how Ma had six of us. Wish they were here now.''

Kent got up to the bench seat and braced his good leg. ''The womenfolk seem to know how to handle it. Guess you'll have to trust them.''

Will nodded and climbed up to the wagon seat. ''Mind my asking if you have a claim up in the Siskiyous?''

''I'm no miner,'' Kent said. ''Came down from Portland, in the Oregon Territory.'' It didn't take long to pull around the corner and go around to the other side of the next block. They stopped in front of the Redwood Saloon across from a nice little cove in the bay.

''Is that near Stump Town?''

''I've heard some call it that.''

Will jumped down to the ground. ''We came down the Columbia and stayed the first winter at Astoria. Some trappers talked about Stump Town, but we never made it over there.''

Kent got down from the wagon and entered the saloon behind Will. The place was large considering the size of the community. Five tables were spread out with plenty of space in between and at least fifteen men could stand at the long plank bar without crowding anyone. There was a woodstove, an unassembled billiard table leaning against one wall, and the proprietor had even hung a large painting of a dark-haired beauty wearing only a sheepish grin. ''Do many miners get down here?''

''From time to time, now they know there's a town here.'' Will stepped up to the bar in front of the bartender. ''Roy, like you to meet Kent Hogarth. Kent, this is Roy Avery, the owner.''

Kent rested his forearm on the bar. ''Glad to meet you. Nice saloon,'' he said, glancing around. Roy Avery was a big man, looked to be in midlife and probably had no trouble keeping rambunctious swizzled gents in line.

Roy chuckled. ''It's roomy, all right. I niver liked feelin' cooped up. What's your pleasure?''

''Two lagers.'' Will looked at Kent. ''I forgot about your leg. You wanta sit down?''

Roy set out two tankards of beer. ''I have a stool you can use if you like.''

''I'd appreciate it.'' When Roy moved the stool in front of the bar, Kent dropped down on the seat. He motioned to the billiard table. ''Change your mind about that?''

''Not at all. It arrived on the ship that wrecked up the coast. Haven't had time to set it up yet.''

Will raised his tankard and paused. ''Roy, Kent's the one who found the shipwreck.''

''I heard about you. Wondered how you did that,'' Roy said, motioning to Kent's leg. ''I was up in the hills that night. Went huntin'.''

''Much game up there?'' Kent took a swallow of beer. In another week or so his leg should be strong enough so he could do a little hunting, too.

''No bears this late in the year, but the black-tailed deer and elk are plentiful.'' Roy drank from a glass of water.

"That's good to hear."

Will shook his head. "Wish I could go with you."

"I'll be glad to share whatever I can bring back." Kent grinned and added, "That's if I bring something back."

"You could talk to Seth Dunn and Franklin Simms," Roy suggested. "They just might be interest'd in goin' with you."

"I'll do that." Kent took another gulp of lager. It was good, so was the company, but he couldn't spend what was left of the afternoon drinking.

"There's good fishing in the river—salmon and a big kinda trout. You could eat for days off just one of those beasts."

"That I can manage. Thanks." Kent finished his beer and stood up. "The lager's good, but I'd better get going. Nice meetin' you. If you want help with that table, let me know." He left the saloon and went to the barbershop and bathhouse on the other side of the vacant shop.

Emma wrapped the pieces of fabric for her quilt in a piece of flour sack and pulled the curtain closed across the front window. Lettie did the same to the side window. "We got a lot done today."

Lettie put out one of the two lamps. "I wonder if Gram talked to Bently about opening the hotel. It really would be a big help for you."

"I'll ask him." Emma put on her bonnet and cape. The shop was quiet and felt like home. If her friend married her brother, she would gladly move into Lettie's room.

"Aren't you going to wait for him? He should bring Gram home anytime now."

"I want to stretch my legs." Emma picked up her bundle. "Why don't you invite him in?" She knew the answer. If only Lettie would let him know she was interested and not be so very proper, although that alone should've caught his attention.

Lettie patted her hair and tugged at the waist of her burgundy dress. "I'll think about it."

"Good. See you in the morning."

Emma started up the street, then cut across the block, walked past the hotel and crossed the road to the bay. It was especially beautiful in the late afternoon and early evening. The tide was coming in and the water was dotted with white-caps. She wandered along the shore breathing deeply as she watched the gulls gliding over the water.

Several of the birds followed her, but she hadn't brought any crumbs. When she came abreast of the livery, she was tempted to visit Bounder but thought better of it. What Mr. Hogarth did was no concern of hers. He did arouse her curiosity, and he smiled easily. She liked that.

Her cheeks grew cold before she reached Meyer's River, and she turned back toward home. Walking alongside the road, she was looking south to avoid the nearly blinding glare of sunlight on the water. She thought she heard someone call her. The sound of the water lapping and the shrill cry of the gulls nearly blotted out other sounds. She slowed down as she glanced around. Mr. Hogarth waved to her from across the road.

Kent crossed the road as quickly as the crutches allowed. "Miss Emma," he said again, as he caught up with her. She seemed startled. "Mind if I keep you company?"

She shook her head, then motioned to the crutches. "You're getting along very well with those."

"I've been practicing. But as much help as they are, I'll be very glad to give them back to Charlie Jenks."

"That's why he only has one pair and lends them out." The pleasant scent of Nate Young's homemade clove hair tonic gave away where he had been. "At least you're getting out, finding your way around town." She was glad he hadn't shaved off his beard, though it shouldn't make any difference to her, but she couldn't help wondering if it felt soft or rough.

"I spoke with Seth Dunn when I boarded Bounder, stopped in to see Charlie Jenks, met Will Talbert. He introduced me to Roy Avery, and then I saw Nate Young." Kent grinned at her. "Did I miss anyone?"

She grinned in spite of her reluctance to do so and looked over at the bay. "There's Mr. Simms, but he doesn't have a shop. You'd have to go to his house to see him."

"Does he own the hotel?"

"No," she said, turning her head. "Mr. Groves built it, but he left last summer." She felt him watching her and briefly stared past him back to the hotel. "It's too bad it's closed up. The rooms aren't fancy like you'd find in the city but they aren't drafty and there's a reading or sitting room. Are you interested in buying it or maybe running it?"

"I've taken a lot of different jobs, but I don't think I could work inside all day." Kent paused and looked at the hotel. "Why did Mr. Groves change his mind?"

"He said he thought the town would grow faster than it has. I overhead him tell my brother he felt cut off from the world here." She shrugged. "The hotel was only open a couple months."

"Not everyone can trade city living for a quiet valley rimmed with high mountains and giant trees." They weren't far from her house, and he slowed down. "You didn't tell me about Nate Young."

"He wrote for a newspaper—in Indiana, I believe. They moved here last summer. His wife, Pauline, is such a warm-hearted person. She was the one who made you comfortable the night you arrived at the house." Emma smiled. "She has that effect on everyone." She stopped at the path to the house. "Is the cabin warm enough? You shouldn't let your leg get too cold."

He gave a short laugh. "It's better than it looks and the fireplace works fine." Chopping wood wasn't easy, but he managed.

"I'm glad, Mr. Hogarth. Thank you for walking me home."

As he watched her hurry up the path, he said, "My pleasure, Miss Emma." When she didn't break stride or turn around, he continued on to his cabin. She was different from other women he'd known. She wasn't coy or saucy, and she seemed content to listen to others rather than herself. That alone set her apart from most women.

After supper Emma carried the fresh pot of coffee into the parlor where the crewmen, Bently, Mr. Brice, and Mrs.

Lewis were sitting. Emma refilled Mr. Green's and Mr. Nash's cups. "Are you feeling better?" They had returned just before supper, limping, pale, and very hungry. Mrs. Lewis's spirits had improved, too.

Mr. Green sipped his coffee and smiled. "I'm about thawed out."

Mr. Nash nodded. "Tomorrow, we'll rent a wagon. Should've done it today."

"I didn't remember the ride being that long."

Mr. Brice chuckled. "It was dark, and I for one wasn't thinking too clearly."

"Mr. Nash," Emma said, "weren't your belongings already removed from the ship?"

"Yes, ma'am, our clothes. But we wanted to find the captain's log and records to take back to San Francisco with us. And the company'll want to know what's left onboard."

Mrs. Lewis continued sewing. "When will you be leaving?"

Mr. Nash shrugged and looked to Bently. "When's the next packet due?"

"This isn't a regular port." Emma looked to her brother.

Bently lowered the book he was reading. "The current around that small island keeps the ships and even the packets from putting in here."

Mrs. Lewis looked up from her sewing. "Then why was the *Julianna* stopping here, Mr. Townsend?"

"I corresponded with Captain Leonard. His boat wasn't as long as the others and had a shallower draft. He thought this would make a good port for him, especially if he was the only one to take advantage of it." Bently rubbed the bridge of his nose. "He didn't have any trouble putting in here on his way north."

"It looks like a natural port," Mr. Nash said. "Don't blame yourself. That storm just caught us at the wrong time."

Tim Ross stared at his shoes and said, "It was Friday. We shoulda waited a day, but the capt'n didn't hold with the old saw that it was unlucky to sail on Fridays."

Mr. Nash looked toward town. "How'd you get all the supplies when you first settled here?"

"Old Captain Link had a flute he'd rescued from the bay at San Francisco. It was spring. The sea was calmer than now. His old flute sailed right into the cove."

Mr. Green perked up. "How do we get in touch with him?"

Bently shook his head. "Heard he was plying the waters south of San Francisco."

"Then we'll have to light a fire or make a flag to signal another ship." Mr. Nash glanced around at his fellow crewmen. "They can send a jolly boat ashore for us."

"We've tried that. I'd be surprised if anyone stopped for you." Bently stood up and walked over to the fireplace. "You might try farther south. There's a harbor at Eureka. It's four or five days by horseback, or you could end up going all the way to San Francisco by land. I brought our winter supplies back. Won't be a wagon through here till spring."

Mr. Nash rubbed his jaw. "That'll take some planning."

Mrs. Lewis waited but no one said a word. "Today Mrs. Nance and I were talking about the hotel. Do you own it, Mr. Townsend?"

"Mr. Groves, the owner, said if anyone wanted to buy it, I should sell it for him. Mrs. Nance asked me about opening it up." Bently met her expectant gaze. "I guess we can, if you would like to stay there. I don't think Mr. Groves'd mind. I'm not sure what supplies were left, but there are enough rooms for all of you."

Mr. Nash glanced at his shipmates, then turned to Bently. "Four'd do us. We can double up. Would anyone mind if we put up there for awhile?"

Emma watched their faces. "Bently, the men would probably like to sleep in beds instead of on the floor."

"Yes, ma'am," Mr. Green said.

Mr. Nash elbowed Green. "He didn't mean no offense, ma'am. It was real generous of you and Mr. Townsend to take us in. But you must be tired of us clutterin' up your parlor."

"Not at all. We can understand how you feel. You've almost recovered. The hotel has a reading room with a fireplace, one small room to rent downstairs, in case climbing stairs is too difficult, and there're six more upstairs." She set the coffeepot down on the hearth. "We could go over in the morning and air it out."

Bently added a log to the fire. "It's up to you. The building's vacant. You might as well use it if you want."

Mrs. Lewis smiled. "I ran a boardinghouse for years. A hotel couldn't be too different."

"I'll go with you, Mrs. Lewis." Mr. Brice looked to the crewmen. "We'll get lazy if we lie around here much longer."

The others agreed. Emma had the feeling Mrs. Lewis and Mr. Brice thought of it as an adventure. After all they had been through, Emma was glad to see them taking an interest in the hotel.

"If there's a room downstairs, Mr. Hogarth could stay there, too." Mrs. Lewis picked up another square and began stitching it to the others.

Mr. Brice fixed Mrs. Lewis with his gaze. "He told you this morning he was happy in the cabin."

She frowned at him. "The hotel's right in town. I just thought Miss Townsend might talk to him about it."

"Women," Mr. Brice mumbled. "Can't leave a man be."

❖ 7 ❖

KENT HOPPED AROUND the corner of the cabin holding a tin cup half full of coffee. The morning air was brisk and there were clouds out over the ocean. He glared at his leg. He'd never felt so confined or hamstrung in his life. He couldn't hunt very easily on crutches, or ride Bounder, or even patch the roof if it leaked.

He'd done all he was going to do to the cabin, and he wasn't about to sit on the log out front as if he were some old codger counting flies. Roy Avery'd said the fishing was good. Kent drained the cup, tossed the dregs into the bushes, and hopped back inside.

After he fashioned a pole from a limb of a nearby tree, he packed biscuits and ham for dinner, banked the fire, and set off for the river. By the time the cemetery came into sight, he figured he'd gone far enough and found a log to sit on.

Once his line was in the water, he stretched out his injured leg on the riverbank and gazed back at the town. The setting was good—would be even better if they put in a ferry crossing near the mouth of the river. With the recent gold claims in the Oregon Territory, a few miles north at Sailor's Diggings and on Jackson Creek last December, the town would surely prosper.

A sharp jerk on his fishing line brought him to his feet, and a few minutes later he landed a fair-sized salmon. He pressed another piece of biscuit to the hook and tried again. The second fish he hooked was a large trout, and he wondered if it was one of the trout Avery had mentioned. When Kent hauled in another one, he decided to quit. Each fish had to weigh over twenty pounds, and he had to get them back to town. He retied the fishing pole to one crutch and did the same with the fish.

It was slow going back to town with the weighty fish swinging, pulling on the crutches with each step. As he lumbered along, he wondered what he'd do with his catch. He wouldn't mind two or three meals, but he had enough for a large dinner party, and he wasn't one to entertain. Emma. He wanted to repay her kindness and the salmon seemed like the ideal answer. He nearly toppled over on the slight incline toward the livery but caught himself.

He stopped at the corner in the middle of town near the hotel and the general store. His arms and fingers felt as stiff as boards. While he worked the kinks out, Jenks waved and came over to him.

Jenks eyed the fish and grinned. "So that's where ya've been."

"Somebody looking for me?" Kent leaned on one crutch, still flexing his fingers.

"Eddie. Said he'd finished his chores an' thought ya might wanta see his pups." Jenks chuckled. "That one's takin' a real likin' to ya."

Kent smiled. "I haven't seen any other boys his age around town."

"Aren't any. The Olsens across the river have a boy and girl, but they're almost grown."

Kent saw Mr. Ross carry two canvas bags into the hotel. "I see Townsend opened up the hotel. Who's moved over there?"

"All of them. They're feelin' better. Been fixin' it up all day."

"They must be hungry. Think I'll give 'em one of these fish for supper."

"Those folks'd probably appreciate it, too."

Kent settled a crutch under each arm. "See you later." He started for the hotel.

Jenks watched him a moment and called out, "Ya're making good time with that catch. Let me know if ya want to make deliveries in town."

"Thanks. I may take you up on that offer."

The door to the hotel and three windows were open. When Kent entered the lobby, a woman came in a back door. It wasn't until she had walked down the short hallway to the lobby and he noticed her arm in a sling that he recognized Mrs. Lewis. She'd done something different with her hair and her cheeks had a healthy glow. "I see you and Mrs. Nance succeeded. Congratulations."

She smiled and adjusted the sling supporting her arm. "Mr. Townsend didn't seem to mind at all."

"That's good to hear. How're you doing?"

"We need to keep busy. Mr. Townsend's hospitality was generous, but to be honest, I was getting spoiled, and I'm getting too old for that," she said with a wink.

He chuckled and glanced around the lobby into a sitting room. "Nice place. Almost looks like home."

"It is. There's even one guest room down the hall. Would you like to move in here with us?"

"Thanks for thinking of me, but the cabin's fine." He'd spent a couple nights in a boardinghouse once but never in a hotel. He didn't like feeling hemmed in so closely with others. He'd even been uncomfortable bedded down in the Townsend parlor.

She looked at the fish hanging from Kent's crutches. "You've been busy."

"They must've been hungry today," Kent said as Mr. Brice and Mr. Green came down the stairs. "Think you could make use of this?"

"Sure do, Mr. Hogarth," Mr. Kirby said, stepping forward. "That's a beauty. It'll make at least two meals with some left over for chowder."

"It's yours." Before Kent could untie the cord holding

the fish, Green untied it. "And please just call me Hogarth or Kent. I'm not partial to 'mister.' "

Mrs. Lewis admired the salmon and looked at Kent. "You will join us for dinner, won't you?"

He motioned to the trout. "Thanks, but I have plans for this one tonight."

"Well, I hope you come by here to visit." Mr. Brice glanced at his fellow boarders. "I for one wouldn't mind keeping you company the next time you go fishing."

"I'll take you up on that offer, Mr. Brice."

"Might as well call me Henry."

Kent smiled and nodded. "Enjoy your supper."

He left the hotel and cut across the bordering lot. He had one more stop to make before returning to the cabin. The wind had come up and the sun hadn't been out all day. He buttoned his jacket and picked his way across the craggy ground. The Hat Box was on the other side of the block behind the hotel. There were two wells in back, one for the hotel, and it looked as if Jenks shared one with Emma and Miss Lettie's shop.

Smoke drifted from the stovepipe, and he wondered if Emma was still there. He swayed and the trout slapped against his leg. "Okay, we're going," he said, as if the fish gave a darn.

Emma shook out the quilt top she was piecing together. Halfway there, she thought. Lydia was sitting in Lettie's up-holstered reading chair by the windows, where the light was better, or so she said. Pauline had come by after dinner and was helping piece together several flour sacks for the bottom of one quilt.

Pauline drew the needle through the edge of two sacks. "I wonder how they're doing at the hotel?"

Lydia looked up from her sewing. "Mrs. Lewis'll keep the men in line. She ran a boardinghouse." She glanced out the window at the hotel. "There's smoke coming from the kitchen stovepipe."

Emma began stitching another patch to the quilt top. "I

hope they didn't feel as if they had to move to the hotel." She glanced back at Lydia. "Are you sure Mrs. Lewis is up to taking care of herself?"

"Oh, yes, dear. I think she just felt a bit left out of things for a while. She perked right up when we talked about moving into the hotel."

"You've probably gotten to know her better than I have."

Lydia squinted. "Looks like Mr. Hogarth's already paid a call at the hotel." She grinned. "He seems to be a good fisherman, too."

He would be, Emma thought. "I'm sure we'll be seeing him around town until his leg heals." And if I look across the way from the front door or lean over the dry sink and peer out the window, I'll see smoke rising from the chimney of the old cabin. The town was so small it would be almost impossible not to see him.

"I hope so. We need more young men in town. Fresh blood."

Lettie stared at her grandmother. "Really, Gram. That's an awful way to put it."

"We buried those poor souls. Now it's time to have some marrying and begetting." Lydia shrugged. "You and Emma should make him feel welcome. He doesn't know anyone very well. Invite him over for supper."

Pauline quickly covered her mouth and coughed. "Hannah and I talked about her idea—for everyone to invite some of the people from the ship for supper." She looked at Emma, Lettie, and Lydia. "Since they've moved into the hotel, why don't we have a potluck supper there? We can serve the food outside. Or if the weather's bad, the sitting room's large enough to seat everyone. Wouldn't it be fun?"

"Oh, yes. A welcoming party and everyone around here'll be invited." Lettie eyed Emma. "You're quiet."

"Sorry," Emma said, gathering her thoughts.

Lettie seemed to be struggling to keep a straight face as she said, "You could still invite Mr. Hogarth for supper. Two evenings out would hardly be excessive."

"Why on earth would I want to do that?" The brass bell over the door jingled, and Emma glanced over her shoulder.

As if she had conjured him up, Kent Hogarth stood outside
the open door, with a grand fish hanging from each of his
crutches. He certainly was a sight.

"Hello," she said, turning in her chair. Why was he standing there? When he didn't come inside, she went to the door.
His bulky coat made him appear even larger than he really
was, which was no runt. "Won't you come inside?"

"I'd better not." He motioned to the fish dangling from
his crutches. "Do you and Miss Morrissey like trout?"

"Yes. I hope you do."

He grinned at her. "I just happen to have an extra one.
Should be enough for a couple meals."

"That's very thoughtful, Mr. Hogarth. Thank you."

He started to untie the cord and hesitated. "It's heavy.
Want me to take it to the kitchen or should I leave it at your
house?"

She darted a glance over her shoulder. If she took the fish
now, she would have to clean it and the shop would reek.
"I'll walk to the house with you."

He smiled at the ladies inside. "These don't smell like
lilacs. I'll wait out here."

"I'll be just a moment." She pushed the door and went
to the back of the shop to get her cape. When she turned
around three pairs of eyes were watching her. "I won't be
long."

Lettie grinned. "There's no hurry. It's almost closing time
anyway."

"Oh, fiddlesticks. He brought a fish for us to share.
It's large and heavy. He's going to carry it home for me.
That's all." Emma fastened the tie at her neck and grabbed
her bonnet. "I'll clean it at the house and bring you half
back."

Lettie's gaze darted to the door. "Please thank him for
me, too."

"He's just being thoughtful," Pauline said with a broad
grin. "We understand, Emma."

"Good gracious, I'm no schoolgirl."

"You certainly aren't." Lettie quickly raised her cup to
her lips.

"Don't keep him waiting too long, Emma," Lydia said. "About time you found a bit of enjoyment."

Such foolishness, Emma thought, hurrying out the door. Kent Hogarth was standing by the side of the road; the fish were swinging from his crutches. He must be tired after walking from the river with that added weight. "I should've told you to go on and I'd catch up with you."

"That's your idea of walking together?"

"Of course not."

"I'm glad." He started down the road with her more than an arm's length to his left, to avoid the swinging fish. "Your shop seems to be popular with the ladies."

"We try to make it comfortable. Women don't have many gathering places." She looked at him out of the corner of her eye. "Men have the saloon, women meet by chance at the dry goods store or hold a quilting bee to get together. Our shop is open every day, except Sunday."

"Interesting idea. But you need a painting of a strapping young man dressed in evening gear for a ball. Serve drinks like . . . a pink slipper and husky tea with brawny ginger cake."

"We're not bawdy women!" She stopped in her tracks, glaring at him. "Keep your blamed fish." She turned on her heel and started back to the shop. Of all the insufferable insults— But she didn't know what hurt most: the words or the fact that he had said them.

"Wait, Emma—" He swung one crutch out and blocked her, the only way he had to slow her down so she'd listen to him. "I was teasing." He waited, but she didn't look at him. "You can't think I was serious—"

She didn't want to believe he was and now that she thought it over, she realized she had once again jumped to the wrong conclusion about him. When she looked at him, his cockeyed expression made her smile.

"You should do that more often." Her brother didn't have the best disposition, and Kent couldn't help wondering if she was out of practice. They passed the old cabin and turned toward the house she shared with Bently. "How's your brother? I haven't seen him around town."

"He's well." The wind grew stronger, and she held the sides of her cape closed. "I think he stopped by the hotel this morning." They reached the front door, and she opened it for him. "Come on inside."

He made his way to the kitchen, swung the biggest fish onto the worktable and untied the cord. "Want me to cut off the head?"

"I'll do it. I learned to clean what I caught." She eyed the large fish. "But I was never as lucky as you were today."

"Emma, is that you?"

"Yes, Bently," she called out. "Mr. Hogarth brought us a large trout." She met Kent's gaze. "He has an office here."

They were shouting again, and Kent decided he'd best leave. "I'll be going." He still couldn't figure them out. She was soft-spoken when her brother wasn't around. "I still have to clean this one for supper." He maneuvered his crutches around and took a step.

"Wait— You can take half of this bread with you. Or do you bake, too?"

He grinned. It was good to know she could return his teasing. "No, ma'am. I make a tasty biscuit but nothing you'd serve for company."

She cut the loaf in half and wrapped up one piece in a towel. Then she realized he couldn't carry it. "Mind if I use that cord you tied the fish with?" He handed it to her, and she quickly secured the bread with one end and attached the other end to the crutch. "There. You need some kind of little wagon to carry your things."

"I could've used one today."

Bently came to the kitchen door. "Hogarth. Glad to see you're getting along so well."

"So am I." Kent nodded to Emma. "Thanks for the bread." He stepped forward.

Bently moved aside, then followed Kent outside. "The hotel's open. You're welcome to stay there. You'd be right in town."

"The cabin's fine." Kent thought if he were a suspicious sort, he'd wonder why everyone seemed to want him out of the cabin. But he knew Townsend's reasoning. However, that didn't hold off his needling him. "I've been thinkin' about hanging curtains and maybe a painting or two."

It started raining during the night. By ten the next morning the roads were muddy and it was cold. Mr. Jenks had already stopped by the Hat Box to ask about the dinner at the hotel. Hannah was next. Word seemingly had spread on the night air. Alicia Simms arrived a few minutes later, her cheeks flushed and her eyes gleaming with curiosity. Emma set another chair at the table. "Put your cloak by the fire to dry."

Alicia moved the chair closer to the woodstove and draped her cloak over the back. "I heard about the town supper but no one seems to know when it will be." She looked around the table.

Emma stood with her back to the woodstove. "Lettie, you and Pauline were talking about it yesterday. Did you set a date?"

"We didn't decide on anything." Lettie poured a cup of tea and handed it to Alicia. "Shouldn't we speak to Mrs. Lewis and the men? We don't even know if they'd like a dinner."

Emma nodded. "Word is spreading so fast someone should do that before they hear about the supper and wonder why they weren't asked about it."

"I don't mind talking to them," Hannah said. "I wanted to pay my respects anyway."

"I'll go with you, Hannah." Lettie glanced around. "Anyone else want to go with us?"

Emma followed the conversation with her friends with practiced ease. "After you set a date, I'll ride out and tell Ginny. I might as well stop by the Chase farm and tell Vera. And the Pools, too."

"Do you think Mr. Chase will want to come?" Alicia shook the damp hem of her dress. "He's not very sociable."

Emma shrugged. "I'll ask anyway. Vera's stuck out there and hardly ever gets into town."

"Makes me wonder why some people marry others who

aren't very pleasant." Alicia raised the cup to her lips.

Her thoughts on the Chases, Emma glared at the wood-stove. "She should just hitch up the horses and come to town without him."

"If she did," Hannah said, "she'd most likely get the back of his hand for it."

Lydia walked over to the table and picked up the teapot. "That's why she should keep a club handy. My piece of maple never let me down. It fit my hand like a glove and was hard enough to crack the thickest skull."

Lettie stared at Lydia. "Gram, I've never seen any such stick."

"You had no need to, dear." Lydia refilled her cup. "In those early days back in Iowa, every woman had to fend for herself, one time or another."

Emma watched Lettie a moment and spoke up. "Good for you, Lydia." Lettie was clearly upset by her gram's outspokenness. Emma admired the older woman's spirit. Her own grandmother had passed on when she was eight, but she remembered her gentle ways, her soft voice that she had never heard raised in unladylike tones.

"Times haven't changed all that much. We're miles from any city. More men will be roaming the mountains now that they've found gold." Lydia carried her tea back to Lettie's reading chair in the kitchen by the windows.

Alicia nodded, staring at the wardrobe. "Lettie, did you make that flannel petticoat with the red ribbons?"

"Yes. Do you like it?" Lettie glanced at the petticoat. "I didn't have any red flannel. But I think the red ribbons are pretty on the white."

"Oh, yes," Alicia said, and went over to take a close look at it. "Your needlework is beautiful."

Hannah stood up and reached for her heavy shawl. "I think I'll walk over to the hotel."

Lettie got her wrap and went over to her grandmother. "I won't be long. Please don't talk about strange men attacking us any more."

"All right, dear," Lydia said, smiling at her granddaughter. "But if you're prepared for the worst, it may not happen." She watched Alicia a moment. "But that isn't easy for everyone."

Lettie kissed her gram's cheek and left with Hannah.

Wearing her fullest skirt, one she had made especially for riding, and one of her brother's old coats, Emma mounted their mare and rode out of town. It had stopped raining but probably not for long. She measured the rainfall all last year. Over sixty inches. Another five and the level would've equaled her height.

She stopped by the Talbert farm and spoke with Ginny. Everyone had agreed to hold the dinner on Sunday. Four days was plenty of time to prepare for it. Ginny was as excited as the others and said she and Will would be there. Since Emma didn't want to get caught in a downpour, she didn't visit very long before she continued on to the Pool farm.

Martha and John Pool had a nice place on the river side of the road. She passed their boys, John, Jr., and Teddy, working in the field on her way to the house. Martha came out to greet her before her feet had touched the ground.

"Emma, what a nice surprise. Come on in. Looks like it'll rain anytime now."

Emma went inside. "How have you been?" Martha wore her dark hair parted in the middle and pulled straight back but her kindly smile softened her features.

"No complaints. I heard you and your brother went up to Astoria. Did you visit the Prices?"

"Yes. In fact we had supper with them one night."

Martha led the way into the parlor and motioned to one chair. "Please sit down. I'll pour us some tea."

"Oh, no, Martha. I still want to call on Vera Chase before it starts raining." Emma told her about the shipwreck survivors moving to the hotel. "Everyone's getting together for a potluck dinner this Sunday, midday. I wish you and your family would join us."

"Why, that sounds real nice. We'll be there."

"Good. Please tell Mr. Pool hello for me." Emma turned

back toward the door. "I'd better get going if I'm going to stay dry."

Martha walked her out to her horse. "See you Sunday."

Emma's last stop, and the farthest from town, was the Chase farm that bordered the foothills.

When she rode into the yard a sopping wet brown dog barked at her. Sheep wandered around at will. She brought the mare to a halt near the front door and dismounted. Still no one came out. She rapped on the rickety door, surprised by the lack of upkeep so evident to her, and called, "Vera, it's me, Emma Townsend."

The door opened slowly and Emma said, "Hi. I was about to give up." Vera's complexion was blotchy and her eyes looked watery. The first months after they settled there Emma had tried time and time again to become better acquainted with Vera but Mr. Chase usually interfered. She was on the plain side with fine brownish hair, but she had the prettiest soft blue eyes—when they weren't red.

"Miss Emma. What're you doing all the way out here?"

After quickly telling her about the shipwreck, Emma explained that the surviving passengers were staying at the hotel. "Everyone in town is having a sort of welcoming dinner for them. Potluck, and I thought you might like to join us."

Vera darted a glance over her shoulder. "That sounds real nice. I'll ask Mr. Chase, but he don't hold with socials much, 'specially on the Sabbath."

The dog came over to the front stoop and brushed against Emma's skirt. "Please do try to come to the dinner. It's been so long since you've been in the shop. Mrs. Dunn and Mrs. Simms have been asking about you." A small fib, but Emma didn't think they would mind.

Vera nodded. "I'll try, Miss Emma."

❖ 8 ❖

THE KEEN RINGING of a bell brought Kent straight up in bed. The only bell he'd seen in town was near the corner by the general store and Emma's shop. He pulled on his trousers and felt around on the floor for his boots. Except for the banked embers, the cabin was as dark as a moonless night. He hopped over to the door, got into his jacket, grabbed the crutches, and headed for the road.

Voices drifted from the center of town, but he couldn't make out any of the words. When he came through the pines, he saw the flames lighting the night and hurried as fast as he could. The fire was either in the back of Jenks's store or the Hat Box. Others were running to help, too. It wasn't until he'd almost reached the corner, where Eddie was ringing the alarm bell, that he knew which building was on fire. Emma and Miss Morrissey's shop. Flames shot up the back corner post and a good-sized section of the roof was gone along with the two windows.

Mr. Kirby appeared at the peak of the roof and dumped a pail of water on the shakes. Nate Young tossed a bucket of water at the flames and exchanged the empty bucket for a full one with Roy Avery. Charlie Jenks manned the well he shared with the women's shop. The crewmen from the ship were running between the hotel's well and the shop. They'd managed to save all the building, save the one corner. Kent made a wide circle around the men to the other side of the well. "Why don't I spell you?"

As Charlie Jenks raised the pail, he glanced over at Kent. "Son, ya can't help with this. Ya might check on Miss Morrissey and Mrs. Nance."

"They weren't hurt, were they?"

"Oh, no. When I noticed the fire, I ran over here and woke them up." Jenks coughed.

There was no wind and the smoke seemed to hang in the damp night air. "Good thing you spotted the fire. Could've been a lot worse." When Kent stepped out of Mr. Green's way, he noticed Townsend drive up with Emma. She'd be better company for Miss Morrissey and Mrs. Nance. "Miss Townsend's here now. I can bail water. I'll man the other well."

Kent went over to the hotel's well. Mr. Brice was raising a pail. "How're you doing?"

"Okay. Too bad they don't have a pump. Would be faster." Mr. Brice poured water in Mr. Green's bucket, dropped the pail back down the well and wiped his forehead with the back of his hand.

Kent stepped up to the rope pull. "Let me take over here. I can't carry buckets, but I can fill them."

"Okay." Mr. Brice hurried away with the full pail.

With his crutches propped against the well, Kent went to work. Half an hour later the flames had been put out. He leaned back against the well. The southeast corner of the shop was gone but miraculously there didn't appear to be any damage to the rest of the building.

Eddie ran over to Kent. "Golly, that was some fire."

"Sure was." Kent looked at the boy. "Do you know how it started?"

"Naw. Ma's in talkin' with Miss Morrissey 'n Mrs. Nance. Oh, there's Pa. Better get goin'. See ya, Mr. Hogarth."

Kent made his way over to the back of the general store where the crewmen were talking with Jenks. "Good thing you have that alarm bell."

"They would've lost half the shop if ya men hadn't been here. I'm not sayin' that shipwreck wasn't a terrible thing," Charlie Jenks said, glancing around, "but we're all glad ya helped out tonight."

Staring at the burned-out corner, Kent got an idea. "Does anyone know if the sails are still on the boat?"

Mr. Green looked at Mr. Nash. "They were pretty ripped up, but they were there yesterday."

Kent nodded. "Think anyone would mind us using some of the sails to cover the corner of the shop until it's repaired?"

Jenks gave Kent an approving nod. "Good thinkin'."

The crewmen exchanged looks, and Mr. Green said, "Don't see why not. We'll take a wagon up there soon as it's light."

"Wish I could help."

Jenks eyed Kent. "I'm sure ya'll find a way."

"Let's hope it doesn't get any colder." Kent stared at the shop a moment longer. He tried to put his weight on his injured leg and winced. Damn, it hurt like the devil. "Guess there's nothing else we can do tonight. I'll see you tomorrow."

He made his way over to the burned-out corner. The dining table had been pushed back near the kitchen stove. At least a ten-foot section of roof was gone. The first thing to be done, though, was to shore up the stone foundation. The stones wouldn't be hard to put back in place. Just then Emma stepped into the kitchen. The hem of her white nightgown hanging below her heavy cloak was blackened from the ash covering the floor and ground.

Emma added hot water to the teapot. She and Lettie owned the building, but Lettie was devastated—as if she had started the fire. Lydia wouldn't stop mumbling that the fire was her fault, and she wouldn't be consoled. Emma glanced around at the charred boards and trembled. They had been so very fortunate. No one had been hurt.

As she searched for the tea, she noticed Kent Hogarth standing outside. She hadn't expected him, but then she hadn't been thinking about much besides Lettie and Lydia. For some peculiar reason, she recalled his first visit to the shop. "Did you mean what you said about being handy with a hammer?"

"Yes, ma'am."

"Do you think you could rebuild this corner? I like fresh air but it's almost the rainy season." She couldn't believe what she'd said. I sound deranged, she thought.

He chuckled. Her sense of humor hadn't deserted her. "Mr. Green and some of the others are going to get a couple sails from the ship to cover the damaged part of the house temporarily. It won't hold in much heat but it'll help keep the rain out." He watched her as she stared at the front of the shop. Her expression turned bleak, and he added, "At least no one was hurt. The building can be repaired."

"You're right." She couldn't help thinking how different it would've been if the fire had started on the other side of the house. "We're so grateful for everyone's help. I'll tell Lettie and Lydia about the sail. They'll be most appreciative."

"Will they be all right tonight?"

"Yes, now the excitement's settling down, they can go back to our house." And Bently will be seeing Lettie more often, Emma realized.

"And how're you doing?"

She shrugged, saying, "All I need is some sleep." She looked at the charred wall, up at the roof and back at him. "Are you sure you'll be able to rebuild this? You said you couldn't climb a ladder."

"I did say that, but I think I can get one or two of the men to help out." He could put up the walls, replace the plank flooring, and build up the foundation, but he'd need help with the roof and putting in the windows.

"I'm glad. One broken limb is enough." She glanced at the teapot still in her hand. "I'd better take this in to them before it's ice-cold."

"See you tomorrow, Miss Emma."

"Good night, Mr. Hogarth." She opened the door to the hallway and paused to watch him leave. He was a striking figure, even on crutches. Too bad there weren't any other marriageable women in town, she thought, besides Lettie. Pelican Cove needed men like Kent Hogarth.

Emma was back at the shop the next morning. After she swept the floor, she helped Lettie clean ash and soot from what remained of the kitchen. They saved enough ashes to make a good supply of soap. The rain had moved on and everything smelled sweet, except the shop. The door and windows were open to help air out the shop but the pungent odor of charred wood still hung in the air.

Lettie finished wiping off the top of the small kitchen stove. "We really were fortunate. That corner was the least cluttered." She dropped the blackened rag in the bucket and took a deep breath. "I'm so sorry, Emma."

"Please don't get all weepy. You and Lydia are safe. That's what matters." Emma added her rag to the bucket. "The walls and roof will be replaced. I know how much you liked your reading chair. We'll get Bently to build another frame, and we'll upholster it ourselves."

Lettie shook her head. "How can you be so nice? Gram started the fire."

"We've been through that."

"Why won't you listen, Emma? She went to bed and left the lighted lamp on the table and didn't even close the window. You know how she sometimes turns the wick up too high." Lettie wrung her hands. "She should know to be more careful."

"She needs more light to sew by at night. If she had *tried* to burn the house down, then I'd be hopping mad. But she didn't." Emma picked up the bucket with the filthy rags. "Right now I'm going to soak these rags in clean water."

When she returned, she built up the fire in the kitchen stove, put a kettle of water on to heat and added a good measure of vinegar to the pot. "Lettie, let's take a walk while the vinegar freshens this place." She took off her apron and hung it on the peg.

"Want to see if Mr. Dunn will let us use his wheelbarrow?" Lettie hung up her apron and put on her shawl. "If we give the floor a good sanding it should help get rid of the stench."

"And wash the drapes and curtains." Emma grabbed her shawl, walked through the shop and out the front door. "I'll be glad when that little lemon tree starts bearing fruit. We can polish every piece of wood with lemon oil."

They went to the livery and Mr. Dunn gave them the use of his wheelbarrow and a shovel. Then they walked along the shore, shoveling dry sand into the wheelbarrow. When they returned to the shop with as much sand as they could manage, Kent and three of the crewmen were there.

While Kirby and Ross nailed the top of the sail to the roof, Kent put a couple nails along one side, fixing it to the south wall. He started back to the wagon to speak to Mr. Nash and saw Emma and Miss Morrissey pushing a wheelbarrow full of sand. "Nash, would you help the ladies?"

Mr. Nash looked up and ran over to Emma and Lettie. "Here, I'll do that for you, ma'am." He took the handles and started pushing the wheelbarrow, then hesitated. "Where do you want this?"

Lettie stepped forward. "Close to the canvas will be fine, Mr. Nash." She went along with him to show him where she meant.

Kent made his way over to Emma. "Do you do that very often?"

Emma was watching the men on the roof and didn't realize Kent Hogarth had come up to her, until something caused her to look at the ground, and she saw one of his crutches move. "Oh, hello. The sail was a wonderful idea," she said, keeping her attention on him. The hammering and other voices were distracting.

When she didn't react to his teasing, he figured she must not have heard him. "It should keep most of the rain and wind out of the kitchen and the shop."

"That's good." He has nice lips, she thought, watching his mouth. So far she hadn't had any problem understanding him. She brushed her hair back and secured a loose hairpin.

"Mrs. Nance and Lettie insist on staying here." She glanced around. "I'd better help Lettie sand the floor. It was my idea." And, she thought, Lettie's feeling so guilty she'll try to do it all without me.

He instinctively reached out and touched Emma's arm. "Don't step near the burned edge of the planks. The boards could give way. I'll put some logs under the floor to support it. I'll see to that right now." She didn't pull away from him, but she seemed to freeze, staring at him as if she were a wary doe. He lowered his hand. What was she thinking? He couldn't believe she thought he'd mistreat her. But something had unsettled her.

"I would appreciate that, Mr. Hogarth."

She hurried to the front of the shop, and he hoped she was all right. He'd only rested his hand on her arm; he hadn't grabbed her. The last thing he wanted to do was frighten her. At times like this, he thought, I know the Almighty has a sense of humor. Why else would men have so much trouble understanding women?

Kirby and Ross had finished what they had to do on the roof and met Kent near the wagon. Kirby motioned to the roof. "That'll hold less'n it blows great guns."

"I hope that doesn't happen. There's one more thing that needs to be done today." Kent explained that supports were needed for the floor and the men offered to take care of it. So far, he thought, I haven't done a damned thing myself. That wasn't what he'd had in mind when he offered to help.

The Hat Box opened as usual on Friday. Emma checked on the drapes drying in Lettie's sitting room and returned to the shop. Lettie was polishing the table. "I wish you'd stay at our house until the repairs are done." Emma glanced at Lettie and added, "Bently asked about you at breakfast."

"He did?" Lettie finished with the table and spread a clean doily in the center. "What did he say?"

Emma shrugged. "I think he missed seeing you."

Lettie eyed Emma. "You mean he didn't know we'd moved back here." Lettie almost banged the sugar bowl down on the table. "If I had any sense, I'd forget about him.

There are other men in town—at least for a while.''

"The dinner is Sunday. You'll have a chance to get to know some of them better." And I'll make certain Bently is there, Emma thought.

Lettie stirred the fire in the woodstove and added more wood. "This may be a waste with that gaping hole in the kitchen."

"If it doesn't help, we'll save the wood until the walls are replaced." Emma glanced around. "With the windows gone and the canvas blocking out the light, we'll need another lamp or two in here. Mind if I bring in one from your sitting room?"

"I'll get it," Lydia said, picking up the cup of tea. "I was taking this to Gram."

"Don't make it too easy for her to hide away in her room." Emma got a rag out of the bin, found the polish, and began wiping off the wardrobe. Bently had built it to display some of their finery—two soft chemises, a dress corset and one for every day, the lace-edged handkerchiefs, a pair of dress gloves, and a full petticoat. She took the latter and the green silk shirtwaist outside and gave them a good shaking. She folded the shirtwaist with care and put it in one drawer. The petticoat was left hanging over one of the open wardrobe doors.

She and Lettie had wanted the inside of the shop to resemble a lady's bedroom and be as cozy. The outside was supposed to look like a hat box, until Bently explained how very costly it would be. They had settled for a small front bay window and yellow paint with white trim.

Lettie brought two lamps into the shop and set them on the table she had just polished. "Emma, you've already cleaned that."

"I know I have." Emma smiled and poked a hanky into one of the gloves. "I like rearranging these things."

"I'm glad you do. I'd rather sew or do needlework."

"That's why we work so well together." Emma put a pair of women's drawers half in and out of the top drawer, leaving the ribbon-trimmed legs hanging over the edge.

She stepped back and nodded. The disarray on the wardrobe gave a homey feeling to the shop. She wasn't a messy person, but she indulged the fanciful side of herself in the shop. After spending the better part of the morning changing different displays around the shop, she sat down at the table with a cup of tea and started assembling a top for another quilt.

It was close to midday when a wagon pulled up beside the shop. Lettie was closest to the side window and looked outside. "It's Mr. Hogarth—with lumber in the back of the wagon." She glanced at Emma, her brows drawn together. "Where would he get the boards? Ours came by ship."

"Let's ask." Emma went out the front door and walked around to the side of the building. He was just putting a crutch under each arm. "Good morning, Mr. Hogarth. It looks like you've been busy."

"That I have, Miss Emma." Kent went over to the canvas, held the right edge and dragged it over to the left, exposing the burned corner of the building. "You were out early, too."

She narrowed her gaze. Had he been watching her? "We open the shop every morning at nine."

He admired her pluck. Neither the shipwreck nor the fire had gotten her down. "I'll start work today. Hope that won't bother you."

"Oh, no. We'd like to have the walls up before the next storm." She held him in her gaze but tried not to look as if she were staring at him. "But you'll have to order the window glass from Mr. Jenks. It could take a year to get it. He'll send in the order next spring when the supply wagon is due and be delivered next fall."

"There was a window on each side of the corner, wasn't there?" When he glanced at her, she seemed to be watching him. She wasn't friendly in an encouraging way, but she kept her eye on him. Maybe she didn't trust him.

"Yes. That won't be a problem, will it?"

"No. I'll fashion some type of shutters you can prop open to let in the sunlight."

"That would be nice." She looked at the canvas. "Couldn't you make the window frames and cover them with a piece from one of the sails? We could cover the canvas with wax to keep the rain out."

"Yes, that would work." He smiled at her. "I might put you to work. How're you with a hammer?" He moved toward the front corner of the shop.

"Slow." She stepped out of his way. "Where did you find the boards? I thought Bently used all the extra ones."

"You have one less outbuilding." He managed to get down on one knee to check the slope of the land.

"Does my brother know?" Bently would have Kent Hogarth's hide if he'd taken the building apart on his own.

"Yep." Kent got back to his feet. "He even helped me take it apart." After talking to Dunn and Jenks, Kent had gone to Townsend about the needed supplies. He explained there was no lumber to be had but offered to give him a hand dismantling a shed. Kent accepted the help.

She moved to his left side, which meant she didn't have to keep staring at him. "Oh."

She sounded surprised, and he gaped at her. "Did you think I just took the shed apart without telling anyone?"

"No—" she said with a smile to cover her embarrassment. "Someone would've noticed." She stepped back. "I'd better get back to work and leave you to yours."

"See you around."

Lettie was waiting for Emma when she came back inside. "I was beginning to wonder if I should bring tea out to both of you."

"He'll be working here the rest of the day." Emma started to go back to the kitchen but paused. "The boards are from one of our sheds. Bently even helped him take it apart."

Lettie smiled. "I'm not surprised Bently helped him." She looked outside. "I thought Mr. Hogarth would have to build the new walls with logs."

Emma stared at the charred wood. "Not unless he runs out of lumber." Emma went to the back of the shop and set out the folding screen, but it only shielded part of the damage. She was pouring hot water into the teapot when Kent Hogarth appeared in the burned-out area, a few feet from her.

"Hi, there." He hopped up and sat on the floor. She'd been caught unawares and clearly was none too happy about it. "This'll be noisy, but I have to cut the burned edges of the floorboards."

"Do whatever you have to, Mr. Hogarth."

He laid the handsaw he'd borrowed from Jenks on the floor and met her gaze. "Why not call me Kent since we'll be seeing so much of each other."

The breath stuck in her throat as she stared at him. "That's hardly a good reason, *Mr.* Hogarth."

❖ 9 ❖

AN HOUR LATER Kent Hogarth sawed off the burned end on the last floorboard. Emma mumbled under her breath, as she had been doing since he had the gall to suggest she address him by his given name. She might choose to think of him that way, but he certainly didn't need to know that.

Lettie glanced from Mr. Hogarth to Emma. "Why don't you make a small pot of coffee?"

"I just poured myself a cup of tea." Emma smoothed the quilt top with more force than she'd intended and strained the stitches. She wasn't about to make coffee and encourage him to sit around visiting with them.

"That sounds good, Miss Morrissey." Kent set the saw aside and stood up in the kitchen. "If Miss Emma doesn't mind, I'll make the coffee."

Emma glanced in his direction. "The coffeepot's in the lower cupboard next to the stove. Coffee beans are in the small crock by the grinder." Never had she been so rude, but the man had deliberately irritated her. She had no doubt. And Lettie had turned pink from her effort to hold in her laughter.

Emma threaded the needle, picked up a long piece of green calico, and began stitching. He bumped the crock against the grinder, dropped a spoon, played with the water dipper, *and* he hummed while he ground the coffee beans. She did her best to ignore him. It wasn't easy. When it seemed quiet, she peered over at the kitchen. He was grinning at her!

Lettie leaned toward Emma's right side. "What's gotten into you? I've never seen you this way," she quietly said.

Emma answered just as softly. "The coffee was your idea. Why didn't you make it?" She spared a quick glance at him. "He's just being tiresome—like any young boy is at times."

"And little girls," Lettie added.

The brass bell rang. Ginny lumbered into the shop. "Why's the canvas over . . ." Her voice trailed off as she stared into the kitchen. "A fire? When did that happen?"

"Wednesday night." Lettie pulled out a chair. "Here, Ginny."

"What happened? Where's Mrs. Nance?" Ginny looked from Lettie to Emma and sank down on the chair. After she loosened her shawl, she stared into the kitchen.

As Emma told her about the fire she couldn't help noticing the movement beneath Ginny's skirt. It was fascinating, as if a hand were moving about beneath the fabric. "Ginny . . . what does it feel like when the baby moves?"

Ginny grinned. "The first few times it felt like a bubble, but now it reminds me I'm never alone. Especially when he kicks my rib." She laid a hand on each side of her enlarged abdomen. "Mostly it's hard to believe a whole babe's curled up in here." She met Emma's gaze. "It's a good feeling."

While the coffee boiled, Kent leaned back against the cupboard and watched Emma. She had a pretty face and her hair looked as soft as corn silk. She could turn any man's head, but he'd bet his next year's earnings that was the last thing she'd want to do. It was clear to him she envied her friend's condition, although he wouldn't say she was jealous. If she wanted a family, he thought, she shouldn't be so standoffish around men.

"I'm not sure Will understands what it's like, either," Ginny said, shifting on the seat.

"It is hard to imagine." Emma couldn't really but knew she would never know firsthand, so Ginny's description would have to do. "I'm sure Will's just worried about you."

Kent cleared his throat. "Maybe he feels like a third thumb." He poured a cup of coffee and set the pot back on the stove.

Emma stared at him in shock. She'd forgotten he was there but even if she hadn't, what gave him the notion *he* should say anything?

Ginny looked at Kent for the first time. "Mr. Hogarth, I didn't see you back there."

"It's the screen, Mrs. Talbert. I think that's why," he said, meeting Emma's gaze. "Miss Emma set it out."

Ginny glanced from Emma to Kent. "Please tell me, Mr. Hogarth, why would my husband feel left out? My goodness, without him—" She quickly put her hand over her mouth and turned her head.

Lettie put her arm around Ginny's shoulder. "Don't take what he said to heart. You know Will loves you."

Emma went to the kitchen and spoke softly. "Mr. Hogarth, just because you're working in here doesn't mean you're to join our conversations. I'm sure you didn't mean to upset Mrs. Talbert, but you did."

"You're right, Miss Emma, guess I shouldn't've butted in. Just thought she might like a man's opinion."

"If she'd wanted to know what you thought, she would've asked you." Emma's glance darted over her shoulder to Ginny and back to him. "Besides, unless you're married and have children, how would you know?"

He gave her a crooked grin. "You know what a hotbed of gossip saloons are. Of course you do." He shrugged. "I'm a good listener."

She gritted her teeth, glaring at him. "You fool! Your prank's upset Mrs. Talbert."

"I'll see if I can set it right." Without his crutches he couldn't move forward without help. He put his hand on Emma's shoulder and hopped forward. "Mrs. Talbert, I meant no offense. I was just thinkin'—your husband hasn't had to share your attention with anyone till now."

Ginny turned in the chair and stared at Kent. "Did he say that?"

"Oh, no, ma'am. He certainly did not." Kent stared straight into her eyes. "He's a good man. He couldn't be more proud of you or more pleased about the little one. I've heard other men talk an' that's what it sounds like to me. That's only my thinkin'. Don't set too much store by it."

"But you make sense, Mr. Hogarth. Thank you for speaking up." Ginny turned back around on the chair, then arched and rubbed her back. "Sometimes I wish Will could spell me and carry this one for a while."

The palm of Kent Hogarth's hand felt warm on Emma's shoulder, but his fingers rested well below, nearly on her chest. She looked sideways at him. He was watching Ginny and seemed genuinely concerned, but she hoped he'd learned to keep his comments to himself. Men hardly ever came into the shop. And this is why I like it that way, she thought. "If you figure out how to do that, Ginny, please share your secret with us."

"Emma, wouldn't that be rich?" Ginny giggled. "Can you imagine the look on his face when the babe moved?"

Emma smiled. "That would be something to see."

Kent suddenly realized he wasn't just resting his hand on her shoulder, his fingers were holding her. Oddly enough, she didn't seem to mind, but he didn't want to press his luck. "I'd better get back to work."

She took a step backward. When he lowered his hand, she looked at him. "I think Ginny'll be all right."

He nodded and reached for his cup. After he gulped down the coffee, he took a closer look at the inside walls, how they'd been finished. With no lumber mill in town, he realized, he'd better save the wood from the shed for the new walls. As he worked on resetting the stone foundation, he planned the next day's work and tried not to listen for Emma's soft voice.

After Ginny left the shop, Mr. Ross and Mr. Kirby came over to help Kent Hogarth. Each time Emma managed to forget him, she would hear him talking or hear him working with the stones. When she started fixing dinner, he left without saying a word. She very nearly felt guilty for not inviting him to eat with them, then her temper flared. The man had turned her quiet, orderly life inside out. No more, she thought, I really must not let him bother me.

Late that afternoon Hannah and Mrs. Lewis arrived. Emma brewed a fresh pot of tea, and served Mrs. Lewis. "It's nice to see you're getting out. How're things going at the hotel?"

"We're settling in just fine, dear. Mr. Kirby's a very good cook, and all of us enjoy the sitting room."

Emma served the freshly brewed tea. "I'm glad you're happy there. If there's anything we can help with, please let one of us know."

"Can't think of a thing we can't do for ourselves." Mrs. Lewis tasted the tea. "We're all looking forward to the dinner Sunday," she said, and smiled at Hannah. "And Mrs. Dunn's sweet-potato pie. I can't believe she can grow them here."

"Hannah has many skills." Emma smiled at her.

"I like sweet potatoes. I babied nine tubers all the way across the prairie and over the mountains. Five survived."

"Ma brought a rosebush root along with us," Emma said, a little surprised she had remembered, "but it was in the wagon when it went down the gully." That had been at least seven and a half years ago. It was hard to believe so many years had passed. At seventeen she had thought she was fully grown and that leaving the States was the greatest adventure of her life. She had been half right.

Hannah glanced from Emma to Lettie. "Emma has the only lemon tree around. She's going to supply us with plenty of juice before long."

Emma laughed. "If you have a secret tonic for plants, please share it with me. I don't even know how long it will be before it'll bear fruit, so don't plan on lemonade next summer." She looked to Hannah. "Want me to bring a tablecloth?"

Hannah nodded. "I'll bring one, too, and the big coffeepot."

"Since Mr. Hogarth isn't interested in staying at the hotel, we've talked about putting up a table in the back room. We can use it for a dining room."

"That's a wonderful idea, Mrs. Lewis," Lettie said.

Mrs. Lewis picked up her cup. "I don't see why the owner of the hotel didn't add a dining room. There's nowhere for the guests to eat."

Emma looked at Lettie and grinned. "Maybe we can talk some of the crewmen into staying here permanently."

"Especially one who can cook," Lettie added.

"Oh, Mr. Kirby's a very good cook." A wide grin spread across Mrs. Lewis's face. "We'll work on him together. This's a nice little town, and he hasn't said anything about going down to San Francisco."

Hannah frowned and glanced out the side window. "That Eddie. He's pestering Mr. Hogarth, probably talking about the pups again. I'd better take him home and get supper on the table. I'll see you all Sunday." She dashed outside and called to her son.

Mrs. Lewis glanced around. "How's Mrs. Nance? I haven't seen her since the fire."

Lettie's gaze went to the door to her sitting room. "She's still feeling a little peaked, but I'll tell her you asked about her."

"Oh, please do. I miss our lively conversations." Mrs. Lewis stood. "It's time I get back. I wish it weren't too late to pick berries. I make a real good berry pie." She crossed her shawl over her chest. "I'll see you ladies later."

"Bye, Mrs. Lewis. Come over for a visit anytime."

After she left, Emma looked at the front window. "Let's see if the drapes are dry enough to hang. We can iron them tomorrow."

Lettie led the way through the door to her sitting room. "We'll have to bake tomorrow, too."

Lydia was sitting by the window, and Emma walked over to her. "You'll ruin your eyes. Why didn't you light the lamp?" She couldn't believe the change in Lydia. She hardly spoke and shied away from lighting a fire or lamp. Emma kissed her soft cheek.

"It's about time I stopped sewing."

Hoping to kindle some spark of interest, Emma said, "Mrs. Lewis stopped by and asked about you."

"She was being neighborly."

"You should call on her tomorrow, Gram." Lettie gathered up the drapes. "But right now you can help fix supper. Emma and I are going to hang the drapes in the shop."

"I'm not very hungry, dear."

"Well, I am, and I need your help." Lettie fixed her grandmother with a stern look. "You've been sitting in here all day. 'Bout time you got up, before you get moldy."

Good for you, Lettie, Emma thought, hiding her smile. She tossed the curtains for the side windows over her arm and went over to Lydia. "I'll walk to the kitchen with you."

"Oh, botheration," Lydia said, coming to her feet. "When are you two going to stop pestering me?"

Lettie grinned at Emma. "When're you going to tell me where you keep that maple stick?"

Lydia laid her sewing on the seat of the chair. "Get one of your own. I'm not ready to give up mine yet."

When Emma walked into the kitchen with Lydia, she was surprised to see the canvas back over the opening. Kent Hogarth had evidently left. The kitchen felt warmer, but she wondered why he had left without saying anything. Not that I've encouraged him to be friendly, she thought.

It didn't take Lettie and Emma long to hang the curtains and drapes in the shop. When they finished, Emma put on her bonnet and cape. "See you in the morning."

"We don't need to start at sunup."

Emma grinned at Lettie. "Don't worry. I intend to get a good night's rest." It was dark when she walked home. The stiff breeze felt refreshing after being inside all day. By tomorrow afternoon, with all the baking for the dinner, the town would be filled with delicious aromas.

As she turned toward her house, she looked at the old cabin. A soft light shone from the bottle window. It might be warmer without windows, but she wondered how *he* liked living in a dark box. Then she remembered he had been asked to stay at the hotel with the others but wanted to remain in the cabin. He didn't strike her as a hermit, not the way he got along with everyone. Everyone except her. But that was her doing.

* * *

After breakfast Sunday morning Kent chopped a good supply of firewood. He washed up, put on a clean shirt and pants, and combed his hair. The day before, Mr. Green and Tim Ross had hewed a corner post from a tree trunk for Emma's shop and helped Kent put it up. He put on his coat and set off to stop by the shop on his way to visit Bounder.

The wind coming in off the ocean was cool. When he made his way around the front corner of the Hat Box, he was assailed by delicious aromas. Of course, he remembered, the town dinner. He'd almost forgotten. It was close to midday and everyone would soon gather at the hotel. He checked the corner of the shop. The canvas flapped in the wind but held tight. From there he went to the livery.

He hobbled inside, and Bounder whinnied. Kent went over to his stall and rubbed behind one of the horse's ears. The animal couldn't understand why he'd left him. He spoke softly and decided to give him a good brushing. He had just run the brush down Bounder's back, when Seth came in the back door. "Hi. Didn't think I'd see you here today."

Seth walked over near Kent. "We're going over to the hotel after I close up here."

"He's not used to being cooped up so long." Kent set the brush down and grinned. "I'm not, either. I'll take him out for a while."

"You must've taken a liking to those crutches. Why not put him out in the corral? Take your time. There's no hurry." Seth leaned on a post by the stall. "Looks like the repairs on Miss Townsend and Miss Morrissey's shop are coming right along."

"The crewmen have done a good part of the work." Kent picked up the brush and continued to groom his horse.

Seth nodded. "Heard a couple of them'll be leaving before long."

"Mr. Green and Mr. Nash wanta get back out on a boat." Kent brushed Bounder's sleek neck.

"Will all of 'em be leaving together?"

Kent looked over at Seth. "Maybe a few'll want to stay

on here. For some, this might be a good place to get a fresh start.''

"Just what I been thinkin'." Seth chuckled. "The few strangers we see are heading up to the gold strikes." He shrugged. "Can't blame 'em none. There's nowhere to get a hot meal."

"I heard Dave Kirby's a good cook." Kent moved to do the horse's rump.

"Well, I'd better get out of here." Seth took a few steps and looked back at Kent. "You're goin' to the supper too aren't you?"

"When I finish here, I'll stop by." Kent moved to the other side of Bounder. "I'll close up when I leave."

"Thanks. See you later."

After he completed Bounder's grooming, Kent was tempted to try riding him. He sat on the top rail at the front of the stall, and Bounder stepped up to him. Kent had the feeling the horse understood he wasn't quite himself. He grabbed onto the stallion's mane and started to lean forward. His injured leg banged against the lower rail. A sharp pain shot upward, and he stiffened. Maybe he'd wait till his leg was stronger.

"Sorry, boy. I hate this as much as you, but I don't want to hobble around any longer than I have to." He went out back, washed the smell of horses from his hands and closed the wide front doors to the livery.

The wind had died down to a breeze and the sun was bright. Nice day for getting together. He made his way up the road. The Townsends' buckboard and Talberts' wagon stood in front of the hotel and in back several men were putting a table together. Seth and Jenks were among them. He went back and stood out of their way.

"Pa," Eddie called, running into the yard. "Oh, hi, Mr. Hogarth. Ain't this gonna be fun?"

Kent chuckled. "Sure is, Eddie. How're the pups?"

"Ma says they're growin' faster'n weeds." Eddie ran over to his father. "Ma wants to know if the table's set up."

"Tell her it's ready."

Kent watched the boy charge back into the hotel. "Too bad there aren't more young'uns 'round here."

Seth grinned. "We're workin' on it."

Kent laughed. "Glad to hear it. Will's doing his part, too."

"What's Will doin'?" Charlie Jenks asked as he joined them. "Need any help?"

Kent looked at Seth, barely concealing his amusement.

"Nope." Seth shook his head.

Others were starting to gather around, and Kent didn't want the jest getting out of hand. "We were just talking about how the town's growin'."

Charlie glanced around. "Good thing, too. We've been tryin' to figure out how to let folks know we're here." Another man walked up. After Charlie greeted him, he said, "Hogarth, don't know if ya've met Nate Young. Nate, Kent Hogarth."

Kent held out his hand. "Hi." He had seen him before and Emma had mentioned him. Now he could put the face and name together.

"Mr. Hogarth." Nate shook Kent's hand. "Haven't seen you since the burial. Glad to see you're getting around."

Hannah came out of the hotel with Pauline. "Seth, what are you boys doing? We've got a supper to get on the table."

Pauline shook out a tablecloth and spread it at one end of the makeshift table.

"If you want to eat, you'd best give us a hand." Hannah unfolded a second tablecloth and spread it on the other end of the table.

Will stepped out of the back door of the hotel and helped Ginny down the two steps. "I'll bring a chair out for you."

She patted his arm. "Thanks, sweetheart. I'll need it later." She tried to take the basket he carried, but he held it out of her reach.

"Where do you want it?"

"On the table."

Kent watched the exchange. Pelican Cove needed more young people like them, but he wouldn't like to see it turn into a boomtown. When he returned to Portland, he'd tell a few people he knew about the place. Roy Avery arrived, pushing a handcart holding a large barrel. Then Mrs. Dunn and Emma came out into the yard.

Kent nodded to her. Emma's dress was straw colored with what looked like light green leaves, the color of her eyes. She'd tied her hair back with a matching ribbon, and she reminded him of a spring day.

Emma returned his greeting and set the pitcher of cold tea down on the table. Gracious, the man's eyes had a way of looking at her that felt as if he'd brushed against her. But what was he thinking? She had an inkling he was very good at hiding his feelings, but they would have nothing to do with her. She brushed at her sleeve and walked over to Ginny. "Where's the other table?"

Ginny grinned and motioned to the men. "Mr. Avery arrived with the lager before the men brought it out."

"I'll get Bently. There's cold tea in that pitcher," Emma said, pointing to the end of the table. "The other one has cider."

"Where's Lettie?" Hannah asked. "I haven't seen her or Miss Lydia."

Emma looked over at the back of the shop. "I'll see what's keeping her. Hannah, would you ask Bently to see about putting up the other table?"

Ginny reached around and rubbed her lower back. "I'll get the glasses."

Emma slipped her arm through Ginny's. "I'll do that. I'd feel better if you would see to things out here and let the rest of us bring the food out."

Ginny heaved a sigh. "I feel like a cow, except they get around easier than I do."

Emma smiled. "Take it slow while you can. Before long you'll have more to do than you ever imagined."

Kent watched the ladies, always a pleasant pastime. With Mrs. Dunn and Emma organizing things, he was sure everyone'd feel right at home.

Ginny walked over to him. "Hello. Aren't you going to have some beer with the others?"

She'd caught him unawares. He tried not to let it show.

"I was just thinking about it." Hell, he couldn't very well tell her what was on his mind. "How about you? Can I get you something to drink?"

"I'm fine." She glanced over at the Hat Box. "It looks like the roof's about finished. You've been busy."

"Not me, Mrs. Talbert. Mr. Green and Mr. Ross're rebuilding the roof. They're doin' a fine job."

Ginny glanced over at her husband. "Thank you for speaking up the other day. Will and I had a nice talk."

"I figured you two'd work it out."

She grinned. "I did, too. I know I shouldn't ask, but are you married, Mr. Hogarth?"

"No, ma'am." She must've led her husband on a merry chase, he thought.

She saw Emma coming out of the hotel and went over to take the napkins tucked under her arm. "I was just telling Mr. Hogarth how surprised I am the repairs are coming along so quickly."

As Emma set the tray of glasses down on the table, she met his gaze. "Isn't it a beautiful day?" That sounded foolish, she thought. His eyes sparkled. If she weren't careful, she could easily forget herself and wonder how many other women he had charmed. She saw Lettie and waved.

Kent smiled at her. "You're busy. I'll see you later, Miss Emma." He'd pay ten cents to know what she was thinking.

❖ 10 ❖

THE CITIZENS OF Pelican Cove are all here, Emma thought. The Dunns, Pools, Talberts, Youngs, Mr. Jenks, Mr. Avery, and the Simms were the last to arrive. Vera and Virgil Chase hadn't come, but Emma hadn't held out much hope they would attend. She surveyed the tables and nodded to Mrs. Lewis. "Everything's ready. Why don't you fix yourself a plate and sit with Lydia?"

"I will, soon as I get the men's attention." Mrs. Lewis went over to where the men were gathered.

Emma only caught a couple of words of what Mrs. Lewis said, but the men appeared to accept it good-naturedly and came over to get their food. Charlie and Roy were the first to reach the table where Emma stood. She saw Kent Hogarth say something to Mr. Ross, but he didn't get in line. She handed Charlie flatware, a plate, and napkin. "Please help yourselves. The soup bowls are by the kettle."

"Thank ya, Miss Emma." Charlie stuck the napkin in one pocket. "Sure smells good."

"I snitched a taste of Lettie's potato soup and Hannah's corned venison. They're delicious—but everything is," she said. "And Hannah's sweet-potato pie never lasts long."

Kent hung back. He'd finally met Franklin Simms, who

seemed to be an easygoing man, and one new couple, John Pool and his wife. Said they had a farm outside of town. Their two boys were at least seven to eight years older than Eddie, too old to pal around with the boy. Everyone Kent had met seemed to be hardworking people, and he wanted to give a favorable report about the town to Mr. Wendell.

Pauline Young walked over to Kent. "I hope you're going to eat with us."

"Yes, ma'am. I was just waiting till the crowd thinned out a bit. It's a real nice crowd."

"I would be happy to fix your plate if you'd point out which dishes you want."

He smiled at her. "Thank you, Mrs. Young. I'd appreciate the help." He followed her over to the table. Nearly everyone had served themselves and still there was more than enough for seconds and thirds.

Pauline picked up a plate and a bowl. "Potato soup?"

"Sounds good, but not too generous a portion."

After she ladled the soup into the bowl, she set a biscuit on the plate and moved down the table. "Mr. Kirby made bread, Mrs. Dunn brought corned venison, the beef stew's Mrs. Talbert's, the vegetables are Miss Townsend's, and there's fried chicken."

"I'll take a piece of your fried chicken," he said, sure he'd guessed right, "and some green beans to start with."

"We don't want you to waste away, Mr. Hogarth." She put two large pieces of chicken and a large helping of beans onto his plate. "Now you let me know when you want seconds." She looked at the long table. "There's room for you at the other end by Miss Townsend."

She was in motion before he could tell her it'd be easier for him to sit on the back steps of the hotel. He made his way over to the end of the table where she quickly set a place for him. "Thank you, Mrs. Young."

"You don't have anything to drink. What would you like? Water, cider, coffee, cold tea—or did you have a glass of beer?"

He chuckled. "I'll take whatever's in this pitcher," he said, motioning to the one in front of Emma. She had been right about Mrs. Young. She surely did her best to make a person feel comfortable. He sat down at Emma's side. "Hello, again."

She glanced at his bowl and plate. "You made good choices. But all the women are good cooks."

"What did you make?"

"The vegetables," she said, pointing to his plate.

"Ah, the beans're good," he said, stabbing his fork into several pieces. "But you made tasty beef-and-onion pie one night. I was hoping you'd bring one today."

Emma was more than mildly surprised that he remembered any of the meals she had prepared. "I didn't know." And it's just as well, she told herself. He's only making polite conversation. Her cooking was filling but certainly wouldn't win any awards at a county fair. She ate a bite of bread and looked down the table to Dave Kirby. "This's wonderful, Mr. Kirby. Would you share your secret with us?"

Dave shrugged. "Just lager, ma'am. And a few herbs."

"You're spoiling us, Mr. Kirby," Mrs. Lewis said. "It won't be easy replacing you after you leave."

Charlie Jenks nodded. "Sure would be nice if some of ya'd stay on here."

Mrs. Lewis glanced from Lydia and Hannah to Bently. "Mr. Townsend, since there's nowhere for hotel guests to eat, I was thinking someone could make the downstairs guest room into a dining room and enlarge the kitchen."

Bently lowered his fork. "That wouldn't be too hard to do, but after everyone leaves, there wouldn't be much of a need for it."

"I could run the hotel until you found someone else," Mrs. Lewis said. "Unless one of the men want to do it."

Dave Kirby shook his head. "I'll cook two meals a day, if anyone's there to eat."

"Good," Lydia said. "Now what about the rest of you? Mr. Brice, I understand you're a shoemaker. Can you do repairs, too?"

"Yes, ma'am," Mr. Brice said. "Later, you tell me what you need fixed."

"Hey, Pa," John Pool, Jr., called out. "Can we get new shoes?"

John met Martha's gaze. "We'll talk about it later."

Charlie raised his lager. "Now we got somethin' else to celebrate!"

It was too good an opportunity for Kent to pass up. "If someone put in a ferry crossing near the mouth of the river, there might be enough business in the coming year to keep him from going hungry." He glanced at Mr. Nash, Mr. Green, and Timothy Ross. "People are bound to travel up the coast to the mines up north."

"I can't speak for anyone besides Mr. Green," Mr. Nash said, "but we'll be leaving in the morning. You folks've been real kind, but we have to set out for San Francisco."

Mr. Green nodded. "If any of you wanta go with us, you're more'n welcome to join us."

Emma smiled across the table at Lettie. "Seems like we've gained a few townspeople."

"I haven't seen a gristmill," Kent said, turning to Bently. "How do you manage without one?"

"Matter of fact, we have a small one." Bently speared a chunk of corned venison with his fork. "We all own a share and take turns working it."

"Good," Kent said.

"Before long you'll need a newspaper to keep track of the happenings around here," Mr. Brice said.

Lettie glanced at Bently. "My, wouldn't that be wonderful. Emma, we could run a small advertisement for the shop."

"And the hotel, too." Mrs. Lewis smiled at Lydia.

Emma ate rather absently as she struggled to keep up with the conversation. She noticed Alicia's keen interest. Her husband, Franklin, seemed pleased with the talk of a newspaper, too. Emma glanced sideways at Kent Hogarth. He talked as if he were thinking about staying in town. If he did, she wondered how she would feel. He grinned at her, and she looked at her plate.

When she continued staring at her food, he asked, "Miss Emma, would you pass the pitcher?"

Forcing herself to eat a bite of beef stew, Emma watched Mrs. Lewis, who was talking with some of the men. At times like this, Emma thought, she hated her hearing loss, but she also realized how much worse it could be. If she were completely deaf, she wouldn't be able to hear the thunderous, stormy surf, the bright call of the warbler or the cry of the gulls, the sound of wind whistling through the tall trees—or the stirring tone of Kent's voice.

Kent waited and watched her, but she seemed lost in thought. So much for his social graces, he thought and reached in front of her for the pitcher.

Eddie tugged on Hannah's sleeve. "Ma, can I have some of that cinnamon custard now? It sure smells good."

Mrs. Lewis grinned at the boy. "If it's all right with you, I'll get the boy a bowl."

Hannah nodded. "What do you say, Eddie?"

"Please . . . thank you."

The dishes were collected and dessert passed out to everyone. The men shared stories about their journeys from back East, and every so often one of the women corrected an amazing account. Eddie tagged along with the Pool boys when they went exploring in the woods north of town.

By early evening, when the western horizon was a brilliant yellow, the dishes had been washed, the bowls and kettles of leftover food covered, and Eddie had fallen asleep on Hannah's lap. The men and women had settled into two groups. Timothy Ross played "Old Rosin the Beau" on his mouth organ. Emma sat between Pauline and Alicia.

Lydia poured a little of her blackberry wine into nine odd-sized glasses and passed them out to the women. "Lager isn't bad, but I like a little of my wine after a good supper."

Martha sipped her wine. "Miss Lydia, when're you going to share your secret recipe for this? It's the best I've ever tasted. And you know it, Miss Lydia Nance."

"Don't worry." Lydia laughed softly. "I won't take it with me."

"Good," Alicia said, raising her glass.

Lydia grinned at them. "But part of the trick is patience."

Alicia looked at her glass. "Oh, I may not have much success with it then."

As Emma sipped her wine, she gazed over at Kent Hogarth. He was sitting on the side of the well her shop shared with the general store. Mr. Ross stopped playing his mouth organ and said something, but she couldn't read his lips. Mr. Kirby nodded, and John Pool made a comment. Kent listened with keen interest, and that aroused her curiosity. For someone passing through, he took an uncommon interest in the town's affairs.

He also attracted interest. She'd seen Ginny cast him a friendly look and Pauline, too. Emma couldn't blame them. He met her gaze and smiled. She felt as if a summer breeze had ruffled her hair. Instantly looking away, she prayed the feeling was only her imagination.

She had fought the attraction, but it was there, whether she wanted to believe it or not. And it wasn't fair. She was damaged goods, and the last thing she wanted was to care for him when she knew it would lead to a broken heart. Oh, what's wrong with me? she wondered. In his eyes I'm no different from any of the other women here.

"Emma—" Alicia said, and then lightly tapped her arm.

Emma gave a start and belatedly realized Alicia had spoken to her. "Yes?" Lettie, Hannah, and the others were standing. Oh, Lordy, Emma thought, I've done it this time.

Alicia rose and shook her skirt. "It's getting dark. Ginny's tired. Martha wants to start home, and I think we should, too."

"Yes, of course." Emma quickly got to her feet and began helping to clear the table. Timothy Ross played "Home Sweet Home." How much of the conversations had she missed because of her musing? She couldn't allow herself to be so distracted by Kent again. As the Pools and Talberts said their good-byes, Bently joined her. "Did you enjoy the afternoon?" Emma asked.

"It was pleasant enough. I didn't think any of the shipwreck survivors would be interested in remaining here." He waved to the Simmses and looked at his sister. "What do you make of Mr. Hogarth?"

She shrugged. "He appears to get along with everybody." She didn't say any more. Her brother was thinking aloud and likely wouldn't hear what she said.

"I don't like the man. There's no reason why he should care if we have a ferry or a gristmill." He shook his head. "Don't like it at all."

"He seems friendly enough." She glanced sideways at her brother. "He may be the sort of person who makes the best of any situation."

"Well, if he came here to rob anyone, he'll be sorely disappointed."

She stared at Bently. "You can't mean that."

"Who's to say what he's up to?"

"Then why did you offer him the wood from the shed? You even helped him take it apart." She returned Ginny's wave and eyed her brother again.

"It was for *your* shop. He'd damn well better use all of it there." Bently glared at her. "And if there's *any* trouble with him, you had better tell me. I can't believe you hired him to repair the damage."

"He's been working very hard, and you didn't offer to help us out."

Lettie came over to the Townsends and touched Emma's arm. "Gram's getting chilled. I'm going to get her inside. I'll see you in the morning."

"She must be tired too but I think she enjoyed herself." Glancing just past Lettie, Emma noticed Kent, and he was watching her. When their gazes met, he waved and went across the yard toward the street in front of her shop. She should've said something to him, but she couldn't very well chase after him, not just to say good-bye.

"She seems to be her old self again," Lettie said, grinning.

"I'm so glad." After Lettie left, Emma started to walk away, then hesitated. "That reminds me, Bently. Lettie's favorite chair burned in the fire. She'd be so grateful if you would build another frame. We can upholster it."

"I'll speak to her about it."

"Thank you." She gave him a quick kiss on the cheek

and went to help finish putting things away. Sometimes she had trouble remembering that Bently hadn't always been so narrowminded or serious.

Emma walked into the general store. "Good morning, Mr. Jenks." She wished there was a new shipment of goods to browse through. However, he only received new goods once or twice a year, and she was familiar with almost all of his stock.

"Hi, Miss Emma. How're ya doin'?" Charlie Jenks sat by the woodstove watching her.

"Just fine, Mr. Jenks." She glanced at the shelves behind the counter where he kept his account records. "Looks like you've made a few sales since the last time I was in."

"Mm," he said, lifting one shoulder. "Green and Nash needed supplies. Sure was sorry to see them go. Hope the others stick 'round." He grinned at her and said, "Be glad when some of those travelers Hogarth talked about'd stop in here."

I wouldn't hold my breath, she thought. "If Eureka grows in size and we can hold out, other towns will start up along the coast, too." She ambled over to the yard goods. "But I don't think it'll happen this winter."

"Think you're right 'bout that, Miss Emma."

She skimmed through the yard goods and paused at the bolt of cabbage-green foulard. If she weren't careful, she'd leave a worn spot on the fabric from running her fingers over it every time she came to the store. Lowering her hand, she stepped over to the counter.

Mr. Jenks went to the other side. "What can I get for you?"

"I need a pound of coffee beans, three nutmegs, cinnamon, and we're also low on peppercorns. Oh, and chocolate. The weather's turning cool."

He chuckled. "Winter's usually cold."

"I don't mind the rain, but I'm glad it doesn't snow here."

"Don't think ya'll have to worry 'bout that account." He set the packages on the counter and entered the purchases in his book.

"That's true." She gathered the small parcels into the crook of her arm. "By the way, have you seen Mr. or Mrs. Chase in the last few days?"

"No . . . not in for a—" He skimmed his thumb down the open account book. "Must be more'n a month."

She smiled. "Thanks." She returned to the shop and went into the kitchen. Lydia and Lettie were preparing dinner, and Kent was working on the new inside wall. Emma put aside half the cinnamon and one nutmeg to take home later, and put on her apron. "What can I do to help?"

"Not much," Lettie said, stirring the pot on the stove. "Gram shredded some of the leftover beef to add to the potato soup."

Lydia set the large knife on the table. "Would you like to slice the bread, dear?"

"Be glad to."

Lydia smiled at Kent. "What would you like to drink with dinner, Mr. Hogarth? Water as usual? We're out of milk, but we have coffee or tea."

Emma's hand slipped and the knife came down hard, just missing her finger. "Fiddlesticks," she muttered, and paid closer attention to what she was doing. She shouldn't have been surprised. Lydia had invited him to eat dinner with them all week, ever since the town supper. The only real concern Emma had was that she couldn't relax with him seated within reach.

"Water'll do fine, Miss Lydia. Don't go to any bother on my account." He put the hammer down. "I split a number of boards for the laths. I think there're enough boards left to finish off the east part of the outside wall. If we can't get any more lumber, I'll have to close up the back wall with split logs."

Lettie looked over her shoulder at Emma. "That will be all right, won't it?"

"Yes." Emma glanced at Kent, then to Lettie. "I'm sure we have a little more yellow paint at the house." He had finished the floor the day before. All of a sudden the room was closing up, but it wasn't like before the fire.

The new planks used to replace the missing floor had been

hewn from one of the giant trees and added a pleasant aroma to the shop. She stole another glance at Kent. He was a fine craftsman. Oh, who was she fooling? She had grown used to seeing him every day and having him around the shop.

"Good," he said, watching her a moment longer before he returned his attention to his handiwork. He couldn't tell what she was thinking, but he decided he'd never play poker with her. "I'll put a coat of plaster on the walls tomorrow 'n start on the window frames." He gathered up the tools. "I'll put these away 'n wash up outside."

"This will be ready when you are, Mr. Hogarth." Lettie moved the pot to the side of the stovetop and saw Lydia searching through a cupboard. "What're you looking for, Gram?"

"What else can we serve? Mr. Hogarth's worked hard all morning. He needs rib-sticking food." Lydia shook her head. "Guess I'll just cut up the end of the roast. We can make sandwiches."

Emma laid the sliced bread out on the cutting board and broke the uneven piece into a bowl for herself. Kent returned a few minutes later, and she held the bowls while Lettie ladled the soup into each one. They sat down at the kitchen table.

Kent took the place Miss Lydia insisted was his at one end of the table. When Emma passed the plate of meat to him, his fingers brushed hers. They hadn't spoken more than a few words since Sunday, but she'd been a mite friendlier. He set two pieces on his plate and held it for Miss Lydia. "I hope you know you're spoiling me, ma'am."

"What you need, Mr. Hogarth, is a good woman to take care of you." Lydia glanced across the table at Emma. "Since you don't have one, we'll do what we can for you."

He chuckled. "I do appreciate your kindness, but I been on the move most o' my life. Not too many ladies'd want to call a camp home." He'd seen how Emma followed the conversations around her but said little. Well, he wasn't going to be in town that long so he knew better than to start something he couldn't finish.

Emma dipped her spoon into the soup. If she didn't waylay Lydia's matchmaking attempt, the dear woman would surely embarrass her. "I'm worried about Vera. Mr. Jenks said he hadn't seen her or Mr. Chase for at least a month."

"I'm not surprised they didn't come to the supper." Lettie broke some bread into her soup. "I hope she's all right."

Kent glanced around the table. "I haven't met them, have I?"

"Not unless you've been out to their farm." Emma took a sip of tea. "I'll ride out there after we eat. She didn't seem very happy when I spoke to her the other day."

Lettie frowned at her. "You're not going out to their farm by yourself, are you? I don't think Bent—your brother would like that."

"I certainly do not need his permission, and I'll be fine. I simply want to see Vera to ease my mind." Emma took another spoonful of soup.

"I'd be happy to drive you out there, Miss Emma," Kent offered, staring straight into her eyes. That earned a reaction. If she'd looked down and suddenly found herself naked, she couldn't've seemed more surprised. He really did want to become better acquainted with her. She reminded him of a piece of cut crystal he'd seen once that looked different with each turn.

Emma gulped down the soup. "That won't be—"

Lydia interrupted her. "Thank you, Mr. Hogarth. With you escorting her, we won't worry."

"Is this Mr. Chase dangerous?" Kent looked at Emma, but she didn't say a word. "Miss Lydia?"

"He's a bitter man."

Emma set her spoon down and met his gaze. "I've never heard of him harming anyone." When he continued staring at her, she added, "It's just that Mrs. Chase seems to be afraid of him, and I'd like to see her again. I don't need a guard."

"Good. It'll be a nice ride, then. A chance to see more of the area." *And maybe we can get to know one another a little better,* he thought.

❖ *11* ❖

Emma handled the reins with ease. Kent had been determined to help her harness the horse, but she had insisted on driving the buckboard. After all, she had no intention of spending the rest of the day exploring to satisfy his curiosity. She glanced at him and pulled her skirt out of his way. "Is your leg comfortable?"

He smiled. If she scooted over any farther, she'd fall off the bench. "Yep. You?"

"Yes, of course." What nonsense, she thought, looking out of the corner of her eye. He was grinning! "You seem to be enjoying your stay here."

"Shouldn't I?"

"That's not what I meant."

"My mistake." He pointed to a farmhouse to the left of the road. "Who lives there?"

"The Talberts, Ginny and Will."

Their place was well kept and confirmed Kent's first impression. "Then the cemetery must be just ahead."

"Yes," she said softly. "Meyer's River's on the other side of those trees."

"Mm-hm." The road slowly curved away from the river. "Are any settlers over there?"

"The Olsens have a good-sized farm. It borders the river."

"It's still hard to believe someone hasn't put in a ferry. That river's runnin' too fast to drive a wagon across it."

"The Olsens have a little boat they use when the water's high."

"What about the others? Don't people travel up or down the coast?" The hillsides and lowlands were green and lush. But he'd have to admit most of the land didn't appear flat enough to farm.

"Not very often. Sometimes we see miners who've come down from the mountains, but most of the claims are closer to Wyreka over on the Shasta River."

He was familiar with that area. Mr. Wendell already had supply wagons running north from Sutterville and Sacramento City, and he wanted to be the first to supply the coastal towns. "Are there any settlements up in these hills?"

"I haven't heard of any. There're too many trees and the land's not suitable to farm." She stared ahead at the densely forested hills. "Not good for cattle, either. I don't know about sheep." She glanced at him. As she thought the question, her heart beat faster, but she had to ask. "Have you changed your mind about settling here?"

"It's real nice here, I'll give you that. But I like movin' around, meetin' people." I'm not old enough to put down roots, he thought.

She wasn't surprised by his answer, but she was strangely disappointed. "What is it that you do?"

"About anything for an honest wage. I've driven supply wagons, ridden shotgun on a stagecoach, built fences, trapped. I've been a guide, tried my hand at finding gold— gave that up real quick; made more money sellin' supplies to the miners." He saw no need to rouse interest in Wendell's project until a decision had been made and that wouldn't happen till Kent reported to him in Portland. He watched her out of the corner of his eye. She wasn't sitting as ramrod straight as she had when they left town, and he'd even managed to get a smile out of her. "What about you? Townsend doesn't seem like the type to make you work."

She laughed softly. "I'd rather spend my days at the shop

than in my kitchen. With only my brother and me at home, there isn't much to do.'' Her gaze darted to him then back to the road. ''I'm his sister, not his maid, mother, or wife.''

''Good for you. But I'm surprised the husbands aren't afraid you'll reform their wives.'' He shifted on the bench and eyed the hem of her skirt. ''You're not one of those bloomer ladies I heard about, are you?''

She stared at him and couldn't help grinning. ''Are you talking about Amelia Bloomer?''

''Don't recall her given name. Let's hope there's only one.''

''Last year I saw a caricature of her in an old newspaper.'' She shook her head. ''It was terrible.''

''Was she smokin' a cigar?''

''Mm-hm.''

''Remember those frilly bloomers? They looked kinda saucy.'' He gave her a crooked smile. ''You might think about setting a pair of those in your front window.''

She kept staring straight ahead, but she was laughing. ''I could call them leg warmers.'' The man was a wicked tease, and she really did enjoy his company.

He liked her pretty smile. It lighted up her whole face. ''Whatever you call 'em, bet you'd have more men walkin' by your window.''

She shook her head. ''We're passing the Pools' farm.''

It was larger than the Talberts', but the Pools had two boys to help out. Kent saw a few head of cattle in the distance. ''The land must be rich. Everyone has a nice log cabin.''

''That was the agreement. Those of us who moved here first made sure each family had their own home and a well. By the time the lumber arrived, we had the log cabins built.''

''The Chase family. Were they with you?''

''No. They arrived a little over a year ago.'' Though you'd never know it by the look of their cabin, she thought. ''That's their place up ahead.''

If she hadn't told him it was a farm, he wouldn't have guessed. Part of the field was planted, the rest was overgrown. A cow and two nags grazed on the far side of the barn. However, someone carefully tended a fairly large garden at the side of the barn. When they entered the yard a barking motley-looking mongrel ran up to the buckboard. When Kent stepped down to the ground, the dog ran off.

Emma walked around to where Kent waited for her. "Are you sure you want to do this? She probably won't ask us inside."

He glanced at the rough cabin. "I wasn't expecting to be invited for supper." He started up the path to the front door.

She shrugged and led the way. She couldn't remember ever meeting anyone with Kent's easygoing disposition. Part of her couldn't help wondering what would trigger his temper. She knocked on the door. Before she had lowered her hand, it opened.

"Hello—" she said, assuming Vera would greet them, but her husband, Virgil, stood in the doorway glaring at her. "Mr. Chase. It's been so long. You may not remember me— I'm Emma Townsend, and this is Mr. Hogarth."

Virgil Chase gave them a curt nod.

Kent moved close to Emma's side. Chase was stocky and not much taller than Emma. He was also rude and, as Miss Lydia had said, seemed to be a bitter man. Kent had seen others like him. But unless the man threatened Emma, he would stay out of it.

"We missed both of you at the supper last Sunday. I've come to see Vera. Is she around?" She had to be, but Emma didn't want to give him an excuse to vent his anger.

"She's scrubbin' the floor."

Virgil didn't budge from the doorway, and Emma couldn't see past him. "Oh, then she may welcome a visit. Scrubbing floors is so hard on the knees." She'd be darned if she was simply going to leave because Virgil was used to intimidating people.

"Look, miss, she's busy."

Emma smiled over her shoulder at Kent and looked back at Virgil. Now she was becoming irritated, and the devil in her faced him. "We've driven all the way out from town. I'm sure if Vera knew we were here, she'd spare us a minute or two and a dipper of water.'' ''We'll share'' was on the tip of her tongue, but she knew he wouldn't even crack a smile.

Virgil called ''Vera!'' over his shoulder with only a slight turn of his head.

Vera appeared at his side, behind her husband's outstretched arm which blocked the doorway. ''Miss Emma, so nice of you—and your friend—to call on us.''

''I was showing Mr. Hogarth around,'' Emma said, crossing two fingers in the folds of her skirt, ''and thought we'd pay our respects.'' She put her hand on Kent's arm. ''I would like you to meet Mr. Hogarth. Mr. Hogarth, Mr. and Mrs. Chase.''

Kent smiled at Mrs. Chase and held out his hand to Mr. Chase. ''Glad to meet you.''

Virgil clasped Kent's hand and gave it a sharp jerk, as if working the handle on a water pump. ''Hogarth.''

He had the grip of a smithy, Kent thought, and his wife didn't quite look him in the eye. However, Emma's behavior interested him more than the dour couple. Women always had confounded and fascinated him.

Emma didn't believe she had ever seen Vera wear her hair down, the way it was today, covering the sides of her cheeks. ''Your garden's doing so well, Vera. What's your secret?''

Vera glanced at her husband. ''I just try to keep the weeds down and use crumbled-up cow pies.''

''It looks nice. I don't have any luck with mine.'' Emma's attention drifted to Virgil and back to Vera. ''We missed you at the supper. We'd hoped you could join us.''

Chase's face was turning red, and Kent quickly said, ''You've got some good acreage here. Must yield good crops of corn and potatoes. You plant winter wheat yet?''

Chase stepped over the threshold. ''What business is it of yours?''

Kent moved up to Emma's side. ''Just curious.''

''Oh, Vera,'' Emma said, ''you'll have to come into the shop and see the quilts Lettie and I have been piecing together. If you're working on one, bring it with you.''

As Vera licked her lips, she drew her brows together and

barely shook her head. "Yes . . . I'll do that one of these days."

Emma put her hand on Kent's arm. "I guess we'd better be on our way. See you the next time you're in town."

"I'll surely try, Miss Emma. We don't get t'town much."

Emma looked straight at Vera and said, "Please try," then followed Kent back to the buckboard. When he was seated, she quickly turned the horse and headed back to town. She waited to speak until they turned onto the roadway. "Now you've met everyone but the Olsens."

"I'm looking forward to that. Is Chase always such a charmer?"

She chuckled. "You met him on a good day."

"Mrs. Chase didn't look too happy about your visit." He shifted on the bench and placed his elbow between them on the backrest.

"I wish she'd stand up to him." It was impossible to avoid every rut. One side of the buckboard bounced, jostling them, and Kent's hand brushed her arm. She instinctively glanced over at him, but he was looking at the river, not at her. He really is a *nice* man, she thought, sliding a bit closer to him. Since the attack, when she lost more than the hearing in one ear, she had known she was damaged goods. He didn't treat her as though she was, but he didn't know her secret and never would.

"Too bad we didn't bring fishin' poles." As he watched the far riverbank, he noticed a strange brown bird with long spindly legs. "That's some bird. What kind is it?" He rested his hand on her shoulder and pointed across the river with the other. He could've sworn she sighed. He relaxed his fingers over her narrow shoulder. For a few coins he could hold an easy woman any way he liked, but he couldn't help wondering how it would feel to hold Emma in his arms, her slim body pressed against his.

She looked to the far bank and smiled. "That's a pelican." His touch was a friendly gesture, but the warmth of his hand stirred a restless, tingly feeling that made her want to edge even closer to him. Instead, she blurted out, "There're a lot of them around here." He didn't seem to be aware his hand was still on her shoulder, but she was glad he hadn't pulled away. She was sure it didn't mean anything to him, but she treasured the moment.

Emma was seated at the table in the shop with Lettie and Alicia. The wind was brisk and blowing in through the two uncovered windows. Emma pulled her shawl up around her neck and hoped Kent was able to keep warm as he put the window frames together outside.

During the two days since their ride out to the Chase farm she had repeatedly touched her shoulder where his hand had rested, but it wasn't the same. She had taken him several cups of coffee, but she couldn't very well stand around as if she were a simpering schoolgirl while he worked. Besides, she firmly reminded herself, she only wanted to enjoy his friendship.

Alicia wrapped both hands around her teacup. "Do you really think anyone would want a newspaper here?"

Lettie nodded. "Yes, it would be so nice to have our own paper and read it fresh off the press, so to speak, not months later. But how could Mr. Simms learn about what's going on?"

"I'm not sure. In Indiana he got newspapers from all over in the mail. Many weren't more than a couple days old. And of course he talked with coach drivers." She traced the cup handle with her thumb. "He won't be able to do that here."

Emma recalled her conversation with Kent. She hadn't really thought of Pelican Cove as being cut off from other towns and cities, but it was. It would hardly be worth Franklin Simms's time to print a paper with local news everyone already knew.

"Haven't carrier pigeons been used in England?" Lettie looked from Emma to Alicia.

Alicia nodded. "But they can only carry short messages, and it would be hard to train them."

"Since ships can't get in here, we need roads." Emma swallowed a sip of tea. "Mr. Hogarth was right about the ferry. Our town isn't very easy to reach." Her brother had

counted on ships being able to land and then taking supplies
upriver by boat to the high country, but that hadn't worked
out, and it would be costly to clear a road over the mountains
to the inland valley.

"From the time he heard about this town, Mr. Simms
wanted to publish the first newspaper in the area." Alicia
continued running her thumb up and down the cup handle.
"Sometimes men get caught up in a dream and don't think
about how to make it happen."

"There'll be a road along the coast. It'll just take time."
Lettie looked at each of them in turn. "We knew that when
we came here."

Alicia looked back into the kitchen at the new wall and
spoke softly. "Mr. Hogarth seems like the kind of man to
help make this town into an important city."

"There will be others—maybe as close as Eureka."
Emma glanced at the window opening in the kitchen. It was
mid-afternoon, and she was certain Kent would be finished
with the frames anytime. "Next spring some of us should
go down to Eureka. After all, we're neighbors. We should
get acquainted."

Lettie grinned. "That's a splendid idea. I hope your
brother'll go with us."

"He should be interested." And it would be a good opportunity for you two to be together, Emma thought. "You
can browse through the stores and see what kind of mer-
chandise they have."

"You'll go with us, won't you?"

"I got to visit Astoria. Now it's your turn." It was quiet
outside. Emma walked back to the kitchen and watched Kent
stand one window frame up on its side. "That looks good,"
she called out to him. "Are you still going to cover it with
canvas?" He smiled at her and her pulse fluttered. Ninny,
she thought. Why should a pleasant smile, something he does
many times a day, send her emotions reeling?

"I was just about to do that." He picked up the piece of
canvas he'd cut to cover the frame. "You still want to coat
it with wax?" If she kept looking at him with that fetching
gleam in her eyes neither of them would get any work done.

"Only the one on the back wall needs it," she said, resting her hands on the opening for the south window. "It gets the brunt of the rain. I'll melt the paraffin while you attach it to the frame."

He chuckled. "Yes, ma'am." Like most women, she gave orders easily.

She got out the old tin teapot her mother had also used to melt paraffin and set aside the long, narrow stick of wood used for stirring. After she broke up some of the wax and put it in the small teapot, she set it over the heat in a pan with water and returned to her chair in the shop. "Looks like we'll have at least one window before suppertime."

"He's done a wonderful job." Lettie turned and eyed the new wall. "Since he painted the kitchen and stained the floor, I can't even tell there was any damage."

"He is a prize," Alicia agreed. "Too bad we don't need more buildings, but we still have two empty shops. Do you think he would like to start his own business?"

Emma shook her head. "He seems to be someone who likes to work out of doors."

"Then maybe he would like to be an expressman. He could bring the news from Astoria, San Francisco, even Sutterville and the gold fields." Alicia grinned at Lettie, then Emma. "What do you think? Would you ask him?"

"Me? Why not you? Or better yet, Mr. Simms. He'd be the best one to ask." Emma glanced at the window and wondered if he had overheard their conversation. She liked the idea of seeing him once in a while. It was better than never seeing him again, which was more likely.

Lettie watched Emma and grinned. "Oh, do speak to Mr. Simms about it, Alicia."

Emma went to check on the wax. As she stirred it with the stick, she considered what Kent's reaction would be to the Simmses' offer. If he did accept, for only a few trips, and she didn't think he would, it could prove to be a great advantage to the town. She knew better than to hope he would make more than two or three treks but that might be enough to . . . what? Coax him into settling here? she wondered. Oh, she was becoming fanciful—and she wouldn't be twenty-four for another six months! At the rate she was going she'd surely be a handful when she was in her dotage.

"Miss Emma," Kent called from the window opening.

She set the pan to the side of the heat and went over to the window. "Are you finished already?"

He moved the covered frame out where she could see it. "Do you want to wax it out here?"

She glanced around the kitchen. "I'll be right out." She grabbed a clean rag from the bin and took the teapot of paraffin outside. He had set the frame across two logs for her.

"I can do that for you." His gaze skimmed down the light green dress that showed off her curves so nicely. "I'd hate for you to spoil your clothes."

"I'll be careful." As she tucked one end of the rag up her sleeve, she noticed the other window frame leaning against the shop wall. "You work fast."

"I try," he said with a grin. He got the other piece of canvas he'd cut earlier and began nailing it to the second frame.

She poured the paraffin onto the canvas and spread it with the stick until the entire frame was coated. There were three leather tabs on one side she assumed were the hinges and she avoided getting wax on them. "It's so cool out here, the wax is almost hard already. You can hang this in a few minutes."

"I'm about done here. I'll put it up first."

He had replaced the burned-out back wall with split logs, but it didn't look bad at all. "Won't you need some help?"

"I can stand on the stump to nail it up, if you'd hold it from the inside."

"I'd be glad to." She touched the wax coating on the canvas. "It's dry." And if it rains too hard, it will probably crack. Beeswax would have softened it, but she didn't have any.

He watched her hurry along the side of the shop and around the corner. She sure was easy on the eyes, and good to talk with, too. He stepped up on the stump, leaned his crutches against the wall, and fitted the window frame into the opening. If he wasn't careful, he might start thinking about coming back—to pay his respects.

"I'm here." Emma held the frame in place. The fit was perfect and kept the wind out nearly as well as the glass.

He put a nail in the leather hinges at each end. "You can let go now." He quickly finished nailing the leather and stepped down to the ground. "Try pushing out the bottom. It shouldn't fall off."

She did as he asked. The window swung out and he was standing below. "It works perfectly."

"Good. I'll cut a stick so you can prop it open." He looked around and saw one of the leftover siding boards. "Help me with the other one?"

She nodded and lowered the window. It was cleverly designed and wouldn't allow the wind a direct path through the kitchen or shop. When he raised the second window frame into place, she held it steady while he anchored the leather hinges.

He checked the sides and bottom of the frame. "Looks okay out here."

"You aren't surprised, are you?" She turned and smiled at Alicia and Lettie. "What do you think?"

"They're perfect," Lettie said, glancing at Alicia. "And we don't have to worry about curtains until he puts the glass in."

Alicia frowned. "Can the windows be opened from the outside?"

Kent came into the shop in time to hear her question. "Not after I put these on." He held up two short leather straps.

Lettie's gaze went to Emma as she said, "You seem to think of everything, Mr. Hogarth. We're fortunate you were here when we needed a good carpenter."

"From the look of the buildings 'round town, I'd say you weren't short of skilled men." He made his way through the shop to Emma's side. "You may not have many strangers coming through here, but I'd feel better knowing you ladies were the only ones who could open the windows."

"Thank you." Emma peered over at Alicia and wondered why she had worried about locking the windows. Glancing at Lettie, Emma didn't think her dear friend feared living alone. And she, of all people, had never felt safer.

"Miss Emma—" Kent waited a moment, but when she didn't answer, he laid his hand on her arm.

Emma gave a start and met his gaze. "Sorry. Did you say something?"

Kent hooked the leather strap over the top of the nail. "Just wanted to show you how this works." If her brother hadn't kept his voice down when they talked, he would've sworn she was hard of hearing.

❖ *12* ❖

SUNDAY MORNING EMMA took a walk along the shore. The ocean was a deep blue-green. Once, when the sunlight hit a wave just right, the crest appeared to be a clear shade of turquoise. It lasted only a few moments. But it was beautiful and so was the sight of windblown sea spray.

She thought about continuing on up the shore to where the ship ran aground and quickly dismissed that idea. It was more than a good stretch of the legs. Instead, she climbed up the cliff and wandered through the forest. She hadn't brought a basket, so she used her old bonnet to hold the comfrey, ginger, mint, and plantain she gathered. By the time she started back to the house, she had also gathered up the lower part of her cape to hold more leaves and stalks.

She was rinsing off a bunch of the leaves when Bently came into the kitchen. "Did you finish working on the ledger?"

"Some time ago."

"Is everything okay?"

"So far, but we need more people and businesses if we're to keep this town going."

"What can you do about that?"

"I left notices with the newspaper in Astoria, ship captains, and with the merchants.'' He shrugged. ''I've also sent information to a dozen other newspapers back east.'' He frowned and stared at the mound of herbs. ''I looked for you along the beach. That is where you said you'd be walking, isn't it?''

''I did. Then I went on to the forest and collected some herbs I needed.'' She rinsed off a bunch of mint leaves and held them out for him to smell.

He brushed them aside. ''You were gone for nearly three hours. Didn't you think I'd worry about you?'' He went over to the stove and refilled his coffee cup.

''Why would you? I couldn't feel safer.''

He set his cup down on the worktable. ''After what happened at Soda Springs, I didn't think you'd venture off without an escort.'' He raised the cup to his mouth, then stared at her. ''Were you alone? Or did Hogarth keep you company?''

''Oh, Bently, do you honestly believe that?'' She faced him, waiting for an answer. She had never given him any reason to distrust her. Although she loved him dearly, she knew how he liked to be in charge of everything. But not of her, she thought, not her.

After a long pause he shook his head. ''I had to ask. We don't know a thing about him, but you seem to have become pretty friendly with him.''

Instead of slapping him, she gave the wet ginger a good shake. ''He did a wonderful job rebuilding the shop, and he seems very nice. I don't see any reason to be rude to him.'' She winced, knowing she had been, and hoped her brother hadn't noticed. There were some people who were genuinely nice, helpful and trustworthy. She had known a few, and she thought Kent Hogarth was one of those people. She honestly believed she had nothing to fear from him—except maybe her own impossible desire to be more than just friends.

She didn't want to discuss Kent or her feelings for him with her brother and changed the subject. ''Why don't you call on Lettie and go for a drive? My life is quiet and predictable, no matter how you try to spice it up.''

He slammed the cup down and stood up. ''That's another

thing. Before the shipwreck, you weren't so impertinent, and I must say I do not approve.'' His frown seemed to reflect his statement.

''I'm fully grown.'' She set the clean plantain on the towel by the other herbs. ''You've kept your promise to Mama and Papa. They'd want you to make a life for yourself.'' She broke a mint leaf and rubbed it on her wrists. ''You turned twenty-eight almost three months ago. Isn't it time you thought about getting married, starting a family of your own?''

''I've plenty time for that.'' His frown slipped away. ''And you'll always have a home here with me.''

She nodded. ''I've been thinking about that. You know how I like being at the shop, and Lettie's apartment is nice. I wouldn't mind living there at all.''

''With Miss Morrissey and Mrs. Nance? Why would you want to do that when you have your own room here?''

''Not with Lettie, with Lydia.'' She watched his puzzled expression. Was he really so dense he didn't understand what she was suggesting? ''Before long some man's going to see what a wonderful woman Lettie is and marry her.''

He drew his brows together. ''Are you trying to tell me she's seeing someone?''

The tone in his voice told her he was interested in Lettie. Emma shook a vine. ''I haven't asked her, but I'm sure she'll meet a man who can find it in his heart to overlook her pointy nose and retiring way.''

''Really, Emm, how can you say such things about your closest friend? Miss Morrissey is a lovely woman. And her nose is not pointy,'' he muttered.

Good, Emma thought, that's a start. ''Well, I'm certain others will share your view. After all, no matter how homely a woman may be, she doesn't want to grow old by herself. Not many women do,'' she said, hoping that would give him something else to mull over.

''Why don't you fix yourself a cup of tea? You must have a weed there that'll sweeten your disposition.''

With her back to him, she grinned as she took out a spool

of heavy thread and cut a length. "By the way, have you started working on the chair for her?"

"There isn't any lumber. I'll find some."

"Oak is good, isn't it?"

"Yes, yes, of course. But we don't have a lumber mill."

She nodded. "If you asked, Mr. Hogarth might help you cut down an oak tree. Between the two of you, I think you could cut enough pieces from one tree trunk to put a frame together. It's just one chair."

"I'll take care of it."

"Good. Oh, did I tell you I invited Lettie and Lydia to Thanksgiving supper? You could walk with Lettie after we eat, discuss the design of her chair," she suggested in case he didn't know what to talk about. "Or go for a ride." There's not much else to do here, she thought, no places where men and women could get together and become better acquainted.

Monday morning Kent dropped in at the general store and visited with Charlie Jenks, then stopped by the hotel. Kent found Timothy Ross huddled over a piece of paper on the table in the sitting room with Dave Kirby. "Hello. You look like you're plottin' somethin'."

Timothy glanced up. "Oh, hi, Kent. Have a seat."

Dave pointed to the paper. "Tim's been thinkin' about what you said. The ferry. We been workin' on the plans."

"That's good news." Kent sat near the end of the table. "I don't know much about building anythin' that floats, but I'd be glad to lend a hand."

Timothy shrugged and grinned at Kent. "Nothin' much to it. Hardest part'll be cuttin' down the trees and splittin' 'em from end to end for the top." Timothy pushed the paper over to Kent. "I drawed what it should look like."

Dave tapped the picture. "That scow'll be sturdy, carry any wagon that comes along."

Kent stared at the drawing. It looked like a raft with a fence on each side and a ramp at each end. Seemed to be plenty big enough for a supply wagon and horses.

"Shouldn't be too hard to build. What about the winch? You goin' to rig up one?"

"Yep. I'll ride out to the ship an' see about a cable."

Kent nodded. "When do we start?"

"Why not now?" Dave stood up. "Let's cut down some trees."

Kent walked down to the livery with both crewmen. They rented a wagon, borrowed heavy rope, and Seth led the way inland to the forest beyond the Chase farm. When it came to choosing which trees to fell, Seth and Kent followed the crewmen's direction and began cutting down oak trees. By the time they started back to town, three tree trunks had been stripped of branches and the sizable limbs put in the back of the wagon.

Dave sat on one side rail of the wagon. "It's a good start."

"Yep." Timothy eyed the timber. "I figure it'll take about nine more trips to cut down enough."

Kent looked over his shoulder at him. "We'll keep cuttin' till you say we're done."

On the way back to town, Timothy chose a spot for the ferry crossing not far from the mouth of the river. "Anyone own this land?"

Seth shook his head. "The town, if anyone, on this side. And I believe the Olsens' land's all tilled, so it looks like this's a good place for the crossing."

Timothy grinned. "We'll leave the logs here. I'll talk with Mr. Townsend when we get back."

Kent figured the river was about a hundred thirty or forty feet across at that point. Almost a natural crossing. He drove the wagon back to the livery. "Timothy, you want to cut down a few more trees tomorrow?"

"Sure do." Dave jumped down to the ground. "Thought you said you'd go huntin'," he remarked, looking at Timothy over the bed of the wagon. "Thanksgivin's Thursday. Never mind. I'll go fishin'. Be better'n venison anyhow."

"We haven't had a storm lately." Seth dismounted and motioned across the road to the cove. "Should be able to catch a few crabs, if you like them."

Dave beamed. "Sounds good to me." He looked at Kent.

"How about havin' Thanksgivin' supper with us at the hotel?"

"Thanks." Kent pulled his crutches out of the wagon. "That's real nice of you. I'd like that."

"Good." Dave dusted off his trousers. "See you later. Have to get supper started," he said, and walked out of the livery.

Timothy called out, "See ya later." He looked at Kent and Seth. "Thanks. I surely appreciate your help."

Kent settled a crutch under each arm. "See you in the morning." Timothy left, and Kent looked at Seth. "Once that ferry's workin', you just may have more business than you'd thought about."

"I wouldn't argue with that." Seth chuckled.

Kent made his way up the road and stopped by the Hat Box. Entering the shop was like walking right into a lady's bedroom without even knocking. The ladies he knew didn't have rooms as nice as this. But as Emma had said, she wanted it comfy for the women, and he didn't imagine she had too many men callers dawdling around there. She was sitting with Miss Morrissey at the table. "Hello, ladies."

Lettie smiled at him. "Mr. Hogarth. Nice to see you."

"Please join us." Emma pulled a chair out for him. He reminded her of a little boy who had been running through the hills all day. There was a slight pink cast to his cheeks and his hair was tousled. "Would you like a cup of coffee?"

"That'd be nice." He sat down on the chair she'd pulled out between hers and Miss Morrissey's. "How're the windows holding up? It feels a bit warmer in here than it was the other day."

"They're fine." Lettie glanced sideways at Emma and back to Kent. "We've missed seeing you here every day, Mr. Hogarth. Have you found other employment?"

"In a way." He stood both crutches at his side and held them with his right hand. "Mr. Ross drew up plans for a ferry. We cut down the first trees for it today."

"A ferry. Emma," Lettie called out. "Did you hear? Mr. Ross is building a ferry for Meyer's River." She looked at Kent. "It is for Meyer's, isn't it?"

He chuckled. ''Yes, ma'am. The Olsens'll be able to come to town anytime they want.'' He watched Emma's smile take shape slowly, as if she had waited to see Lettie's reaction. He thought Emma would've been pleased as punch with the news.

''Excuse me,'' Lettie said, standing up. ''I'll see if Emma needs help.'' She went into the kitchen and stepped to Emma's right side. ''Did you hear what Mr. Hogarth said?''

Emma shook her head. ''Was it good news?''

Lettie darted a glance over her shoulder at Kent and said, ''Mr. Ross has started cutting timber to build the ferry.''

''Thanks for telling me.'' Emma had looked away from him when he mentioned the windows. How was she to make coffee *and* watch his lips at the same time? ''I'll have to be more attentive.''

Lettie put her hand on Emma's shoulder and spoke softly. ''Why don't you tell him that you're a little hard of hearing? I don't see why he wouldn't understand.''

''There's no need. After his leg heals, I won't see him again and it won't matter.'' Emma set the coffeepot on the stove and returned to the table. ''The ferry is good news. Does that mean Mr. Ross intends to live here?''

''I'd say so.'' Kent sensed a difference in her. ''He won't put that ferry together overnight.'' Suddenly she seemed very serious. Had Miss Morrissey said something that upset Emma? Somehow that didn't seem likely.

Emma lowered her hand and ran the fingers of one hand along the edge of the chair. ''What kind of trees will he use?''

''Oak,'' he said, keeping an eye on her. ''Does it make a difference?''

Ignoring his question, she asked him, ''Has my brother spoken to you recently?''

''No. I haven't seen him since the supper. Was he looking for me?''

She glanced at Lettie. ''I thought so, but I may be wrong. Oak is used in furniture, isn't it?''

''It makes fine pieces. Does your brother need some?''

"Yes. For a chair. One tree would be enough, wouldn't it?"

"Plenty. I'm going back to take down some more trees tomorrow with Mr. Ross. I don't see why we can't bring one log back for Bently."

"That would be wonderful."

Her smile was brighter than sunlight. For that he'd bring back all the logs she wanted.

Lettie observed their exchange. "What does Bently want with a whole tree?"

"For the frame of your chair. Have you forgotten?" Emma met Kent's curious gaze. "I spoke to him the other night. With no sawmill nearby there isn't any lumber to make the frame."

From the way Miss Morrissey's eyes lit up, Kent got the feeling she had more than a passing interest in Bently. "Where do you want me to leave it?"

"In front of the house will be fine." He'll see it every day to remind him of his promise. Emma noticed steam rising from the coffeepot and hurried to the kitchen. She hadn't meant to let it boil so hard. She moved the pot to the side of the fire. While the hot liquid cooled off a bit, she set out a cup and a plate full of pinch-offs.

Lettie cleared a space on the table as Emma set the tray down. "I'm glad you remembered Gram's cakes. Please try some, Mr. Hogarth. She likes to bake—often much more than we can eat." She held the plate out to him. "I'm afraid she's spoiled us."

"The cakes look good." Kent put two on the plate Emma set in front of him. "Now tell me, what have you ladies been doin' to keep busy?"

"We've grown lazy without you to keep us on our toes." Lettie grinned.

"It's been quiet," Emma added, coming close to smiling. "Lydia spends her afternoons at the hotel with Mrs. Lewis and most of the women have been busy putting up late vegetables for winter."

He finished chewing one of the little fried cakes. "Please

give Mrs. Nance my compliments,'' he said, picking up the second cake.

"Thank you, young man," Lydia said, coming into the shop from the kitchen.

Lettie swung around on the chair to see Lydia. "Gram, I didn't hear you."

"Of course not. You were too busy talking with Mr. Hogarth." Lydia removed her heavy cape and hung it up. "But I don't blame you."

Kent raised his cup in a salute to Mrs. Nance, then took a drink. She must have been a right interesting lady in her youth. She had a lively spirit. "You're looking well, Mrs. Nance."

Lydia gave him a curt nod. "You seem to be staying busy, too."

"I try." He noticed Emma was quiet, but her attention appeared to be fixed on them. "And how is Mr. Brice?"

"Fit. He's been taking a lot of walks around town." Lydia helped herself to one of the pinch-offs and sat down across from Kent. "He's a man looking for something. And he'll find it."

"What do you mean, Gram?"

"He said he's worked since he was ten—he's not used to being idle." Lydia reached for another pinch-off. "I don't think he will be for long though. He and Mrs. Lewis are spending quite a lot of time together."

Emma grinned at Lydia. "I'm happy for them. She's worked hard, too."

Women, Kent thought, always happy when a man loses his freedom. Although at his age Brice might not look at it that way.

Emma watched Kent over the rim of her cup. He looked amused. He had a nice smile, the kind that was catching, but she couldn't help wondering what he found so entertaining. "Mr. Hogarth, do you know Mr. Brice very well?"

"I've talked with him. He seems to be a likable sort." Kent held Emma's gaze a moment. "Are you worried about Mrs. Lewis's reputation?"

"Should we be?"

He shrugged, then shook his head without cracking a smile. "Mrs. Lewis probably knows her own mind. I wouldn't worry about her."

"Of course not. Irene Lewis is a most sensible woman," Lydia said, staring straight at Kent. Then she frowned at him. "You rapscallion. You shouldn't taunt an old woman."

He glanced around. "I don't see any old people. Do you, Miss Morrissey?"

Lettie was laughing. "Don't ask me. You two are a good match—both about fourteen, wouldn't you say, Emma?"

Trusting Lettie and not completely certain she had heard every comment, Emma nodded. "Good thing you didn't eat a pinch-off, Lettie. Maybe there's something in them." She picked up her half-eaten fried cake and teasingly eyed it. "Think it's safe?"

Kent grinned at her. It was an unexpected pleasure to see her so lighthearted. "Why not take a chance?" What was she like at fourteen? Eighteen? Or twenty? he wondered. When she was eight, did she climb trees and chase rabbits?

"I didn't realize I hadn't," she said, and popped the rest of the cake into her mouth.

Lydia followed Kent and Emma's banter with interest. "Mr. Hogarth, would you like to stay for supper?"

"I'd sure like to, ma'am," he said, with a heartfelt smile, "but I've got a kettle of stew I'd better polish off or find some pigs to slop." He drank the last of his coffee and got to his feet. "Thank you for your hospitality, ladies. Those little cakes were real good." With a look at the kitchen he added, "If the windows give you a problem, let me know."

He didn't sound lonely, but Emma didn't want to think of him spending the upcoming holiday by himself. "Surely the stew won't last all week. Won't you join us for Thanksgiving supper at the house? We're having roast of beef and baked chicken with all the fixings." She sounded as if she were hawking meals on the street corner, but she hoped he wouldn't think so. As she watched his mouth, she wondered how his lips would feel pressed to hers. Would his beard chafe her chin or tickle? Not now, she thought, I don't want to miss a word he says.

The gleam in her eyes would melt rock candy. He surely didn't want to turn down her offer. "Thank you for thinkin' of me, Miss Emma, but Mr. Kirby's already invited me to eat at the hotel with them."

She nodded. "He's a fine cook. You'll have a good supper." She shouldn't be surprised that he'd had other invitations, but it didn't lessen the disappointment she felt.

"Have an extra portion of chicken and roast for me, Miss Emma." He set the crutches under his arms. "Anytime you wanna go fishin', my offer still stands."

I'm glad. "I'll remember." *How could I forget your offer?*

❖ *13* ❖

Eᴍᴍᴀ sᴇᴛ ᴏɴᴇ of the baked chickens on the platter and put the pan on the top of the stove. She glanced over at Lettie. "Soon as I make the gravy, everything'll be ready."

"These are ready to go in the oven." Lettie put the last biscuit in the pan and stepped over to the stove. "The whole house smells delicious. Mr. Hogarth's going to miss a wonderful meal."

"Fiddlesticks." Emma shook her head as she sprinkled flour over the drippings. "From what I've heard, he won't miss a thing. I'd trade these chickens for a couple of crabs in the beat of a hummingbird's wing." She added a couple of pinches of salt and pepper to the pan and stirred the browning flour.

Lettie picked up the bowl of butter and dish of pickled cucumbers and looked over at Emma. "What would you give to have Mr. Hogarth here right now?" Without waiting for a reply, Lettie left the room and passed her grandmother on the way out.

Lydia stepped back when her granddaughter brushed past. "She's certainly in a rush. Isn't there something I can help with?"

"I don't believe there is, unless—" Emma poured the last

of the milk into the browned drippings and continued stirring the gravy. "Would you see if the teapot's empty?" She didn't think Lettie had ever teased her as much as she had recently about Kent. Of course, Emma thought, if I didn't care a whit about him, it probably wouldn't bother me.

She moved to the side of the stove and peered out the window toward the old cabin. A thin ribbon of smoke rose from the chimney. He would be at the hotel by now. With the way Lettie was carrying on, it was just as well.

Lettie returned and checked the biscuits. "They're almost brown." She started mashing the potatoes.

Emma set the pan of gravy on the worktable. "Is Bently grumbling about supper yet?"

"Mm-hm," Lettie said, grinning. "He's as bad as a little boy when it comes to waiting for mealtime."

"I used to think when he was fully grown he would learn patience," Emma said, spooning the dressing from the chickens into a bowl. "I was wrong. Maybe you'll have more luck with him."

"I wouldn't mind trying." Lettie finished mashing the potatoes and scraped them into the serving bowl.

Emma poured the gravy into a bowl. Unless Bently became deathly ill in the next half hour, she would see that he spent time alone with Lettie. Hog-tying came to mind. They served supper in the parlor. Bently was seated at one end of the table with Lettie on his right, Lydia on his left, and Emma at the other end.

Lydia spread butter on a biscuit and glanced at Bently. "That's a nice log in the front yard, Bently."

Bently looked down the table at Emma, but she was wiping up a spill on the tablecloth. He met Lydia's canny gaze. "Emma's responsible for it."

Emma looked at him. "You can't build the frame for the chair without wood, and you told me you hadn't found any. When Mr. Hogarth told us he was cutting down trees for the ferry, I asked if he would bring one log to the house."

"Mr. Townsend," Lettie said, "don't feel you have to build the chair frame. Mr. Hogarth has offered his help."

Lydia nodded. "That man's good with tools."

"Yes, he is." Emma looked her brother in the eye. "You should come by the shop. You wouldn't know there had been a fire. The new wall matches the old one perfectly."

Bently wiped the napkin across his mouth. "I don't doubt Hogarth's ability." He turned to Lettie. "But you misunderstood me, Miss Morrissey. I don't mind building the frame for you." He cut a bite of the beef roast. "Later you can tell me what kind of chair you want."

She smiled at him. "I'll be glad to."

Thank goodness, Emma thought. "I've been meaning to ask you, Bently, have you spoken with Mr. Brice recently?"

He nodded. "Yesterday, matter of fact. Any reason why?"

Emma shrugged. "I'd heard he has been looking around town. He's a shoemaker, isn't he?"

"Yes. He's renting the small shop between the barbershop and saloon."

"Glad to hear it," Lydia said.

"Does he have the tools or equipment to start business?" Emma had hoped he would settle there. It would be grand to have a shoe store right in town. The windows rattled. The wind seemed to come from nowhere and buffet the house. She looked outside. The ocean was dotted with whitecaps. Winter was setting in, she thought.

"Yes. A lot of the crates were removed from the ship and stored at the livery." The windows rattled, and Bently glanced toward the ocean. "He's been going through them, and fortunately for him, he finally found his gear there."

Lettie took a sip of tea and set her cup down. "Has Mrs. Lewis said what she wants to do?" She glanced around the table. Bently shook his head, and Emma tipped hers to one side. "Gram?"

"She's happy running the hotel. Mr. Kirby does the cooking, but she keeps the place clean, does the laundry—keeps the men on the straight 'n narrow."

"Oh, Gram."

"Well, she would, if this weren't such a quiet town." Lydia laughed and dug her fork into the mashed potatoes.

Emma chuckled. "Bently, is there any reason Mrs. Lewis can't continue running the hotel?"

"None I know of. When the ferry starts up, she may even rent some rooms."

Lettie nodded. "We'll have more people coming through town next spring. We knew it would take time to get the town going."

Emma looked at her brother. "Have you given any more thought to a sawmill? We need one, especially if we'll be putting up more buildings."

He let out a long sigh. "We'll have to call a town meeting to talk about that. I'd hate to have so many logs float downriver that we lose the fish."

"I don't want the river fouled like some back East." Emma gazed out to sea. It was so fresh and clean here. "Why can't we control the mill? See that the river stays clean?"

Bently sat back in his chair. "Don't start fretting. We may not be able to put in a mill. We've been lucky so far. The miners haven't filled the streams with debris or stirred up the river bottom."

Emma managed to finish her portion of chicken and slice of the roasted beef. When the others appeared to be done eating, she stood up and began gathering the dishes to clear off the table. "Everyone ready for dessert? There's gingerbread and molasses pie."

"Oh, not now, dear. Maybe after we clean up," Lydia said. "I brought blackberry wine, but I'm even too full for that."

Lettie placed one hand on her waist. "I can't eat another bite right now, Emma."

Emma stared at her brother. "Bently?"

He shook his head. "I ate like I hadn't had a hot meal in months."

Emma glanced from Lettie to Bently and stared outside. "Looks like the wind's died down." Emma moved the bowl of pickled cucumbers closer. "Why don't you two take a walk?"

Lettie looked at her with eyes as big as saucers before she stared down at her lap.

"That's a good idea." Bently stood up and dropped his

napkin on the table. "Miss Morrissey, would you like to take a walk?"

"Yes—" Lettie came to her feet so quickly, she nearly knocked her chair over. "I'll get my cape."

Emma carried a stack of dishes back to the kitchen and returned to the parlor for more. After Bently and Lettie left the house, Emma grinned at Lydia. "Hasn't it been a lovely Thanksgiving?"

"It is now, dear. Why don't we taste the wine—just to make sure it hasn't turned to vinegar."

Against her better judgment and her resolve to keep her distance from him, Emma watched for Kent each day. She had seen him twice since the holiday, both times at a distance. She waved and hoped he would stop by the shop. He didn't. She couldn't even be certain he had noticed her. From what she had heard, he and Mr. Ross had gone into the hills to cut down trees every day.

After a week of peering out through windows, looking for smoke from the old cabin, and glancing over her shoulder every time she thought she heard the sound of his crutches, she knew she needed to get out of the shop for a while. She draped the lavender-edged hanky over a small pewter picture frame. The brass bell jingled and Pauline came in. "Hi. We've hardly seen you."

"I don't know what's gotten into me. It takes me forever to do the simplest chore." Pauline went over to the woodstove. "Hello, Lettie."

"Pauline. Good to see you."

Watching Pauline as she moved the brush-and-comb set closer to the picture frame, Emma noticed her usually bright smile had dimmed a bit. She poured a cup of tea and set it on the table for her. "Sip on that. Maybe it'll help."

"Thank you, Emma." Pauline took a drink and set the cup down. "Have you seen Hannah this morning?"

"She hasn't been in."

"Pauline," Lettie called from the kitchen, "would you like to have dinner with us?"

Pauline pressed her hand on her stomach. "I'd better not. I need a couple of things from the general store, and I have enough ironing to keep me busy all week."

"I did mine last night." Emma laughed. "And I'm thinking to tell Bently to iron his own clothes."

"Emma," Lettie said, "you wouldn't!"

"Don't be too sure. It's about time he either gets a wife or hires someone to play the part."

Pauline laughed. "Unless Mrs. Lewis hires out, his best chance is for a wife." She grinned at Lettie. "Any volunteers?"

Emma shook her head. Lettie's cheeks were deep pink.

Pauline went over to the wardrobe and picked off the chemise. "I'll take this shimmy. Maybe it'll perk me up."

Lettie took the chemise and folded it up. "I like the little tucks across the front. I'll have to make another one."

"The other one's nice, too, but this is prettier. Would you put it on account?" Pauline finished her tea.

"Of course," Lettie said, handing the package to her.

"I'd better go. Thanks for the tea."

"Anytime," Emma said, walking her to the door. "I hope you're feeling better soon."

"Me, too." Pauline opened the door and called out, "Bye, Lettie," smiled at Emma and left the shop.

Emma went back to the kitchen where Lettie was cooking dinner. "Do you mind if I leave? I won't be gone long."

"Of course not. Don't you want to eat first?"

Emma swung her cape around her shoulders. "I'm not really hungry." She set her bonnet on her head and tied the strings. "I'm just going for a ride. I'll eat when I get back."

"Okay." Lettie studied her a moment. "I can manage here. Take the rest of the day off."

"A couple hours'll be enough. Thanks, Lettie." Emma walked through the shop. She had always felt at home there, until the past few days.

"If you stop by the Simmses' place," Lettie said, moving the kettle to the side of the fire, "tell Ginny hello for me."

Emma paused at the door and looked back. "I thought I'd ride up to the shipwreck."

Lettie frowned. "Oh, do you think you should?"

Opening the door, Emma again glanced at Lettie. "Want to close the shop and go with me?" Lettie shook her head, and Emma waved as she pulled the door closed.

"Be careful—"

I always am, Emma thought and hurried back to her house. It didn't take her long to change clothes, comb her hair and tie it back with a ribbon, saddle the mare and put a flask of water in the saddlebag. After she tied her cape to the back of the saddle, she rode north along the coast. Every once in a while a puffy white cloud drifted by.

She let the mare stretch her legs for a short distance then slowed her down. It was as warm as a summer day. Emma would've liked to race, but she didn't want to lather up the horse. To her left, from the shore to the horizon, was the deep blue ocean, and on her right were the giant redwoods, which seemed to reach the sky, some with trunks so big around it would take several men with outstretched arms to circle just one. The forest was a dense green, nearly dark as pitch in places, while in other spots shafts of sunlight filtered through the trees creating a magical setting.

The first months after their arrival, she had often wondered if all this was real or if she had dreamed it up. Rarely did it freeze or get too warm. It seemed the best of all worlds. She came to a clearing and realized she had reached the wrecked ship. She dismounted and stood at the top of the path she had climbed the day of the accident.

The waves had battered the *Julianna* against the cliff until her sleek sides had snapped and split apart. As the water surged in and out, a deep wrenching sound drowned out the roar of the surf, as if the ship had groaned. Emma shivered and held her cape close. The mast that Kent had climbed was gone—in fact it looked as if most everything was missing. She had thought about looking around the ship but that was impossible now.

Holding the reins, she glanced across the road and noticed a little pink bloom. It was late in the year for sour clover. She walked over, and as she bent to pick one of the leaves, she heard what sounded like muffled sobs. "Who's there?"

There was only silence. She called out again. Just when she had decided she'd been mistaken, the ferns on the far side of the huge redwood shook. She quickly stood up and moved back. A trapped animal? She wound the reins around a woody stalk and gingerly made a wide circle around to see what kind of little creature had startled her.

It was a child! A little Indian girl curled into a ball on one of the bushy ferns. The child couldn't be more than four or five years old with large sad eyes. Dried bits of leaves and twigs poked out of her tangled hair, her soft hide shirt was caught on a dried thorny vine, and tears streaked her cheeks. Emma smiled, pulled her hanky out of her sleeve, and dropped down to perch on her toes. "Hello."

The child cringed, trembling, but didn't utter a sound.

"It's all right." Emma dabbed the handkerchief on her own cheek, then reached out to dry the little girl's tears, but the child frantically looked around. Emma laid the cloth on the girl's knee and pulled her hand back. "I won't hurt you."

The child's lips quivered and fresh tears spilled down her cheeks.

Emma looked all around hoping to find her mother, or brother or sister. It was hard to believe that such a young girl would be alone so far from her village. She called out in her loudest voice, but again, no one answered. When she turned back, the little girl was clutching the hanky in her hand.

Emma pulled the prickly vine away from the girl. When she started to pick her up, the child struggled but Emma firmly held on and sat down with the girl on her lap. "Now, let me see if you are hurt." The child's thin legs had only a few scrapes but there was a deeper gash on one arm below her elbow that had almost stopped bleeding. Emma tied the hanky around her arm and tried to soothe the little girl's fears.

She couldn't sit there and hope someone would come looking for the child. It was early afternoon, more than enough time for her to take the child to her village and return home before dark. Her next problem, however, was to find the village. She'd heard it wasn't too far away, but she had never been there.

"Come on, little one. Maybe you'll help me once you understand I'm trying to take you home." Emma stood up with the little girl held close. When the child saw the mare, she relaxed. Emma let her drink from the flask before she mounted the horse.

The little girl sat in front of Emma and held on to the mare's mane.

After loosening the child's grip, Emma put the little girl's hands on the saddle horn, wrapped the cape around them, and started the mare walking through the forest. She fervently hoped to come upon the child's relatives or someone from her tribe. Eventually, they came to a creek and followed it to a well-used path.

Suddenly they were surrounded by Indians. And they were barely clothed! She counted ten, on foot—all but one had only a small piece of leather over their most private parts, the other one wore a pair of homespun trousers. *Never* had she seen a man's body so boldly exposed. She quickly looked away, but she didn't think she could ever forget their images.

The Indians stared at her. One grabbed the hem of her skirt and started to lift it. She slapped his hand, then pulled back in horror. They eyed her, speaking amongst themselves. Deciding to show bravery, when at that moment she felt none, she looked at one man and pointed to the little girl. "She was lost. I was bringing her back to you," she said, handing the child down to him.

In the blink of an eye, one of them grabbed the mare's halter and started running. They wouldn't take the child, and she couldn't simply toss her to the ground. Emma held on to the little girl and kicked the mare. Normally the horse would have shot forward, but the Indian held tight and the mare could only balk.

Her fear nearly overwhelmed her. The Indians had her surrounded, trapped; no one said a word she could understand and she hadn't even thought to bring the rifle, not that it would be any use now. She wrapped the reins around her hand and gave a sharp pull to her left. As if the Indian had expected the move, he countered it.

The Indians kept running, taking her deeper into the forest. As she prayed for a chance to escape, she tried to commit to memory the direction they were going. She would sneak away and walk back to town if need be.

After leaving Ross at the livery, Kent started back to the cabin. He passed the general store and slowed down as he came to the Hat Box. He'd spent so much time cutting down trees he hadn't seen Emma in days. He kept going and had just passed the bay window when Miss Morrissey burst out of the shop. "Hello, Miss Morrissey."

Lettie stood there wringing her hands. "It's Emma. Have you seen her?"

"Not in days," he said, taking a gentle hold of her arm. "What's wrong?"

"Emma went for a ride. Said she wouldn't be gone more than a couple of hours." She looked up at him. "That was almost four hours ago. It's not like her to be late."

"She kept her seat on my stallion, so she can handle a horse. Maybe she's visiting with friends and lost track of time. I'm sure she's all right."

"That couldn't be. She rode north. There aren't any homesteads up there, just the Indian village." Lettie drew in a deep breath. "She wanted to see the wrecked ship."

Now he began to feel uneasy. "She wouldn't try to get back on that ship, would she?"

"Oh, my, I hope not. I hadn't thought about that." Lettie stared northward. "The Indians fish on the coast and collect seashells. By now they must have already searched through the ship. But what if—"

"Don't fret, Miss Morrissey. From what I've seen, they keep to themselves."

"But—"

Again, he cut her off. "I'll ride up there and see what's been keeping her." He patted her wringing hands. "Have you told anyone else? What about her brother? Does he know?''

"Oh, no. I'm afraid he's going be very angry with her.''

"Then he's a bigger fool than I thought,'' Kent muttered. "Don't you worry. I'll bring her back as safe as when she left. She's prob'ly on the way back now.''

"Thank you, Mr. Hogarth.''

He hurried back to the livery, rented a rig, stopped by the cabin for his pistol and rifle, and headed north to where he'd found the ship. On horseback it wouldn't have taken so long. When he reached the cliff above the wrecked ship, he stopped and stood by the path staring down at the remains of the ship. Even though her horse wasn't in sight, he shouted her name. The path didn't have any fresh shoe prints. That was a relief. He looked around.

Good God A'mighty, he thought, she could be anywhere. He made his way to the other side of the rig and studied the ground for any fresh tracks. Several yards away he found a set of footprints and tracks from a horse going toward the woods. He went to the other side of the road. After a short search, he found a crushed fern at the base of a tree and more horse tracks heading deeper into the forest.

What was Emma doing? Had she taken a walk through the big trees? She might be hurt or lost. But he couldn't drive the rig through the woods. A roadway cut through the forest not far from there. It was the best he could do. He tried putting his weight on his leg, but he knew it wasn't strong enough to trust on horseback. He returned to the buggy and set off for the road. Townsend had been worried about Indians that first night, but Kent hadn't heard of any trouble with them.

Once he turned onto the road, he slowed down to survey the woods. About a quarter mile in, he stopped and listened for the sound of her horse. A bird called out and a squirrel ran up a tree trunk, normal sounds. He called her name and listened for her voice.

He managed to frighten a couple of birds, but that was all. He continued on up the road. At least a mile farther on he came to a small clearing with what looked like a footpath leading north. He knew what lay ahead, so he turned the rig into the field.

The trail was nothing more than trampled grass and brush but it looked as if it had been made recently. At times it seemed to disappear altogether. It wasn't difficult to hold the horse to a slow walk. The path snaked around trees but seemed to lead back toward the coast. He didn't know how far he'd gone before the trees thinned out. He brought the horse to a halt and listened. He heard the pounding of the ocean waves. He'd been right. He had doubled back.

And he heard voices.

His instinct was to continue on foot, and he'd learned to listen to it. Using his crutches, he moved along the line of trees. Just ahead there were a handful of wooden buildings. In front of one was a totem pole decorated with a large bird and fish. Some of the Indians were roughly clothed, others wore only loincloths, and a few of the women only painted hide skirts. Several children ran past a group of elders. He watched, searching for any sign of Emma, until two braves left the group.

In his experience, Indians respected strength. A man on crutches would be at a definite disadvantage—whether they were friendly or not. He returned to the rig and drove into the middle of the village, the crutches shoved back under the seat, the rifle within easy reach. As he expected, the group turned to see what was happening. Standing in the center was Emma, pale, wide-eyed, and quaking, but seemingly all right.

As he headed straight for her, he smiled and waved. "Emma, about time I found you. I told Miss Morrissey you'd called on friends and forgot the time."

❖ *14* ❖

Emma couldn't believe her eyes. Kent? His wonderful smile gave her a weightless, heady feeling. He was the most welcome sight in the world. Her knees trembled so violently she pressed them together and prayed she wouldn't collapse. One of the older women, with marks on her chin and arm and wearing only a leather skirt, touched her hair—again. Sheer willpower kept her from flinching or running away.

He rode right up to her as if she were standing in front of her shop. "Kent—I'm *so happy* to see you." She stepped up to the buggy—laid one hand on his leg, gripped the wheel with the other—and she said softly, "Can you get me out of here?" Her heart pounded furiously and so loud she feared she wouldn't hear him and focused on his beautifully shaped lips.

So this was what it took to get her to say his name, he thought. He pried her fingers off his leg, raised her hand to his lips, and pressed a kiss to her knuckles. "I won't leave you, Emma." Still holding her hand, he looked at the brave standing directly behind her. "I've come to bring her home."

The brave frowned. He pointed from Emma to Kent. "Yor wo-man?"

Kent gave him a curt nod. Lifting their hands, he said,

"Mine," and pointed to his chest. He couldn't deny wishing it were true. It sounded real nice. Her hand had felt too good on his leg. But he reminded himself it had only been an act of desperation. She was scared. The Indian seemed to accept his claim and spoke to the others. "Emma, where's your horse?"

"On the other side of that last building." She looked out of the corner of her eye. "But can't I ride with you?"

"You sure will. But I'd just as soon they don't see the crutches. Are you strong enough to walk over and bring your horse back?"

Staring into his winter-brown eyes, she felt a calmness settle over her. "Now?"

He gave her hand a reassuring squeeze. "Just walk over there as if you were at home. I won't let anything happen to you. Trust me?"

How could she not? He'd proved to her that he could do just about anything he put his mind to. And he had even worked his way into her heart, but he would never know that. "With my life."

He let go of her hand and watched her, hoping her courage would stand by her just a while longer. She walked away with her back straight, head held high, and she didn't look back. She's definitely a lady, he thought with admiration, she just wasn't his woman. The Indians were silent and moved out of her path.

She put one foot in front of the other, over and over, but the end of the small village appeared to be a mile away. Before Kent rode in, she had wondered how much longer the Indians would keep crowding around her, touching and poking her. When she'd arrived there, she had been relieved to find that most of the Indians were clothed in pants, shirts, and skirts, but she hadn't been prepared for their curiosity. The one Kent spoke with had apparently claimed her. Even though none of them had raised as much as a knife to her, the mounting fear that they would was wearing her down.

She neared the shack, marched around the corner and saw her mare. Not daring to waste time, she slipped the reins free and walked the length of the yard again. As she approached the rig, the little girl she had found stepped up to her and held out a beaver skin. Emma smiled at the child. She didn't even know her name.

The girl pushed the pelt into Emma's hand and ran away. Emma sank her fingers into the dark fur. "Thank you." She smiled at the little girl peering from behind one of the women.

After Emma tied the horse to the back of the buggy, she quickly climbed into the rig and sat at Kent's side. "Now what?"

He pulled off his jacket. "Put this on." He put it around her shoulders.

She slid her arms into the sleeves and crossed the lapels over her chest. The faint scent of clove hair tonic was comforting, and so was Kent's arm around her shoulders.

He lowered his arm and gazed into her wide eyes. "Now, smile and wave to the little girl." He looked back at the Indian, nodded and drove out of the village. "Is she what brought you here?"

"I found her in the woods. I couldn't leave her there all alone. But when the Indians found us—" She moistened her lips and added, "They wouldn't take her or let me go."

Even though he was sure there was another, shorter way back to the road along the coast, he left the way he'd come. When they started back down the rough path he patted her leg. "Take a deep breath and let it out slowly."

She did as he suggested, but she couldn't stop shaking. She gripped the pelt with both hands and stared straight ahead, seeing nothing. She was cold, so cold. She couldn't believe the Indians had just let them ride out of there so easily.

After he reached the road leading to the coast, he put his arm around her shoulders and pulled her close. "Better?"

"Mm—" She rested her head on his chest. She felt his steady heartbeat, but she couldn't hear it.

He glanced down at her and smiled. There must've been an easier way to get her into his arms. "Want to tell what happened?"

"I . . . I—" Her teeth chattered uncontrollably. Now that

she was safe, the fear seemed even more real. She swallowed and tried again. "I . . . wanted to see the ship. Then I found that little girl." She started crying. She'd been frightened from the moment they surrounded her, but when they had hauled her down from the mare and everyone crowded around, pressing against her, she'd felt trapped by their bodies. She'd tried to run away but one brave easily tripped her and pinned her on the ground with his body. Then suddenly she was seventeen again and that trapper was on her, tearing at her clothes, trying to . . .

He stopped the buggy just before they reached the road on the coast. He turned and wrapped his arms around her. She felt so small in his heavy jacket. "Didn't you wear a coat?"

"Cape. One of the men . . . took it." The Indian had pulled it off and nearly choked her when the tie didn't let go. She couldn't stop sobbing. It made no sense. She was all right. And Kent was holding her close.

"You're safe now." No matter how firmly he held her, she still shook like a leaf. "Did they hurt you?"

His voice was so gentle she burst out crying anew.

"Emma, what happened? Did they—"

She shook her head before he could say any more. "They didn't hurt me, but they wouldn't . . . stop touching me, crowding me. I couldn't move." She clamped her lips together and closed her eyes. "The one you spoke to—he smelled me and p-pinned me on the ground. It was just like b-before."

He started rubbing her back. "You were captured by Indians before?"

"White man. A trapper."

He tipped her chin up so he could see her face. "He kidnapped you?"

"Not really. He dragged me into the bushes . . . he—" Dear Lord, she had held it inside for so long she needed to tell somebody what had happened to her. She wanted it to be Kent, but how could she say the words? The act was so vile, but describing it might be even worse.

He felt his muscles tighten along his jaw. "You mean he forced you?"

She nodded and waited for him to push her away. But he didn't. In fact he held her as if he thought she might try to escape. "Aren't you repulsed?"

"I'll kill him. When I'm through with him, there'll be nothing left for the coyotes and wolves." That trapper was the lowest kind of creature. Kent had never understood how any man could treat a woman so foully. "When? Where'd it happen?"

"Seven years ago. Our family was coming West. Papa said we were more than halfway to our new home, then the wagon went down a ravine. Our parents were killed." That was so long ago, she thought, and not the worst of it.

Kent held on to her. If he could've made things easier for her he would have. But no one could do that for her. It was a hard part of healing, of surviving.

"The wagons stopped at Soda Springs." She peered up at him. "Bently and I were alone . . ." The sound of their wagon tumbling down the hill had haunted her dreams for months afterward—her mother's frightful scream, the sound of splintering wood, then the deafening silence.

Her voice had softened to a whisper, and he'd bent his head to hers. Whatever had happened to her had left a deep scar. "Didn't another family take you in?"

"The Stuarts made room for the few things Bently was able to get out of the wagon. We had both been riding that day, so we had our horses."

Many had been left with much less, but he didn't think she was ready to hear that right then. "You must've been scared."

She nodded. "When we stopped at Soda Springs, I volunteered to look for firewood. I wanted to get away from the wagons, the people. All of a sudden that awful man . . . he dragged me away." She rubbed her cheek on his coat sleeve. "I tried to fight back." She bolted up and stared into Kent's eyes. "I did. I fought and kicked 'n I tried to scream, but he . . . he put his filthy hand over my mouth." Oh, Lord, she still remembered the foul smell of his hand. She shuddered.

"Sh— I believe you."

"Bently said no one would, but *he* was so big . . . and so strong—" She trembled and sagged against him.

He watched to see if she'd passed out. She'd buried her face into his chest. He smoothed her hair back and kissed the top of her head. Whatever had happened, she'd survived. He wanted to hold her and keep her safe, but that wasn't what she needed. He waited for her to complete her story.

"I don't know what happened— I fell. Next thing I knew, Bently was bending over me. He said my head had hit some rocks and if anyone asked, that's all I was to say." She grabbed the front of Kent's shirt. "But that *wasn't* all. My ear was bleeding, and I couldn't hear anything with it—and there was more," she whispered. "Bently said that man hurt me even more—that he ruined me—but he said it'd be our secret and no one would ever know."

Kent well understood her brother's need to protect her, but she had suffered so much. Belatedly, what she'd said about her ear sank in. "You're deaf in one ear?" That'd explain why she seemed to ignore or misunderstand him sometimes, and why she watched people so much.

"Mm-hm," she said without leaving the warmth of his chest.

"But you can hear me."

The surprise in his voice made her almost smile. "This is my good one," she said, touching her right ear, the one away from his chest. "I don't always hear what people say, though."

I wish I'd known, he thought. "You don't miss much."

She tipped her head back and gazed into his eyes. "Why are you being so nice to me?"

"Why wouldn't I be? You did nothin' wrong, nothin' to be ashamed of." Her lips parted, as if she'd said "oh," and the look she gave him stirred him more deeply than it should have. He drew one knuckle under her eye and skimmed his finger down her cheek and under her chin.

He wanted her to know how much he cared, and he needed to show her in the only way he knew. Slowly, giving her time to pull back, he bent his head and pressed his mouth to hers. She flattened her hand on his chest, then slid her arm around him. If there was a heaven, he was closer than he'd ever been before.

She had never been kissed like this. His lips felt gentle and hot, and wonderful, and her insides seemed to turn to jelly. She leaned closer and hesitantly slid her hand over his back. His shirt was soft but the muscles beneath her fingers were taut. Her mind whirled dizzily, and she wished they could hold each other forever. No one had ever showed her such tenderness. She didn't want it to end. Would he be sorry? Think she was brazen because she allowed such liberties? Then, as slowly as it began, the kiss ended, and he was looking at her ... with the same wonder she felt? It didn't seem possible. Not her. She stared at his beard and touched it with her finger. It wasn't scratchy.

"You're lovely. But if you keep looking at me that way, it's going to take a lot longer to get you home." He kissed the end of her cute nose. "I think we'd better get back before your brother has every man in town after us."

Lovely? She smiled. Even if he didn't really mean it, it surely sounded nice. She glanced around for the first time and saw that it was dark. "Yes, we'd better. I didn't realize it was so late."

He smiled. "Neither did I." He tucked her arm through his and picked up the reins.

She hugged his arm and rested her head on his shoulder. Why would such a clever man, who got along with most everyone, bother with her? She didn't want to wonder about it, but she couldn't stop the doubts from flooding her mind. She was damaged goods, and he knew it. But he treated her as if she were a real lady, not a woman of easy virtue. After her scare with the Indians, she couldn't believe how good she felt.

When they left the forest and turned onto the coast road, the horizon was pale yellow. He smiled down at her. "It's not so late."

And Bently will be furious, she thought, staring out at the ocean. And Lettie— "How did you find me?"

"Miss Morrissey was worried when you didn't return. I offered to track you down."

"Thank goodness, but how did you know I was in the village? Or find it?"

He smiled at her. "She told me where to start looking. I found tracks in the woods 'n hoped for the best." He shrugged. "Guess I was just plain lucky."

She didn't believe it was that simple. "I'm very grateful. I don't know how I can repay you."

"Next time you wanta take a ride, I'll go along with you. I'll even let ya drive the rig, if ya ask real nice."

She chuckled. "Alright, I will." The tide was coming in and the waves surged toward shore. They were almost home and soon she would have to let go of his arm. She nearly asked him to slow down. "Have you seen other Indian villages?"

He nodded. "A couple. Was that your first visit to one?"

"Yes, and I saw more than I wanted. I don't understand why they—well, some of them—weren't wearing much. Don't they get cold?"

He laughed. "Their idea of clothes is different from ours. This band doesn't seem to be weavers. It isn't real cold, so they're probably comfortable wearing much less than we do."

"But—" She shouldn't be discussing this with him. However, she thought he would answer her questions, and she was sure her brother wouldn't.

He had a good idea what was bothering her. "They aren't embarrassed about their bodies. From childhood they know the difference between men and women."

"Indeed." Now that he mentioned it, she didn't remember the children paying any attention to the adults.

He grinned at her. "I don't think loincloths will sell too well in town. Do you?" He glanced back at the road and noticed rising dust ahead. "Someone's comin'. Probably your brother."

"Lettie was likely frantic when you didn't return, either." She stared at the approaching riders. "Oh, Lordy, he's brought most of the town with him." She didn't let go of

Kent's arm. "I'd hoped we could speak to Bently quietly. *Everyone* doesn't need to know what happened."

"They still don't." Kent slowed the horse but didn't come to a halt until he was beside her brother. "Evenin', Townsend. Thought we'd be back before now."

Bently glared at his sister. "*Where* have you been, Emma? I've been worried sick about you and so has Miss Lettie."

"We've been talking," she said, and felt Kent hug her arm to his side. He was right. She didn't need to announce to one and all why she'd been so terrified. "I found a little Indian girl and returned her to the village. Mr. Hogarth arrived and escorted me out." She looked at Mr. Dunn, Mr. Jenks, and the two crewmen. "Good evening gentlemen. I'm sorry about this. As you can see, I'm fine."

Mr. Jenks moved forward. "Glad to hear it, Miss Emma." He gave Kent a nod. "Nice night for a ride." Then he glanced at the others and said, "Guess we'll be gettin' back."

"Seth," Kent called out. "I'll turn the horse out in the corral. No need you waiting 'round for me."

Seth chuckled. "I'm not worried."

After the others left, Kent looked at Bently. "Don't you think we should get her home? It's gettin' cool."

Bently's horse sidestepped, and he noticed Emma's arm linked with Kent's. "What the hell's going on here? She's wearing your coat and practically sitting on your lap."

Without missing a beat, Kent said, "She lost her cape and was kind enough to keep my arm from freezing." He slapped the reins on the horse's rump and the animal took off. "I'll speak to him at the house. If he's concerned about your reputation, he shouldn't air his laundry in front of half the town."

She nodded. "When he's worried, he loses his temper easily. If Lettie was upset and told him you went after me, he probably thought both of us were dead." Or worse, she realized. Sometimes she had the feeling her brother blamed her for her earlier attack. Will he hold me responsible for this, too? she wondered.

And I bet he wouldn't be too disappointed if I was, Kent

thought. "He'll have time to cool off on the ride back."

Bently caught up with them. "Emma, I insist you give his jacket back to him. Take mine."

She gazed at Kent. "You're cold, aren't you?"

"Not a bit," he said just loud enough for her to hear.

She looked at her brother. "We're almost home, Bently. It makes no sense to swap jackets now." It would take him a while to calm down this time, but it would've been nice if he'd been glad she was safe. "How's Lettie? Didn't she tell you Mr. Hogarth had come after me?"

"Of course she did. But dammit, Emma, you've been gone for hours! Him, too. If he'd found you near the ship, you would've been back long ago."

"Townsend," Kent said, glancing at him, "she's had a rough afternoon—"

"If you've disgraced her, Hogarth, so help me I'll kill you." Bently kicked his horse and charged ahead of them.

Kent gave Emma a gentle nudge. "You okay?"

"Mm-hm. He will be, too." She rubbed her thumb on the lapel of his jacket as she watched the lights grow brighter. When they reached the house, her brother was waiting for them at the front door. As Kent pulled up to the steps, she slipped her arm free of his and took off his coat. "You don't need to come inside." She whiffed the clove hair tonic and smiled to herself.

"Yes I do." He stepped down from the rig and pulled his crutches out from under the seat.

"Don't bother, Hogarth." Bently came down the steps. "You're not staying."

"You have a nasty habit of thinkin' you're always right, Townsend. This time you're wrong." Kent walked around the buggy and waited for Emma to go on ahead of him.

Emma motioned for Kent to go on into the kitchen and spoke to her brother. "Did you make supper?"

"What difference does that make?"

"I haven't eaten since breakfast. I'm hungry and thirsty."

Kent had just gulped down a dipper of water when Emma joined him. He plunged the dipper in the pail of water and held it out to her.

"Thanks." She drank half the water before she remembered the flask. "I brought water with me this afternoon. I'm sorry I forgot it."

"You were having so much fun, it's not surprising." He glanced at the doorway. Her brother watched them as if he expected them to be carrying on right there in front of him—the fool.

Bently sat down at the worktable and leaned back in the chair. "Looks like you two had a pleasant afternoon."

Kent moved to the other side of the table. "Emma didn't enjoy being scared half out of her wits." He sat down opposite Bently. "She was tryin' to take the little Indian girl back to her people when she met up with some braves. They took her back to their village. I offered her a ride home."

Emma put the coffeepot on the stove. "The little girl couldn't have been more than four years old. She'd scraped her legs, and she was afraid." She passed out plates and flatware.

"Oh, Emma. How do you think she got out there?" her brother asked.

She set out slices of cold beef and bread. "Children wander off. Anyway, I was trying to find the village when the Indians surrounded us." Keeping busy helped. She uncovered a bowl of baked beans and handed a spoon to Kent. "And they took me to the village."

"Oh, my God—" Bently stared at her as if she were standing in cow dung. "Did you try to get away?"

She stared at him. "You ask that as if you thought I'd chosen to stay there." Turning her head slowly in disgust, she said, "Of course I did. It was frightening—but not because they tried to hurt me. Fortunately, Mr. Hogarth arrived."

Good, Kent thought, she's keeping it simple and sticking to the truth. But the strain showed in her eyes and in her brittle voice. It was incredible that her brother didn't seem to notice how difficult this was for her. However, it confirmed his opinion of the man. He put a piece of meat on a slice of bread, folded it in half and took a bite.

"That village isn't far from where the *Julianna* was

wrecked." Bently rested his forearms on the edge of the table
and leaned forward. "Did you two get lost in the woods on
the way home?"

Kent gulped down his bite. "You're so damn ready to
convict her. Of what?" He shook his head. "The only trail
I found leading to the village veered off the road a ways
inland. We left there by the same route. I figured it was likely
the long way around but the safest way out."

Bently rolled his eyes. "What will people say? Or think?"
He scowled at his sister. "Why? Why did you have to go
off on your own? We've worked so hard—"

Kent ate another bite of the sandwich. He understood more
than her brother realized but he wasn't about to say anything.
She'd been through enough.

"If you or Lettie had been missing, I'd thank the Lord
you'd come back safely—not accuse you of scandalizing our
good name." She noticed Kent's expression out of the corner
of her eye, and she didn't want to know what he was thinking.

"That goes without saying. But it simply doesn't make
sense for those Indians to capture you—for a visit. *What else
happened?*"

Kent had listened to about all he could stomach. "When
I rode into the village, *Townsend,* Miss Emma was surrounded by Indians. They weren't just standing around chat-
ting, they were pressed close to her, touching her hair and
her clothes. They were curious, Townsend. Curious. That's
all." He ate the last bite of sandwich, then an ugly thought
crossed his mind. "You're not thinking about riding up to
the village, are you?"

Bently took a long look at his sister. "Guess not. Don't
know what good it'd do."

Emma sighed and absently stirred the beans. Kent had
earned her gratitude for the third time that day, but she
wouldn't be surprised if he never wanted to see her again.
He not only knew their family secret, her brother had given
him every reason to keep his distance from them.

"Glad to hear it." Kent stood up and grabbed his crutches.
"Well, Miss Emma, thank you for the pleasure of your com-

pany." He tipped his head to her and made his way to the kitchen door. "I'll be seein' you."

Emma jumped to her feet. "Don't you want something else to eat?" He had saved her, and she hadn't even given him a proper meal for his effort.

He stopped in the doorway. "I'm not too hungry now."

"I'll walk you out, Mr. Hogarth." She caught up with him as he stepped outside. "I don't know how I would've gotten out of the village without your help."

He smiled at her. "They probably would've had a brave take you back to the road."

"I appreciate your concern and help just the same." She untied the mare from the back of the buggy.

He stopped at her side and gave her hand a light squeeze. "My pleasure, Emma."

His hand felt rough and strong. When she gazed into his eyes, she wanted to feel his lips on hers again. "Stop by the shop, Kent, anytime." For an instant, she thought, hoped, he would kiss her good-bye, but he climbed back into the buggy.

He picked up the reins and looked at her. "I'll stop by the shop and tell Miss Morrissey you got back."

"Thank you. She'll rest easier." She ran her hand down the mare's neck and watched him until he pulled up in front of the shop. "Happy dreams, Kent. I know mine will be."

❖ 15 ❖

Emma refilled Lettie's, Lydia's, and her own teacup, then reached for a second apple roll. "Lydia, I'm so glad you baked these this morning. I didn't know how hungry I was."

Lettie broke off a piece of her roll and eyed Emma. "I'm still surprised by how well you're doing after your ordeal. Last night Mr. Hogarth told me not to worry—I thought he was just being kind."

"He said he'd speak to you, Bently and I were still talking when he left." Emma reached out and gave Lettie's hand a squeeze. "I did have a fright, but they didn't try to hurt me. My fear that they would overshadowed my common sense." Emma slowly shook her head. "When they wouldn't let me go, I was so sure . . . they'd—I don't know. Maybe it was all those terrible stories we heard crossing the plains."

Lettie shuddered. "They gave me nightmares, too."

"Those stories grew with each telling," Lydia said, stirring her tea. "And the boys loved taunting you with them."

"Lettie, I hope you know how grateful I am that you asked Kent to come after me. He said they would've let me go. But I don't know if I would've had the strength to ride the mare home."

The little brass bell over the door rang, and Hannah hurried inside. "Seth just told me what happened. Are you all right, Emma?"

"I'm fine, Hannah, but thank you for asking." Emma pulled a chair out for her and poured another cup of tea. When she climbed into bed last night, she'd filled her thoughts with Kent—the curve of his smile, the times he had teased her, the pitch of his voice. She indeed felt very well this morning.

Hannah sat down. "I overheard some of what Mr. Hogarth told Seth about the Tolowas' village. I thought all Indians lived in tepees, but he said they had wood buildings."

"It was a surprise to me, too. And they make baskets that hold water—without leaking. I saw a woman pouring hot water from one."

Lettie leaned forward. "What are they like? Were they friendly?"

Emma looked at Hannah's and Lettie's anxious expressions, then she saw the Tolowa Indians from the safety of her memory. "After talking with Kent, I realized they were probably just curious. They touched my clothes and hair, but I didn't see any weapons."

"Thank goodness," Lettie said.

Hannah thought a moment. "The Indians we saw hanging around the forts were dressed in clothes not so different from ours. Weren't the Tolowas wearing shirts and pants, and the women dresses?"

We're no different from them, Emma thought. "Some were. The braves that took me to the village wore what Kent called loincloths. Some of the women in the village were bare chested, but most wore cloth or leather dresses."

Lettie and Hannah exchanged glances.

"They've been here longer than we have, and it was warm yesterday," Lydia said. "I don't mean to be nosy, dear, but I'm curious about that beaver pelt you brought in this morning."

Emma went to the kitchen where she'd left the skin and brought it back to the table. "Isn't it nice? The little girl I found gave it to me when I was leaving."

Lydia ran her fingers through the fur. "It's soft. The pelt's big enough to make a collar and muff."

"It was kind of Mr. Hogarth to stop by last night to let us know that you were safe." Lettie idly fingered the pelt. "He must be very brave, Emma. Tell us how he rescued you. He didn't say anything about that."

Emma smiled at her. "I was standing in the middle of the village, and he drove the buggy right up to me—as if I'd been waiting for him." She picked up her teacup but hesitated before taking a drink. "I believe the Indians were even more surprised than I was." She recounted the events, leaving out their kiss, repeating what she had told Bently the night before. What passed between her and Kent was private, not some bit of gossip to be spread around town.

Hannah sipped her tea. "Seth said Mr. Hogarth knew how to handle himself. Good thing you asked for his help, Lettie."

"That was more luck than planning." Lettie gave Emma a sheepish look. "I was about to get Bently."

"I'm glad you didn't. The Indians really were peaceable." Emma draped the pelt over the back of her chair and glanced out the window at Hannah's little boy. "Is Eddie training the puppies?"

Hannah laughed. "That's what he calls it, but he does have fun with them. We've got to find homes before they're full grown. We don't need three dogs." She eyed Lettie. "Wouldn't you like one? They're gentle."

"Oh, no," Lettie said, shaking her head. "I'm afraid a dog would turn this place upside down. I'm not even sure we could manage a cat in here."

"I'll remember that when Sassy has a litter next spring." Hannah looked at Emma. "How about you? Wouldn't you like a pup?"

"Bently's enough for me," Emma said. "I'm here at the shop all day." Hannah laughed, but Lettie didn't seem to appreciate her little joke. "When he marries, I wouldn't mind having a cat."

"Why not a husband?" Hannah swirled the tea in her cup.

"They're more trouble, and you'd never train one to sleep at the foot of your bed, but he'd be better company on a cold winter night."

Emma choked on her tea.

"Mr. Hogarth'd be a good catch, but I've the feeling he'd be a hard one to tame," Hannah said with a wink at Emma. "But if he doesn't interest you, Mr. Ross seems to be an enterprising man, and Mr. Kirby's a good cook." She chuckled. "You wouldn't even have to fix his meals."

Oh, Lordy, Emma thought, if I don't go along with her teasing, she may become serious about this matchmaking. But Hannah was right about Kent. He had been roaming the countryside far too long to take up farming or open a store— or settle for only one woman. "You forgot Mr. Jenks. And what about Mr. Brice? I'd have free shoes for life."

"Mm—I've a feeling Mrs. Lewis has her bonnet set for him. Don't you, Lydia?"

Lydia nodded. "I do believe that's the way the wind's blowing."

"Good for her." Lettie picked up the plate of rolls and held it out to Hannah. "Today they're apple."

Hannah took one and looked at Mrs. Nance. "Your sweets are so good, Lydia. You should open a shop. It wouldn't have to be open every day, maybe two days a week."

Lydia laughed. "Oh, my, no. If I had to bake, it wouldn't be half as much fun. Besides, I'd miss seeing all of you here and the latest goings-on."

Emma grinned at her. "If you want to set up a counter in here, you can."

"Good thing I don't have your knack for baking, Lydia." Hannah finished the roll and licked her fingers. "If I did, I'd be as big as the livery. And I'd better find out what that boy of mine's up to now. He still has to do his sums. See you ladies later."

"Good luck with the pups." It was too bad there weren't more puppies, Emma thought. By the time Hannah found homes for them, she might have lost interest in matching her up with some man.

*   *   *

Kent leaned the axe handle against his leg and rubbed his shirtsleeve across his forehead. He and Ross had spent all day hewing planks. Kent arched his back. It felt good to be working instead of just watching others. "Looks like we might be in for a storm."

Ross stared out to sea. "Sure does." He looked around at the logs and the growing stack of planks. "This's comin' right along. I appreciate your help, Kent. Don't know how much use it'll be, but you'll have a free crossing anytime."

"Thanks. Could come in handy. Never know when I might need it." Kent picked up the axe and cut two more planks.

Ross added his to the stack. "That's enough for today. It's almost dark."

"Fine with me." As Kent pulled on his coat, he looked toward the south end of the bay. He'd seen pictures of towns back East. There'd been houses almost on the water in some places. It could happen here, he thought. Once the ferry was running, the roads'd be traveled more often. Mr. Wendell wouldn't be disappointed. "Think the ship's owners'll try to salvage what they can?"

Ross wrapped the axes in canvas and left them near the planks. "They'll figure there isn't much left worth their trouble till Mr. Green and Mr. Nash report." He grabbed his jacket. "Then they'll likely send another ship to get the cargo we stored."

Ross walked back with Kent as far as the saloon. "I'm gonna have a lager. You wanta join me?"

"I'll take you up on that another time. I have a stop to make before it gets dark."

Ross pushed the saloon door open. "If it's rainin' tomorrow, don't bother about helpin' out."

"Sure 'nough." Roy Avery came to the door. Kent waved to him and continued on up to the corner.

Word had spread about Emma being taken to the Indian village. The men were concerned with safety and some questioned the likelihood of an Indian attack. Since there hadn't been any trouble, it wasn't hard to ease their concerns.

Women, he'd discovered, though, looked at things differently.

Emma was respected and well liked, so he wasn't too uneasy about the women giving her a rough time. She'd seemed fine when he left her last evening. But fear was a strange beast and could pop up out of nowhere at the worst moment. The lights were bright in her shop when he stepped up on the board walk in front and entered the Hat Box.

Miss Morrissey was in the kitchen, and Emma was setting cups on a tray at the round table near the woodstove. "Hello. You still open?" Emma's smile seemed brighter than usual or maybe he just wanted to think it was.

"Kent— Come on in." As she cleared the place nearest the woodstove for him, her heart beat wildly. "I was just straightening up. Here." She pulled the chair out for him. "Can I get you something to drink?" After the scene with her brother the night before, she didn't believe he would stop by the shop again. She had never been happier about being wrong.

"Thought I'd see if you wanted company on your walk home." From her wide-eyed gaze and parted lips, he would've guessed he'd startled her if he hadn't known better. "I don't mind waiting. It's up to you." The longer he knew her, the more questions he had. Her response to his kiss had been sweet—inexperienced, and passionate. That last one bothered and intrigued him most.

"That would be nice." She carried the tray of dishes to the kitchen.

Kent turned around to the kitchen. "Hello, Miss Morrissey. How're you doing?"

Lettie smiled at him. "Fine, thank you, Mr. Hogarth." Stepping closer to Emma, Lettie said, "I thought he'd pay you a call." She added one more piece of wood to the stove firebox and closed the door. "He's here to see *you*. Why don't you keep him company?"

"I will," she mouthed, pouring a dipper of water into a glass. She set the drink down on the table and moved a stack of clothes. "I wanted to fold these and put them away before I leave."

"Take your time," he said, picking up the glass. "I'm in no hurry." He took a drink. "How was your day?"

When she looked into his eyes, she understood what he was asking. "Not too much out of the ordinary. You were right. Thanks for the advice."

He nodded. "Most people don't go around hoping for the worst for others." She'd likely find it hard to believe anybody did, he thought. "How was your brother after I left?"

"He didn't say much." She held up a petticoat and quickly folded it. "He has a good heart. He really does, and he's been good to me. I wouldn't have any of this," she said, sweeping her arm in an arc, "if not for him."

"This's a nice shop. I haven't seen anything like it, not from Oregon City to Sacramento City." She beamed, and he stared at her. If she'd do that around the right sorta men, she'd have her pick. But he was glad she wasn't already taken.

"That's nice to know. When more people settle in the area, maybe the women will shop here." She finished folding the clothes and put them in a wardrobe drawer. "Lettie, I'll see you in the morning." She set the jug and butter crock in her shopping basket, and grabbed her cape and bonnet.

"Enjoy your walk."

Kent stood up and watched her tie the ribbons on her bonnet. When she'd lowered her hands, he took her cape and settled it around her. Resting a hand on each shoulder, he asked, "Ready?" She trembled, and he caressed her—wishing he could take her in his arms, knowing he couldn't since they weren't alone—and lowered his hands.

"Mm-hm." Oh, I could get used to this. But she knew she mustn't. She reached the door first and opened it for him.

He eyed her, then chuckled. "Thank ya, ma'am. But don't you go spoilin' me just b'cause o' these crutches."

She closed the shop door. "I have a feeling that wouldn't be easy to do." She paused on the board walk. "Do you mind if we stop in at the general store?"

"Not at all." He maneuvered the crutches so he wouldn't trip her. "I was goin' to come back by there." In another week, he'd try walking without them.

"Did you know Mr. Brice's opening a shop here?"

"He talked about it. Glad to hear he decided to. He seems to like it here."

She paused at the door to the general store and gazed over her shoulder at him. "It's a nice place to live."

"Hello, Miss Emma," Mr. Jenks said, reaching his arm around to hold the door open. "Hogarth."

"Jenks. How's it goin'?" Kent stepped inside.

"Nothin' t' complain about." He caught up with Kent and said softly, "What ya did fer her was right nice. She's such a genteel li'l thin'."

When Emma moved closer, Kent turned to her. "You go first. I don't need much."

"Why don't you? I want to look at a couple of things first."

Jenks chuckled. "The ladies enjoy browsin' 'round more'n the gents do."

"You'd know." Kent grinned. "I'll need a slab of bacon and ground coffee beans."

"Sure thing."

Emma left the jug and crock on the counter. She sauntered by the spice drawers and stopped to look at a newfangled potato masher. A pewter candlestick also caught her eye, but she didn't need another one. She picked up a small white pitcher, smiled and set it down again. If she bought every pretty candlestick and pitcher she liked, she would have a house full of them.

"I'll take a couple chickens, too, and— Never mind. That's enough." He'd come back next week when he could carry more . . . What the hell was he thinking? When his leg had healed, he was leaving—wasn't he?

Charlie Jenks wrapped the bacon and chickens in paper and did the same with the ground coffee. After he tied a length of string around the bundle, he looped one end and knotted it. "Can ya manage that?"

"Yep." Kent reached into his pocket.

Jenks waved his hand. "I'll put it on account."

Kent laid enough coins on the counter to cover his purchases. "I'd rather pay my way. Too easy to run up a bill and forget what all I've purchased when the money's due."

"Okay." Charlie laughed. "I don't usually turn down cash." He turned to Emma. "What can I get fer you?"

"I need a dozen eggs, molasses, and butter," she said, scooting the containers over to him. She noticed Kent's package. "I'm glad this wasn't a waste of time for you."

He grinned. "I remembered a few things besides coffee."

Charlie set the jug of molasses and crock of fresh butter on the counter. "Mrs. Pool brought fresh churned butter and four dozen eggs in this mornin'." He counted out the eggs and put them into her basket. "Anything else today?"

"That's all I can think of, but if you get in any honey, I wish you'd save some for me."

"I sure will, Miss Emma."

"Thank you, Mr. Jenks." She hung the basket on her arm and picked up the crock and jug. She looked at Kent. "Ready?"

"Yes, ma'am." He started toward the door.

Charlie hurried around a table, beating him to the front door and opened it for them. "Oh, Hogarth, you still inter'sted in odd jobs?"

"Sure am. What do you have in mind?"

"Drive a wagonload of supplies up to old Sourdough. Take ya 'bout six hours to make it up there."

Kent glanced at Emma out of the corner of his eye and nodded. "Let me know when you'll need me."

"Good. Stop by for coffee sometime if ya git tired o' that old cabin."

"I will. Thanks." Kent made his way down the two steps to the ground. A gentleman'd carry her packages for her, but he was doing good just managing his own.

As they walked past her shop, she didn't have to look at the window to know their passing hadn't gone unnoticed. She looked at his crutches then at him. "You won't have to use those much longer, will you?"

"By my reckoning, another week. I suppose it'll take a while to get the strength back."

"It usually does." But she didn't think it would be long before he'd be able to ride again—and then he would leave.

However, until he did, she wanted to enjoy his company. "It might be a little easier if you start putting some weight on that leg before you give back the crutches." A stiff breeze billowed her cape. A storm was blowing in and the air already smelled fresher. Kent was like a winter storm, she realized. He arrived, stirred things up, then he would ride out as suddenly as he'd come. Lordy, she didn't want to think about that now. "How's the work going on the ferry?"

"Ross seems to know what he's doing. We've got about half the planks cut."

She stopped at the turnoff to her house. "Will you be here to help launch it?" She had to ask. The wondering would've given her fits.

"Not unless we finish it in the next ten days," he said, wondering if she'd miss him. She suddenly looked away, and he added, "Ross said I could ride free anytime. I just may come back and take him up on his offer."

At least now she knew, now she could prepare for his leaving. "That could be a long journey for a free ride." She stared at him. She hadn't meant to say that aloud.

He chuckled. "That may be true. But don't you think it'd be worth my time?"

Thank you, Kent, she thought, and tried to sound lighthearted. "All depends on how bad you want to cross the river, I guess."

"If I was coming north, I'd wanta cross *real* bad."

His voice reminded her of Eddie, and she giggled.

Emma tied off the last stitch on the quilt. "I was beginning to wonder if I'd ever complete it." She glanced over at Lettie. "What is so fascinating outside?"

"Eddie. Come look." Lettie held the curtain back. "He's walking the puppies."

Emma went over to the side window by her. "He's sure going to miss those pups. But I'm surprised Hannah hasn't already given them away."

As she continued watching, Lettie smiled. "Does Bently like dogs?"

"Mm-hm. He used to have one. It was reddish-brown."

Emma kept her attention on Eddie. "You should ask him about it."

"Do you think he'd like a little black dog?"

Emma turned her head away and smiled. "You might ask him that, too."

Lettie frowned at her. "You're no help at all."

"On the contrary," Emma said, facing her. "I'm trying to give you an excuse, if you need one, to speak to my brother." When she looked back outside, Eddie was gone. "If you don't do something to nudge him along, you'll both be in your dotage and barely holding hands."

"Emma, that's a dreadful thing to say."

Emma picked up the quilt and, satisfied with her handiwork, began folding the bedcover. "Then do something about it." Listen to her, she thought, giving advice so confidently. If she were half so assured, she might try taking her own words to heart.

"Looks like the rain's finally stopped for a while. Let's pay a call on Mrs. Lewis. We've been cooped up in here all week." Lettie set her cup in the dry sink. "I'll put a note on the door, 'visiting Mrs. Lewis.' "

Emma's gaze strayed to the window. "You go on. I think I'll weave a yellow ribbon around the neck of that plain camisole."

"That can wait." Lettie lifted their capes off the pegs. "And Mr. Hogarth probably won't stop by for another hour or so."

Emma stared at her. "Don't be foolish. I am not waiting around for him."

Lettie grinned. "If you're not, it's the first time in the last week." She draped Emma's cape across her shoulders. "Next time he walks you home, why don't you ask him if he likes cats?"

"You're impossible." Emma straightened her cape and started for the door. "Well, aren't you going to write that note?"

Lettie quickly wrote out the message and tacked it on the front door when they left. First they walked down to the bay. "Emma, are you afraid to sail on a ship again?"

"I don't think so. The sound of the ocean is comforting, and the roll of the ship put me right to sleep. No, I wouldn't pass up another trip on a boat, but I would like to learn how to swim first." Emma smiled.

"I feel safer on the ground. Give me a buggy, coach, or wagon."

They crossed the road and entered the hotel. Emma peered into the reading room. The upholstered sofa had been cleaned, the furniture rearranged, and a painting of a horse in a meadow now hung over the fireplace. "See what Mrs. Lewis has done. Isn't it nice?"

Lettie walked into the room. "If any travelers stop by here, they won't want to leave."

"Mrs. Lewis knows how to manage a hotel." Emma heard voices coming from the back room and ventured down the hall. Motioning to Lettie, Emma stepped into the kitchen. Mrs. Lewis and Lydia were sitting at the small table. "Hello."

Mrs. Lewis looked and smiled at them. "Please come in."

Emma took a closer look at the doorway she'd just walked through. "Opening up that wall makes the kitchen feel larger."

Mrs. Lewis nodded. "We'll need it when the dining room's completed." She set out a tray and put cups and saucers on it. "We made a fresh pot of tea. We can sit in the reading room."

"Here," Emma said, reaching for the tray. "I'll carry that for you."

Lydia got a plate out of one cupboard. "I'll bring the rest of the butter biscuits." She eyed her granddaughter. "It's nice to see you two getting out of the shop together. Any special reason?"

Lettie shook her head. "Do we need one?"

"Of course not. But I am surprised Emma left the shop so late in the afternoon." Lydia looked at her granddaughter. "Doesn't Mr. Hogarth usually stop by around this time?"

Lettie grinned and picked up the plate. "That's another good reason to get out for a while."

❖ 16 ❖

KENT LEANED BACK on the chair by the woodstove in the general store, his legs stretched out in front of him. It had been raining for days. He had a lager with Roy Avery one afternoon and stopped by the hotel another day. And he had walked Emma home each evening. But yesterday when he arrived at the Hat Box at about his usual time, he'd found a note on the door. Maybe she'd grown tired of seeing him every day. If he had a lick of sense, he'd leave her alone.

Jenks refilled his cup of coffee and sat back down. "Sure ya don't wanta keep the crutches a few more days in case yer leg gits tired?"

"No, thanks. I'll never work the kinks out if I don't use it." Kent sipped the hot drink. "Last week you said somethin' about me drivin' supplies up to one of the camps. You still need a driver?"

"Yep. Can you do it tomorrow?"

"Sure. You said it'll take about six hours?"

Jenks nodded. "I'll draw ya a map. The camp's not hard to find. I'll load the wagon tonight an' ya can leave anytime ya want in the mornin'."

"Might as well start up there around sunup. Any reason why we can't start packin' the wagon now?"

"We can start if ya want. I'll go to the livery and drive it over."

Kent sat up. "I'll do it."

"Nah, rest easy. I need to talk to Seth about hitchin' up the horses in the morning."

Kent stood up, gulped the last of the coffee, and set the cup on the floor by the chair. "I'll go over with you. He can show me which horses, and I'll do it. No need for him to start the day so early."

They went to the livery, and Seth didn't have any objections to Kent's taking the horses. Then Jenks and Kent started packing the back of the wagon with the supplies. He wanted to keep busy, so busy he didn't think about Emma. But it wasn't working. If he wasn't remembering something she'd said, her smile drifted into his mind.

Near sundown, Jenks brought out canvas to spread over the back of the wagon. After it had been lashed down, he held up his hands. "We're done." He looked over at Emma's shop. "She'll be expectin' ya."

Kent eyed Jenks.

Jenks lifted one shoulder. "'Bout time someone walked her home. She's a special lady."

"That she is." Kent dusted off his trousers, rinsed off his hands in the trough, and put on his coat. "See you tomorrow, when I get back."

"If the store's closed, bang on the door. I'll hear ya."

Kent cut across the corner and paused in front of the Hat Box. There wasn't a note on the door. If she didn't seem glad to see him, he'd leave. Figuring he didn't have anything to lose, he went inside the shop.

When Emma heard the door latch an instant before the little bell rang out, she completely forgot Alicia and spun around. It was *him*—and walking without the crutches. She thought back to the shipwreck and how he had walked on deck with such confidence before his fall. Her pulse fluttered, and she prayed her voice wouldn't fail her. "Congratulations."

"Thanks." He smiled, and greeted Lettie and Mrs. Simms.

"There's a fresh pot of coffee." Emma took a step toward

him. "Would you like a cup?" She hid her hands in the folds of her skirt to keep from appearing as anxious as she felt. She had understood why Lettie didn't want her to look as if she were waiting for him every day. What Lettie didn't understand—and Emma did—was that soon he would be gone, and she wouldn't see him again.

Alicia smiled at him. "I haven't seen you since the supper. You seem to have recovered very quickly from your accident."

"Yes, ma'am." He sat down at the table. "Did I interrupt something?"

Lettie laughed and shook her head. "No, Mr. Hogarth. We were talking about making a journey down to Eureka next spring."

Alicia nodded. "The ferry will be working by then, won't it, Mr. Hogarth?"

Emma set a steaming cup of coffee in front of him, pulled her chair out a little ways and sat down. Since he was on her left, no one would think anything of her watching him. And if they did, she realized she didn't care.

He smiled at Emma before he answered Mrs. Simms. "It should be."

"Wonderful." Alicia glanced at Emma and Lettie. "Most of us haven't been any farther south than the river. A group of us wants to see Eureka and let the people there know we're here—in case they don't already."

"That's a good idea. Who's going?" He raised the cup to his mouth and gazed at Emma over the rim. As far as he could tell, she looked happy to see him. Funny how one of her sweet smiles made him feel eighteen again and start thinking about holding her in his arms all night long.

"Lettie will be going, and Bently." Emma glanced at Alicia. "And we hope Mr. and Mrs. Simms. Maybe Mr. Brice, too."

Alicia took a sip of her drink. "There's time. I think Mr. Simms will also be interested." She grinned. "He'll want to know if someone's publishing a newspaper there." She scooted her chair back and stood up. "It was nice seeing you, Mr. Hogarth. Lettie, Emma, I'll talk to you soon."

As Alicia left, Lettie stood up and pushed her chair to the table. "It's about time to close up." She pulled the curtains together across the front window.

If she'd been closer, Emma would have kicked her under the table. "Finish your coffee," she told Kent. "I'm part owner. She won't boot us out."

Lettie laughed as she passed the table. "Don't be too sure. I also live here."

Kent held up his hand. "Enough, ladies, or you'll turn my head." Lettie laughed even harder, but Emma's cheeks were bright pink.

"I guess we aren't wanted here," Emma said, half joking. "Would you walk with me?" She couldn't remember ever feeling so foolish. Lettie is taking full advantage of the situation, Emma thought. She knows I won't make a scene in front of him.

"I would be happy to keep you company." He eyed Miss Morrissey, but she kept her back to them. Women. If any man ever figured out how to read their thoughts, he'd become rich selling his knowledge.

Emma got her cape and bonnet and left the shop with him. "I'm sorry about that. Lettie wasn't quite herself." And I'm not going to explain, she left unsaid. She stopped on the board walk, plopped her bonnet on her head, and swung her cape around her shoulders.

He grinned and slipped her arm through his. "How was the rest of your day?" They started down the road.

"Quiet. You were in on the most exciting part." They walked slowly, and she suddenly realized what was different. They were arm in arm and it was so much nicer than keeping her distance. "Did you give the crutches back to Mr. Jenks?"

"Today. I took your advice and practiced in the cabin." He hugged her arm. "Those things got in the way at the worst times."

She smiled, then noticed her brother driving the buckboard in their direction with something at his side. When he stopped near them, she remained at Kent's side with her arm through his. "You finished Lettie's chair?"

He gave them a curt nod. "Thought I'd better take it over to her and give you a ride home."

"She'll be happy to see you. We're almost home. I'll meet you at the house."

Kent took a closer look at the chair frame. "Nice work. Didn't know you were a cabinetmaker."

"I *know* how to do many things, Hogarth." Bently stared at his sister. "It's getting cold. Don't stand out here and take a chill." He slapped the reins on the horse's rump and continued toward the shop.

"I'll walk you home." He took a step and realized she hadn't.

She stared at the rickety old shack. "I've never been inside your cabin, and I admit I'd like to." She looked into his eyes and decided to heed her own counsel. "Would you show me what you've done?"

"If that's what you want to do." Didn't she know that wasn't very wise? However, he'd abide by her wishes.

"Mm-hm," she said with a nod and turned toward the shack.

He walked up the path with her. "From what Eddie said, the old man who lived here wasn't too sociable."

"No. He said we crowded him out. He didn't like all the ruckus in town." When he stopped to push the door open, she glanced back at her house. She had wondered what he could see from there. The front of the house was visible, if someone stood in the front doorway, but certainly not to anyone looking out of the kitchen window—not even if her nose were pressed to the glass.

He went in ahead of her and lighted the lamp. "It's cleaner. But nothing else has changed." He watched as she slowly moved around the room clutching her cape, charmed by her willowy grace. The hem of her cape swayed, taunting him with hope for a glimpse of her ankle.

She looked over at him. "It's better than I'd expected. It doesn't seem to lean on the inside, but that doesn't make sense." The room was clean, his belongings were folded or neatly set aside, and even his bed was made. The room was

dark, though. It was no wonder he didn't spend his days in
here.

"That surprised me, too. But the roof hasn't leaked, so
I'm not complaining."

And it's private, she thought, almost like camping out with
a roof overhead. Suddenly she realized she was standing at
the foot of his bed and quickly crossed the room to get a
better look at the bottle window. Now when she thought of
him at night she could imagine him in here.

She's skittery as a doe, he thought, and she should be,
since she's in a man's cabin. He still hadn't figured out why
she wanted to come inside, but he *knew* her reasoning was
innocent. "Sorry I haven't a pot of coffee on the fire. I
wasn't expecting company."

She grinned at him. "I'm not thirsty. Just nosy, I guess."

"I don't mind, but your brother sure would."

"He'd do better to worry more about himself."

Kent grinned but said nothing. If he really wanted to do
what was best for her, he wouldn't stop by to see her so
often and walk her home each evening. He wasn't the right
man for her, but hellfire, he was having trouble remembering
that. Especially now. "I'd better walk you home now."

She stepped in front of him. "Yes, I suppose so." She let
go of her cape, uncertain what to do. She wanted to kiss him.
She could never admit her love for him, but she could show
him. Two kisses to last a lifetime wasn't asking too much,
was it?

He got a crazy idea. It was reckless—but oh, so tempting.
"I'm goin' to deliver supplies up to a camp in the mountains
tomorrow." The light was low, but the sparkle in her eyes
was spellbinding. "Would you like to ride up there with
me?"

"Yes . . ." She smiled and rested her hands on his chest.
"I'd like that. I'll pack a dinner basket."

He could feel her warm breath on his cheek, and her hand
surely'd leave an imprint over his thudding heart. "I'll have
to leave early. Sunup—or just after. That too early for you?"
He'd lost what little God-given reasoning he had. He wanted

to take her in his arms, hold her body close, and feel her mouth on his.

"I'll fix the food tonight." She grinned. A whole day together. She could hardly believe it. "I'd better get busy," she said, and impulsively stood on tiptoe, slid her hand around his neck, and pressed her lips to his. She felt his arm circle her waist, and she leaned into him. She was in heaven.

When her mouth caressed his, he couldn't believe it at first. Then she slanted her lips over his, and he put his arms around her and held her close. She didn't feel as fragile as she looked. Her strength, her determination to prolong the kiss, overcame his better judgment, his common sense, and he deepened the kiss. She opened up as if she were a bloom in the sunlight. But as soon as she moaned, he knew he had to step back and take a deep breath. He pressed a kiss to her forehead and gazed down into her shimmering eyes.

She had never imagined how wonderful a kiss could be. She'd thought the first one was glorious, but this time . . . she felt light-headed and filled with a wondrous energy that seemed to promise even more. Slowly, she gathered her wits. There was so much to do. "I'll meet you in front of the general store at sunrise."

He straightened her cape. Her cheeks were glowing, and her eyes were still bright. She couldn't know, but he had never faced the danger she posed for him. "Sure you want to go tomorrow? Maybe it's not such a good idea." Alone with her all day. He wouldn't hurt her for the world, but— What was wrong with him? His thoughts were spinning out of control.

"I haven't been up into the hills. It'll be fun exploring with you." She stepped back and said, "See you in the morning," and dashed outside. So much to do. When she reached the road, she saw the buckboard in front of her house.

There was one thing she had to do before going home. She nearly ran down the street to the shop, knocked on the door, and burst inside. Lettie was in the kitchen, and Emma hurried back there to her.

"Emma, what's happened?" Lettie dropped the spoon she had been holding and grabbed her apron strings. "Did Bently have an accident?"

"No. Why would—"

"You've been running," Lettie said, pulling off her apron. "You're flushed and— *What* is it?"

Emma caught her breath. "I just wanted to let you know I won't be in tomorrow. I didn't want you to worry and send a rescue party after us."

"Us?"

Emma nodded. "I'm going with Kent when he delivers the supplies to one of the camps in the hills." Lettie gave her an odd look Emma didn't understand. "What is it? If you don't want to open the shop by yourself, then don't. We can close it for one day."

"You've called him Kent all day. Emma, do you think you should go off for that long a time with him—by yourself?"

Emma laughed and clasped Lettie's hands. "I like him. I just want to spend one day in his company before he leaves." Emma replaced the word "love" for "like" in her mind. Her feelings were too fragile, too private, to share with even her dearest friend. "We'll be fine. And I don't want you worrying about me."

"I don't know. Bently will kill Mr. Hogarth." Lettie narrowed her gaze. "You're not telling him, are you?"

"There's no reason. For all he knows, I could be out riding around the countryside. I won't lie to him, but I don't need to tell him, either."

"Oh, Emma— You know when he finds out he'll come after you."

"Who'll tell him? And if he finds out, I'm hoping *you* will convince him to be sensible. We should be back by late afternoon." Emma cocked her head. "Please, Lettie. If he becomes too unreasonable, agree with him, but do make him see that it'd be better to wait for us."

"I've never seen you so happy or excited about a man." Lettie shook her head. "I shouldn't. I have a feeling we'll both be sorry." She stared at Emma a long moment. "Oh, all right. But you better return by the time we usually close the shop."

Hugging Lettie, Emma said, "Thank you," and started to leave, then she paused. "Didn't Bently visit with you?"

"He brought the chair in, and I offered him a cup of coffee. But he said he had to get home because you would have supper waiting."

"I'd better see to that. I'll stop by here when we get back." Emma ran all the way home. She had never felt more alive and had no idea how she would get a wink of sleep that night.

All the while Kent harnessed the team of horses, he wondered if Emma would be waiting for him in front of the general store. In the end, he'd convinced himself she'd realized it would be a mistake to go with him. She wouldn't be there. Besides, it was cold and foggy. With a firm grip on the cheek strap on the near horse, he led the pair over to the wagon in front of the general store. He was positioning the animals, when he saw her standing by the wagon.

He smiled, not quite sure if he was glad she was there. "Mornin'." The hood of her cape framed her face, the only part of her that wasn't covered up. Her cheeks had a pink cast and her eyelashes seemed to glisten. She certainly was bright eyed and cheerful for so early in the morning. "Been waitin' long?"

"Not at all." She walked around to the other side and helped him get the horses backed up to the wagon. "I put the basket under the seat. Did you pack a box of food, too?" Maybe he hadn't thought she would really show up this morning. She assumed the rifle and ammunition under the bench seat were his and thought the other food might be his, too.

"Jenks must've put it there. Hope he didn't forget the map."

She peered over the backs of the horses. "Don't you know how to get there?"

He grinned at her. "Feeling adventurous?"

As long as we're together. "You found me, didn't you? I'm not worried."

He finished hitching the horses up to the wagon and went around the back, making sure everything was in order. When he met her gaze, she smiled at him, and he was glad she hadn't changed her mind. "Ready?"

"Is everything packed in the wagon?"

"It'd better be." He put his hands on her waist and lifted her off the ground. She felt as light as a bushel of feathers. When her face was above his, she braced her gloved hands on his shoulders. "You'd better stay out of a strong wind. I don't wanta lose you."

"I haven't blown away yet." And *I'm not likely to,* she thought, not with him holding me so close.

He swung her up to the seat and lowered his arms. "You going to be warm enough?"

"I have enough clothes on for two women, and I brought a couple of blankets. I thought we could have a picnic dinner." She moved over so he would sit on her right, and it would be easier for her to hear him.

He climbed up to the seat beside her, picked up the reins, and started the horses around the corner. "Sounds good to me."

She settled back and crossed the sides of her cape over her lower legs. "I love mornings like this with the fog hanging over the river and in the trees. Isn't it wonderful?"

He nodded. "Ever notice how quiet the animals are when the fog's down so low?"

"Mm. It's as if there's no one else within miles."

He glanced at her and grinned. "There won't be in a little while."

They passed Ginny and Will's farm, but Emma knew better than to expect to see them out at that hour. "Have you seen Eddie this week?"

"Yeah. With the pups. He sure was havin' fun."

"He's going to have to give them away. His mother doesn't want three dogs. He won't be happy about that."

The sky was growing light and the fog was lifting. When they rode by the Pool farm, she saw one of the boys go into the barn.

"No, but that's part of growin' up, isn't it? Besides, he'll probably visit them."

With his gumption and patience, she thought, he would be a wonderful father. "Do you have any brothers or sisters?"

"Two of each."

"In California? Or were you the only one with the wanderlust?"

"Nope. Nate's up in the Washington Territory, and last I heard George settled in the Nebraska Territory with his new wife. They must have a son by now. I'll have to write."

She narrowed her gaze. "You haven't heard from him?"

He shook his head.

"Then why're you so sure they would've had a boy? They could have had a daughter. It's been known to happen." His grin was so confident, she laughed. He was teasing her again.

"Firstborn's always a boy in our family. That way on both sides."

"Always?"

"Yep. With our pa and ma, and theirs, aunts and uncles."

"All of them? You're so good at making almost anything sound sensible, I'm not sure you're teasing."

"Let me see now," he said, resting one boot on the footboard. "My grandpa Edward was the oldest, as was his pa, Uncle Chester, and Uncle Herbert, then there was Edward, Jr., Edward James—"

"Stop . . ." she said, laughing. "All right. I believe you." For all she knew he had made up the whole tale, but she had the feeling he would recite names all the way up to the camp.

After they had passed the Chase farm, she felt as if they were really on their way. All that was familiar lay behind as they made their way into the pine-covered foothills. Sunlight now touched the top of the tallest trees. Emma turned and stared back toward town. "What a wonderful bird's-eye view." The sky over the ocean was still dark but soon it would be bright and the water a deep blue.

Kent halted the horses and looked back. "That it is. Surprising someone hasn't built a cabin up here.'' He started the team going again. He didn't see any signs of a creek and figured digging a well up there could be a devil of a job. But it'd be a good spot for a picnic, though.

She turned around and pushed her hood back. ''How far is the turnoff?''

''Bored already?''

''Just wondering. You said Mr. Jenks was supposed to leave you a map.''

He frowned. ''You said there was a box of food. Would you check in there?''

She slid off the bench, reached underneath and pulled the box forward. Tossing back the cloth covering the food, she found the map wedged between two bundles. ''Here it is,'' she said, handing the folded page to him.

He flattened the paper on his thigh and traced the road. ''We've a ways to go. I figure we're about here,'' he said, pointing with his finger.

She moved closer to him, and as she leaned forward to see where he pointed, she brushed against his arm and rested her hand above his wrist. The first thing she noticed were his fingernails. Clean and smooth, unusual for a man who worked with his hands. ''Hope that big old tree hasn't changed. I wonder how long it's been since Mr. Jenks came up here.''

He glanced at her. ''I didn't ask.'' She'd put her hand on his arm. It was still there. And it felt nice. He couldn't remember the last time he'd gone riding with a lady, but he'd never known a lady like Emma. That was his problem. She had become too important to him. He caught her yawning and smiled. ''Close your eyes if you're sleepy. You can rest on my shoulder if you want.''

It was tempting, but she didn't intend to sleep the day away instead of enjoying their time together. ''Maybe later. Do you know any interesting stories about mountain men or other settlements?''

He chuckled, and then thought of some tall tales he'd heard. ''Ever hear about Old Stoney?''

''Uh-uh. Who's he?''

"A trapper. It happened a few miles north of here in fact."
He met her gaze and nodded.

She grinned.

"Stoney was checkin' his traps b'fore the first snow.
When he got to the last one, he found it'd been sprung. Only
thing left were some bits of gray fur caught on the teeth of
the trap." He shook his head. "He reset the trap and decided
to hide in the bushes and see who'd been messin' with it.
He waited—one, two, three days. Well, feelin' whatever'd
stolen his game wasn't comin' back, he fixed to leave." He
looked at her out of the corner of his eye and lowered his
voice. "All of a sudden this walloping grizzly bear grabbed
him."

She gulped. She had heard stories about grizzlies and how
the huge animals could easily shred a person's flesh with one
swipe of the paw.

"This ol' bear hauled him off. No matter what Stoney did,
he couldn't break free of the beast. The bear dragged him
back to his cave, through a narrow passage, and leaves him
in this little space just big enough for the man to lay down
in."

Kent seemed to be lost in thought, and she waited. However, she began to suspect he might be joshing her again.
Finally, she said, "Well . . . what happened to him?"

"What? Oh, he's still there. The bear throws him meat
every so often, a few berries. Poor fellow must be skin and
bones by now." He glanced at her. "I hear the bear's real
happy with his pet."

She burst out laughing. "I guess I asked for that, didn't
I?"

His tomfoolery had the desired result. Her laughter was
beautiful. And the sound had the same effect as when she'd
pressed herself against his body and kissed him. He sat up
taller, stared straight ahead at the road, and urged a little
more speed out of the horses.

• 17 •

By MID-MORNING IT had turned icy cold, and Kent knew he'd made a mistake bringing Emma with him. It wasn't long after that when the first snowflakes started falling. "This's turned into some trip. I didn't think it snowed in these mountains." They were past the halfway point and didn't know how badly the miner needed the supplies. He wanted to go on, but he didn't want to take any risks with her.

"I don't remember seeing snow up here last year."

He put his arm around her and held her close to his side. "Do you want to turn around? We're still about two hours away from the camp."

It was worth being cold, she thought, to be so close to him. "If the snow doesn't stop, another wagon wouldn't be able to get through, either, would it?"

"Hard to say."

"Keep going."

He kissed her brow. "Better put one of those blankets around you."

She kneeled on the seat and grabbed one of the blankets. After she wrapped one end around him, she put the other around herself and snuggled as close to him as she could without sitting on his lap.

He concentrated on the road ahead but still he nearly missed the big tree marked on the map. Jenks had noted it was another mile from there to the camp. Kent just hoped he'd be able to see it when they got there. At last they came to what he hoped was the right place. A sturdy-looking shack seemed to grow out of the side of the hill. He stopped at the edge of the camp and called out. He was fairly certain the miner would've heard their approach, but he waited to make darn sure the fellow wasn't going to greet them with a load of buckshot.

A man who must've lived at least five decades stepped into the clearing. Kent waved to him. "Charlie Jenks sent these supplies. You Sourdough?"

"Only one here. Come on in."

Emma lowered the edge of the blanket from her face. "He doesn't sound very friendly." It was hard to tell what the man looked like underneath the woolly cap and all that hair.

Kent pulled into the camp and climbed down from the wagon. "I'm Kent Hogarth and this's Miss Townsend," he said, lowering her down beside him.

"Su'prised you got through the pass with all this snow." Sourdough peered under the canvas covering the wagon bed. "You got a barrel o' flour there?"

"Yep." Kent walked to the back of the wagon and started unloading the supplies. "What pass're you talkin' about?" He sure didn't like the idea that he'd missed seeing something that big.

"'Bout four miles back. It don't look like much, less'n you trigger a snowslide."

While Emma stretched her legs and tried to warm up, she couldn't help hearing what the miner had said about a snow-slide. Didn't they have enough to worry about? She took a better look at the man. All she could see, besides his heavy clothes, were his light brown eyes and reddish nose. She picked up a box of supplies and carried it over by the shack. A sudden gust of wind-driven snow whipped her cape out and billowed her skirts. The weather was growing worse by the minute.

After the barrels and boxes had been stacked, Kent watered the horses while he spoke to Sourdough. "You got any mail or messages you want me to take back?"

"Nah. Jist see that Jenks gits this," Sourdough said, shoving a leather pouch into Kent's hand. "'N tell him thanky."

"Be glad to." Kent swung Emma up to the wagon and climbed up beside her.

"Don't us'ly git snow this early. But th' first one nev'r lasts more'n a day."

Aren't we lucky— Another two hours could be disastrous, Kent thought, waving to the old miner as he headed the team of horses back down the trail.

"You must be as hungry as I am, and I'm starved." Emma reached under the seat and pulled the basket forward. "I made sandwiches. We don't have to stop to eat."

"Good thinking. Did you bring something to drink, too?"

"Just water." She gave him a sheepish smile. "I should've brought coffee, but I didn't think you'd want to bother with a fire." The snow began falling harder. She unwrapped the first sandwich she came to and handed it to him. "Beef okay?"

"Sounds great." He took a big bite. His stomach had been complaining for the better part of the last hour.

"I made three beef and two chicken. Thought they'd be easier to eat than a fancier meal. We also have dilly beans and bread 'n' butter pickles." She laughed and added, "But there're butter cakes for dessert."

"Thanks. This's sure good."

She took a bite of a chicken sandwich, then poured water into one of the tin cups. "I'll hold the sandwich while you drink."

"Mm," he said, gulping down the bite. "I've missed your cooking."

She chuckled. "When you're this hungry, *anything* tastes good." She made the exchange and when he had finished the water, she handed the sandwich back to him. She ate the rest of hers and dusted the snow off both of them. "Have you tried mining?"

"Yeah. This fella showed me a handful o' nuggets. Said he'd just picked 'em out of the riverbed." He laughed. "I used a tin plate and sifted through half a streambed. Guess it was easier for him than me." He smiled at her. "I did better delivering mail and supplies, and I didn't get wet unless it rained."

"Do you want another sandwich?" She chafed her hands and wondered how he managed to look as if it were a spring day.

"Thanks but not now." They'd be even hungrier later—especially if they had trouble getting through that pass.

The deeper the snow, the harder it was on the horses. He pulled his hat down and concentrated on the road. But it was impossible to see much beyond the horses. He wasn't familiar with this territory and had to trust the animals' instincts.

She pushed the basket back under the seat and tried to see what lay ahead. "How far do you think we've come?"

"Not nearly as far as we would've on a clear day. I don't like this. We may have to stop and wait for the storm to move on." He spared a moment's glance at her. "I'm sorry about this, Emma."

She tried to smile at him but her face was too cold. "You're not to blame."

He chuckled. "Your brother'll have every right to beat my skull in for inviting you to come along with me." If she'd been his sister, he'd kill the son of a bitch who'd taken her.

"H-he may agree with you, but I don't see it that way. Besides, I'd hate to learn you were up here in the storm alone." She rubbed her hands together until she felt a bit of warmth, then did the same to her cheeks. "I don't know where we are. Is it level off to the side of the road?"

"There's one way to find out," he said, bringing the team to a halt. "I don't think we've gone through that pass Sourdough mentioned. And we need to know when we reach it."

"What are you doing?"

He handed the reins to her. "Hold on to these. I'm going to walk around." He slipped the edge of the blanket down, kissed her cold lips, and covered her mouth again with the blanket. Looking into her eyes to make sure she understood him, he said, "I won't be long."

He stepped down into the snow, tested the ground a few feet out from the wagon and did the same on the other side. "It's level here." He stomped his feet. "I'd feel better leading the horses."

"Here, you'll need this—" She grabbed the other blanket and handed it to him. "Please be careful." She held onto the reins, but he guided the team. She was so cold. She moved her feet so they wouldn't become too numb, but it wasn't enough. "Kent, stop the horses a moment. If I don't walk around, my feet will freeze."

He stopped and looked at her. She was pale and shivering badly; she needed to move around. "Okay." At least, he thought, they were heading away from the storm.

She climbed down and struggled with the first steps before her legs limbered up. She walked by the side of one of the horses with one hand on the animal. With no sun to mark the time, it didn't seem to pass. As she trudged through the snow, she pictured Kent's cabin—what was on the shelf, his clothes neatly folded—and she wondered what kind of meals he made for himself. The snow became deeper. Her cape and skirt dragged along the top, leaving her lower legs more exposed to the cold.

Kent figured they had come about a mile and there'd been no letup with the snow. How much longer could she continue? They had two choices—ride the horses on and hope they found their way down the mountain or camp out under the wagon until the weather cleared. "Emma, can you ride without a saddle?"

She knew he had said something, but she couldn't understand the words. "You'll have to shout. I didn't hear you."

He asked her again, still unsure which would be the best choice. One misstep could mean falling down the side of the hill. If he were alone he wouldn't think twice about riding out. But could he risk her being injured?

"I never tried."

He knocked the snow off his hat, went around the animals, and walked with his arm around her. "We could go on for hours and still not get out of this. Or we could ride the horses—but I can't see more'n five feet ahead. Or make a shelter under the wagon.''

''I—I don't think I can r-ride. But I'm not ready to stop yet.''

''All right, if you promise to let me know when you've had enough.''

''I w-will.'' She was afraid to stop, afraid she might not be able to move again. And it wasn't half as cold with him at her side. ''Aren't the snow-covered trees pretty?''

''Yes, but I'd rather be inside looking at them through a window.''

She nodded. ''When we get back, I'm going to build a huge fire in the parlor and sleep on the hearth.'' And if Bently wants to argue, he'll have to wait until I've thawed out. Or maybe she should have Mr. Jenks ask him to make another delivery up here, and she'd arrange for Lettie to go with him. Emma liked that idea and grinned.

All of a sudden she had the biggest smile on her face and it was catching. ''What're you thinkin'?''

''I shouldn't.'' But she wanted to tell him, and she did trust him. ''Lettie's had her cap set for my brother for almost a year, but he hardly pays her any attention.'' She glanced at him. ''It won't sound as funny aloud.'' She shrugged and continued. ''I was thinking that if Bently and Lettie were stuck together for a while like this he might realize he liked her.''

Kent laughed. That was some picture she'd drawn.

His laughter was deep, and for a moment, she forgot her stiff feet and legs. Then she heard a sound she couldn't identify. She pulled on his arm. ''Hear that?''

Instantly, he stopped in his tracks. Once heard, the sound of a snowslide isn't forgotten. He pushed her down, shoved her under the wagon, and rolled in beside her. And waited.

In less than a minute, she was huddled under the wagon, and her mind went blank. The thunderous sound went on and on, and grew louder and louder. Then it was silent. Eerie, unnatural—terrifying.

He ran his hand over her head and down her back. ''You okay?''

"Yes. What happened?" Her heart was still pounding, but they were safe.

"Snowslide. We can get out now." He crawled out and helped her to her feet. While he brushed off her clothes, he saw the rising cloud of snow caused by the slide. Damn, they'd been lucky.

"Are you sure it's stopped?" She stared down the road. If the snow had given way on top of them, she knew they would be dead.

He scrutinized the area. "I think we're safe here."

She dashed after him and held on to his arm. "You aren't going into that, are you?"

"Not me. We'll have to camp here. If the storm blows through while it's still light out, we'll ride the horses back to town. But I'm not chancing that till it clears up, and we can see where we're goin'."

"Can we start a fire?" The thought sounded ridiculous, but if she had known there might've been a danger of being stranded, they could have been better prepared. They had food, however, but could they keep warm?

"In a while."

"What about the horses? How'll they stay warm?"

He looked around. "I'll stake them under the trees, over there," he said, pointing to a sheltered spot. "The wind's not down to the ground there. Good place for the wagon, too. It's the best I can do." He led the team to the protected area and positioned the wagon with a bank of snow on one side.

She paced around chafing her hands and stomping her feet. It didn't seem to be snowing as hard, but they were hours away from town.

"I want to go through that crate Jenks packed. You'll be warmer if you put your arm over the horse's neck and rest your cheek on him." He climbed in the back of the wagon and started rummaging through Jenks's crate. "We're in luck," Kent called out. "Coffee and a pot, bread, a chunk of smoked venison, and a knife."

She walked back and looked over the side of the wagon. "We have three more sandwiches, beans, pickles, and butter cakes, too.'' She met his smiling gaze. ''Do we have matches?''

''They would make starting a fire easier.'' He set the goods on the bed of the wagon. When he picked up a clean rag, he saw the small tin, held it up for her to see and chuckled. ''Good thing he's a cautious man.''

She gathered wood, got a fire going, and put a pot of coffee on, while he tended the animals and packed snow around three sides of the wagon. After he told her they would sleep underneath, she couldn't think of anything else. She collected vines and branches from bushes, stripped the leaves to cushion the cold, hard ground. Sometime late in the afternoon it stopped snowing.

She kept busy until the fire was their only source of light. He had covered the horses with the canvas from the wagon. After she and Kent had eaten their fill, she sat in front of the fire watching him out of the corner of her eye. She was weary, and she was anxious about sleeping at his side. Most of the day she had clung to his side, supposedly for his warmth, but it was more. So much more. She had never felt so alive as when she was close to him. What if she put her arms around him in her sleep, responded to the feelings he stirred in her? She feared her reaction to his nearness—not him. Never him.

Kent yawned and stretched his arms. She'd been so fidgety he was surprised she'd finally sat down on the log. But no matter how hard she tried to appear alert, she wasn't fooling him. It was a wonder she hadn't fallen asleep before then, but he had a pretty good idea why. She'd already spread a blanket over the bed of leaves. He couldn't think of any more excuses to put off the inevitable.

He stood up and banked the fire. ''We'd better turn in now. Tomorrow won't be any easier than today,'' he said, holding her gaze, and reached out to take her hand. ''I plan to sleep the night through.'' Trust me, Emma, I wouldn't disgrace you. ''Emma?''

Oh, fiddlesticks. She had spent the last hour or so trying to think of a reason to stay up or a way to stay awake, but she hadn't come up with anything. ''Go on to bed.'' She glanced at her cup. "I want to finish my coffee, and I need to take a short walk." She made an attempt to smile but the way he looked at her had her belly fluttering. "I'll . . . turn in in a little while." She had come close to saying "come to bed" but that sounded much too close to what she really wanted to do.

He shook his head. The difficult part was not laughing. "I'll wait for you. You have to sleep on the inside." Her eyes were wide open now. "In case coyotes or a mountain lion come sniffin' around. Do what you have to. I'll meet you here." He watched her stand up and walk away as if she were on her way to the gallows. He'd give her about three minutes on that bed before she'd be sound asleep. He took a short walk in the other direction and returned to the fire.

She tended to her needs and went back to the wagon. Her willpower had never been tested as it would be that night. When she saw him standing by the fire with his hands in his coat pockets, she drew in a deep breath and joined him.

He took her hand and led her to the side of the wagon. "Once you lie down, make sure to pull your hood up and lie close to me. I'll put the blanket over both of us." He grinned. "It'll be warmer than you think. Go on now."

"I'm sure it will be." She dropped down to her knees and slid under the wagon and onto the blanket. "You'd better hold this side of the cover or I'll end up with it bunched under me."

He got down and anchored the blanket for her.

She stretched out on the far side, pulled the hood up over her head, and made sure the front of her cape was closed. "Okay. You can get in now." All of a sudden she didn't know what to do with the arm resting on her side. She never slept stiff as a board. She was in the habit of bending her knees and usually had her arm somewhere in front of her.

He set the rifle behind the wheel and within his reach. Her eyes were closed. Was she expecting him to strip before he crawled in with her? "Emma, take this," he said, handing the second cover to her. He rolled onto the blanket and stretched out just shy of the middle—she was barely on the other side. "Move closer. We have to share that blanket you're holding."

She scooted over, but she hadn't expected him to tuck the covers in around her back. He was gentle, but when his hands pressed against her bottom and slid down to her legs, the most wonderful sensations whirled around and through her. She thought he had to know what she was feeling and waited for him to ease her back and kiss her.

"Better?"

"Mm-hm." Oh, Lordy, yes. "What about you?"

"I'll be fine. I'm half asleep right now." He settled the hood over her cheeks. He'd thought about having her in his bed so many times, but he'd never quite pictured this. "Sleep tight, Emma." He leaned over and kissed her, then rolled over. He pressed his back to her and pulled the top blanket over him. "Warmer?"

"Oh— Yes." The sound of her pounding heart seemed to fill the small space. His kiss left her wanting more; her desires were unfulfilled. His backside was jammed against her and her arm—the darn thing still felt like an extra limb. She tried to get comfortable but her fingers kept brushing his coat or his trousers.

He felt sorry for her. Sleeping so close together had to be awkward for her. "Here," he said, putting her arm around his waist. "Better?" He curved his hand over hers and smiled as he closed his eyes. Now all he had to do was sleep.

"Mm—" Yes and no, she thought, stretched out next to him from shoulder to knee. She hadn't realized how bulky his coat was until then, but her hand was inside it, on the leather belt around his waist. She nestled her head against the back of his shoulder. He smelled of pine and smoke and something she could not place, but it was wonderful. She had wanted to spend the day with him so she would always have the memories of what love could have been like. This, however, was more than she had hoped for, or even allowed herself to imagine. A giggle bubbled up, but she refused to give in to it. She'd never be able to explain it to him this time.

He'd actually started to rest when he felt the unmistakable

shake of laughter. There were so many layers of clothing separating their bodies, he hadn't thought he would feel the shape of her body. He was wrong. With each breath she took, her breasts gently pressed on his back and every so often she'd move her hips against him. His body responded. He wanted to make love to her. He wasn't going to, but that didn't lessen his need for her.

He forced his thoughts in a different direction. Think about tomorrow. About facing the town. That did it. Now he would sleep.

Sometime during the night, he awakened. A coyote howled but that wasn't what woke him up. No. It was the small hand exploring his chest, the thighs molded to his, and the garbled murmuring at the back of his neck. She was asleep but his body answered her tender seduction. He groaned and shifted his position slightly.

She didn't want to wake up, but she wasn't asleep, either. He moved his leg, and she realized she had slipped her fingers under his belt. Her eyes opened wide. It wasn't a dream. She stared at the back of his head, uneasy about waking him if she moved her hand. Please be asleep, she thought. It was black as pitch but his handsome face was so ingrained in her memory she didn't need to see him.

If only she didn't feel so restless, she could doze off again.

❖ 18 ❖

As she lay there, she wished he would turn over, take her in his arms and make love to her. She thanked God she had no memory of the attack that left her ruined beyond repair. Losing her virginity was a heavy price to pay for a sin she hadn't committed.

She didn't believe it was wrong to want one night of love with the only man she trusted and had come to love. She smiled and listened to his breathing. She knew what she wanted, but she wasn't sure if he felt the same way about her. He had been right about it being warm in the space under the wagon. In fact, she dearly wanted to shed her cape.

She snuggled against him, drew her knee over his legs, and skimmed her hand over the soft fabric of his shirt. She lowered her hand to his waist. As she fingered the smooth leather of his belt, her palm rubbed the hard ridge in his pants.

He mumbled and brushed at her hand, hoping to end the agonizing temptation, but her hand stayed put. That confirmed his suspicions. She was awake. And playing with fire. He slipped his hand under hers and said, ''That's a dangerous way to wake a man, Emma,'' as he dragged the hand up to his chest.

"Oh, did I hurt you? I didn't meant to. I—" She looked at him, though it was too dark to see. Since she had never done this before, she wasn't sure if she should blurt out what she had in mind, or not.

"Not in the way— No. Can't sleep?" He had slept off and on, but it was impossible with her hand roaming over his body, arousing him after he'd finally put his physical needs aside.

"I just woke up a little while ago. I'd been dreaming . . . about you—" This is my chance to tell him, she thought, touching the ends of his beard. "Lying here with you, like this, I don't want to sleep." She slid her hand up to his chin and traced his lips with her finger. "I can do that every night."

He kissed her finger and gently pushed her hand back to his chest. "You have to stop or I'll have to spend the rest of the night with the horses. I care too much for you to take advantage of this situation." Oh, how I want to, he thought. But in making love to her, he would be committing himself to her, as surely as vows spoken in front of a preacher. And he wasn't ready to take that step, not yet.

She smiled, her heart racing. Leaning over, she nudged him onto his back and kissed him. His lips were warm and soft, and his beard tickled her neck. When he put his hand on her shoulder, she brushed her chest over his, and it felt as if her body had just come alive.

One kiss. Surely he could enjoy one before he had to be responsible and stop this. He lay as still as he could with her sweet mouth on his, her tongue exploring, arousing, and demanding his response. When she rubbed her breasts on his chest, he wrapped his arms around her, stilling her movements. "We have to stop. I promised myself I'd protect you. I've been doing a fair job of it so far." He ran his fingers through her hair. "You'll be sorry if you don't wait. Your husband should be the one to teach you about love."

An icy wave of regret swept down her spine. She shivered, but she refused to be distracted by her doubts. "Is it because I'm damaged goods?"

"No! You're *not*— You're the most kindhearted, loving

woman I've ever known. Any man'd be proud to have you for his wife.''

Does that include you? she wanted to ask, but it really wouldn't make any difference. She had made that decision years ago. "I'm not getting married. But I want you to show me what it's like to make love." She laid her cheek over his heart and felt the steady beat. It pounded as fast as hers, creating a strange rhythm her body understood and responded to. "I've never . . . even my skin feels different, more sensitive . . . so aware of the texture of your lips when we kiss. Can't you feel it?"

"Oh, yes. It'd be hard to miss." And I'm not dead, yet. "But you can't do everythin' that feels good." Though God knows, he thought, I haven't always abided by that, either.

She was no good at games and wouldn't start playing any now. She might as well ask and find out once and for all. "Don't you want to make love to me?" His breath fanned her good ear. At least she'd given him something to think about. While she waited, she settled more comfortably with her hips over his. A shower of tantalizing sensations rippled in widening circles. She shifted her weight and increased the tension.

If he could only see her face, he'd know if she heard everything he was saying, and he'd be able to see how she was taking it all in. "Yes. I want to make love to you. But you're a lady, Emma, and I'm trying my best to remember that." This was a first for him. Did that mean he was already committed to her? He'd lay down his life for her, defend her honor with his last breath, and he'd been thinking about offering to manage the office Wendell would likely open in town. That was closer to being bound to someone than he'd ever been before.

"Don't ladies make love?"

Oh, Emma, he thought, don't make this so difficult for us. "Of course they do—with their husbands." But not always. However, he wasn't about to add that. It would only spur her on. Belatedly, he realized she was lying on top of him, and she was sliding her hips over his. Against his will, he couldn't deny his unmistakable desire for her.

"What if they never marry?" She couldn't be still. Something stirred inside that wouldn't be ignored. The slightest movement, the briefest thought increased her need for him.

"That's why they're old maids." He wasn't making much sense but the whole conversation was outrageous. The last thing he wanted to do was talk, but she had no idea how appealing she was to him.

She braced an elbow on either side of his chest and stared at him. "I can never be an old maid, and I'll never be a wife." She thought a moment and said the first thing that popped into her mind. "I don't think I'd like being a fancy woman."

"What?" He rolled over, putting her on her side, and sat up—until he rammed his head into the bed of the wagon overhead. Even that didn't ease his hunger for her.

"Here." She placed her hand on his forehead. "When you said you cared for me, I thought—hoped—you felt what I do."

Her hand was cool but it was inspiring definitely heated desires. "Emma, you've offered me the highest compliment a woman can give to a man. If you're feeling half of what I am, that's why you're doing this. It's the most natural thing in the world, but one of us has to be—"

She put her hand over his mouth. "Sh— I want you to kiss me the way you did yesterday, and I want to feel you inside me." She hadn't thought she could be so outspoken, but it felt right. Maybe the darkness brought out this streak of boldness in her. "And I believe I'll need your cooperation."

"Why're you being so stubborn about this? You'll be sorry tomorrow. You will." And I'll want you even more than I do right now, he thought.

She lowered her hand to his knee and slowly moved upward. "If I do, I'd never blame you. Lordy, look at the trouble I'm having trying to convince you that I need *you*. Tonight."

He pulled her hand away from his privates. No woman had ever meant as much to him as she did, and he'd never refused a pretty woman's comfort before. But she wasn't *any woman*, he admitted. Hadn't he been courting her, after a fashion? The thought of another man touching her chilled him to the bone. God help him, and her, he wanted to be the one to show her the wonders between a man and woman.

"Oh, Em—" He covered her mouth with his and parted her lips with his tongue. She was so sweet. He felt as if she held his heart in her small hands—with her, it would be safe. He stretched out on his side in front of her. He still hadn't convinced himself he had the right to her affections. Besides, this was a hell of a place to make love for the first time.

She put one arm around his waist and rolled onto her back. She felt his kiss all the way down to her toes. Her breasts ached for his touch and her need for him grew stronger by the moment. She pulled the sides of his coat from between their bodies and did the same with her cape. That was so much better. Holding him close, she let one hand drift down to his pants. When she pressed on his backside, his hips seemed to leap to hers, and she felt an emptiness inside only he could fill.

As he trailed kisses over her cheek and down her neck, he worked the buttons free on the front of her dress and skimmed his lips along her satiny flesh at the edge of her chemise. With more haste than he'd planned, he parted the shimmy and stroked her full breasts. If only he could see the body that felt so perfect and was driving him beyond reason. But as he mapped her curves, he formed a clear image of her in his mind.

She fumbled with his belt, the buttons on his pants, and yanked his shirt up so she could run her hands over his back. Each time a new feeling washed over her, another replaced it. Wherever he touched her, her skin tingled and yearned for more. She rolled her hips, wanting to get even closer to him and the evidence of his desire. Then he leaned back from her and drew her skirts up. When he lay down on her, his hot skin rubbed against hers and sent a new, consuming swell of longing through the very core of her. She swayed her hips over his throbbing member and felt light-headed from the pure pleasure of his touch.

As he entered her, his mouth covered hers, and he buried

himself deep within her heated body. There was a moment of tightness, but he drove through it before it registered in his hazy brain. Had she gasped from pain? He held completely still. "Emma— Did I hurt you?"

"Oh, no." He filled her completely and her body molded around him. Wasn't that normal? She rocked her hips, saying, "Don't stop. Please don't." She pulled his head down and greedily pressed her parted lips to his. Never had she known such a hunger to be touched and loved existed, and some part of her wondered if it was possible to ever satisfy this need. He filled her and yet she knew there was more, something her body instinctively sought. She met each thrust and welcomed the next.

Although he'd hesitated, she held on to him, and he had never felt such overpowering love and acceptance. He'd thought he was going to show her the wonders of passion, but it was she who'd shown him the kind of love he'd heard about and only had seen a few times in others. He savored her awakening passion and the awareness that she cared for him. He waited for her shuddering climax and gave in to his own. It was as if this were his first time—and maybe it was. If this was love, the others had not been.

She gulped in the cool air as the aftermath of their passion slowly rippled through her belly. She kissed his neck and tightened her arms around his back. "Is it always this wonderful?"

He dragged his parted lips over her cheek and kissed her chin. "No. This was very special, and so are you." He had the feeling that every time would be special with her because of her ability to love with such trust.

"Oh, I feel sorry for maiden ladies." She snuggled against him. "I don't want to move. Can we sleep this way?"

"The ground's too cold and hard." He covered her lips with his one more time, shifted his weight to her side and pulled the blanket over her. "I'll be right back."

He'd tried to ignore it, but he couldn't forget that tightness he had felt when he'd first entered her. He would've sworn she'd been a virgin, but that couldn't be, not if she had been violated by that trapper. He took a napkin from the basket, dampened it, held it until his hands had taken the chill off and crawled back under the wagon.

He bathed her private parts, folded the linen and put it in his pocket. If his suspicion was right, he'd have to tell her. And then what? They'd have a lot to talk over.

He pushed her skirts back down over her legs and spread the blanket over both of them. "You'll be warmer if you put your back against my chest."

"I was warm before."

"Now it's my turn to curl up around you." When she'd settled against him, he fit his arm around her waist and closed his eyes.

A couple of hours later when Emma woke up, Kent left the shelter of the wagon with her. After he rekindled the fire, he took the napkin out of his pocket and unfolded it. Blood. Not much, but unmistakably blood. Dammit! How could that be? He tucked the linen in his pocket and checked on the horses. He sure as hell wasn't looking forward to telling her. But she deserved to know the truth. Somebody had lied to her or made an awful mistake.

After a heavenly good morning kiss, Emma started fixing breakfast. The sun hadn't been up long, but it was going to be a beautiful day. It was already much warmer than yesterday afternoon and the snow was melting. The pass they couldn't see the day before didn't appear as frightening in the light of day, but Kent would have to return in a few days for the wagon. By the time she had heated slices of venison, the coffee was ready, and she had set out bread and the beans.

She filled their cups with coffee and watched him. He was using a stout piece of wood to knock the snows away from the wagon wheels. "I thought we were going to ride the horses back to town." She handed one cup to him.

"We are. But I want to move the wagon under the trees." He took a sip and smiled at her. She was so happy, but he couldn't put off telling her much longer. "What're we havin' to eat?"

She picked up his plate and handed it to him. "We'll have sandwiches for dinner, and the butter cakes."

He chuckled. "Sounds good. And one way or the other, you'll be home for supper." He thought that would make her happier. But her smile slipped from her pretty face, and she nodded. "Aren't you eating?"

"Mm-hm." She put a slice of meat on bread, folded it and took a bite. She wasn't nearly as eager to return as he seemed to think she would be. Explaining why she had gone with him to her brother wasn't going to be pleasant, but after last night, she felt she could do just about anything.

"These beans're good."

"Glad you like them." She ate another bite.

He set his plate on the log and sipped the coffee. His stomach was knotted up and wouldn't get any better till they talked it out. "How're you feelin' this mornin'? About last night?"

She grinned at him. "Can't you tell? I've *never* felt better." She gazed into his eyes. "You aren't sorry, are you? I'm not."

"I didn't do anythin' I didn't want to." He wrapped his arms around her and combed his fingers through her hair. "You're wonderful—" He pressed a kiss to her head. "But we need to talk about something."

She nodded. "By the time we get back everyone will know we were gone overnight."

"There's that, too."

She leaned and looked at him. "What else is there? What's wrong?"

He continued holding her within the circle of his arms. "Emma, how did you find out you'd been assaulted?"

She frowned. "Bently."

Just what he feared. "Was there a doctor? Or did the women help you?" The color drained from her face, and he didn't think he'd ever hurt anyone more than he'd just hurt her. But he'd see her through it.

She shook her head. "He found me and carried me back to the wagons. My ear was bleeding—my skirt was torn . . .

He had to wake me up." She swallowed. "Just tell me what's wrong. You're scaring me."

"You weren't violated, Emma." He showed her the napkin. "When we made love . . . it was your first time. If that man had violated you, there wouldn't've been any blood after we made love." A tremor shook her, and he tightened his hold on her. God, this was tearing him up inside.

"Why would he say it if it hadn't happened?" It didn't make sense, but she was holding the proof in her hand. "He's been so good to me. I can't believe he'd be so cruel."

He raised her chin with his finger and kissed her. He'd meant to comfort her, but she put her arms around his neck and melted into him. As the caress deepened, he realized how very much he loved her. No matter what happened when they got back, they'd weather it together.

She stood on tiptoe and welcomed the intimacy. Slowly, she understood what he had really told her, and rained kisses over his face. "You were the first . . . Do you know how happy that makes me? And last night was all the more special."

"I sure do." He smiled and swung her around. "I'm so glad you're not angry." He kissed her again and set her on her feet. "You know what that means, don't you?" The smile slipped from her eyes and face.

"Bently has much to explain."

"He sure does." He wanted to hold her close to him, but she needed to hear him. "We'll face this together. I won't leave you to tell your brother alone."

"Thank you." She couldn't begin to tell him how grateful she was that he hadn't insisted they marry. That would have crushed her and her glorious memories. "I'm not sure I will tell him. I'll decide later, but you have nothing to face. Aren't you hungry?"

"I'm starved. Any more meat left? I'll take one of those butter cakes, too."

She started laughing. "Anything you want." Oh, she was angry, but not with him—with her brother.

They finished eating and packed up the few things they had with them. When the horses were ready, he looked over at her. "You're sure you want to ride astride?"

She grinned at him. "It would be more fun sitting sideways in front of you, but we might never get back." She studied the snow in the pass. "Can we get through that?"

"I'll try it first. If we can't lead the horses through, we'll go around." He picked up his hat and a long branch he'd broken from a tree. "Wait here."

"Don't take any chances. I'm not sure if I could dig you out."

He brushed his lips across hers. "I'll be back."

She watched him make his way up the snowslide, poking a branch into the snow before taking each step. With her skirt and cape pulled to one side and tossed over her arm, she paced back and forth across the slushy road. Fortunately, he wasn't gone long at all.

"We can't go that way." He stared at the trees on the south side of the pass. "We'll try goin' around, through those trees. Looks like there's a gully on the other side of the pass. Are you ready to leave?"

She walked over to the horses. "Give me a hand up?"

"Better than that." He grabbed her by the waist, lifted her to his height, gave her a quick kiss, and set her on the horse's back. "Think you can stay on him?"

"I'm going to try." She straightened her skirts and wrapped the cape close around her. "Lead the way." The first half hour was the hardest, then she became more confident and enjoyed the ride. They circled around and found the road some distance from the pass. He set a good pace. They stopped to eat at midday and rode out of the mountains a couple of hours later. She smelled the tangy scent of the ocean. They were almost home.

When Pelican Cove was in sight, he looked over at her as he'd done so often in the last few hours. "Are you all right?"

"I'm fine. Everything will be."

"We'll go straight to your house. Afterward, I'll see Jenks and take the horses back to the livery."

She nodded. After she talked with her brother, she would go to the shop. Lettie must be frantic, Emma thought. They stayed on the bay road. She was relieved that no one was in front of the hotel. When they arrived at her house, she hurried inside. The house was empty. "You might as well go talk to Mr. Jenks. I'll see you later."

"I'm not leaving you alone to defend yourself." He held out his arm.

She slipped hers around him. "Okay. Let's try the shop. Maybe Bently's there with Lettie." When he arched one dark brown brow, she gave him a wry grin. "I can hope, can't I?"

He shook his head. The next hour could be interesting. He kept pace with her until they reached her shop. He took her reins and tied both to the post.

She put her hand over his. "You don't need to come in with me." She glanced at the door, shoved her hand into her skirt pocket and felt the soiled napkin. She was ready to face her brother.

"I'll just pay my respects," he said, tucked her hand in the crook of his arm and walked her up to the door.

She didn't argue. He opened the door, and she stepped inside. Lettie cried out. Her brother scowled, and Lydia smiled. Emma looked up at Kent. "We only have to explain it once."

Lydia went over to Emma and hugged her. "We're so glad you're back safe and sound."

Kent held Bently's attention and hoped the man understood that Emma was under his protection. Kent took off his hat, nodded to Lettie, and looked back to Mrs. Nance. "We haven't had a warm drink since mornin'. I'm sure Miss Emma would like some tea."

"I agree, Mr. Hogarth. I think all of us could use a drink." Lydia gave him a still smile. "You two sit down at the table."

Lettie pulled two chairs out for them. "I'll put the coffee on." She held her arms out and embraced Emma. "I'm so glad you're okay." She sniffed and brushed at the sudden tears that had sprung to her eyes. "You certainly have given me a few scares lately."

Emma grinned. "Was my brother any comfort?"

Lettie nodded. "He's been wonderful. I don't know what I would've done without his support."

"I'm glad." At least someone appreciates him, Emma thought.

Kent slipped Emma's cape off and held the chair for her. He put his coat and her cape over the back of the chair next to hers and sat down. He looked across the table at her brother. "Townsend, have you talked to Charlie Jenks?"

Bently glared at him, grinding his teeth. "He said you were making a delivery for him, but he didn't know you'd taken Emma with you."

Kent nodded. "This'll be easier if we explain it to all of you at the same time."

Bently leaned over to Emma's right side. "Don't say any more than you must to make them believe your story. When we return home, you'll damn well tell me what really happened!"

He'd spoken just loud enough for her to hear him. Emma stared him in the eye and replied just as softly. "I want to put Lettie's and Lydia's minds at ease, then *we will* talk, Bently."

❖ *19* ❖

B<small>Y THE TIME</small> Bently, Kent, and Emma left the shop, Lettie and Lydia understood what had happened. Emma knew better than to expect her brother to believe even part of what she'd said. However, she hadn't finished with him yet. She opened the front door of the house and went straight into the parlor and started a fire in the fireplace.

After he followed Bently into the house, Kent closed the door. Emma was holding her own. In fact, she seemed even calmer now that she was home. He took a chair by a window facing the ocean, leaned back, set his hat on his knee and waited. Townsend's face had been growing redder by the minute all the way to the house. When Bently stopped at a cabinet and carelessly poured himself a glass of whisky, Kent sat up in his chair. Liquor and flaring tempers were a bad mix.

Bently gulped the whisky, slammed the glass down on the cabinet, and turned to face Kent. "Now tell me exactly what did happen. And don't expect me to believe you slept with the horses or in the snow!"

"You already know. Whether you choose to believe is up to you. Emma's *your* sister. Why're you so primed to believe the worst about her?"

Roaring, "You lying bastard!" Bently charged across the room and lunged at Kent.

Kent heard Emma scream at the same time his fist connected with Bently's rock-hard jaw. Kent shook his hand. "Damn—"

Emma looked at her brother and snatched Kent's hat off the floor. "Please leave now. I can handle him."

Kent shook his head. "Not all liquored up you can't."

"If you go, he'll be fine." She pushed the hat at his hand. "Please, Kent. What I need to say to him should be in private. I'll talk to you soon."

He held her in his arms and pressed a kiss to her temple, then released her. "I'll see you tomorrow for sure. If you need me, I'll be at the cabin after I return the horses."

She nodded and noticed that her brother was coming to. She tugged on Kent's hand. "Please—" This wasn't the way she wanted to part from him, but under the circumstances, it was the best. She hurried to the door and opened it for him. "Don't worry." She loved him so very much, but she would have to be very careful not to let it show. Kent left, and she eased the door closed behind him.

Bently got to his knees and shook his head.

When he managed to stand up, Emma dampened a cloth and handed it to him. "Do you want to talk now?" Seeing her brother like that was disheartening, and his defense of her honor felt more like condemnation. However, this time she could defend herself.

Bently lowered himself onto the chair. After he rubbed the cloth over his face, he slumped forward with his forearms on his knees. "What's happened to you, Emma? First you end up with the Indians and Hogarth rescues you, then you take off into the hills with him and spend the night." He lowered the cloth and stared at her. "Before he came, you were most biddable, considerate of your reputation."

"And now I'm not?" she asked softly.

"It sure as hell don't look like it."

She drew her right hand into a fist crushing her skirt. "It was snowing—so hard we couldn't see five feet ahead of the horses. We just barely missed being buried under a snowslide. What should I have done? Thrown myself down a ravine? But I thought only virgins were sacrificed."

"Contempt and vulgar language don't suit you." He stood up and stepped over to the window. "Start at the beginning. Why did you go away with him? Did you think I wouldn't find out?"

She started pacing. "Mr. Hogarth's an interesting man. He's thoughtful and kind. I wanted to keep him company. We would've returned by late afternoon, if not for the snowstorm." She turned on her heel. "What've you been doing while I was gone? Did you see Lettie last evening? Have supper with her? Ride around with her searching for me? Did you ease her fears?" She already knew the answer, but he needed to think about the questions.

"How dare you question me! Or Lettie's or my integrity. You're the one who spent the night with that scoundrel!"

Good for Lettie, Emma thought. "Would you rather I froze to death?"

"Dammit, Emma. Just tell me—did he have his way with you?"

Knowing he had lied about her virginity, she came close to hating her brother, and that enraged her as much as his lies. She straightened a candle. "What do you mean?" She wanted him to say the words aloud before she asked him what she needed to know. A gull screeched, echoing her despair.

"You want to hear the word, fine. Assault. Did he ruin you? Or did you—"

"*Ruin?* You tell me—*now,*" she demanded, too infuriated to speak reasonably, "about my assault seven years ago, Bently. It was so embarrassing for you. But you protected me, didn't you? Tell me now!" He stared at her with his look that usually softened her, but she met and matched his anger.

"How did . . . Are you still a virgin?"

Without flinching, she said, "I might be, if I'd known I was. But you convinced me I'd lost my virginity." She had increased her pace, almost running up and down the length of the room, when she stopped in front of him. "How could

I lose it a second time?'' She spun around and resumed her stride.

"Oh, my God. You've been uneasy around men, kept your distance from them. Why now?"

As if she didn't hear him, she continued. "I didn't see it before. But you've done your best to feed my fear of men." She stared blindly out the window shaking her head. "I don't understand *why* you wanted to ruin my life. I believed you, Bently, believed I was soiled. I believed no decent man would marry me. I was damaged goods.'' She glared at him with all the contempt she felt. "You did that to me."

"You have the shop. It's what you wanted."

"It was a *lie*! The last seven years of my life have been a lie.'' Suddenly, she felt very weary and dropped down to the hearth. "I'm your sister. Do you hate me so much?"

"Oh, God, Emma, no." He went over to the cabinet, opened a drawer, and took out a pipe. He turned around and held it out for her to see. "This was Papa's. Remember?"

She bit her lips, her eyes filling with tears, and nodded.

"He was dying, when he made me promise to take care of you . . . keep you *safe*."

"You didn't tell me." She could hear their father's gravelly voice.

He fingered the old pipe and closed his fingers over the bowl. "I didn't—keep you safe—though, did I?"

"It wasn't your fault or mine." It hadn't been fair of their father to put such a burden on a young man—any more than the one Bently had placed on her. "I still don't understand why you wanted me to believe I was a fallen woman. Did you realize that made me afraid of everyone? The first time a woman smiled at me, I cringed."

"No, I didn't think about what you were going through." He returned the pipe to the drawer. "I thought if you didn't trust men, you would keep your distance from them and you'd be safe. I wasn't blind—men leered at you, and I overheard some boys talking about you."

Fresh tears washed down her cheeks, and she dried them with the hem of her skirt. "I was collecting fuel for the fire that day. It was so hard to find." She could almost remember the smell of the dry grass— "I didn't know he was there until he grabbed me." The rest of that day was better locked away in the back of her mind.

"I shouldn't've let you leave camp alone."

"I wish you would've talked to me about it. Being attacked was terrifying. Losing my dignity, my dreams, made it so much worse." It made more sense now, she thought, but that didn't make it right.

"No one knows what happened, Emma. I kept my promise. Never told anyone. And everybody here respects you. I thought you were happy."

"I have been. But your lie stole my dreams away from me. I couldn't hope to fall in love, marry, and raise a family. No man wants damaged goods." She watched him until he looked at her. "Would you?"

He shrugged, then shook his head. "But *no one knows*."

"I do." She was too exhausted to get angry again, but she felt it building up. "Don't you think my husband would've found out on our wedding night?"

"But you'd be married. He'd come around." He walked over to her and stood there looking down at her. "You'll be married. Hogarth *will* do his duty. He has no choice."

"You can't make me marry him!" she said, jumping to her feet, and came up nearly nose to nose with him. "If I *ever* marry, it will be *my* decision. Stay out of it, Bently."

"But he—"

"*Don't* say any more about it." She walked away from him.

"Well, of course I can understand why you don't want to marry him. We'll move. It'll take me a while to settle up here, but we'll leave as soon as I can arrange it."

"What is wrong with you? I *do not want to marry. And I will not move away.* Just forget about this." She left him standing in the middle of the parlor looking completely confused, and went into the kitchen. If Lettie wanted him, Emma prayed her friend would have every success.

The next morning Emma went to the shop as usual. She dusted and rearranged the display on the wardrobe. All the while she kept wondering if anyone would really believe the story she told about her night with Kent. No matter what might be said, it would remain a cherished memory. She felt no guilt, no regret, only a sadness about what might have been. And she'd not spend what remained of her life thinking "if only."

She opened the bottom drawer where they stored fabric. After searching through the folded yard goods, she found the wine-red muslin. There were two pieces, one a remnant. She took that one out, closed the drawer, and showed the cloth to Lettie. "Think this will make a pretty bonnet? It'll brighten up the display in the window. I've been so distracted, I nearly forgot about Christmas."

"I've always liked that fabric. What kind of bonnet do you have in mind?"

"Remember the old straw bonnet with the deep brim?"

Lettie frowned. "The one the dog ran off with?"

"That's the one. I put it away. I thought it'd come in handy sometime." Emma draped the material over her arm and held it up to the light. "This should be enough to line the underside of the brim with ruching and maybe even a puffy crown."

"There should be a matching piece of mousseline de soie." Lettie looked in a small drawer and brought out the fine cloth. "Here it is." She glanced at the bay window. "Didn't we find some holly bushes in the woods last year?"

"Mm-hm. Not far behind the old cabin." The one Kent's staying in, but Emma didn't need to add that. She pleated the muslin with her fingers and wondered what he was doing. If he came by the shop late in the afternoon, it wouldn't seem any different from all the other days he had stopped to walk her home. A delicious ripple floated down her back, and she smiled.

"I'll take a walk later and cut some branches for the window. And we saved the red ribbon from last year."

Without thinking, Emma said, "You shouldn't go alone." Giving advice was much easier than following it, she realized. "Why don't you ask Bently to go with you?" She noticed the gleam in Lettie's eyes. At last.

"Maybe I will. He said he'd stop by here today." Lettie stepped over to the table and laid the sheer fabric over one side of the muslin. "Perfect."

"It is. Glad you thought of it." Emma glanced at the wardrobe. "I put the silk emerald-green shirtwaist in one of the drawers. That would look nice in the window, too."

Lettie nodded. "Are you going to put up a tree?"

"If Bently cuts one down . . ." As Emma folded the muslin, she glanced through her lashes at Lettie. "How about you?" Emma went to the wardrobe and found the silk shirtwaist.

"Maybe a small tree."

Emma stepped over to the bay window, deciding where to put the blouse. "I've been out of the shop so much I feel a bit guilty. Why don't you go with Bently to pick out a couple of trees? You might even be able to talk him into cutting down some mistletoe from one of the old oak trees."

Lettie held up the sheer remnant of mousseline de soie and peered through it. "I think I will ask him."

"When were you expecting him?"

Lettie shrugged. "I'm not sure."

Emma slipped the sheer wine-red material from Lettie's fingers. "I don't believe we have thread this shade here at the shop." Grinning, she handed it back to Lettie. "Since you were going to take a walk, would you stop by the house and look in my sewing box for some?"

Lettie chuckled. "I wouldn't mind at all." The brass bell rang, and Franklin Simms came inside. "Hello, Mr. Simms."

"Miss Morrissey, Miss Townsend. I hope you can help me choose a gift for Mrs. Simms."

Emma dropped the muslin and smiled at him. "We would be happy to, Mr. Simms. What did you have in mind?"

He looked around the shop. "I thought you might know what she's had her eye on. You have so many nice things."

Lettie glanced around at the various items displayed around the shop. "I remember—" She went over to the wardrobe and picked up the white flannel petticoat trimmed with red ribbon. "She admired this, Mr. Simms. Emma, can you think of anything else?"

Emma picked up the carved ivory fan. "She might like this, but I believe the petticoat is best."

Mr. Simms nodded. "Would you wrap it for me? I don't want her to see it before Christmas."

"It won't take me long." Lettie folded the full, ankle-length petticoat, wrapped it in a remnant of green calico and tied it with gold-colored ribbon.

"That is lovely, Miss Morrissey." Mr. Simms paid for the gift and put it under his arm. "Thank you, and Merry Christmas, both of you."

"You, too, Mr. Simms." Emma grinned at Lettie. "I wish more husbands would ask our help. Now, I'd better find that straw bonnet." She walked back to the kitchen and paused. "If you're still going to see Bently, don't forget to take a basket for the holly branches and mistletoe." The way Lettie beamed at the mention of Bently, Emma believed they only needed a little nudge. The best of luck, she thought, and glanced out the window. Maybe it would rain and they'd have to take refuge in a cave or under a thick stand of trees.

Kent worked with Ross on the ferry all morning. When the sun was overhead, they stopped. Kent rinsed his hands and face with river water and combed his hair back with his fingers. "I'm goin' by the general store. You need anything?"

"No. We've done about all we can now." Ross covered the tools with the canvas. "I'll be helpin' Kirby. We'll be puttin' up the new walls for the dining room and kitchen. Or tryin' to."

"Need another hand?" Kent intended to see Emma, but he didn't want to hang around her shop all afternoon. And he felt sure she wouldn't be able to leave for very long. But maybe they could take a short walk.

"Sure. Kirby and Mrs. Lewis're real anxious to get those rooms finished."

Kent chuckled. "I'm glad she's doin' so well after the shipwreck. I don't mind admitting I was concerned when she didn't leave her room those first days."

Ross nodded. "I only saw her onboard a couple of times."

"Being on that ship was something." Kent pulled his jacket on. "Think you'll miss sailing?"

Ross stared toward the ocean. "Mebe. But Kirby an' me were talkin' 'bout givin' it up an' goin' into business t'gether." He looked at Kent. "This seemed to be the right time."

"Well, you both have your own businesses. Now you might want to claim some land—a parcel on each side of the river and one big enough for a cabin—before someone comes along and starts selling parcels." Kent walked into town with Ross and stopped at the corner by the hotel. "I'll be over in a while."

Ross waved and kept on walking. "Anytime. We'll be there."

Kent saw Jenks sitting out in front of his store and stopped. "How're you doin' today?"

"Can't complain. Have ya thawed out yet?"

"Yep. Built the damnedest fire that ol' cabin ever saw." He chuckled. "Half expected you to charge in leadin' the fire brigade."

"Good." Jenks looked off in the distance. "Townsend stopped by earlier."

Kent rested his foot on the edge of the board walk, wondering what Jenks was getting at. "He lookin' for me?"

Jenks shook his head, then grinned. "Jist paid his account 'n eyed a few gewgaws. Mebe he'll get more'n one this year."

Kent had no idea what Jenks was talking about. "Is Miss Emma havin' a birthday?"

Jenks laughed. "Ya fergit 'bout Christmas?"

"Already?" Kent couldn't believe it. Had that much time passed? "Thanks for warning me." What with Thanksgiving and the snowstorm, he should've known. But his mind had been on Emma, and the nights hadn't been cold enough to feel like wintertime. He lowered his foot. "The snow should be melted in the next couple of days, and I'll go back for the wagon."

"That'll be fine. Sure didn't 'spect it s'early."

Kent laughed. "Neither did I."

He went around the corner to Emma's shop. When he opened the door, something smelled good, but he didn't see anyone. "Miss Emma? Miss Morrissey?" There was a half-finished bonnet lying on the table. Somebody must be there.

He walked through the shop to the kitchen and heard someone coming. When she came into the room, he relieved her of the bucket of water she was carrying. "Hi. Where is everyone?" She looked wonderful. He'd been worried she might have a change of heart once she was home and had time to think over what had happened. Seeing the gleam in her eyes, he didn't believe she had.

Emma hadn't expected him. The sight of him made her heart beat faster. "Lettie's out with my brother. They're looking for trees to decorate for Christmas. They might even bring back holly and mistletoe, too." She grinned at him. "Think they'll get caught by a sudden storm?"

He laughed. She seemed to be feeling fine and the way she looked at him roused thoughts of them spending a whole night together in his cabin, sleeping on his bed instead of on the ground. But he couldn't help wondering how she'd managed with Bently the night before.

"I was about to have some soup." She set the coffeepot out and reached for the crock of coffee beans. "Would you like to stay? I'll share with you."

"Smells good. I'll chance it." He glanced around again. "Where's Mrs. Nance?"

"Visiting with Mrs. Lewis." She ground a scoop of coffee beans and started a pot of coffee.

Watching her was pure pleasure. Her hands were fine boned, delicate, but they'd felt surprisingly strong the other morning when she explored his body. "We're alone?"

"Mm-hm." As she gazed at him, she noticed a tiny gold fleck in his left eye. She remembered picturing his brown eyes before they made love in the dark. A delicious trickling sensation slithered down her spine and below her belly.

He tossed his hat aside and wrapped his arms around her. "You're awfully pretty today. Did you sleep well last night?"

"Yes." But I was alone, she thought.

He lifted her up and covered her parted lips with his. She molded herself to him, and he realized he would want more each time they kissed. And he couldn't allow that to happen. Not again. He set her down and pressed one more kiss to her forehead. "Now I'm really hungry."

So am I. "It's ready," she said, turning to the stove. His kiss convinced her he had more than one reason for calling on her. She knew what the other one was.

He picked up his hat and set it on a small table by the window. "Where're the bowls?"

"In that cupboard," she said, pointing with the spoon she'd used to stir the soup. She set out the flatware and a cutting board with a knife and a fresh loaf of bread.

He put two bowls on the table. As he searched for a cup, he said, "What'd your brother have to say after I left?"

She stirred the beef soup one last time. "He had spent a good part of his anger on you. After another outburst, he calmed down."

She'd already told him about the attack, so he was puzzled when she appeared to be more interested in the soup than in telling him. "He didn't hit you, did he?"

"No!" She whirled around and shook her head to emphasize her claim. "The more we talked, the better he was." She ladled soup into the bowls and put them on the table. "Sit down, please."

"Yes, ma'am," he said, hoping it would encourage her to continue.

She sliced several pieces of bread and sat down across the table from him. She would be able to hear him, and she needed to see his full face. "I was the one who lost my temper." She pushed the cutting board between them. She might as well just say it, but she wasn't going to share every detail. "I kept asking him why he lied to me, and he finally admitted he'd done it to protect me."

Kent held the spoon over the soup. "That's a hell of a way." The better he got to know her brother, the lower his opinion was of the man.

"I didn't say it that way, but he understood." She lowered her gaze to her bowl. "Believe me, I told him how his lie had made me feel.'' And, she decided, she was not going to say anything about Bently's threatening her with marriage. It didn't exist. And he was so blamed honorable, he'd likely go to Bently.

''About time he understands how terrible it must've been for you.''

''He knows. And he told me why he did it.'' For a brief moment, she lost herself in his gaze. ''Just before Papa passed on, he made Bently promise to keep me safe. It was difficult for us after our parents died. Bently tried so hard to take Papa's place.'' She picked up a slice of bread and broke off a piece. ''I'd gone off alone to gather fuel for the fire. When I didn't return, he came looking for me.'' Again, she met Kent's gaze. ''I think he first did believe I'd been ruined, then he used it to frighten me. He believed if I were afraid of men and stayed away from them, I'd be safe. But he never told anyone else. It was our secret.''

At least he did that for her, Kent thought. The poor bastard. ''And didn't he see what that was doin' to you?'' He reached out and held her hand. ''Does he—''

She nodded. ''I don't think I really knew how angry I was until I lost my temper . . . and it all came out. But it's okay now. I doubt he'll mention it again.'' He was rubbing his thumb on the inside of her wrist and she was having a terrible time concentrating. ''While we were gone,'' she said, trying to ease the increasing tension below her belly, ''he kept company with Lettie. I'm sure she won't disappoint him.''

''I hope he understands there's no reason for him to be upset with you.''

''Or you, either.'' She brought his hand up and pressed a kiss to the smooth skin on the back. ''I don't regret anything.'' And with a little luck, she thought, her brother might discover how wonderful it feels to love someone.

✦ 20 ✦

AFTER KENT LEFT, Alicia Simms stopped by for a short
visit that afternoon, and Mr. Dunn came to find a Christmas
present for Hannah. He decided on the blue bonnet, and
Emma put it in a pretty hat box for him. Then she was on
her own. She worked on the wine-red bonnet and was close
to finishing it, when she heard Lydia.

"You're back early." Emma wove the needle into the red
muslin and arched her back. She was surprised when she
glanced up and realized how late it was.

Lydia came through the kitchen and into the shop. "Why
is it so dark in here, dear?" When she noticed the bonnet,
she smiled at Emma. "That's a handsome one, but you
shouldn't be sewing. You can't even see."

"I'm almost done, but it can wait until morning," Emma
said, coming to her feet. "I'll light the lamps."

"Mr. Hogarth was putting on his coat when I left the
hotel. He'll probably be here soon." Lydia glanced around.
"Where's Lettie?"

Emma looked outside as she closed the drapes over the
bay window. There still was no sign of them. She smirked,
then quickly sobered. She didn't want Lydia curious about

anything else. "She went with Bently to pick out trees for Christmas. They shouldn't be too much longer."

Lydia grinned. "About time, but I am surprised. You know, dear, sometimes your brother is too concerned about propriety."

"And Lettie's been too modest." Emma pulled the curtain closed over the side window and smiled at Lydia. "She wasn't today, though." They were laughing when the bell over the door rang.

Kent walked in and closed the door. "Sounds like I'm just in time for the party."

"Come on in." Emma lighted another lamp.

"Hello, again, Mr. Hogarth." Lydia hung up her cloak. "You men accomplished a lot this afternoon. Mrs. Lewis is so pleased with your progress."

He chuckled. "She's ready to start rearranging furniture." He watched Emma a moment. "They aren't back yet?" Emma's eyes sparkled with devilment. Who would've thought he'd find such a wonderful woman when he'd least expected to?

"Uh-uh," Emma said, not trusting herself to say more. She couldn't wait to do her sisterly duty and give him a hard time.

"Can I walk you home?" He struggled to keep his face blank. She was fairly bursting. He had the feeling Bently'd be on the receiving end for once.

She wanted to say yes, knowing they would have more than a few minutes together, but she couldn't leave Lydia alone. "I'll be here a while longer. Will you come by tomorrow evening?"

"At least take a walk with him, dear," Lydia said. "I'll start supper."

Kent took Emma's arm. "Walk me to the door."

Emma nodded and spoke to Lydia. "I'll be right back." She went outside arm in arm with him. "I don't want to leave her alone."

"I understand. Want me to look for them?"

"Thanks, but I don't think that'll be necessary." She

leaned her head on his shoulder. "Knowing those two, they'd both have to have two broken legs to stop them from coming back tonight."

He kissed the top of her head. "If I take a walk later, I'll come by."

She smiled and rubbed her cheek on his coat. "You're a nice man, Kent Hogarth."

"Glad you think so." He stepped down to the board walk. "If you need anything, come get me."

She stood eye to eye with him and rested her hands on his shoulders. "I will. See you tomorrow?"

"Count on it." Holding on to her waist, he pulled her against him and kissed her. Each time was a little different, and he knew he'd never tire of loving her.

She slid her arms around him and held on to him. His bulky coat felt like a wall between them. She ran one hand through his soft hair and felt her body responding to his. She moaned and nestled closer.

He leaned back and smiled at her. "You'd better get inside." He turned her around and gave the back of her skirt a playful swat.

She laughed and hurried into the shop. The only explanation she had for her bold behavior in front of the shop was a reckless desire to store up memories. When she was Lydia's age, she could smile at young couples and remember what it felt like to be in love.

She began clearing the kitchen table. "Have you seen Mrs. Chase around lately?"

"No, dear. I haven't seen her for . . . since late summer, I guess. Weren't you out there a couple of weeks ago?"

"Mm-hm. But I'm still worried about her. She usually comes to town every few months, and she hasn't."

"Why don't you ask Mr. Jenks? They'll probably be in to do some shopping before long."

They talked about Christmas and soon had supper ready. Emma was slicing bread when the buckboard pulled up out front. "They're back."

"I'll set two more places," Lydia said, reaching for the plates. "You will have supper with us, won't you, dear?"

"I shouldn't." Emma moved toward the hall door so Lettie and her brother would see her. "In fact, I'm going home right now. But do ask Bently to stay. I'm sure Lettie won't object."

She peered around the corner, grabbed her cape, and left by the back door. They didn't need her hanging around, and her brother might feel uncomfortable courting his sister's closest friend in front of her. She walked around the hotel and up the bay-front road. Smoke curled up from Kent's chimney. It was good knowing he was there.

During the next week Kent brought the wagon down from the mountains and helped Ross and Kirby close up the enlarged rooms in the hotel. Mrs. Lewis and Mrs. Nance decided to have a Christmas dinner at the hotel for those who wouldn't be having a family supper. Each day the plans grew, and Mrs. Lewis asked if the new dining room would be completed in time. Kent told her the inside walls wouldn't be plastered before the supper, but they could dine in there.

He walked Emma home every evening. And each time he said good night, even with a few stolen kisses in the shadow of a pine tree, it became harder and harder to let her go. But he had no choice. The town was so small, he couldn't be certain of a moment's privacy. However, they'd spend Christmas together with the others at the hotel. He wanted to give her some small trinket to remind her of him, but as soon as he thought of something, he quickly discarded the idea.

Two days before Christmas, he waited in the dining room with Ross, while Kirby escorted Mrs. Lewis in to see what she thought of their handiwork. It hadn't been easy to keep her out of there the last few days, but they'd managed.

Mr. Kirby led Mrs. Lewis to the middle of the room and waved his arm in an arc. "What do you think?"

Mrs. Lewis turned around slowly, taking in the whole room, and ran her hand along the window ledge. "It's wonderful. And since the walls haven't been plastered yet, we can put up some greenery and won't hurt anything." She smiled at each of the men, and then at Mr. Kirby. "Christmas supper will be a perfect way to christen the room. Don't you think?''

"Yes, ma'am, I do."

Kent noticed a movement out of the corner of his eye and looked into the kitchen. Mr. Brice was standing at the far end with a pair of shoes in one hand, watching Mrs. Lewis. Kent went over to him. "She seems happy with the room."

Mr. Brice nodded. "It's all she's talked about lately." He glanced down at the shoes in his hand. "I don't suppose she'll want to see these now."

Kent looked at the brown leather lady's slippers. "Did you make them here?"

"Yes. She complained about her shoes pinching. Said men had no idea how to make shoes for women." Mr. Brice frowned. "I'll see her later."

"Why not go over there and show them to her now? From what I've seen, you hold your own with her." Kent looked over at her and gave Brice an encouraging slap on the back. "She's already seen you. Might as well."

Mr. Brice crossed the room and presented the slippers to Mrs. Lewis. "I just finished them and thought you would like to see how your ideas turned out."

Mrs. Lewis took one shoe and carefully inspected it. "Very nice, Mr. Brice. And you softened the sole like I asked. It's just enough." She held the slipper up. "Look, everyone, Mr. Brice's first pair of shoes." She smiled at him. "They are wonderful."

"I'm glad you like them."

"You should take these over to the Hat Box and show them to Miss Emma and Miss Morrissey."

"They're for you."

She beamed at him. "Thank you so much, Henry."

He nodded. "You wear them and let me know if they give you any problem, Irene."

"Oh, I will."

"Congratulations," Kent said. "Before long, you'll be busy filling orders." It didn't occur to him till he'd heard himself, but that gave him an idea. When Brice started to leave, Kent went up to him. "Mind if I walk with you?"

"Not at all. Can I interest you in a new pair of boots?"

Kent chuckled. "These're broke in just right. I may have you fix one of the heels, though. Can you make gloves for a lady?"

"I'd be happy to, but she'll have to come in so I can make a pattern of her hands."

"I'm sure she won't mind. Do you have any nice, soft leather?" They arrived at his shop, and Kent followed Mr. Brice inside. There was a cowhide and one that looked like that of a pig on a sturdy plank worktable.

Mr. Brice glanced at Kent. "I don't make just boots and shoes. I can make or repair almost anything from leather— belts, feed bags, pouches, straps," he said, motioning to a shelf on the far wall. "If you can think it up, I can make it." Mr. Brice picked up the smaller skin and held it out to Kent. "Feel this. Pigskin gloves will be soft and strong."

"That might be just the thing for Miss Emma." He hoped she'd like a pair of dress gloves and that he'd also get to see her wearing them.

Mr. Brice went over to his worktable and rummaged through the papers. "I don't know where I put those drawings. But I'll find them tomorrow."

"They're for Christmas, so you won't—"

"Oh, I am sorry, Mr. Hogarth, but I can't possibly have the gloves done by then."

"I wouldn't expect you to. I'll tell her about them Christmas day. She won't be in to have the pattern made till next week."

"Ah, that's much better." Mr. Brice laughed. "Thought for a minute there I'd have to turn down my first sale."

Kent chuckled. "Don't you worry about that," he said, and settled up with him for the cost of the gloves. "I'll be back and have you look at my boot."

"Anytime, Mr. Hogarth. And thank you for the order. I hope Miss Emma will be happy with her new gloves."

"Me, too. See you on Christmas day."

As he walked past the saloon, Kent waved to Roy Avery and went on to the livery. Kent strolled out back and found Seth in the corral. "Hi. How're you doin'?"

"Stayin' outa trouble. You?"

"Trying to do the same." Kent rested his elbows on the top rail of the fence. "Sure as hell isn't easy, is it?"

"You got that right." One of the pups darted into the corral and startled two of the horses. Seth bellowed, "Edward Dunn!"

Eddie came around the back of the house and slowed his pace when he saw his father's face. "Yeah, Pa—"

"I told you to keep those mongrels away from here. If they spook the cow, you'll drink her milk. You understand me, son?"

"Yes, sir." The pup saw Eddie and took off into the livery with the boy running after him.

Kent laughed. A boy like him would do any man proud. He hadn't given much thought to having a family, but the idea certainly appealed to him now. Emma would be a wonderful mother. He wasn't so sure how he'd be at fathering, though.

Seth shook his head. "That boy an' his dogs. Never shoulda let him have the bitch. She'll throw pups till he's mostly grown."

"I won't keep you. Just wanted to let you know I'm takin' Bounder out to stretch his legs."

"That's a fine animal. Ever think about breedin' him?"

"When I settle down. Be nice to find a good mare. I'd like to be around to see the foal." Kent waved and headed for the livery.

"I'll watch for a good breeder—" Seth called after him. "Who knows? You just might be back."

When he found himself wishing Seth good luck, Kent chuckled. After he gave his stallion a good grooming, he saddled him and rode through town. Once he'd passed the Townsend house, he let the horse run. Damn, it felt good. He headed up the coast. When he thought they'd passed the Indian village, he reined in a bit.

Kent had been running free since he was fourteen. Could he be saddle-broke? He recalled breaking Bounder. Kent had won him playing poker. The loser had had a good laugh, saying the horse was a rogue, but when Kent had looked into that animal's eyes, he knew different. It'd taken him a full month to win the horse's trust and now they seemed to know what the other was thinking. When Emma gazed at him, he could almost understand how his mount may have felt. Hell, she already had him bridled. And he didn't think it would take much to saddle-break him.

He returned near sundown. He was giving the horse a rubdown when Eddie came in with the little black pup at his heels. "Hi. What're you up to?"

"Nothin' much."

Kent finished with Bounder and closed the stall. "Is that the one that scared the horses earlier?" Kent dropped down on one knee and rubbed the pup behind its soft floppy ear. Its coat was thick and the chocolate eyes were clear.

"Nah. This's the boy. The girl's the one always gittin' me in trouble."

Kent laughed. "They'll do that sometimes." *Even when you think you're too old to bother with.* "Does he have a name?"

Eddie shook his head. "I just call him 'boy.'" He watched Kent. "He likes you. He don't sit like that for no-body. You want him, Mr. Hogarth? He wouldn't be no trouble. Bet he'd foller you 'round and never get lost."

Kent looked over at Bounder. They were both black as pitch. He picked up the pup and stepped closer to the stallion. "What'd you think?" The horse snorted and finally smelled the pup. *They just might get along,* he thought, putting the pup down. It was a cute li'l mongrel. But the last thing he needed was a dog.

"Wanta take him for a walk? I bet he minds you real good."

Kent covered his smile and cleared his throat. "Not today, Eddie. I'm sure I'll see him next time I come in." He grabbed his coat and started walking to the road.

Eddie ran after him. "But what if someone takes him? Don't'cha want him?"

Kent paused at the door and looked at the boy. "Just find him a good home. He'll be a beauty when he's grown up." He ruffled the boy's hair and left. After the holidays, he had to return to Portland and that pup wouldn't be able to keep pace with Bounder, not for months.

Christmas morning Emma woke up and sat on the side of her bed, before she remembered what day it was and crawled back under the covers for a few minutes. Sunshine poured in her window. She stretched and curled up again. Her Christmas wish was for Bently and Lettie to marry soon and have a baby by next December. Children made some holidays special, the way they were when she and Bently were growing up. Maybe if it had snowed and they could take a sleigh ride . . . But that wouldn't change what really bothered her. Kent would leave soon, and she didn't know how to say good-bye to him.

Not about to spend the day in bed, she stepped onto the cold floor before thinking twice. Splashing her face with cold water brought her wide awake. She stepped into her slippers, put on her woolen wrapper, and went through the house lighting fires to take the chill out of the air. By the time she took the sticky buns out of the oven, Bently had joined her in the kitchen for his usual eggs and bacon.

He went over to her. "For a minute, I almost thought you were Mama standing here. I didn't realize how much you look like her." He cleared his throat. "You made her buns, didn't you?"

Tears sprang to her eyes, and she blinked them away. She had always thought their mother was so beautiful with her thick, wavy honey-blond hair. "I don't know why I haven't before."

He gave her a brotherly embrace and kissed her cheek. "Happy Christmas, Emma."

She smiled and kissed him. "You, too." This was the Bently she adored, but not many people ever saw this side of him. "Sit down. This's getting cold."

He sat in his usual place.

When she set their plates on the table, she noticed the small package tied with red ribbon by her place. Grinning, she reached into the lower cupboard and set his gift on the table.

He eyed the present. "Are you sure you didn't get mine mixed up with Lettie's? It's so big."

"It's all yours." She'd had the coat made for him when they were in Astoria and was anxious to see if it would still fit him.

He moved the package closer, then picked up his fork. "Remember— We can't open them until after breakfast."

"You haven't forgotten." She glanced at him. He was serious, but she couldn't resist teasing him. "We aren't children. Why wait?" she said, picking up her present.

He smiled at her. "You haven't changed all that much."

You have, she thought, you've almost forgotten how to laugh. "Are you going to call on Lettie before the supper?" She broke off a piece of the bun and ate it.

He lowered the sticky bun. "I've been thinking about it. Do you need to go by there today?"

"I hadn't planned to." She ate another large bite and washed it down with coffee. "Did you notice our display in the window?"

He finished chewing the bite and swallowed. "Yes. Very nice. Didn't I tell you the other day?"

"Uh-uh. I hope it was Lettie you complimented." She smiled and popped another piece of bun in her mouth.

"Must've been."

She laughed. "Have you seen the new dining room at the hotel yet?"

He nodded, chewing a piece of bacon.

She ate the last bite of the sticky bun and licked her fingers. As soon as she had swallowed, she took her brother's half-full plate away from him. "We're done. Open your present."

He chuckled. "All right."

She pulled the tail of the bow and unwound the ribbon, unfolded the soft cloth, and found a small silver sailing boat much like the *Julianna*. "It's beautiful, Bently. Thank you." She picked it up and felt the pin on the back. "It's perfect!"

He sighed. "You enjoyed sailing so much that when I saw this in Astoria, I thought you would like it. Then after the shipwreck . . . If it reminds you of that, put it away."

She ran her finger over the smooth surface of the sails. Whenever she wore it, she'd know a bit of Kent was touching her heart, but that was her secret. "Oh, no. I'll always treasure this." She pinned it on her wrapper. "Go on, open yours."

He pulled the green ribbon off and quickly folded back the calico wrapping. "A waistcoat?" He held it up and smiled. "It's handsome. I almost ordered one when we were in Astoria."

She laughed. "That's where I had it made for you. See if it fits. The tailor said the rounded corners and piped pockets were the latest fashion."

"It's grand." He pulled off his coat and slipped on the new one. "Perfect."

She watched him strike a haughty pose and giggled. When he started around the table, she stood up and stepped into his open arms. "Happy Christmas."

"Well," he said, stepping back and smoothing the lapels on his new waistcoat. "I think I'll call on Lettie."

"Don't forget to look for the mistletoe. We put some in the shop, and I hung a couple of sprigs in her parlor." She grinned. "We also gave several pieces to Mrs. Lewis to put up in the hotel. You're bound to catch her under at least one." When he smiled and left the room, she resisted the urge to congratulate or tease him.

She did step over to the window and crane her neck to see Kent's old cabin. When she saw smoke rising out of the chimney, she began humming.

Bently stopped in the doorway. "I'm leaving now. I'll see you at the hotel."

"All right." She added wood to the kitchen stove to bake the eighteen potatoes and large pan of scalloped onions. While they cooked, she worked on readying herself for the supper.

Her prettiest petticoats plus four others were laid out, the good white cotton stockings she'd only darned once, her nicest shimmy, and her fanciest dress—the dark emerald-green muslin. The bodice was plain with a low shoulder line and the skirt so full that when she spun around it floated out like a cloud. She pinned the silver sailboat to the bodice and smiled. Today she'd wear her hair down and loosely held back with a ribbon.

She might be approaching spinsterhood, but she didn't have to dress as if she'd been put on the shelf.

❖ *21* ❖

Emma arrived at the hotel just after midday. She waved to Mr. Brice and Mrs. Lewis standing out front. It was nice to see them gazing at one another with obvious affection. Emma had barely stepped down from the buckboard when they came over to her. "Happy Christmas. Isn't it a beautiful day?"

"It surely is, Miss Townsend," Mrs. Lewis said.

Mr. Brice stepped forward. "Can we help carry something for you? Seems everyone's arrived loaded down with food."

She smiled at him. "I'd appreciate your help. There's a warm pan for each of you." She handed the baked potatoes to Mr. Brice and the scalloped onions to Mrs. Lewis. "Thank you. I'll be right in."

Emma carried the basket with her gifts for Lettie and Lydia, and the little carved bear she had found for Kent. She hurried through the front doorway and past the mistletoe hanging over it, exchanged Christmas wishes with Mr. Ross, Mr. Avery, and Mr. Jenks in the entry. She made her way into the kitchen, put the basket under a wooden chair in one corner and draped her cape over the chair. She had stacked the pans and was setting them on top of the stove when Mrs. Lewis came over with Mr. Brice.

"Your dress is beautiful, Miss Emma." Mrs. Lewis studied the gown. "I do like that dark green. Do you sell dresses in your shop?"

Emma smiled. "No. We have a lovely silk shirtwaist almost this color in the window, but mostly we have assessories, everything but dresses. I like yours, Mrs. Lewis. The silvery-gray is splendid with your hair."

"Thank you, Miss Emma. If I were twenty years younger, I'd want one like yours." Mrs. Lewis took a closer look at Emma's pin.

"It's a gift from my brother."

"What a thoughtful gentleman he is." Mrs. Lewis glanced at Mr. Brice and leaned closer to Emma. "I believe he's with Miss Lettie out back."

Emma beamed. "That is good news." She lifted the lid on another pan on the stove. "Mm. Fried chicken."

"Be careful of that, dear. Grease stains would ruin your dress."

"You're right. I brought my apron. I'll remember to put it on before I help serve." Emma smiled and stepped away from the stove. "If you'll excuse me, I'd like to pay my respects to Lydia."

"I believe Mr. Hogarth asked about you."

Emma swallowed and struggled not to appear overly interested. "Thank you." She walked toward the dining room and hesitated. "Mrs. Lewis, when did you want to serve supper?"

"In a little while. Oh, and the spiced cider's in the reading room."

Emma nodded and went to look for Lydia. She greeted Mr. Kirby in the dining room and found Lydia by the punch bowl in the reading room. "Happy Christmas. How's the cider?" She kissed Lydia's soft cheek.

"And you, dear. Mr. Avery made this cider. Good. Very good."

"It smells delicious." Emma gazed at the blaze in the fireplace.

"I'll pour you a cup." Lydia picked up the ladle and cup and softly said, "Mr. Hogarth's over in the corner—looking at the books. He's read the spines many times over." She handed Emma the cup. "I also caught him eyeing the mistletoe."

Emma giggled. "Thank you for warning me, Lydia."

Lydia whispered, "Be surprised, dear. Men like to believe we have no idea what they are up to." She grinned and left the room.

Kent was leaning back against the bookcase watching Emma. She was a vision in green. She had almost floated into the room. Her dress brought out the same color in her beautiful eyes and her hair reminded him of the first rays of sunlight. He wasn't one for fancy dress balls, but he sure wouldn't mind dancing around the floor with her in his arms. He picked up his empty cup and went over to the punch bowl. "Merry Christmas, Emma."

She met his gaze and a thrill coursed through her. Now she understood the glances that Ginny shared with Will. And for once, Emma thought, she could've used a fan to cool her warm cheeks. "Happy Christmas to you, Kent." He was wearing a deep red flannel shirt with dark gray trousers and his boots had been polished. And he was the most handsome man she had ever seen.

He refilled his cup with cider and raised it to her. "To the prettiest woman it's been my pleasure to know." There was a fine ripe peach glow to her face that spread down her neck. He drained his cup and set it down on the table.

"I'm flattered," she said, and drank to his toast. It sounded so nice. It wasn't true, but she appreciated his kindness all the more. "You're very handsome yourself. Have you been here long?"

"I'd just walked in here when Mrs. Nance joined me— about the time you arrived." He thought of something he'd love to have. A daguerreotype of her—just the way she was gazing at him in that moment. "Would you like to walk outside?"

She smiled and set her cup by his.

He lightly touched the back of her arm and followed her down the hall and out to the backyard. "It's so nice out, hard to believe it's Christmas."

When she saw Lettie and Bently over by the well, Emma took Kent's arm and strolled in the other direction, to the far end of the building. "It did feel more like winter in the mountains." She looked at him and belatedly realized how that may have sounded. She didn't ever want to forget that time with him and hoped he felt the same way.

He hugged her arm and laughed. "Emma, you're a treasure." They walked around the corner and stopped. "That's a pretty pin." He took a closer look. "Looks like the boat you were on."

"I does to me, too. Bently gave it to me because I enjoyed sailing."

"I would've thought the last part'd be something you'd just as soon forget."

"I very much enjoyed the journey until then," she said, and smiled. "And I met you on the deck of the boat." She glanced down at the pin. "That's what makes it especially dear to me. Feel the sails. They're smoother than glass."

He put his hand over her chest. As he traced the sails, the heel of his hand brushed against her breast. He heard her soft gasp and wanted to crush her to him. Each night since their return, falling asleep without her in his arms became more difficult. He wanted her, needed her in his life, but he had to complete his business in Portland before declaring himself to her. "I wanted to give you something, but I wasn't sure what you'd like. But I arranged with Mr. Brice to have him make a pair of gloves for you."

Doesn't he know how much he's already given me? she wondered. "Thank you. That was very thoughtful of you."

He shrugged. "He has a good piece of soft leather. But you'll have to stop by his store so he can make a pattern of your hands. He'll stitch the gloves the way you want." He raised her arm and kissed her hand. She's beaming at me as if I'd given her a big nugget of gold.

Bracing herself for his answer, she asked him the question that was never far from her thoughts. "Does that mean you'll be here when they're finished?" She put her free hand on his chest and felt the thundering beat of his heart.

One of the qualities of hers he most admired was her

straightforward way of speaking. But this was a hell of a time for it. "Not unless he's done with 'em by the middle of next week—"

She nodded, relieved to know when he would be leaving, but she certainly wasn't looking forward to it. "I have a gift for you, too. Wait here. It's in the kitchen." She took a step. "I'll be right back." She dashed inside, took his present out of the basket, and hurried back in a very unladylike fashion. She slid to a stop right in front of him. When she handed the small package to him, she hoped he understood its meaning and wouldn't be disappointed.

Her gift was about the size of his pistol grip. "You didn't have to get me anything." He untied the bow, loosened the red silk ribbon, and grinned at her. "Give me a hint?"

"Uh-uh. Open it up."

He felt something hard and unrolled the object from the calico. Folding back the last corner, he found a carved bear and grinned at her. "Old Stoney's bear. He's wonderful!" He felt strangely comforted to know their day together meant as much to her as it did to him. He drew her a step farther from the corner of the hotel. "Thank you," he said, and pressed a tender kiss on her lips.

"I'm glad you remembered." She grinned. "Poor Mr. Jenks just shook his head. I didn't tell him who it was for. If he asks Bently about it, they'll both be surprised."

"I don't think he'll do that. He can't afford to lose any customers in a town this size." He tucked the bear in the pocket of his shirt over his heart and patted it.

"I'd better help Mrs. Lewis. She shouldn't have to do all the work."

"All right. Wouldn't want anyone to come looking for you." He slipped his arm around her waist, held her close and kissed her thoroughly.

She melted against him and gave in to her need to show her love for him. When he released her, she realized she wanted so much more. "See you in a few minutes." She turned on her heel, and promptly stepped into Lettie. "Oh— I didn't see you."

"How could you?" Lettie said, clinging to Bently's arm.

She smiled at him and looked back at Emma. "We thought we would take a walk along the bay. Want to go with us?"

It was clear Bently wasn't happy with Emma, and Kent was surprised Lettie had suggested such a thing. But he'd gladly go along with whatever Emma wanted.

Emma glanced at Kent. "I promised to help Mrs. Lewis set out the food."

Lettie slipped her arm from Bently's. "Maybe we can take that walk after supper."

"Yes, of course. That would be better," Bently said. "I'll go in with you." He gave Kent a curt nod and left with Lettie.

Emma covered her mouth and waited until they were near the door before speaking. "Isn't that wonderful?"

"You seem pleased."

"Oh, I am. If he didn't care for her, he wouldn't escort her that way." She stood on tiptoe and gave Kent a quick kiss. "Now, if he'll just ask for her hand, all will be well." She peeked at the back of the hotel again, then at him. "Isn't this a wonderful Christmas?"

"The best." He watched her dash off, her skirts flying and her hair swinging down her back. She was a vision all right, even lovelier than he'd dreamed.

For the next few days, Emma waited for Bently to announce his betrothal. Lettie hadn't said much at all. She had a dreamy smile plastered on her face most of the time, hummed while she embroidered pieces for another quilt, and had been caught lost in thought several times. Wednesday was no different until Pauline came in to visit.

"Lettie . . . ?" Pauline glanced at Emma, shrugged and said, "Lettie, you were telling us what Mr. Townsend gave you for Christmas."

"Oh." Lettie looked around and put her hand on one side of her lace collar. "Well, he gave me a pin." Her fingers brushed over the lace. "A silver bow," she said, lifting the collar.

"It's lovely. That was very thoughtful." Pauline smiled at Lettie. "I'm glad you had such a nice Christmas."

Emma grinned. "It's beautiful. You should pin it on top of the collar."

Lettie's smile grew wider. "I think I will," she said, reaching for the pin.

Emma turned to Pauline. She said she hadn't been feeling well, but she didn't seem ill. Maybe it was her serene smile. It was different. "Pauline, are you sure you wouldn't like a cup of tea? You look like you could use a warm drink."

"I'm . . ." Pauline smiled. "We're going to have a baby," she said softly.

"Congratulations!" Emma was closest and gave her a hug.

"That's wonderful news!" Lettie said, hurrying around the table. "I'm so happy for you."

"That's it. I knew I should've recognized it. You reminded me of Ginny. When is it due?"

"June, I think—I'm not too sure."

"Can any woman be?" Emma laughed and glanced at Lettie. She had that dreamy lost look again.

Pauline pulled her shawl back up around her shoulders. "I'd better go. It doesn't take much to wear me out these days."

"If you need anything, just let us know." Emma walked her to the door, then went into the kitchen.

Kent said he would be leaving by mid-week, and Emma was a wreck waiting for the final good-bye. The night before, Bently had returned home and interrupted her saying good night to Kent. She hadn't seen him that morning and prayed he would stay just one more day. She stirred the simmering stew. After tasting a bite, she put the spoon back on the saucer.

Lettie glanced up from her embroidery. "Emma, why don't you pour a fresh cup of tea and sit down for a while? You're as jumpy as a beheaded chicken."

Emma was tearing up a slice of bread in a bowl. "I'm going to have a bite of stew."

"It's not ready yet, is it?"

"Close enough. I'll have some broth on bread." She spooned the liquid over the bread, grabbed a spoon, and sat down at the table in the shop with Lettie. "I keep thinking about Vera. No one's seen her, and I can't help worrying."

Lettie nodded. "I've asked, too. Mr. Chase hasn't been around, either."

"I'm going out to call on her after I eat. Want to go with me? We can close the shop for a couple of hours."

"We haven't seen Ginny, either."

"It's too near her time for her to ride to town."

"You're probably right, but go on without me. Bently said he'd see me this afternoon." Lettie snipped a thread and tied it off. "What about Mr. Hogarth?"

Emma knew he wouldn't ride out of town without seeing her. "He probably won't stop here until later."

Lettie stared at her. "You didn't have a disagreement, did you?"

"What gave you that idea?"

Lettie shrugged. "I wouldn't want to miss seeing Bently. Don't you think Mr. Hogarth will stop by here this afternoon?"

"I expected him this morning, so I hope he didn't leave already." Emma gulped down the last of her stew. "I won't be gone long. Just out to the Chase farm, make sure Vera's okay, and back." She washed and dried the bowl, and tossed her cape over her shoulders. "Why don't we call on Ginny in the morning? I'll bake sticky buns to take to her."

"All right."

Emma hurried home and soon rode the mare out of town. She had let her hair down and her bonnet hung by the strings. She realized she felt driven to ease her mind about Vera. For the first time in days and with the wind in her hair, she felt calmer knowing she was resolving what had been bothering her. And, she had more than a wink of hope that Lettie and Bently would make an announcement—hopefully soon.

She rode past the Pool farm. Mr. Pool and John, Jr., were working in the distance, and she waved to them. Farther down the road, when she came to the Chase farm, she looked for Virgil Chase. The fields were poorly tended and there wasn't a person in sight.

When she entered the yard, it was like the other times.

The dog barked and no one appeared to be around. The house seemed closed up for such a sunny day. Most everyone else was taking advantage of the respite from the winter storms. She secured the reins to the fence post and started up the walk.

The front door flew open. Virgil came out and stood at the edge of the porch. "What'd'ya want now, missy?"

She stopped in the middle of the path and stared at him. "I came to see Vera. She looked poorly the last time I called. Is she here?"

"Ain't none o' yor biz'niss. She's my missus an' she's jist fine." He went down the two steps and clamped his hands on his waist. "Ya go on back to yor fancy li'l store. Leave me an' mine alone!"

She had watched for some sign of Vera, but the woman didn't show herself. "I'm not leaving until I speak to her— *alone.*" He was nothing but a bully, and Emma wasn't going to allow herself to be run off.

Virgil took another step toward her. "Ya shouldn'ta come out here where ya ain't wanted. Now git the hell off my property and don't ya come back!" he bellowed, shaking his fist at her.

Emma's heart pounded in her throat, but she wouldn't let that oaf frighten her away. She cupped her hands around her mouth and screamed, "V-e-r-a— Vera, come out here—" If he'd do this to her, how did he treat his wife?

Virgil charged at her.

She started shaking and took a step backward, then another. This had happened before . . . seven years ago— No, no, not again! No one was going to hurt her without a fight— she *wouldn't* let it happen. She darted to her right. If she could get around him and into the house, she would be able to find a weapon to use against him. Something—anything.

"No ya don't, ya meddlin' bitch!" Latching onto her left arm, he yanked and shook her.

When he jerked her off her feet, she became frantic. She swung her arm at him. But her fist hit his belly with less force than she would've used swatting a fly.

He started dragging her across the front yard. "I'll teach

ya what happens when ya poke yer nose where't don't b'long.''

She gritted her teeth and scrambled to get her footing. Slowly, as she stumbled along, she closed her fingers tight and pressed her thumb onto her first finger. Then with a burst of energy, she bolted ahead and around him. She'd caught him off guard. She pulled and twisted and lunged until she had him off balance. When he teetered, she immediately pulled her arm back, aimed her knuckled fist at his eyes, and swung with all her might. This time she punched him hard.

He bellowed, flung her away from him, and covered his eyes as he fell to the ground.

Vera came running out of the house. "Oh, God— What've you done to my man?"

Emma bent over and braced her hands on her knees, gasping for air and staring at Virgil. Her mind seemed to whirl like a dust devil, but she hadn't missed Vera's blackened eye and red cheek. Then Emma noticed her own thumb. It was covered with blood. Carefully, she stepped closer to Vera. Putting her other hand on Vera's shoulder, Emma said, "Come on. He won't bother us—at least not now. Let's get back to town."

Vera sprang to her feet and shoved Emma's hand away from her. "Leave us be! Ya've blinded him."

Emma couldn't believe what she'd heard. "Didn't you hear me? You're safe now." Doesn't Vera understand? "Look what he's done to you. You don't have to take this, Vera. Leave with me."

"Why would I do that?" Vera wiped her husband's face with the hem of her skirt.

Emma heard a horse approaching and looked toward the road. Kent. Thank goodness. Maybe he could talk some sense into Vera.

He stopped Bounder and quickly dismounted near her side. "What's goin' on here?" He studied her before he eyed Virgil. Whatever'd happened, Emma wasn't the one on the ground.

"He got angry when I wouldn't leave without seeing Vera." She glanced over at Virgil.

He held her hand while he reassured himself she really wasn't hurt. He knew she hadn't attacked the man for no reason. "Did he hit you?"

She shook her head. "I'm not sure where he was dragging me, but I finally managed to knock him off balance. And I punched him in the eye." She spared another glimpse at Virgil, then she looked at Kent. "My thumb went into his eye. I didn't mean to do that. I just wanted to get away from him."

She was flushed, breathing hard, and her hair was messed, but Kent didn't see any marks on her. "You okay? He didn't try to—"

"No. He grabbed my arm, and I panicked. I felt I had a second chance to do what I couldn't all those years ago."

He put his arm around her shoulders and held her. "He must be twice your size—and you stopped him. You saved yourself, Emma." He kissed the top of her head. "I'm so proud of you."

"What if I blinded him?" she asked softly. Just the thought sent a shudder down her back.

"Emma," he said, lifting her chin so he could watch her eyes. "You defended yourself. He had no business grabbin' you. Let's go. I promised Lettie we'd be right back."

"We've got to take Vera with us. Look at her. He beats her."

"Emma—" She didn't listen, and he watched her walk right up to Mrs. Chase. He followed her over and made sure Chase saw him.

Emma stood out of Virgil's reach and spoke to Vera. "We're leaving now. Come with us."

"Haven't you done enough? He's not much, but he's all I got!" Vera helped her husband sit up.

Kent gently clasped Emma's hand. "Ready?"

Emma watched the Chases. How could any woman settle for an animal like him? "Vera?"

"Come on, Emma. She wants to stay here."

"But—" Emma stared into his eyes. She still didn't understand. "I guess."

After she mounted up, Kent did the same, and they left.

When they'd gone down the road a ways, he slowed to a walk. "You sure you're all right? Why don't you ride in front of me?"

She gave him a weak smile. "I'll be fine. And don't worry. I'll not go back to see how Vera's doing again." She felt stronger by the minute. "How did you get out here so quickly?"

"I stopped by the shop to see you. Lettie admitted she'd never trusted Chase and asked me to ride back with you."

"I'll be sure to thank her. And I'm very grateful you came to my rescue."

"I didn't do a thing. You had him under control." He smiled and added, "When this gets around, you shouldn't have to worry about anyone bothering you."

She stared at him. "You can't. Oh, please, Kent, don't tell anyone." Oh, Lordy, what had she done?

"I don't think you should try to keep this secret. What if he gets mad at some other woman? He's like a smoldering fire—ready to burst into flame. And it won't take much to set him off." He held her gaze a moment. "It's up to you. I won't say anything if you don't want me to."

There was one other point he hadn't mentioned, she realized. When Virgil finally did come to town, people would ask about his eye. "All right, but please don't make too much out of it. I only protected myself. Nothing more." And I discovered I could protect myself, she thought. She didn't have to be so afraid.

❖ 22 ❖

Kent NOTICED THE cloud of dust farther up the road. It looked like a wagon, but he couldn't make out who was driving. "Someone's in a hurry."

Emma frowned. "I think that's Will Talbert . . . Oh, no," she said, urging the mare to a run. "Must be Ginny—" She met up with him and stopped at the side of the wagon.

"Sure am glad I found you, Miss Townsend." Will took off his hat, rubbed his arm over his forehead, and slapped the hat back on. "It's Gin— I just left Miss Morrissey at the house. She told me to bring you back, too." He looked at Kent. "Would you mind keeping me company?"

Kent nodded. "We'll meet you there."

Emma didn't wait to hear any more. She pressed her heel to the mare's flank and took off down the road. The baby was early, or was it? Some women were good at figuring when to expect the birth, but this was Ginny's first. Emma turned down their path and dashed inside before Kent arrived. She called out to Ginny and Lettie.

Lettie came out of the bedroom. "Come on in. It may be a while, but I'm certainly glad you got here so fast."

"We met Will on the road." Emma looked out the window at Kent and followed Lettie into Ginny's room. "How's she doing?"

"Just fine so far. She put the big meat cleaver under the bed. Said if a knife cut the pain, the cleaver would work even better. And she wanted a pan of water with a cinnamon stick on the fire. She likes the smell." Lettie took a hard look at Emma. "Where's your cape? And *what* happened to you?"

Emma gave a slight turn of her head and stepped to the side of Ginny's bed. "Hi. You look better than Will."

Ginny smiled and moved onto her side. "I wish he'd go to town for a while. He'll be in here every two minutes." As she sat up, she slid her legs over the side of the bed.

"No he won't. Kent's with him." Ginny seemed surprised, then Emma realized what she'd said and shrugged. "Mr. Hogarth?"

Lettie glanced at Ginny and laughed.

Emma gave Lettie a playfully stern look. "I don't think Lydia would be shocked if you called my brother by his given name."

"Recently, it's been harder not to," Lettie admitted.

That's good news, Emma thought. "Did you leave a note in the shop for him or Lydia?"

"Gram was there when I left, but he hadn't arrived. I told her to tell him both of us would stay with Ginny. I didn't want him to worry."

"Good." Emma didn't want him fretting, either. She glanced at the bed just to reassure herself that the knife and string were handy.

"Ooh, my," Ginny groaned. "Another one."

Emma held out her arm, and Ginny latched onto it.

Lettie did the same on Ginny's other side. "How close are they?"

Ginny shook her head. "I'm not sure."

The door flew open and Will stared at his wife. "You okay? Why aren't you in bed, Gin?"

"She'll do better if she walks around, Will." Emma saw Kent's shoulder, though his back was turned to the open door. "Kent, why don't you and Will make a fresh pot of coffee, maybe a pot of tea, oh, and put on a kettle of water. Let it simmer until we need it."

"Yes, ma'am." Kent put his hand on Will's shoulder. "Come on. We're not needed, yet." Kent chuckled. "You could have a long wait."

Will pulled the door closed. "What've I done to her? Dear God, if she survives this, I'll never touch her again."

"Whoa, just a minute," Kent said, leading the younger man to the fireplace. "You really think she'd be happy if you never held her in your arms again? Never showed her how much you care for her?" He shook his head. "After that babe gets born, and your wife rests up a bit, why not ask her?"

"No, no, no," Will said, shaking his head. "I don't wanta lose her."

Kent handed him the bucket and walked outside with him. "You think you're the only one who got any pleasure from your foolin' around?" He shook his head. "Any woman who looks at her man the way your wife does surely doesn't dread her 'wifely duty.' You hold that bucket. I'll work the pump."

Will held on to the pail. "You think that's really true?"

Kent smiled, the memory of Emma too clear in his mind. "Yeah, I do. But Mrs. Talbert's the one you should ask."

Late that evening, Emma dipped a large cloth into the pan of hot water, held it up to cool a bit, squeezed it out, and pressed the warm linen against Ginny's lower back. "Does that feel better?" It was almost time, and Ginny was squatting by the side of the bed, just the way her sister had written and told her to do.

"Mm—" Ginny sighed and rested her head on her arm. "I thought that cleaver was supposed to help cut the pain."

Lettie glanced at Emma and said, "Maybe it would be much worse without it."

"Leave it there. I don't want to find out—" She rocked her head from side to side, then she screamed.

Emma changed the warm cloths. The back of Ginny's

loose gown was soaked. "I've got to open the door. It's too cold in here."

Ginny groaned and gasped. "Go ahead. I don't care."

Emma opened the bedroom door all the way and went into the main room. "Will, you need to build up the fire. We're going to leave the door open to the bedroom."

Kent was sitting with his back to the bedroom and decided to keep it that way. "Want me to wait outside?"

Ginny's scream filled the small cabin.

Will dropped the log in his hands. "Oh, God. Can't you do something for her, Miss Townsend?"

"We're doing all we can, Will. Childbirth's never painless, but I don't think it will last too much longer. Just build that fire up and keep a kettle of water heated."

"Yes, ma'am."

Emma gazed at Kent. Oh, if only she could have his— She didn't dare finish that thought. "You don't need to go out. In fact, he'll need you now more than before."

"If you want anythin', call. I'm not leavin' till you do." She'd tied her hair back with a string and rolled her sleeves up. He smiled, wishing he could hold her for a moment. But that'd have to wait.

When Ginny's next shrill cry rang out, Emma hurried back to help. She changed the cloths again and rubbed Ginny's back. "Remember, Ginny, the closer the pains are together, the closer the birthing."

Ginny screamed again, this time longer. When the pains ended, she gasped and whimpered. "If I die, I want you to send my sister Beth a hank of my hair. Lettie, I want you to have my blue bonnet." She doubled up and started panting. When it passed, she blurted out, "Emma, take my claret shawl. My heavy dress goes to Hannah. Have Will send my diary to little Louisa, m-my baby sister—"

"Sh—" Emma said, interrupting her. "You're not going to die." She changed the cloths again. "It just feels like it."

". . . wrote everything down— Ohh!" Ginny shrieked.

Emma heard Will's and Kent's voices, but she couldn't make out what they were saying. Just the deep sound of

Kent's voice had a soothing effect on her. After the confrontation with the Chases and the long vigil with Ginny, Emma was beginning to feel worn out. But I'm not nearly as tired as Ginny, she thought.

Ginny yelled louder than before.

Lettie drew Emma aside and whispered, "I've never helped with this part. How can we deliver the baby when we can't see it coming?"

"Midwives do it without looking, but I can't. We'll put a blanket up to shield her and raise her skirt. I'm not taking any chances with her baby."

Lettie nodded. "I'll put up a blanket."

Emma bathed Ginny's face and applied another warm cloth to her lower back. "You're doing fine."

Ginny wailed, "It's—"

"There's no time to hang up a blanket." Lettie ran into the main room. "You two have to go outside!" And she ran back to help Emma. "What now?"

Emma had tucked Ginny's skirt under the edge of the mattress to keep it out of the way. "Grab a towel and one of the little sheets she made for the cradle."

Ginny howled and her legs trembled violently.

"Lettie, help hold her up." Emma knelt and bent over as the top of the baby's head appeared. She put her hand under the infant and supported it until the tiny legs slipped out. "Lettie, help her lean forward and lie down with her legs hanging over the edge of the bed."

"It's a boy!" Emma patted the baby's back. The baby cried out, and she turned the tiny body over. "Ginny, he's beautiful, and he's perfect." She wiped out his mouth and smiled. He had his mama's dark hair and his papa's eyes.

Lettie held the baby while Emma tied two pieces of string on the cord and cut between them. "I'll clean him up."

"Good. You might need the practice," Emma said, smiling at her. "There's nothing so wonderful as the birth of a babe, is there?"

Lettie cradled the infant in her arms. "I'd forgotten how tiny new ones are."

Emma smoothed Ginny's hair back from her face. "Just a little longer."

"Emma, the pains're starting again."

Quickly wringing out a cloth, Emma bathed Ginny's face. "The afterbirth has to be delivered. It won't be as bad." Emma hoped that would be true as she rubbed Ginny's back to ease her weary muscles. "We've got good news. Pauline's in the family way, too. She thinks it's due in June."

"Oh," Ginny sighed. "That's nice."

When the ordeal was over, Emma bathed and dressed her in a fresh gown. "I'll get some tea."

Ginny reached out and grasped Emma's hand. "Thank you. Both of you. I was so sure I might die like my sister Mary."

Lettie placed the dressed and wrapped baby in Ginny's arms. "He's the prettiest baby I've ever seen."

Ginny gave her a weak smile. "Thanks, but you'll feel different when you have yours."

Lettie grinned and pulled the covers up over Ginny's hands. "I'll add more wood to the fire."

Emma called to Will, then smiled at Ginny. "He's paced a ditch out front."

Will stepped up to the side of the bed, rubbing his hands on his trousers. "Oh, Gin, you're all right and . . . he is, too." He bent over and kissed her. "Boy, he's so little."

Ginny gazed at Will. "He looks just like his papa."

Emma left them alone. She paused in the main room. "How're you doing, Lettie?"

Lettie put a log on the fire and sat on the hearth. "We were all so tired—until the baby came. Now I'm not. Isn't it odd?"

"Not really. But I won't have any trouble sleeping." Emma stretched and arched her back.

"Want me to stay in with Ginny tonight? One of us should."

"Would you? I'll sleep in the barn. Will can stay in here." Emma drank a dipper of water. "I'm going outside for a minute."

Lettie grinned at her.

Emma met Kent in the yard. Lordy, he looked good, if a little tired, but they all were. ''The excitement's over.''

''Just in time. I don't think Will would've lasted much longer.'' He draped his arm around her shoulders. ''You must be almost as worn out as Mrs. Talbert.''

She grinned and rested her cheek on his solid chest. ''Oh, this feels good, but I shouldn't keep you here.''

He skimmed his hand over her head and lightly massaged her back. ''I told you I'd see you home. I unsaddled the horses hours ago. They're already asleep. I'll sleep in the barn.''

''That's where I'm staying.'' She looked up at him. Those wonderful tickling, unsettling feelings were making her weak in the knees again.

Her gaze was saying what he wanted to hear but this sure as hell was the wrong time and place. ''Aren't you stayin' in with Mrs. Talbert?''

''Lettie's going to sleep on the pallet in her room. And Will won't want to be any farther away from Ginny than the main room.'' She closed her eyes a moment and almost fell asleep.

Will stood in the front doorway. ''Kent, come see my new son! He's really somthin'.''

Kent woke up before dawn. During the night Emma had nestled at his side, but she was still securely wrapped in her cape and a blanket. Her brother could've walked in at anytime and wouldn't't've had a reason to be upset. She was out before he had tucked the last cover over her. He drifted off again watching her.

The rooster's rowdy crowing finally roused Emma. Kent was curled around her with his arm holding her in place, and she didn't want to break the spell. When he had walked her to the barn early that morning, everyone was too exhausted to question their sleeping arrangements. Besides, she had assured Lettie that if she was needed, for any reason, to come wake her up.

It wasn't as easy to lie perfectly still as she had first supposed. A piece of straw poked her neck, and she had a nearly irresistible urge to wriggle closer to him. But she didn't. His deep, slow breathing sounded reassuring, then he mumbled and spoke her name so sweetly she almost didn't recognize it.

"Mornin'," he said by her good ear, moving his arm back to rest his hand on her hip. "Why didn't you wake me?"

"There wasn't any reason." She scooted over and rolled onto her back so she could see him.

He pushed the sides of her hood away from her face and pressed a kiss to her chin. "Feeling better?"

"Much. Yesterday seemed two days long." She started to brush a few strands of hair out of her eyes and realized her right hand was curled into a fist. And her fingers were stiff. She really had hit Virgil. And he didn't hurt me, she reminded herself.

He'd been watching her. "Sore? Soak your hand in cool water for a while. It'll loosen up. You slept peacefully. You're not afraid he'll try anything else, are you?" he asked, studying her expression.

"Yesterday I learned I don't have to be afraid." She looked at him. "I'm not going to be. *I'll never be like Vera.* No woman should live like that."

"You're right. If she liked herself better, she probably wouldn't stay there. But she isn't as strong as you." His fingers traced the line of her jaw. "I've seen bullies like him. They take great pleasure in telling their wives how stupid they are. After a while, the women believe them."

"How can a person be so cruel? I *won't ever* need a man that badly. No woman should." Kent looked worried. Once again, she had thought aloud instead of keeping her notions to herself. "It's over with, and I'm fine." She rose up on her elbow and peered down at the door. "I wonder if Lettie and the Talberts are awake yet. I didn't hear the baby cry. Did you?"

"Not a peep." He wasn't comfortable with the change in her. She'd switched horses midstream; it didn't sit well with him. He had to leave tomorrow, and he didn't want to go away with her in such an unsettled state.

"The baby's so adorable. Nothing feels the same as a new-born baby in your arms. Ginny was positively glowing when she held him." She grinned. "So was Will. Did you see his face?"

"Mm-hm." He chuckled. "Bet he can't wait to take Lettie back to town and do a little braggin'." Emma was smiling and her voice had lost that hard edge that bothered him. Maybe he'd been wrong. She was a sensible woman, and he'd sure hate to see her lose that sparkle in her smile.

"Lettie's so proud of the baby, you'd think he was hers. I have a feeling Bently's going to hear about it for a while." She laughed softly. "I can't wait for them to start a family."

"Aren't you going to get them married first?"

"Of course," she said, laughing, and nudged him with her elbow. "Being Lettie's sister-in-law and an aunt to their children will be wonderful."

He watched her in the growing light. "Sounds like you're not planning to have any of your own. That would be a shame." And highly unlikely, he thought, knowing her nature, maybe better than she did.

"No. Besides, I've looked forward to playing with his children for years." Although the reason had changed, she still wouldn't be considered marriageable and that was all right. She had known a happiness many married women had not.

He had seen her gazing at the baby with such longing he couldn't understand why she seemed to be denying it now. "But after you marry, won't it be up to the good Lord and your husband?" He wanted children and trying for them was half the fun.

She already knew the answer, but she wasn't about to say anything that might make him feel obligated to *do the right thing*. "What about you? How many children would you like?"

He chuckled. "Whatever comes along. My brothers an' sister an' I had fun growin' up. Think our parents did, too."

"Our papa whistled a lot, and Mama hummed while she did chores." She had forgotten, until now, but that's how she remembered them. And after her brother married, just maybe he would be more like Papa. "I'm ready to see if they're up. If I can't make coffee, I'll settle for water."

"Sounds good. They probably wouldn't mind waking up to the smell of fresh coffee." He got up and pulled her beside him. "This makes twice I've seen you first thing in the mornin'. Both times you've been pretty as a sweet little pansy." His ma was partial to them and pointed out that each flower's face was different. It'd been a long time since he remembered that.

She grinned. "That's the second-nicest compliment I ever received."

"The second?" He arched one brow teasingly.

"The first you paid me at Christmas. Don't tell me you've forgotten—"

He laughed and gave her a big hug. "Let's see about that coffee."

When they went into the house, everyone was awake. She and Lettie made breakfast and fussed over Ginny, who told them she had named the baby after his father. After they had eaten, Emma carried baby Will in the crook of her arm while she straightened up.

Kent was captivated with the sight of her holding the baby. She'd been dead wrong about not having one of her own. They'd have several, if trying counted.

Lettie went over to Emma. "Mr. Talbert's taking me back to town. Are you ready to leave?"

"The mare's here. I'll ride her home and see you at the shop after I change clothes." Emma skimmed one finger over the baby's velvety cheek. "I won't be long. You can ride double with me if you want to."

Lettie grinned. "I think I'll pass, but thanks for asking." She put her little finger under Will, Jr.,'s tiny fist. "I can't wait for Pauline to have hers."

"Me, either, but I'm getting anxious to be an aunt. Get busy, sister dear."

Lettie gave her a wide-eyed gaze. "You're terrible." She put on her cloak and looked at Emma. "We haven't really kissed. Don't expect too much."

"Then don't wait for him to do it." Shocking her was one

way to plant an idea, Emma thought, as she kissed Will, Jr. "You'd better go on. I can't leave until Will returns."

After they left, Ginny fell asleep, and Emma meandered around the cabin with the baby in the curve of her arm. When Will came back, Kent had the horses saddled and ready. Emma kissed the baby one more time and put him in the cradle. She went outside, with Will following in her wake. "If Ginny or you need any help, just ask."

"I can't thank you enough, Miss Townsend. And I'm lucky Mr. Hogarth was with you. He's a good man to have around in a predicament." Will shook Kent's hand.

On the way back to town, Emma held the mare at a walk. She glanced at Kent. Something was on his mind. Could he be as uncomfortable saying good-bye as she was? "Are you leaving today or tomorrow?"

He shouldn't have been surprised. "You go right for the throat, don't you?"

"It saves time." She looked around and saw a stand of trees up ahead by the river. "Mind if we stop?"

"Not if you want to." They turned off the road and pulled up under the alder trees. He dismounted and lowered her to the ground. "What's wrong?"

She took his hand in hers and strolled toward the river. "I'd rather say good-bye to you here, without so many people around."

"I decided to leave in the mornin'." He held her hand a little tighter. "I was goin' to see you later this evenin'." He stopped and faced her. "You want me to leave today?"

"No— Oh, no, Kent." She brushed her fingers over his beard. "I'm not very good at good-byes. I hoped it might be easier here."

"Emma," he said, wrapping his arms around her. "I wasn't goin' to wave to you and ride out of your life." He tipped her face up and held her gaze. "I'll be back."

"To try out the ferry." She stared downriver toward the bay. "You've helped all of us. You'll be missed. I'm sure Mr. Ross would like you to help him launch the ferry."

"He'll do fine without my help." He released a pale

golden strand of hair caught in her eyelash and ran his thumb over her soft cheek.

She slipped her arms around him inside his coat. "I don't know how to say good-bye to you."

"You're doin' just fine. This's a good way to say hello, too." He covered her lips with his and kissed her thoroughly. No woman had ever made him feel as if he could do anything in the world—as long as she was at his side. "Love" was a word he'd heard often enough, but he'd always connected it with his family. Until he met Emma. She'd completely disarmed him. He trailed kisses over her brow and along her jaw and down to the base of her throat.

She stirred against him, hungry to feel the heat and weight of his body on hers. What better way to say good-bye, she thought. Her heart pounded, and she ached with desire.

Watching the glint in her eyes, he slid his hands under the edge of her cape. "Maybe we should get back to town."

"Not yet . . ." She worked his buttons loose and ran one hand through the dark curls on his chest.

"No, not yet—" He spread her cape on the ground and lay down with her.

As she explored, his muscles grew taut beneath her fingers. She wanted to touch every part of him, to see him without clothes in the sunlight and by the light of a fire—feel him inside her. A tremble of longing washed through her.

Every time she shuddered it created a new spasm of desire. He opened the top of her dress, untied the ribbons on her chemise, and caressed her full breasts. He kissed her silky skin and grazed his beard over her belly. She was even more beautiful than he'd imagined, and he'd have a lifetime to explore her more slowly. He felt her hand slide over his hip. Brushing her skirt aside, he skimmed his hand up over her stockings, her firm thigh, and fondled her lower belly. She raised her hips, urging him on, and he couldn't deny her. He slid his body over hers, and she moaned, a rich, throaty, arousing appeal.

With each stroke of her hands over his arms and down his back, she marveled at his strength. She rocked her hips against his. Then with one incredible thrust he filled her. She braced her hands on his shoulders and increased the pressure. Wave after wave pulsed through her belly and spread out in magical ripples. She welcomed each thrust and stroked his hard-muscled backside. When he withdrew, she rolled her hips, impatient for his next thrust. A deep tremor thundered through her. At last—all too soon—she cried out and crushed him to her. They were one as those heavenly sensations burst within.

He felt as if he'd shattered into millions of pieces and was slowly coming back together. He gasped the cool air and rested his cheek on her breast. In his youth he'd dreamed of passion like theirs, but he never expected to find it. He pressed light kisses over her breasts and smiled at her. "That sure didn't feel like you were sayin' good-bye."

She smiled and sank her hands into his thick hair. "A woman once told me that in some language one word is the same for 'good-bye' and 'hello.' "

✦ 23 ✦

Kᴇɴᴛ ᴡᴀʟᴋᴇᴅ Eᴍᴍᴀ to her door. "Sure you want to work in the shop today?"

"It's not work." She opened the door. "Come by there later?" She still felt weak-kneed, but it was a wonderful feeling.

He gave her hand a gentle squeeze. "Try and walk home without me."

She smiled and closed the door. And found herself face to face with her angry brother. "Hello." She frowned at him. "Lettie said she had left a message for you. You do know we spent the night at the Talbert farm?"

"So I was told."

"Ginny had a beautiful baby boy, Will, Jr." She stepped back and hung up her cape. "What is wrong with you, Bently?"

"*Me?* You have the effrontery to ask me that? Look at yourself," he said, waving his arm from her feet to her head. "Even Mrs. Nance could figure out what you've been doing." He turned his back on her, paced to the hallway and back, flexing his hands with each step.

Blindly wandering into the parlor, she felt as if she had plunged from euphoria into Hades. She had always believed he loved her. If he did, how could he do this to her? "I slept in these clothes last night—in the hayloft." She gritted her teeth to help stay the furious tremor gripping her. She still felt the effects of her ordeal with Virgil yesterday, but she wasn't about to mention it to Bently. It would likely add fodder to his rage.

He dogged her steps. "Don't lie to me! Your lips're too red and so're your cheeks. You allowed that bastard to have his way with you *again*! Didn't you?"

She spun around with her arm raised and slapped him soundly on his jaw. "Get out of my way."

He rubbed his hand over his cheek and jaw. "What the hell's wrong with you?"

She glared at him. "I've always believed I had a loving brother. Now I see I do not. You are a mean-spirited man, Bently, with no forbearance or understanding for anyone but yourself." She marched to her bedroom, packed enough things for a few days, and grabbed her cape and bonnet on the way out of the house.

"Emma—" Bently shouted, running to the front steps. "*Where* are you going?"

She paused halfway to the road. "If Lettie doesn't have room for me, I'll be at the hotel."

"You can't do that! What will people say?"

"With your imagination, you'll think of something." She continued on to the road and straight to town. An awful notion refused to be ignored—if she had misjudged her brother so badly, how could she possibly be sure how Kent felt about her? As if she had pulled a loose thread in the fabric of her mind, her thoughts began unraveling. By the time she entered the shop, her resentment of her brother—his lies and the pain they had caused her—had doubled.

Lettie looked up from her sewing. "I was beginning to wonder what had happened to you." Then she noticed the valise in each of Emma's hands. "What's wrong?" She dropped the quilt piece and went over to take one of the bags.

"Would you mind if I stay with you for a while? If you don't have room in the parlor, I can go to the hotel." Emma wasn't sure what to expect, but Lettie smiled and hugged her.

"Of course the parlor's yours. Come on. We'll put your things in there now." Lettie went out the front door of the shop and in the facing door that opened into her parlor. "That sofa's too short to sleep on. We'll make up a bed later." She set the bag under the window.

Emma put the other one next to it. "I appreciate this." She dropped her cape and bonnet on top of the valises. "I'll tell you what happened over a cup of tea."

They returned to the shop and sat at the round table. Emma hoped what she would say would be enough. Some things were just too private to share with even her dearest friend. "He got angry once too often. I'm tired of it. He'd be happy if I never went anywhere. I had to defend myself against Virgil Chase yesterday—I don't want to have to do the same with Bently."

"Oh, Emma, he was just worried about you. You know how his temper flares when he's distressed." Lettie ran her thumb around the rim of the cup. "He's strict with you because he cares. I think that's sweet."

Then why don't you upset him, Emma thought—her temper getting the best of her—and see just how sweet he can be? "I don't." She finished her tea and changed the subject. "Did Will stop by the general store to announce his good news?"

Lettie laughed. "Mr. Jenks was sweeping the walk, and Will stopped to tell him."

"He's so proud. In a few days we should call on Ginny with Alicia, Hannah, and Pauline to see how she's doing." As Emma added more wood to the woodstove, she said, "Lettie, Kent's leaving in the morning . . . and I don't want him to know I'm staying here."

"I won't say anything." Lettie watched her. "Did you ask him to stay?"

"No. I've known from the beginning that he wouldn't."

"Aren't you sorry to see him go?"

"I was surprised he's stayed this long." Emma brushed off her hands and shrugged. One reason she allowed herself to love him for a while was because he would leave. Now she didn't know what to think *if* he had been serious about returning. "I am glad we became friends." She went to the kitchen and added wood to that stove also.

"Sometimes, Emma, I don't understand you. If Bently had paid that much attention to me, I'd be crushed if I never saw him again." Lettie eyed her. "Maybe he's coming back. Is that why you're not upset?"

"There's a small chance he will." As Emma scooped flour into the bowl, she wondered if she'd been too eager to believe that, too. She could throttle her brother for raising these doubts.

She made dinner, and after they had eaten, Hannah stopped by wearing her new bonnet and asked about Ginny. Alicia came to thank Lettie for remembering to tell her husband about the petticoat. Emma kept busy. Later in the afternoon, she put a pot of coffee on the stove. Kent stopped by near closing.

Only Lettie and Emma were in the shop when he entered. "Smells like fresh coffee."

"Emma just made it." Lettie put her sewing away. "I think we have some of Gram's molasses cookies left, too."

"I have the drinks." Emma picked up the fresh pot of tea and carried them into the shop.

"Thank you, Miss Morrissey. I'll have a couple. Any more'd spoil my supper." Emma seemed a little jittery to him, but she'd been through a lot in the last day and a half. "How was your day?"

She smiled. This was their last visit, and she wasn't going to let her brother's nasty comments spoil it for them. "The women have been in asking about baby Will."

"The men I talked with knew about the baby, too."

"Everyone likes good news." And gossip, she thought. And lately she had done enough to keep tongues wagging for months—if they ever found out.

Lettie set the plate of cookies on the round table and put her cloak on. "Emma, do you mind if I leave for a while?"

"Take your time. I'll put the stew on to heat."

"Oh . . . yes. Thank you."

Kent eyed Lettie as she hurried out, then shifted his attention to Emma. Both of them seemed a little out of sorts. "You're not smiling. Does that mean she isn't going to see your brother?"

Fiddlesticks, she wished she did know where Lettie was going. "I don't know. She didn't tell me she'd be going out."

He chuckled. "Maybe she's borrowing a page from your book."

Emma tried to look happy, but that was an unsettling idea. She broke a cookie in half. "Have you told anyone you are leaving in the morning?"

He nodded. "Settled my bill with Seth, had a lager with Roy, and purchased supplies from Charlie Jenks. Saw Mr. Brice. He said you hadn't been in. Don't forget to stop by his shop. He can't start the gloves till he has a pattern of your hands." He had also told Charlie to watch out for Chase, if the man came into town, and explained that he might still have a grudge with Emma.

"I won't forget." She ate a piece of the cookie. "How long do you think it'll take you to get to . . . Portland?"

"Couple weeks, longer if there's an early snowstorm. I'm not sure when I'll get back." He took a drink of coffee. "Isn't it about time to close the shop?"

"The stew—" She hurried to the kitchen, took the kettle out of the cold cupboard, and set it on the stove. On her way back to the table, she closed the curtains on the side windows. "I did say I'd warm it up."

"Shouldn't you move that pot to the side? It could burn if Lettie doesn't get back soon." He closed the drapes across the bay window for her. "Ready to walk home?"

"I'm not going home yet." It was only a little fabrication, she told herself. "But I'd like to take a walk with you."

"Okay. Better wear your cape. The breeze comin' off the ocean's cool."

"I'll be ready in a minute." She moved the kettle of stew to the side of the fire, put on her cape, and met him at the door. She only had to keep up the charade until morning.

*   *   *

Emma didn't have any trouble waking early the next morning. She'd had a restless night and was up at dawn. She had told Kent she would meet him at the shop. She didn't like deceiving him but neither did she want him fighting with her brother. She dressed in the shop so she wouldn't wake Lettie or Lydia, and started cooking.

She had just taken two pans of cinnamon buns out of the oven when Kent came into the shop. She pulled off her apron and hurried to meet him. "Good morning."

"Hello. You've been cookin'?"

"I thought you might like to take some buns with you." She studied his face, the wave of hair that had slipped down on his forehead, the curve of his wonderful lips when he smiled. She didn't want to forget any of his handsome features. "Do you have time to eat now?"

"Come here," he said, pulling her into his embrace. "I'll have to eat mine on the trail." He bent down and kissed her. It'd have to last them at least a month, he thought, deepening the caress.

She slid her arms around his neck and stood on tiptoe. She didn't want to think about how much she was going to miss him. She held him close and wished he didn't have to leave. When he ended the kiss, she gazed into his winter-brown eyes. "Have a safe journey."

"You'll be with me every mile of the way." He pressed a kiss to her forehead. "Walk me outside?"

"I'll wrap up the buns." She quickly had the package ready and went out with him. She waited on the board walk to see him off.

He put the buns in the near saddlebag and smiled at her. He wasn't one for drawn-out farewells and neither was she. He gave her one more hug and kiss, and he mounted Bounder. "Don't forget me while I'm gone."

"No," she said, shaking her head and hoping her smile looked more convincing than it felt. "I won't." She watched until he rounded the curve in the road near the old cabin and headed north. When she stepped back into the shop, she felt the tears running down her cheeks.

* * *

The next week passed at a slug's pace for Emma even though she gave herself little time to daydream about Kent. She went to Mr. Brice's shoe store, and he traced a pattern of her hands for the gloves. Lettie went walking with Bently every day, and that gave Emma hope. She, Alicia, Hannah, Pauline, Lettie, and Lydia went out to visit Ginny and give her their gifts for baby Will. Emma hadn't missed the side-long glances—a mixture of curiosity and sympathy—directed at her.

Kent had been gone ten days when she changed the display in the bay window and remembered that he had teased her about making fancy bloomers for the window. It was just the thing for a new display. Emma found a length of dove-gray muslin and cut out the bloomers. It wasn't until she held up the two long trouserlike pieces that Lettie took any notice. "What do you think?"

Lettie stared a moment, her stitching forgotten, her mouth agape. "What are they?"

"Bloomers. I'm going to trim the legs with ruffles and eyelet woven with plum ribbon." Emma folded the pieces together.

"Whatever possessed you to make those?"

Emma smiled, thinking more about Kent than the bloomers. "Just a notion."

Lettie went back to piecing the quilt top together. "What's happened to you? You never used to give Bently any reason to be concerned about you. But lately you seem to go out of your way to give him grief."

Emma watched her while folding up the unused length of muslin. "What has he said about me?"

"Just that he's worried," Lettie said with a shrug. "If this keeps up, he'll grow old before his time."

"He shouldn't fret so much." Emma put the rest of the muslin away and searched for the eyelet. "I don't see how you can tolerate his narrow opinions. But you're not his sister, or his wife, yet, so I suppose he doesn't fault you—not that you give him any reason to."

"We are in accord on most things, Emma." Lettie set the quilt top on the table. "I know you get aggravated with him, but I love him for those same reasons that upset you."

"I realize that." Emma brought the eyelet and ribbon over to the table. "And I am happy for you. Honestly." She re-filled their cups with tea. "Brothers and sisters weren't meant to live together beyond childhood. But I don't want this to come between us, Lettie . . . and I'm looking forward to moving into your room when you marry him."

"Me, too," Lettie said, grinning. "I just wish he'd ask me."

"Why, Miss Lettie, you're blushin'," Emma said, laughing.

Kent wished he could let Emma know how uneventful his trip to Portland had been. He arrived late on Thursday after fourteen days on the road. He spent all the next day with Mr. Wendell, a man in his midlife who seemed to thrive on work and starting new businesses. He'd asked Kent to make a rough map of Pelican Cove while they talked.

Kent moved the map closer to Wendell and pointed out where each of the businesses were located. "The livery's the last building along here. You shouldn't have any trouble buying the piece of land on the other side. The ferry's goin' in about there," he said, pointing near the mouth of the river. "Five minutes from the heart of town."

Wendell sat back in his chair. "You did a fine job, Kent. I knew you were the one to determine whether Pelican Cove could support the supply company. Sorry to hear about that shipwreck. How's your leg now?"

"Fine. Sorry I couldn't get a message to you. There wasn't any way. The townspeople don't know about your plans to route supply wagons through there. Didn't want to get their hopes up till you'd made a decision."

"I knew you were the right man. That whole route depended on Pelican Cove." Wendell sat up and reached for the jug on the floor by his desk. "How about a drink?"

Kent nodded. "There's one more thing. I'd like to run that office." He picked up the glass Wendell set in front of him.

"It's yours." Wendell raised his glass in a salute and took a gulp. "I was going to offer you the Sacramento City office to manage.'' He had another swig. "But I thought you'd give me an argument over staying in one place. I'll have to get down to Pelican Cove sometime.''

Kent smiled. "Might as well tell you. I'll be getting married when I get back there.''

Wendell smacked his flat hand on the desk and grabbed the jug. "Congratulations! She must be special. I'm happy for you, Kent.''

By the time he'd finished his whiskey, Kent had arranged for the supplies—including window glass—to be ready by the following evening so he could get an early start the next morning. After a sound night's sleep in the boardinghouse, he set out to make a purchase and find a circuit preacher. Portland had grown some while he'd been gone. He looked in three stores before he found the right thin gold ring he wanted to get Emma. He paid the clerk. As he put the ring in his deepest pocket, he decided to ask about a preacher. "Seen a circuit rider or preacher in here?''

The clerk handed Kent his change. "Wouldn't rightly know, mister. People don't usually tell me what they do.''

Another man stepped over to Kent. "Excuse me, sir, but I overheard you. I'm Preacher Jones, Obadiah Jones. Have you need of my services?''

Kent pocketed the coins. "Maybe. Why don't we go outside?'' He figured the preacher was about his age. Now to see if he'd agree to ride directly to Pelican Cove without stopping to save souls at every settlement on the way.

Preacher Jones followed Kent out to the board walk. "Is it your family? I'd be glad to help any way I can.''

"I'm getting married.'' Kent walked to the corner of the building. "You marry people?''

Preacher Jones smiled. "Every chance I get. Is your bride-to-be here in town?''

"No. South of here. You ever done any circuit ridin'?''

Preacher Jones smiled and nodded. "After my missus an' me were blessed with our third child, she told me I had to put down roots. We just got to town a couple of days ago. How far south?''

*   *   *

Winter had really set in, which wasn't unusual for the end of January. Emma was stirring the pot of hot chocolate when the brass bell rang. Her brother came in and was staring at the display in the front window. She kept stirring. The chocolate was almost done, and she wasn't about to scald it. When it was ready, she filled two cups, put the pan on the old trivet on the stove and carried the cups into the shop.

"Lettie'll be back from the general store anytime. I poured a cup of hot chocolate for you."

Bently grabbed the bloomers out of the window display and marched toward her shaking them at her. "What're these doing in the window?"

She caught hold of the waist, staring him in the eye. "I made them, now give them back—" They had spoken only a few words since she had moved in with Lettie, and now this. "Bently, let go!"

Lettie hurried into the shop saying, "Goodness, it's cold—" As she pushed the door closed, she stared. "Bently, what are you doing?" She dropped her packages and rushed over to him. "Bently? Emma?"

He suddenly opened his hand, and Emma stepped back.

Emma looked at the pretty plum ribbons on the legs. All the tiny stitches and work were worth it. "I guess he doesn't like the bloomers."

Lettie put her hands around his arm. "Please, Bently, sit down." She pulled off her cloak and looked from him to Emma. "What were you two doing?"

Emma arranged the bloomers so they poked out from the short skirt in the window. "He pulled them out of the display. I wanted them back." The women had laughed and joked about them.

Lettie sat down next to him. "Please tell me what's wrong."

He stared at his sister. "Emma— Why would you put those things in the *window*? Have you no shame?"

"They gave the women something to laugh at." Emma set her cup by Lettie. "Take this one. I'm going for a walk."

"It's so cold. Won't you stay and talk this out?"

Emma looked at her brother. He had reminded her of Vera

and Virgil more than once in recent weeks. And that had only made her more determined not to *need* any man, which shouldn't be a problem—she didn't expect to see Kent again, and she certainly wouldn't meet another man like him. She put her cape on over her shawl and left.

By the time she had strolled down to the river and walked up to the old cabin, it was dark out but not so dark that she couldn't see the chimney. She pushed on the door and stepped inside. It felt so empty, which was foolish. She knew it would be, but it seemed as if she were snooping in Kent's house. She backed out and pulled the door closed.

When she returned to the shop, Bently had left, and Lydia was drying dishes. Lettie washed. Emma ate a biscuit and excused herself. It was becoming uncomfortable staying with Lettie and having no room of her own to withdraw to, but Emma knew she couldn't return to her brother's house. The old cabin became more appealing each day. Everyone knew she and her brother had had a difference of opinion, so she doubted anyone would be shocked if she moved in there.

Emma had dressed for bed and was reading by the fire in the parlor with Lettie, when someone banged on Lettie's door. Emma laid the book down. "That doesn't sound like Bently."

Lettie put down her sewing. "He wouldn't call at this hour."

"I'll see who it is." Emma opened the door and was surprised to see Roy Avery standing there in his shirtsleeves. "Mr. Avery."

"Miss Townsend. It's your brother. I'm afraid he's gonna need help gettin' home."

Lettie rushed to the door. "Is he ill?"

"Oh, no, ma'am. Passed out on the floor."

Lettie gathered the lapels of her robe together. "We'll be right over."

"Mr. Avery," Emma said, as he started to leave. "Couldn't you just close up and leave him there? Let him sleep it off on your floor?"

Mr. Avery seemed surprised, then chuckled. "Sorry, ma'am. I can't do that."

"Thank you. I'm sure Miss Morrissey will help him." Mr. Avery left, and she closed the door. Served her brother right even though he wasn't in the habit of imbibing to the point of unconsciousness.

Lettie ran back into the parlor. "You aren't dressed yet! Hurry."

Emma didn't want to punish her friend, just her brother. "I'll help you hitch up the buckboard, and you'll have to take him home."

"How can you be so unfeeling?"

"You might think it was a good chance to care for him. Bathe his face with a cool cloth and . . . show him how much you care." As Emma pulled on her shoes, she realized it was easier dealing with other people's problems rather than her own. However, sharing her burden wouldn't change it. She retrieved her cape from the shop and wrapped it around her.

They ran to his house. After Emma hitched up the buckboard, she sent Lettie off and walked back to the shop. Let her worry about him, Emma thought. That's the way it should be.

The next morning, Lydia tapped Emma's shoulder until she woke up. "Emma, dear, Lettie's not home. Do you know where she is?"

"She's all right, Lydia." Emma sat up on the pallet. "Bently . . . wasn't feeling well, and she offered to tend him. I'm sure she'll be back soon."

"My, my—" Lydia sat down heavily on the sofa.

Emma got up and went over to her. "Don't worry."

Lydia patted Emma's hand. "I won't, dear. In fact . . . I feel like cooking. What sounds good?"

"You're spoiling me."

"I'll make potato pancakes or apple fritters, if we still have apples." Lydia glanced down at her robe. "I think I'll dress first."

Emma laughed and set to putting away her bed. It was bad enough having to move into Lettie's parlor without leaving her pallet there for all to see. She dressed and started the fire in the shop woodstove. The morning passed like any other day, except that Lettie returned home around ten-thirty. Emma poured her a cup of tea to go with the fritters Lydia had left for her.

Lettie hung up her cloak and sat down at the table as if in a daze. "He's feeling better."

"I would hope so." Emma hid her grin behind her teacup. "You look tired, though. Why don't you rest after you eat? If we're overrun with customers, I promise to wake you."

Lettie looked at the bite of fritter on her fork as if she hadn't known it was there, and set it back on the plate. "I think I will." She walked to the hall door and paused. "Bently said he wanted to see you this morning. I hope you don't mind."

Lettie sounded almost dreamy, and Emma quickly said, "We'll be okay."

She puttered around the shop until midday, when Bently finally arrived. He definitely looked worse for his evening of drinking. "Come on in. Lettie's resting."

"Good. She was up most of the night. Besides, I wanted to speak to you alone." He went back to the kitchen and sat down at the table.

Emma followed him. "I made tea or would you rather have coffee?"

"I don't care. Tea'll do." He glanced at her. "About last night—"

She set the cup of tea in front of him. "Yes?"

"Do you know what you've been putting me through? How hard it is to face people? Everyone knows you're staying here." He held the cup with both hands and sipped.

"By now they also know where you were last night. I hope they don't find out that Lettie had to help you home."

His cup clattered on the saucer. "What do you want me to say? I'm . . . not perfect." He lowered his face to his open hands. "I never claimed to be."

"That's reassuring, but why do you expect more of me?" She wanted to reach out to him, but she wouldn't make this easy for him.

"I—" He sat up and faced her. "You're a woman."

"I'm glad you noticed."

"But women should be above reproach. You know that."

"And not men?" She stared at him. "Have you explained this to Lettie?" It was hard for her to believe he was her brother.

"Emma—" he growled, then seemed to crumple.

"You don't look well, Bently. Go on home." It was a start, she thought. "Have you eaten today?"

"Ugh— Don't mention it." He shoved the chair back and braced his hands on the edge of the table.

"Finish the tea. It will help." Obediently, he gulped down the tea and got to his feet. "Emma, will you move back home? You must be tired of sleeping in her parlor."

"I'll think it over."

After he left, she made two meat pies with odds and ends of other meals. She ate one and kept the other warm. She was putting the clean dishes away when Lettie came into the kitchen. "Feeling better?"

Lettie smiled. "Much." She found a cold biscuit and went over by the woodstove. "He asked me," she said softly.

Emma turned around. "What? I didn't hear what you said."

Grinning broadly, Lettie said, "Bently asked me if I would . . . marry him."

"Oh, Lettie!" Emma hugged her. "I am so very happy for you. Did you set a date?"

"Not really. Didn't he tell you?"

"He wasn't feeling very well."

"He should have stayed in bed." Lettie turned to warm her back. "Emma, do you realize we don't even have a preacher to marry us? We'll have to go up to Astoria or Oregon City."

"Bently could ask up to the gold camps. There might be one there."

Lettie thought of other possibilities, and Emma cleaned the lamp glass while they talked it over. The brass bell rang out. It was Alicia. "Hi." Emma started to blurt out Lettie's news, then motioned for her to do it.

Alicia looked around the shop. "Where is everybody? The whole town seems to be sleeping."

Emma put the tea tray on the table. "In this weather, it's a good way to keep warm." Especially if you don't sleep alone. She regretted that thought, but not the vivid image of Kent it brought to mind.

"Emma, you look peaked. Are you feeling ill?"

"Oh, no. I'm sorry, Alicia. I just remembered something." Emma poured the tea. "Lettie—"

Alicia narrowed her gaze. "You're positively glowing."

Lettie was still grinning as she said, "I just became betrothed to Mr. Townsend."

"That's wonderful!" Alicia gave Lettie a quick peck on the cheek. "I'm so happy for you!"

Lettie talked about the wedding for a few minutes, then asked about Pauline. "She hasn't been in since we went out to visit Ginny."

Alicia tasted her tea. "I stopped by her house. She's still feeling queasy but she's started sewing clothes for the baby."

Emma smiled. "By summer we'll have a wedding and two new babies in town. Isn't it wonderful?"

Alicia nodded. "Yes, it is."

Emma glanced out the window and saw Hannah. "I'll get another cup."

Hannah rushed into the shop. "Emma, have you heard the news?"

Oh, no, Emma thought, what now? Please don't let it be gossip about Lettie. "What?"

"*He*'s back! I saw him at the livery!"

Emma stared out the window. Her throat tightened up, and she couldn't breathe. Kent? No. Bundled up in the cold, a lot of men could resemble him.

Alicia looked from one to the other. "Who? *What* are you talking about, Hannah?"

"Mr. Hogarth. He's back in town." Hannah studied Emma. "Aren't you surprised, Emma? Or at least happy to know he returned?"

"I thought—" Emma looked at each of them.

Lettie grinned. "I told you he hadn't left for good."

"What a day!" Alicia said. "First Lettie's betrothment and now this."

Hannah stared at Lettie. "He asked you? Now, isn't that something. Today's certainly been a red-letter day."

The brass bell rang, again. Then Emma heard the booted footsteps and choked on her tea. She didn't need to turn around to know who it was. If she hadn't recognized his footsteps, the looks on her friends' faces gave him away. She stood up and slowly faced him. Her heart couldn't have beat any faster if she'd just run twenty miles. "Hello. Come over by the woodstove. You must be frozen."

Kent smiled at her, and the others. "I would like to warm up my hands. How have you been, Miss Townsend?" He stuffed his gloves in his coat pocket and held his hands over the stove, biding his time. She was even lovelier than he remembered. And he was definitely glad to see the others there, too.

"Welcome back, Mr. Hogarth." Lettie jumped up and went to the kitchen.

"Thank you, Miss Morrissey. You're looking very pretty today." His gaze slid to Emma. She grinned and gave him a slight nod. So her brother had spoken up. Good, he thought. Now it's her turn.

Lettie laughed and began grinding the coffee.

Kent unbuttoned his coat, reached into his deep trouser pocket, and brought out the ring on his little finger so no one would notice. Emma was still standing by the table. He walked up to her, dropped down on one knee with his back to the others. "Miss Emma," he said, taking her left hand in his, "would you do me the honor of being my wife?"

She was completely befuddled, and whispered, "Get up."

"Not until you accept my proposal." He held up her hand and wagged his little finger. "I brought a preacher back, and I'd like you to wear the pretty green dress." He grinned at her. "This floor's gettin' hard. Won't you say yes?" Tears glistened in her eyes and her cheeks were the color of ripe peaches. He was glad he'd managed to surprise her, but he didn't know how long he could wait to take her in his arms.

"You don't have to do this—" She gave his hand a tug, but he wouldn't budge. "Please . . ."

"Yes," Lettie called out.

Hannah said, "Yes, she will."

Alicia agreed.

"Sorry, ladies." He held her gaze, pleading silently. "Her answer's the only one that counts."

Emma tried to moisten her lips but her whole mouth was dry. She wanted to marry him, but she didn't want to *need* to marry him. With her friends staring at them, she couldn't say much. But, oh—

He mouthed, "I like the bloomers. Will you model them for me?" so the others couldn't hear.

She burst out laughing. How could she deny what they both wanted? "If you're willing, I am. Yes." He came to his feet and raised her over his head in one fluid move. When he swung her around, she feared she might kick the lamps over. "Kent, do put me down."

"Anything you want, Emma." He lowered her till they were nose to nose and quietly said, "I love you, Emma."

"I do love you, Kent." As she kissed him, she put her hands around his neck. She might be able to live without him, but life certainly wouldn't be as wonderful as she knew it'd be with him.

The door flew open and in darted Eddie with a large puppy in his arms. "Mr. Hogarth—"

"Eddie," Hannah said, "get home with that dog."

"I can't, Ma." Eddie made his way over to Kent. "Ya left the livery before I got back." He held the pup out to him. "He's yours. A present." He glanced at Emma and said in a rush, "Mr. Ross took the girl. I saved him for you."

Emma lowered her hand and petted the puppy. It was cute, and Eddie had even tied an old ribbon around the dog's neck. She smiled at Kent.

Kent lowered Emma to his side and ran his finger under the faded red ribbon. "Have you named him yet?"

"Gosh, no. You gotta do that." As Eddie struggled to keep from dropping the dog, he scrunched up his face. "He's gettin' heavy. Would'ya take him?"

Kent took the pup and held him in the crook of his arm.

He put his other arm around Emma. ''Looks like we've already got a start on our family, and we aren't even married yet.''

''You gettin' married to Miss Emma? Wowee!''

Kent grinned at her. ''Yeah, we're gettin' married.''

Dear Reader,

Kent and Emma have led me on a merry chase. The redwood country on the northern California coast is one of my favorite areas, so I was delighted when Emma showed me around her small town there. I hope you enjoyed *The Hat Box* and the citizens of Pelican Cove. Becoming involved in so many characters' lives is a little like being a snoop or a mind reader, and I will miss visiting with them.

However, Caroline Dobbs and Daniel Grey are anxious for me to begin writing their story. It will be the Christmas 1997 Homespun, which as of this date is untitled. The beginning of Caroline's story overlaps with the ending of *Maggie's Pride* after the crest of the 1861 flood of the Willamette River. Caroline helps deliver twins and promises the infants' dying mother that she will raise the babies as her own. By the time Daniel completes the repairs on her house, he discovers a love he cannot turn away from.

I hope you will mark your calendar and watch for Caroline and Daniel's story in December 1997, and please note that it will be a Jove Homespun, which I publish as Deborah Wood.

Best Wishes,

Deborah

Deborah Lawrence's Web address is
http://www.tlt.com/authors/dwood.htm

Our Town ...where love is always right around the corner!

●●●●●●●●●●●●●●●●●●●●●●●●●●●●●

__*Harbor Lights* by Linda Kreisel   0-515-11899-0/$5.99

__*Humble Pie* by Deborah Lawrence   0-515-11900-8/$5.99

__*Candy Kiss* by Ginny Aiken   0-515-11941-5/$5.99

__*Cedar Creek* by Willa Hix   0-515-11958-X/$5.99

__*Sugar and Spice* by DeWanna Pace   0-515-11970-9/$5.99

__*Cross Roads* by Carol Card Otten   0-515-11985-7/$5.99

__*Blue Ribbon* by Jessie Gray   0-515-12003-0/$5.99

__*The Lighthouse* by Linda Eberhardt   0-515-12020-0/$5.99

__*The Hat Box* by Deborah Lawrence   0-515-12033-2/$5.99

●●●●●●●●●●●●●●●●●●●●●●●●●●●●●

LOVE BY CHOCOLATE

♥

Four Irresistible Stories by Bestselling Authors

Rosanne Bittner
Elizabeth Bevarly
Muriel Jensen and
Elda Minger

Chocolate is the ultimate aphrodisiac. And these four enchanting stories of love, passion and chocolate are guaranteed to melt your heart. Each story features a decadent chocolate dessert recipe to satisfy your sweet tooth and your hunger for romance all year round...

___0-515-12014-6/$5.99

VISIT THE PUTNAM BERKLEY BOOKSTORE CAFÉ ON THE INTERNET:
http://www.berkley.com/berkley

If you enjoyed this book,
take advantage
of this special offer.
Subscribe now and get a

FREE
Historical
Romance

No Obligation (a $4.50 value)

Each month the editors of True Value select the four *very best* novels from America's leading publishers of romantic fiction. Preview them in your home *Free* for 10 days. With the first four books you receive, we'll send you a FREE book as our introductory gift. No Obligation!

If for any reason you decide not to keep them, just return them and owe nothing. If you like them as much as we think you will, you'll pay just $4.00 each and save at *least* $.50 each off the cover price. (Your savings are *guaranteed* to be at least $2.00 each month.) There is NO postage and handling – or other hidden charges. There are no minimum number of books to buy and you may cancel at any time.

*Send in
the Coupon
Below*

To get your FREE historical romance fill out the coupon below and mail it today. As soon as we receive it we'll send you your FREE Book along with your first month's selections.

Mail To: **True Value Home Subscription Services, Inc., P.O. Box 5235
120 Brighton Road, Clifton, New Jersey 07015-5235**

YES! I want to start previewing the very best historical romances being published today. Send me my FREE book along with the first month's selections. I understand that I may look them over FREE for 10 days. If I'm not absolutely delighted I may return them and owe nothing. Otherwise I will pay the low price of just $4.00 each: a total $16.00 (at least an $18.00 value) and save at least $2.00. Then each month I will receive four brand new novels to preview as soon as they are published for the same low price. I can always return a shipment and I may cancel this subscription at any time with no obligation to buy even a single book. In any event the FREE book is mine to keep regardless.

Name

Street Address   Apt. No.

City   State   Zip

Telephone

Signature
(if under 18 parent or guardian must sign)

Terms and prices subject to change. Orders subject to acceptance by True Value Home Subscription Services, Inc.

12033-2